MIDAS

MIDAS

RUSSELL ANDREWS

TIME WARNER
BOOKS

TIME WARNER BOOKS

First published in the United States in 2005
by Mysterious Press, Warner Books
First published in Great Britain in April 2005
by Time Warner Books

A CIP catalogue record for this book is
available from the British Library.

Hardback ISBN 0 316 72539 0
C format ISBN 0 316 72540 4

Typeset in Minion by M Rules
Printed and bound in Great Britain by
Clays Ltd, St Ives plc

Time Warner Books
An imprint of
Time Warner Book Group UK
Brettenham House
Lancaster Place
London WC2E 7EN

www.twbg.co.uk

TO LEN AND LOUISE RIGGIO

My heartfelt thanks for your extraordinary generosity – a generosity that pretty much spreads to all aspects of my life. Most relevant, special thanks for Camp Riggio West, without which this book would not have been written. And here's the official warning: I've definitely got my eye on Camp Riggio South for the next book.

Who lives better than we do?

acknowledgements

This is getting to be a familiar list.

Thanks to . . . Esther Newberg for, as always, going way beyond the call of duty, especially when it comes to her newfound culinary skills . . . Bill Goldman for reading, teaching, critiquing, and haranguing . . . the superb and supportive publishing team of Colin Fox, Susan Richman, Larry Kirshbaum, Jamie Raab, and Hillary Hale . . . John Alderman for his insight and willingness to answer any and all questions, and for putting me in a room with financial whizzes Adam Usdan of Trellus Management, Michael Aronstein of Preservation Capital (who basically gave me the solution to the whole puzzle), and D. B. Lifland of Trellus Management . . . Bill Bainbridge, who educated and terrified me about all things explosive . . . Marv Donnaud for teaching me about anything aviation related and for actually being able to make me understand what a manifold is . . . Andy Barzvi and Chris Bauch for their efficiency, remarkably pleasant way of badgering me to finish the book, and willingness to swig alcohol at a moment's notice . . . Jack Dytman, who amazes me constantly with his hard work and enthusiasm and the fact that he still always calls me back . . . Josie Freedman (this is advance thanks for the work I know you're about to do as soon as I hand over the manuscript) . . . and, of course, Janis Donnaud for her support during the entire process.

Banking establishments are more dangerous than standing armies.
                                                    – Thomas Jefferson

It's good to be king
And have your own world
It helps to make friends
It's good to meet girls
                        – Tom Petty, 'It's Good to Be King'

prologue

chapter 1

From the Houston Chronicle
Reuters News Service
September 14

**Environmental Surprise From
The Anderson Administration**
Led by Vice President Dandridge
A New Direction in Land Preservation

In a move equally surprising to both foes and supporters, Stephanie
Ingles, the Administrator for the Environmental Protection Agency,
announced yesterday that over eight million acres in Alaska's
National Petroleum Reserve have been designated as a national
monument and have thus become permanently off-limits to oil
companies that have been pressing the administration to let them
begin drilling in the region.

The National Petroleum Reserve is not a name that conjurs a
vision of pristine space but it is, in fact, the largest expanse of
untouched wilderness left in the United States. In 1923, President
Harding established the region as a petroleum reserve, stipulating
that the oil fields be drilled only in time of pressing national need.

Large and influential oil and energy companies such as EGenco and Halliburton have recently been lobbying the administration to open the fields for exploration, saying that if ever there was a national need the time is now. President Thomas Anderson has, in the past, been sympathetic to the needs of such companies, as has Vice President Phillip Dandridge, and environmentalists had been expecting Ms Ingles to announce that the administration had bowed to the pressure. However, despite the recent rise in oil prices – yesterday's closing left the price of oil at $44.78 per barrel – Ms Ingles said that the President was standing firm on this issue. 'Despite what is perceived as this administration's close ties to the oil industry,' Ms Ingles stated, 'Vice President Dandridge is a committed environmentalist. He is well aware of the wildlife that swims in and roams around the Colville River Watershed, Kasegaluk Lagoon, Teshekpuk Lake and the Utukok Highlands, and he has no intention of allowing the ecological balance within those areas to be disturbed. The Vice President took the lead in this initiative and the President wholeheartedly concurs with the stand that's being taken.'

Members of the President and Vice President's party did not offer unanimous support after the announcement. Speaker of the House Lester Swannig said that he was 'withholding any final judgment on this decision, but I am dismayed at the potential rise in oil prices it may cause. We have been trying to keep the cost of gasoline down since it affects every American citizen. Shutting off this acreage from drilling will certainly not help that effort and I have to say I don't understand this shift in priorities.'

Environmentalists warily applauded the decision. Christine Herr, co-chairperson of the Save the Earth Foundation, said, 'I am pleased by the decision although I admit it did rather shock me. Over the past seven years, environmental protection has taken a backseat to just about everything else one could name. However, as everyone knows, Vice President Dandridge is beginning his push to achieve his party's presidential nomination next year and I imagine his advisers are telling him he needs to make some concessions to "kooks" like us. But even if this decision was made for political reasons, it's a decision I'm glad this administration had the courage to make.'

Vice President Dandridge is the presumed presidential nominee for his party in next November's election. Heading into primary season, he has a substantial lead in the polls in nearly every state, with very few opponents within the Republican Party. The Vice President does, however, currently trail both of the men competing for the Democratic nomination, Indiana Senator Martin Vance and Georgia Governor Oren Childress. All of his potential Democratic opponents supported this decision on the National Petroleum Reserve and voiced their hopes that in the last year of President Anderson's final term he will take even more of a lead in protecting the environment.

chapter 2

From Bloomberg.com
Bloomberg Financial News
October 8

Energy Prices

PETROLEUM ($/bbl)

	PRICE*	CHANGE	% CHANGE	TIME
Nymex Crude	48.1	0.4	0.96	13:51
IPE Crude	43.4	0.5	1.32	14:12
Dated Brent $	44.55	0.37	0.95	13:59
WTI Cushing $	48.05	0.45	1.08	14:08

PETROLEUM (¢/gal)

	PRICE*	CHANGE	% CHANGE	TIME
Nymex Heating Oil	2.12	1.85	1.76	13:53
Nymex Gasoline	147.3	0.27	0.19	13:52

chapter 3

East End Harbor
Long Island, New York
November 4

Bashar Shabaan had seen death before. Seen it up close.

The first time, he had been sitting in a car in Basra, minding his own business. Bashar was just slouched in the front seat, behind the wheel, waiting. He wasn't waiting for anyone or anything. He was just waiting. It was during the first Gulf War.

In front of him was a truck. It looked like it was going to fall apart, like it couldn't drive one more mile. There was a family inside, a mother and a father and some children, two teenaged boys. An American army jeep pulled up alongside and then the broken-down truck started to drive away. One of the boys rolled down a window, put his hand out to wave to the American soldiers, and the next thing Bashar knew there was gunfire everywhere. The tires on the truck exploded and then sagged, and the rickety wooden slats that had been built to hold the truck's cargo splintered and just disappeared. The truck's windows shattered and everywhere there were bullet holes. The woman was crying, weeping tears of rage and despair. The man and the two boys were dead, Bashar could see parts of their bodies dangling from the seats. Soldiers were yelling. He heard an officer, angry and loud, saying, 'You stupid fuck! It was just a fucking kid! What the fuck were you thinking?' Then more soldiers came and the crying woman was taken away. Then the truck was taken away. Then it was as if nothing had ever happened. Except that Bashar knew that it had.

Another time, years later, he saw death come when it was not so unexpected. He was across the street when his cousin Hamid stepped onto a Jerusalem bus and martyred himself. Bashar saw the geysers of blood and the severed legs. He saw a little girl with lovely blonde hair, soft and curly, maybe seven years old, get on the bus right before Hamid. He also saw her body on the street moments later, her fair skin charred black, her blonde hair on fire.

Death did not shock Bashar Shabaan. Or terrify him. Or even make him curious in any way. He did not welcome it or embrace it. He was not like Hamid. But he understood that death was a part of life. And that life was largely about death and dying. There were no surprises to life, Bashar believed, because it always ended the same way.

Well, perhaps there was one surprise: Bashar Shabaan did not understand why he could not stop sweating.

It wasn't hot outside. There was even a pre-winter chill in the air. It was the kind of damp autumn weather that Bashar detested. He liked heat, the baked feeling that came from standing in the glowing sun. He did not care for the American fall or winter. It gave him colds and the flu. For the three years he had lived in this country, he had shivered from November through February, no matter how many layers of clothes he had on. Bashar preferred warmth. The kind of warmth that radiated from his country.

But on this November afternoon, he felt none of the day's coolness. He was burning up inside. His stomach was hurting and his mouth was dry and his throat was tight. Sweat was pouring from his forehead and palms.

And as he walked he suddenly understood the reason. The surprise was not really such a surprise. Yes, Bashar had seen death. But he had never before been the cause of it.

He had always wondered whether murderers, even ones who believed their causes were just, like Hamid, got nervous before they committed their crimes. Whether any of them, soldiers or martyrs, ever felt guilt or remorse or fear. Now he knew.

Murderers got sweaty palms and stomach cramps before they killed their victims. Murderers were afraid.

There was a big crowd of people milling around the street, about two blocks away from the restaurant. At first Bashar thought they were there for him, that it was some kind of giant trap. There were cameras and lights and policemen and suddenly his feet couldn't move; they refused to take one step. But then he realized they weren't there for him at all. It was a movie. They were shooting an American movie. There were long trailers and large men with larger bellies drinking beer and yelling into walkie-talkies. The policemen were actors, dressed in costume. He saw one actor, someone he recognized, sitting in a chair, doing a crossword puzzle. Bashar knew who it was, had seen him on television, on one of the late-night talk shows, but couldn't think of his name. He waited a few moments, tried to remember, finally gave up. By then his feet could move. And they did. One step, then two, and then he was walking again, leaving the movie behind.

He was almost to his destination. He wiped his hands on his raincoat and, as he'd done at least a dozen times in the past two minutes, reached into his right coat pocket to feel the cell phone and make sure it was there. He ran over his instructions one more time, his lips moving ever so slightly in conjunction with the words in his mind.

9

Go inside.

Give the person at the front the right name.

Go to the table. Hand the briefcase over. Put it down on the floor.

Turn and leave. Don't run. Walk slowly. Be polite.

Once outside the door, take the cell phone. Call immediately. Say that the job is done. Go to the alley to the left of the building. Then run.

Run as fast as you can.

Run like the devil himself was chasing you.

Bashar thought about running. He thought about his weak legs and fiery stomach.

He thought about getting paid for his few minutes of work. Fifty thousand dollars. It was a lot of money. More than he had ever seen before.

He thought about what was going to happen.

Then he thought about how the devil really would be chasing after him.

Bashar wondered if he'd have enough money to bribe the old bastard if they ever met.

He thought that just maybe he would.

Jimmy Leggett felt uncomfortable.

The woman across the table from him was looking at the wine list and that was one reason Jimmy felt edgy: he wasn't used to eating in such fancy restaurants. Harper's was new, open a couple of months and already filled with money. Hamptons money, which meant direct from Wall Street, Hollywood, or simply handed over from wealthy parents who could afford Long Island oceanfront property as their second, sometimes even their third home. The people eating their Cobb salads on their carb-free diets wore casual-looking sweat-

10

shirts made of cashmere and they paid with Platinum credit cards. He wasn't a total rube, he'd been around some, but this was a little too refined for his taste. They didn't just have fish, they had fish with a pistachio crust. The steak wasn't just steak, it was pink peppercorn coated steak. It was like everything on the menu was pretending to be something it wasn't. The martinis had flavors – apple and caramel and lemon cream – and there wasn't a bottle of wine on the wine list that cost less than forty-eight bucks. He'd checked it out and even muttered something before the woman he was eating with had removed the list from his hands to take a look herself.

The second reason Jimmy Leggett was uncomfortable was that he was pretty sure the woman was taking him to lunch because she wanted to have sex with him and Jimmy had been married for twenty-seven years without once having cheated on his wife.

He glanced at the woman now, as she ordered a bottle from the waiter. She was a weekender. East End Harbor, where Jimmy had been police chief for nearly thirteen years, had a lot of weekenders these days. Not always. Although only fifteen minutes' drive from the choicer part of the Hamptons, it used to be a year-round community, nicely blue-collar and unpretentious. You had kids and they stuck around, they were able to buy a nice house just a few blocks away from where they grew up. It was the un-Hamptons town in the wealthy and chic Long Island beach community. But the past decade had brought prosperity. Even to East End. Things had slowed down somewhat in the past couple of years, along with the economy, but there were still clothing stores that sold hundred-dollar T-shirts and food stores that sold nothing but truffles and caviar and champagne glasses. The next generation was moving upstate or mid-Island, they couldn't afford to live in their hometown anymore – small two-bedroom Victorian houses were going for seven hundred grand. The burger joint on the corner was now a sushi bar. The take-out

Chinese was a creperie. And this attractive fifty-year-old weekender whose ex-husband had paid her a tidy sum of money to get away from her and who'd clearly had a couple of face-lifts and probably a boob job, thought it would be sexy to have a fling with the local head cop. She came into the station the first time to complain about kids with boom boxes. Then she came in again to ask advice about an alarm system for her house – prosperity had brought crime along with expensive T-shirts – and then everyone in the station knew that the next few times she showed up she was coming in to flirt with the boss. Times have changed, Jimmy thought. And he was trying to decide now if he was going to finally change along with them.

But none of that was what was really bothering him at the moment. He'd get over the price of the lunch. And he'd deal with whatever he decided to do about the woman, one way or the other. Something else was making the hair on the back of his neck stand on end.

It was the guy at the front of the restaurant, the sweaty guy with the briefcase.

He looked Middle Eastern. Maybe Indian. Jimmy was never too good with that kind of thing. People were people as far as he was concerned. He never paid too much attention to where they came from. The guy was walking past the hostess, going straight for a table just a few feet from Jimmy's. He was carrying an expensive leather briefcase. Large. It looked like it was heavy.

The guy found the table he was looking for. There were three men sitting there. One of them wore a pinstriped suit and tie, an outfit that was none too common out there, especially at lunchtime. The other two men were more in keeping with the community dress code. One wore khakis and a tennis sweater. The other had on pressed jeans and a starched, long-sleeved button-down blue shirt with a two-tone collar. The sweaty guy said something to Pressed

Jeans, and put the briefcase down on the floor next to the man's chair. Pressed Jeans nodded, didn't look surprised or alarmed at the delivery. He didn't tip the guy either. But the sweaty guy didn't wait for a tip. The moment he released the briefcase, his back was turned and he'd taken two quick steps toward the door.

Jimmy stood. He wasn't sure why. Cop's instinct. There was something funny about this guy. Something was up. So Jimmy took a step forward, didn't even look at the woman at his table, didn't see her disapproving frown. He was watching the sweaty guy, who suddenly stopped walking and looked down toward the pocket of his raincoat. The guy looked confused all of a sudden, like he couldn't believe what was happening. Jimmy didn't know what the hell was happening either. All he knew was that he heard a muffled ringing sound.

The sound of a cell phone receiving a call.

Bashar Shabaan froze in place. Something was wrong. Something was very wrong.

The phone was not supposed to ring. They were not supposed to call him. He was supposed to call them. This was very, very wrong.

And then suddenly he understood. There was no question in his mind. It wasn't wrong at all. It made perfect sense. It was exactly as planned.

Exactly as *they* had planned.

Bashar wanted to scream, but he didn't. He wanted to run, but he didn't do that either. Instead, Bashar stood still, completely still, and thought about his faith. He thought about Hamid and what he must have felt stepping onto that bus. And he prayed for his mother and father. He thought that when he first saw death, when he'd seen the soldiers kill that family, he was young. So very young. And now he was so very old.

Twenty-nine years old.

As old as he'd ever get, he thought.

Then he closed his eyes and thought about how he'd never get his money.

He'd never find out if he could bribe the devil.

A real pity.

Because he knew without a doubt he'd be meeting the old bastard any moment now.

First came the noise.

Jimmy Leggett heard that. It was so deafening, so loud that it seemed to have a physical force all its own. And then it got louder because soon there were screams and moans and crying and prayers.

Then the blood came.

Jimmy Leggett saw that. At least some of it. Mostly what he saw was his own blood, which spurted because something ripped into his chest, tearing him apart. That same something lifted him up and carried him backward so fast he felt like he was flying.

There was a lot more blood than just Jimmy's because the initial explosion also ripped many other bodies in half, mangling and crushing anything in its ferocious path. The impact shattered almost all the glass in the restaurant – the windows, the mirrors, the chandeliers – sending fragments and shards, some mere slivers, some the size of checkerboards, hurtling through the air; deadly, jagged projectiles slicing through skin and bone, splashing the white stucco and beige tiles of Harper's Restaurant with gallons of blood, as if being hurled from hundreds of paint cans, blood that was thick and dark, dark red.

And then just as quickly it was washed out and pink, because the sprinkler system burst into action and then a water main was severed, and the new mix of blood and water flooded across the restaurant floor like a river, streaming into the street through what was left of the front of the restaurant. It looked like a slaughterhouse being hosed down after the working day. Jimmy felt that because he was still alive then, his body broken and wet and dying.

Other debris swept past Jimmy as he lay there: pieces of furniture, shoes, plates, silverware, vases, even jewelry, much of which was still attached to severed fingers and ears. And that's when Jimmy Leggett smelled the death that surrounded him. The bloody rags that just moments before had been well-cared-for clothing but were now scattered everywhere: stuck to whatever walls remained, wrapped around table legs, flapping against unmoving bodies. The arms and legs that had been ripped from their sockets, that were dripping red and were piled up so thick they looked like stacks of firewood.

And then Jimmy's senses got fuzzy. He was barely aware of the ceiling plaster that was plummeting in chunks, dropping into the frenzied activity below and onto the deafened, terrified survivors, making them think that the sky itself was falling. He understood that there was new movement, but didn't know it was the emergency medical workers and doctors who arrived within minutes after the blast went off and were doing their best to move anyone still breathing into waiting ambulances. He felt heat, great heat, but didn't realize that volunteer firemen had arrived, too, and were waging battle with the fire that broke out when a gas main in the kitchen ruptured. By the time those customers at Harper's who were not killed by the explosion had burned to death in the raging fire, Jimmy could see, hear, feel, and smell nothing at all.

Jimmy Leggett's last thoughts were about his wife. He saw her face, wanted to tell her not to be so sad. Mostly he wanted to say that he probably wouldn't have slept with the weekend woman no matter how much the goddamn lunch had cost. Within seconds of his death, the streets had been cordoned off and no one was allowed

15

within three blocks in any direction of the devastation. And within three hours after it had begun, the worst was over. The dead had been removed, the living were in Southampton Hospital. Where there had once been life, all that remained was a sudden quiet, an absence of movement, an eerie vision of things that remained untouched and unchanged. A photograph of Main Street in East Hampton that still hung on the restaurant wall, unscarred. A candle that stood unbroken in its candleholder. Mere feet from the center of the room, the point of the explosion, was a round table that stood absolutely intact – flowers still blooming in a small glass vase; the tablecloth neither torn nor sullied; knives, forks, and spoons sitting exactly as they'd been placed. There were two plates on the table. One held a half-eaten steak with a nearly untouched baked potato. It looked as if the diner would be returning from the bathroom momentarily to finish his or her meal. The other plate was filled with small, thin pieces of pasta. It also had a severed hand next to it, a fork still clutched in the fingers.

The FBI showed up, taking over from the overwhelmed and shell-shocked local law enforcement, and the human tragedy was quickly turned into an impersonal crime scene. The TV cameras stayed, of course, positioning themselves as close as they were allowed, and settled in for a long siege. Print journalists churned out copy, spoke to witnesses, and searched for theories while TV reporters stood in front of the cameras and made an instant and unanimous proclamation, sending it out over the airwaves: a terrorist bombing.

A message from America's enemies to its citizens: No one is safe.
Anywhere.
Anymore.
Ever.

part one

chapter 1

'We'd like people to take their seats, please.'

Justin Westwood nodded at the usher, who had leaned over in his direction to make the polite request, but he made no move to honor it. The usher waited, swiveling his neck back and forth, as if his shirt collar was too tight. Then he moved on to tell other, more obedient people to sit down so things could get started.

Justin watched the mourners filing into the church. They were moving slowly; their tears and grief seemed to be weighing them down, preventing them from walking down the aisles at normal speed. In the three days since the explosion at Harper's Restaurant, Justin Westwood had noticed a lot of people moving slowly. His sense was that the entire country was moving along in slow motion right now. People seemed to be in a state of shock after the explosion. There wasn't the same kind of anger that was prevalent after the World Trade Center attack. This was different. There was something obscenely grand about that event, operatic in its horror, that made it all seem vaguely unreal to anyone outside of the city. September eleventh had heroes and villains and scope. This attack seemed small. It wasn't just deadly, it was demeaning. It seemed to bring everyone down to the level of other countries, small countries. It made everyone feel vulnerable, which Justin knew was the worst feeling there was. So people moved slowly. They were in no rush to reach their destination, whatever it was, because that destination no longer seemed safe.

Justin, on the other hand, wasn't moving at all. He was standing toward the rear of the room, leaning against the wall, facing the last pew. He was in mourning, too, but that didn't affect his speed or his ability to move. Justin had learned long ago to use his grief to keep himself separate from normal activity. To stay one step away from whatever pain was due to come next.

He was standing, several feet from the rest of the crowd, because he didn't know what he was supposed to do. He didn't know how to act or what to say to the people passing by. He was being counted on to be strong but he was not feeling much strength. What he felt was what he'd so often felt in the past: numb. He had spent years seeking to reach just such a state, to avoid any unnecessary emotion. After everything that had happened the previous year, he thought he'd finally passed beyond that point, thought he had crossed back to the side of the living and the feeling, but now the numbness was back again. And he understood that it wasn't Jimmy Leggett's death that had brought it back. It was his funeral.

Justin Westwood had sworn that he'd never go to another funeral. He didn't believe in them. They did nothing for the dead, who were well beyond hearing or caring what was happening in a cramped little room filled with crying people. Funerals were for the living. They were to provide comfort and the hope of an afterlife; they were to ease the pain that came with loss. Funerals were to let people know that when their time came, they would not only be going to another place, a better place, there would be other people left behind to mourn them, to miss them, to grieve over their absence. To show them that they had been loved.

Justin knew better.

He did not have any faith in an afterlife. If there were such a thing, he was not willing to concede that it would be any better than what was here on earth. Justin thought that the world had been fucked over plenty. It didn't give him confidence that those in charge could do any better elsewhere.

He also wasn't comforted by funereal rituals. Nor did he think he could fill a church with mourners. Justin had long ago come to grips with the fact that there would be few, if any, people to grieve him or miss him. He had not felt much love in his lifetime. There was no reason to think he'd get much of it after he died.

Two people had truly loved him. That he knew. He'd missed one of their funerals. His eight-year-old daughter's. He'd been in the hospital, shot up in the attack that killed her. He didn't know she'd been buried until two weeks after she'd been put in the ground.

Hc did go to his wife's funeral. Alicia had not coped well with the loss of their daughter. Justin knew that she blamed him, an accusation that had quite a lot of merit to it. He shared her belief. But Justin did his best never to blame his wife for her own death. One year after Lili had been killed, Alicia took Justin's pistol out of his closet, put it in her mouth, and pulled the trigger. He blamed himself for that one, too.

It took him years after that to feel anything close to love. He thought it was happening about a year ago. With a woman in town, Deena, and her small daughter, Kendall. It turned out to be all sorts of things with Deena – friendship, passion, safety, compassion – but it wasn't love. And on her part it was something else, too. It was fear. Fear of what was lurking inside him. Not the numbness. Fear of what was beneath the numbness.

They had given it their best shot. Dated for several months. But after a few weeks, there were signs. He would go to touch her unexpectedly, come up behind her and kiss her on the neck or stroke her bare arm, and she would flinch. The motion hardly noticeable. But he noticed. He could feel her discomfort when he was around Kendall. He was crazy about the little girl, and in some ways, separating from her was the hardest part to deal with. But when he understood that Deena was tormenting herself over the relationship – he had, literally, saved her life; she did not want to add to the pain of his life – he made it easy on her. He sat her down, said that he understood that it wasn't working, gave her an out. And she jumped at it. He was surprised just how quickly she did jump. But he told her that if she ever changed her mind, he'd wait around for a time. It was a pledge he knew he could keep, but he also knew it was a pledge that would never come into play. Deena's heart might waver, but her mind was unchangeable.

It was after Alicia's burial that Justin had made an earlier pledge: never to go to another funeral service. But he couldn't stay away from the church today. Jimmy had helped him when he most needed help. Jimmy had stood by him. They'd worked together for nearly seven years. And he still couldn't quite believe that such a decent man had been killed in this random way. Like everyone else in the country, he was still stunned by the attack. And still waiting for some kind of explanation, something that would give it some kind of sense.

He'd gotten a phone call minutes after the explosion from a sergeant at the Southampton station, the largest station in the area, telling him what had occurred and telling him that all East End cops should be on alert in case they were needed at the bomb site. Eventually they were told their presence wasn't necessary. By that time they were all aware that Jimmy hadn't returned from lunch.

'Maybe he just can't get back,' Gary Jenkins, a young cop, had said. 'The streets are closed so maybe he's just stuck over there.'

'Yeah, maybe,' Justin had said. But somehow they all knew.

At six o'clock, when Jimmy still hadn't returned, Justin went to

Duffys Tavern with Gary and a couple of the other guys and they watched the TV above the bar, stunned at the horror being shown and reported. The president addressed the nation, the vice president and the attorney general by his side, saying that evil had struck again but that, once again, it would be defeated. Justin wondered when the hell evil had ever been defeated, but he kept quiet. Nobody said anything about Jimmy, either. None of them wanted to be the one to jinx things. It turned out no jinx was needed. Justin got the call around midnight that night. It came from Jimmy's son. The FBI had managed to tap into the restaurant's computer records; they'd gotten the names of everyone who had a lunch reservation at Harper's that day. Carolyn Helms was one of the women listed. She died in the blast. So did the person dining with her. Two of the cops at the station knew that she was Jimmy's lunch date. Before Jimmy's son hung up, he said that his mother would like Justin to speak at the service. Lying in bed at midnight, Justin had nodded at the son's request, then realized that the man on the other end of the phone couldn't see him, so he just said, 'Sure,' because he didn't know what else to say. And now here he was.

The service was about to begin. Justin started to move down toward one of the front pews but he felt a hand pulling on his arm. It was Jimmy's wife, Marjorie.

'Why was he there, Jay? Why was he in that restaurant?'

Her voice was loud. And shrill enough that it resonated throughout the room. Justin answered quietly, hoping she'd follow his lead. 'I don't know, Marge. I really don't.'

'I know what people think,' Marjorie said. 'I know what everyone here is thinking.'

'I'm not thinking anything, Marge.'

'I want to know what happened, Jay. I want to know why this happened.'

'I just know what it says in the papers.'

'I don't give a shit what it says in the papers. Or on television!' Her voice was very loud now, and shrill. Heads turned as she spoke. 'I want to know what he was doing there. And I want to know why my husband is dead! I want you to find out for me! You owe me that. You owe *him* that!'

She realized she was being too loud, understood that she was on the edge of hysteria. Marjorie Leggett released Jay's arm. Her hands hung down by her sides now, as if she no longer knew what to do with them. 'I'm sorry.' She spoke almost too softly this time. 'I'm sorry.'

'Okay.'

'Thank you,' she said, a whisper now.

'No,' Justin told her. 'I don't mean that it's okay that you were yelling. It is okay that you're yelling. It's your husband's funeral, you can do whatever the hell you want. I mean, okay, I'll try to find out.'

She nodded, too drained to smile. Too exhausted even to say thank you again. She patted him lightly on the arm, then went to sit down.

Justin sat through three eulogies before it was his turn to speak. He went up to the pulpit, pulled out a piece of paper that had his prepared speech. He stared at the words he'd typed up, decided they were idiotic, that he couldn't say them, then turned the paper over so all he could see was a blank page.

'I'm not very good at this kind of thing,' he began. 'But I just decided to toss my little speech away. What's written here suddenly seems so fake, like I'm talking about a stranger. So . . . To be honest, I don't know if there's all that much to say about Jimmy, except that he wasn't a stranger. At least to anyone in this room. He was a pretty normal guy. But maybe that's what made him special. He wasn't rich, he didn't do things that changed the world. He was just decent.

He worked hard and he liked people. Some people he loved. But whether he liked you or loved you or not, he did his best to help you. Maybe that's why I'm feeling so sad today. Because I don't know all that many normal people who are like that.'

He hesitated, thought he should say something about Marjorie and the kids, maybe something a little more personal. He was distracted, though, by a muffled bang. It sounded like a thunderclap. Or a car crash. Everyone was on edge, half expecting another bombing, so most of the audience turned toward the back door or jumped nervously. This wasn't an explosion, though, Justin knew. His guess was car crash. Some kind of collision. Maybe even something large falling off a truck. That clearly was the general consensus because the fear seemed to subside. People were turning back to face him now. The interruption was over.

And then he realized that a cell phone was ringing.

Two, three, four rings. Jesus Christ, talk about inappropriate.

A fifth ring. Then silence. He waited to make sure it really had stopped before he continued. He turned toward Marge, said one of the ways you judge good people is by the relationships they maintain with other good people . . .

And there it was again. The ringing cell phone. He was about to say something, after the second ring he began to tell the person with the phone to get the hell out.

Then he realized it was *his* cell phone that was ringing.

His mouth dropped open in embarrassment. For a moment he almost had to laugh, it was just too awful, but he realized that laughter was even less appropriate than the call. It was ringing a third time now, at least two more to go before his voice mail picked up. He wondered if people knew where it was coming from, and, looking out at the sea of faces staring up at him, he realized they sure as hell did. Everyone knew. Every single person in the church. His mouth

25

went dry. He couldn't even name anyone who might possibly be calling him. Everyone he knew was at the goddamn funeral.

There it was – the fourth ring.

Justin looked out at the mourners, all of whom were staring at him in disbelief. He swallowed, coughed to clear his throat, and then he said, 'I'm really sorry about this. Excuse me.'

Then he reached into his suit pocket, took out the phone, saw from the digital display that the call was coming from the East End police station, and he answered it.

'Jay, it's Mike.'

Mike Haversham was the only cop who wasn't at the funeral. Someone had to stay behind to mind the store.

Justin kept his voice low, put his hand over his mouth to muffle his words even further. 'I'm in the middle of the funeral, you idiot.'

'I know. I know.' The young cop's voice was trembling. 'I'm really sorry. But it's an emergency.'

Justin looked at the people in the pews. With his eyes and the briefest shrug of his shoulders, he did his best to convey that this wasn't his fault.

'It *better* be a fucking emergency,' he breathed into the receiver. 'What is it?'

Mike Haversham told him. Justin clicked off the phone, lifted his head to stare back out over everyone who was there to mourn Jimmy Leggett.

'I think Jimmy would understand this,' he said to the crowd. 'At least I hope so.' He tapped the cell phone lightly against his forehead, then said what he knew he had to say. 'But either way, I've got to go.'

Chapter 2

'We've got plenty of witnesses,' Mike Haversham was saying. 'A few people at the airport saw a lot of it. Bunch of people saw the crash. Drivers, bicyclists, pedestrians. I'm sure a couple of people in their homes.'

Judging by the crowd that was rapidly gathering, Justin was sure that Haversham was right. Witnesses would not be a problem. 'What the hell happened? Give me the short version first.'

'The guy took off from the runway. Everything seemed okay. He was only up in the air a few minutes and seemed to lose control. He kind of circled around for a while and then . . .' The young cop exhaled a deep whistle and made a diving motion with his hand. 'Looks like he tried to land on the road here, and just couldn't do it.'

'Tried to land right in the middle of fucking town?'

'Hey, who knows what was goin' through his mind? The guy thought he was going to die.'

'Yeah, well, he was right about that, wasn't he?' Justin stared again in disbelief at the wreck, something he'd already been doing for a good two minutes now. He walked up to the small private plane, which had crash-landed maybe thirty yards from the busiest intersection in East End Harbor. It had come down in the middle of the road that led in and out of town, missing by ten feet the concrete bridge that spanned the bay. The brand-new concrete bridge, Justin thought. The town council would have had a shit fit. The bridge had taken six months longer than it was supposed to take to be built. It had just opened two weeks earlier. Ten more feet. He almost smiled at the thought. Ten more little feet . . .

The plane was at a forty-five-degree angle and looked to be compressed to about two-thirds its normal size. The nose and most of the front half were crumpled after colliding with the road.

Beneath the pilot's-side wing, a man's body was sprawled on the ground. His neck was clearly broken. Next to the man's body was a small puddle of vomit.

'I got sick,' Mike Haversham said quietly. 'I never saw anything like this before. I knew I had to get the guy out, see if he was still alive. But when I got the door open . . .'

'Don't be embarrassed,' Justin told him. 'It happens.' When Mike nodded quickly, gratefully, Justin went on. 'So you pulled him out of the plane?'

'With that guy's help.' Mike pointed to a man who was standing about twenty feet away next to a Lexus SUV.

'Who is he?'

'Just some guy who was passing by. There were a few other cars but he's the only one who stopped. You might think about hiring him. At least he didn't puke his guts out.'

'And who's that?' Justin now waved his hand toward a second man who wore jeans and a light gray sport coat over a long-sleeved white shirt and gray-and-blue tie. He was pacing off to the side and quite upset. Curiously, Justin thought he didn't look upset about the crash, more like he was angry about something else. Maybe it was the man's comb-over. It wasn't pretty.

'He's pissed because I wouldn't let him leave,' Haversham said.

'Why not? He see something?'

'I don't know. But he was in the plane, you know, and then he wouldn't talk to me, so—'

'What do you mean, he was in the plane? A passenger?'

Haversham shook his head. 'No. After the crash.'

'What the hell was he doing?' Justin asked.

'I don't know. He's whaddyacallit, you know, the agency that deals with planes and shit.'

'FAA?'

'Yeah, I think that's what he said.'

'How'd he get here so fast?'

'I think he was already here. You know, doin' some business at the airport or somethin'. I figured you'd want to talk to him so I told him to stick around.'

'So what's his problem?'

'I don't know, but he didn't like that. He wanted to beat it. So I told him if he tried to leave, I'd arrest his ass.'

Justin stared over at the man, who was still pacing angrily.

'Should I have let him go?' Mike Haversham asked.

'No,' Justin told the young cop. 'You did the right thing.'

'You wanna talk to him?'

'Yeah. But first talk to me about two more minutes, act like we're having a real serious conversation. Then go tell him I'd like to see him.'

'Why wait? He's only gonna get more pissed off.'

'Yeah,' Justin said. 'I know.'

The crowd was growing now. Not just the people who'd seen the plane go down. These were the gawkers. The ones who can't resist a peek at disaster. The same people who slow down and rubberneck on the highway, desperate for a clear sight of a crumpled fender or a lifeless body. Justin never understood the attraction. His instinct was, whenever possible, to run like hell from anything even resembling tragedy. Disgusted, he waved them all back, kept Haversham by his side for more than the agreed-upon two minutes because the ambulance arrived. It wasn't from Southampton. Justin didn't recognize either of the two EMWs. One of them explained that they'd come from mid-Island.

'After the nightmare at the restaurant,' he said, 'you're lucky they sent anyone. We've been a little overworked. Carrying bodies all over the fucking place. No disrespect intended.'

Justin told him that none was taken, nodded his sympathy, and watched as they put the pilot on a stretcher and made the expected comments – the one who'd already spoken just said, 'Holy shit!' when he saw the damage, the other muttered something about how lucky it was that no one else was hurt – then they carried the stretcher into the back of the ambulance and drove off. As soon as they were gone, Justin sent Haversham to get the FAA agent. The man in the jacket and tie and bad hairstyle immediately strode up to Justin, pumping his arms back and forth as if that would help him get there quicker.

'Officer,' he began, 'I'm sure you and your buddy there think you're doing your job. But—'

'You have any ID?' Justin said.

'What?'

'You have anything identifying you as working for the FAA? That's what you told the other officer, isn't it? And just for the record, he is an officer, not my buddy. This isn't exactly a social occasion.'

The man closed his mouth and stared at Justin for several seconds. Then he reached into his back right pocket and pulled out his wallet. He fished for a card, slipped it out of its plastic sleeve, and handed it over.

Justin saw the man's name, Martin Heffernan, and made a show out of reading the rest of the information very carefully. He took so long to squint at the small print on the card, the man in the sport jacket couldn't restrain himself any longer. 'Look, it's right there in black and white and it's pretty clear. I'm FSDO out of New York.' He pronounced it as 'fizzdough'.

Justin looked away from the card. 'FSDO? Sounds like a cute government acronym.' He looked at the card again. 'Flight Standards District Office?'

'That's right. Local FAA office in New York.'

'The city?'

'Yeah.'

'What are you doing here?'

'I was making a routine ramp check. Airport safety. We do it all the time. The whole tri-state area.'

'So it's just a coincidence, you being here and this accident.'

'That's right,' Heffernan said. 'I saw the plane going down and drove here as fast as I could.'

'And as long as you were on the spot, you thought you'd jump right in, see what was what.'

The man rolled his eyes, exasperated. 'I work for an agency that oversees any and all air traffic. When there's an accident, we investigate. We make reports. And that's what I'd like to do now. Leave, so I can make my report.'

'Which is going to say what?'

'Excuse me?'

'You hopped in the plane, you checked things out. What are you going to say in your report?'

'I don't have to tell you that. The FAA has jurisdiction over local law enforcement when it comes to things like this.'

Justin chewed on his lip for a moment. 'I don't know the legal details about this kind of jurisdictional dispute, Mr Heffernan, but

I'll tell you what – I think you're full of shit. For the moment, however, let's say I take your word for it. Maybe you don't have to tell me what you found. But I'll tell *you* that only a big-time asshole would worry about jurisdiction at a time like this. A man's been killed here, and all you can think about is who's in charge? That sucks.'

The man let some anger fade from his face.

'I just want to know what happened,' Justin continued. 'So why don't you tell me? Before you rush back to your shitty little one-bedroom apartment in the city and make yourself a martini and watch a video or whatever the hell you have to do that's so important. Or you commute from Jersey?'

The FSDO agent exhaled a long breath, then quietly said, 'I can't. I mean I can't tell you exactly what happened because we'll have to do a further investigation. But just from my quick look around, I'd say it was a simple case of pilot error. The plane looks to be in good shape . . .'

'Other than the fact that it's smashed to pieces.'

The man almost smiled. But not quite. 'Yes. Other than that. I don't see anything out of order. But, again, all I did was give things a quick once-over. We'll have a mechanic check things out thoroughly. I've already called over to the airport to get the thing towed there for a proper inspection. If you want my guess, though, it's what we see all the time: another guy who thought it'd be fun to fly and doesn't bother to learn how to do things properly. Now, can I rush back to my shitty little one-bedroom apartment? In the city.'

'After you give your name and contact information to my buddy over there, yeah.'

Justin turned away. He didn't like this guy and didn't want to give him the satisfaction of any further eye contact. He didn't glance in his direction again until Heffernan was in his car and driving away. By that time, the media had arrived: a young reporter from the local East End paper was making his way through the crowd jotting down comments from eyewitnesses, and a cameraman from a network affiliate was already set up. An on-air reporter in jeans, T-shirt, and leather jacket was finishing a quick summation of the accident. When he was done talking, he waved over in Justin's direction. Justin didn't see any way around this, so he nodded and gave his name and title to the guy in the jacket and, as the camera swung over to film him, began answering the reporter's questions.

"Officer Westwood, are you in charge of this investigation?'

'It's not much of an investigation yet, since it happened just a few minutes ago, but yes, for the moment I'm in charge.'

'The obvious question,' the reporter said earnestly, 'is whether or not this is connected to the recent terrorist bombing at Harper's.'

'It's an obvious question but there's no obvious answer yet. All indications are that there is no connection. An agent for the FAA has already been on the scene and his initial instinct is that this is nothing more than pilot error. Although we will be investigating and doing a thorough examination of the aircraft.'

'So you believe there's no connection to the tragedy?'

'It's pretty tragic for the pilot,' Justin said, 'but as I said, there's no indication that this is connected to what happened at Harper's.'

'Do you know the identity of the pilot yet?'

'We're not releasing any information. We've barely had time to gather any, so there's nothing to be released. Besides, we haven't even had a chance to inform the man's family. Now if you'll excuse me, I've got work to do.'

The reporter threw out a few more questions, but Justin shook his head and walked away, over to Mike Haversham. The reporter finished his stand-up. Justin heard the words 'small-town policeman' and 'certain the FBI will soon be making an appearance,' shook his head again, and said to Haversham, 'Okay. Now for the fun part.' He sighed. 'I've got to notify the next of kin. Who is he?'

'I don't know.'

'What does his ID say?'

Haversham looked like he was going to cry. 'I don't have his ID.'

Justin decided to hold his temper. Mike was just a kid. He'd never done anything remotely like this before.

'Call the hospital immediately, tell them we have to get the wallet back. Mike, the first thing you do, always, once you know you can't save the guy, is check for ID.'

'I know. I checked.'

'And?'

'He didn't have any. No wallet, no ID.'

'You checked on his person?'

Haversham nodded.

'And in the plane?'

The young cop nodded again. 'I looked everywhere I could.'

Justin Westwood looked off down the road, in the direction Martin Heffernan's car had just disappeared.

'Don't let anyone else near this plane,' he said to Mike. 'Especially inside. Anyone I don't say is okay tries to get in, you have my permission to shoot him. You got that?'

'I don't have a gun.'

'Then beat him to death with your cell phone, okay?'

When the cop nodded for a third time, Justin headed back to the station. It was no more than a five-minute walk. When he got there, he immediately went to his desk and picked up the phone. He called the Southampton force, got their fingerprint guy, and told him what had to be done. Jimmy Leggett's funeral was over by now and two young cops filed back in. Everyone seemed to assume that Justin was in charge, so he decided to go with the assumption. He told the two cops to get to the site of the crash. He explained to them how to deal with the traffic problem that would definitely ensue. Then he inhaled a deep breath. He didn't feel as if he exhaled until nearly three hours later. By that time, he'd spoken to the fingerprint expert, who'd told him that, other than Mike Haversham's, not one print had come up, that the entire inside of the plane had been wiped clean. Justin had also spoken to an administrator at Southampton Hospital, who told him that no ambulance had been dispatched to any plane crash site, not from them, not from mid-Island, not from anywhere. Nor had any crash victim been picked up. And he'd spoken to Morgan Davidson, a local doctor who also served as the ME when needed. Davidson told him that no body had been delivered to him – and that there had been no alert that a body was expected. When Justin heard that, he hung up and said, 'Goddamnit.'

Gary Jenkins glanced up at that point, caught Justin's eye, and said, 'Problem?'

That's when Justin felt himself exhale. And that's when he answered Gary. 'Yeah,' was his answer. 'We've definitely got a problem.'

chapter 3

The East End Airport had, not so long ago, been small and anachronistic. It was a place for local flyers to park their single-engine planes. And it was a friendly stopover for nonprofessional pilots traveling up and down the East Coast. For years, there was one charter company based there. They flew commuters back and forth to Manhattan on Fridays and Mondays on a seaplane, and occasionally flew families up to Martha's Vineyard, Nantucket, and Block Island.

Over the past decade, like everything else in this part of Long Island, the airport had gotten larger, noisier, and less friendly. Corporate and time-share jets were now hangared there. Private helicopters – the new toy for millionaires who didn't like to deal with highway traffic – flitted about ubiquitously. Commuter planes operated several times a day, seven days a week. And there were three charter companies now. All of them thriving.

Ray Lockhardt had worked at the airport for fourteen years, the last four as manager. Two years before his promotion, he'd been arrested by Justin Westwood. Justin had only recently arrived in East End Harbor, and was new to the police force. Jimmy Leggett had been keeping an eye on a drug dealer named Manual, who'd been dealing out of the black section of the Hamptons on Route

114 – the section the snobby Bridgehampton and Southampton locals referred to as 'Lionel Hampton'. Leggett had been looking for an opportunity to take Manual off the streets and, having had some experience in this area, Justin was assigned to shadow him part-time. On his watch, he caught Ray Lockhardt buying an ounce of grass and some downers. Lockhardt was stand-up when the arrest went down. He didn't argue or deny anything. He just said to Justin, in a fairly even voice, 'I've never done anything like this before. And I'll never do it again. I'm going through a divorce, I haven't slept in a week, and I thought this shit would help. If I'm busted, I'll get fired. Ask anyone about me, they'll tell you this isn't my style.' He blurted it all out as if it was one long sentence. If it had been delivered a little more smoothly, Justin would have thought it had been rehearsed. But it wasn't smooth. The words were nervous and heartfelt. It was Justin's first major decision on the job. If he didn't arrest Ray, he couldn't make the bust on Manual stick. On the other hand, all he had was a small amount of marijuana and a few pills. No way Lockhardt deserved to have his life ruined – or at least put on hold – for doing something that Justin did himself whenever he could. And there wasn't a chance in hell Manual was going to do time for this. He'd get a minuscule fine and be back in business in hours. It wasn't much of a decision. He said to Lockhardt, 'I better not find out you're lying.' That was all he said. Lockhardt was out of there in seconds. Then Justin turned to Manual, who couldn't believe his luck. 'I'm not worried about you. You'll do something a lot stupider than this and you'll do it soon. Then we'll get you.' Manual swore that he was changing his whole life. His stupid days were over thanks to Justin's generosity. It turned out that Ray Lockhardt was telling the truth. His divorce went through, he never got in trouble again, and eventually he got promoted to airport manager. Manual, on the other hand, was definitely lying. Three weeks after the aborted

bust, he was shot and killed in the South Bronx. A coke deal gone sour.

Ever since that day, Ray Lockhardt treated Justin Westwood like his best friend. They didn't socialize or even bump into each other very often. But if they happened to be in the same restaurant, Ray always sent over a drink, which Justin acknowledged gratefully. And if they passed each other in the street or bumped into each other in the supermarket, Ray always went out of his way to say hello and ask Justin how he was doing. Justin always replied that he was doing just swell. Even if he wasn't.

So normally Ray wouldn't have been unhappy to see the police officer walk into the airport terminal two days after the plane crash by the bridge. But Justin thought he spotted something in Ray's eyes. Something that said he wasn't thrilled with the visit. The look disappeared quickly, though, then Ray gave him a happy wave of his hand and said, 'What can I do for you, Officer Westwood?' Normally, Justin would have said what he always said: 'Call me Justin.' But today he let the appellation stand. He had a feeling today it was better to keep things formal.

'I'm here about the crash,' Justin told him.

The look on Ray's face definitely turned to unhappy.

'Your mechanic finish his inspection of the plane?' Justin decided he could now officially describe Ray as looking pained.

Ray Lockhardt nodded. Then he shook his head. 'Yeah, it's finished. But I did it myself. The inspection.'

'That normal? I thought you were more the executive type now.'

Ray didn't crack a smile. He just looked even more pained, then said, 'You know, the FAA can cause a lot of trouble for me. Fines. Heavy fines. They could even shut me down.'

'You doing something wrong?' Justin asked.

'No. Not a thing! Everything here goes strictly by the book.'

'So what's the problem?'

Ray didn't answer.

'Ray, is there some problem I don't know about? Remember, I'm pretty good at solving your problems.'

Ray hesitated again. Then he picked up a copy of the *Daily News* that was sitting on the counter in front of him. He turned to page sixteen, showed Justin a small story at the bottom right of the page. The headline said: PILOT ERROR CAUSE OF LONG ISLAND CRASH. The story went on to say that an FBI spokesperson revealed that the FAA had determined there was no connection between the small plane crash and the bombing at Harper's. The spokesperson was quoted as saying that this was just a terrible coincidence. The pilot's name was still not released, because his family had not yet been reached.

'This based on your report?' Justin asked. 'You talk to this reporter before you talked to me?'

Now Ray licked his lips, which looked dry and cracked. 'I haven't talked to any reporters. And I haven't given anyone my report yet.'

'Not even the FAA?'

'Hell, no.'

'Then how can they already have made this kind of determination?'

'Don't know. But I was told that they had.'

'Who told you? Martin Heffernan? The guy who was here the other day?'

'Right. The GAS agent.'

'GAS?'

'General Aviation Safety.'

'What is it with you guys and your acronyms? He called himself something different. FSOD?'

'FSDO.' He too pronounced it 'fizzdough.' 'Flight Standard District Office. The GAS guys work out of FSDO.'

'Well, with all those acronyms behind them, I guess your report's gonna say the same thing as theirs, right?'

Ray Lockhardt didn't answer.

'Ray? Is your report going to agree with Heffernan?'

Lockhardt lowered his voice, even though no one else was in the building. 'He didn't just tell me what their finding was.'

Justin spoke casually. 'No? What else did he tell you?'

'He said I shouldn't tell you anything. Said I shouldn't tell nobody anything. But especially you.'

Justin nodded, as if the news didn't surprise him. Which, in some ways, it didn't. He hadn't exactly made a pal of Martin Heffernan. 'Well, I don't want you to get in trouble with the FAA, Ray. You don't have to tell me a thing.'

'FAA, hell.' He tapped the newspaper on the counter. 'You read this story? You think I want to mess around with the goddamn FBI?'

'No. I don't think you do. And I don't think you should.'

It was an exit line, but Justin didn't leave. He waited. He waited until he could see Ray struggle to figure out what he was going to say next. And what he said was, 'That guy's a little weasel!' He practically spit the words out.

'Heffernan, you mean?'

'Yeah,' Ray said. 'Heffernan. Normally these guys check us out once a year, maybe twice. He's been here a lot lately, over the past couple of weeks. Hassling us. Even made some late-night checks. I knew something was up. I mean, what the hell's he hassling me for? So fuck him. He can't stop me from telling you the truth.'

'You sure?' Justin said. 'I mean it. I don't want you to get in trouble.'

Ray Lockhardt laughed. 'You're good,' he said. 'The more you tell me to shut up, the more I want to spill my guts. You must be hell in the interrogation room. I'd like to see that sometime.'

Justin did his best to laugh back. 'We don't have an interrogation room,' he said. 'There's nothing to see.'

And now Ray wasn't laughing or smiling. His lips were together and his eyes were grim. 'Well how 'bout if I show *you* something, then?' he said. 'How 'bout I show you something pretty fucking amazing?'

They were back in one of three hangars on the airport property. In the middle of the enormous space was the wreck of the crashed airplane. Ray led Justin toward the wreckage. He hopped up onto one of the damaged wings, indicated that Justin should follow. Then he ducked down and slipped inside the plane. Justin stepped forward and peered in.

'You know anything about planes?' Ray asked.

'Now's probably a good time to mention this. I'm not the most mechanical guy in the world.'

'All right, I can keep it simple.' And as he spoke, he began pointing, indicating various knobs and tubes and gadgets, some still whole, some twisted and gnarled from the impact. 'This is a Piper Saratoga. A single-engine piston airplane.'

'I'm with you so far.'

'There are two weird things about this particular plane. First is, look here in the back. Should be a four-seater but the two backseats are ripped out. Somebody ripped 'em out so they could put this thing in.' He tapped a large, heavy-looking tank that took up much of the back half of the plane.

'And what is that?'

'A long-range gas tank.'

'Okay, now you've got to explain.'

'These planes aren't meant to fly long distances. It's not what

41

they're made for. They're easy to fly, they're not complicated. It's why a lot of them get stolen. And when they're stolen, the guys who steal 'em sometimes put in these long-range tanks.'

'Why?'

'Look, I only know this because I hear the pilots talk. This is pretty common knowledge . . .'

'Ray, I'm not interested in where you get your info. I just want to know what it is.'

'These are drug planes. A lot of 'em get stolen in Florida. They steal 'em from weekend fliers, they get the new tanks, they're good for long trips to South America and back.'

Justin tried to digest this information but it didn't add up to much. It had no context for him other than it opened up one vague possibility: the crash was connected to some kind of drug smuggling scheme. So he just filed it away in the back of his head. 'You said there were two things that were strange about the plane. What's the second?'

'Can you take a little lesson in heating systems?'

'Hey, you can dish it out, I can take it.'

'These kinds of planes, the cabins are heated by heat from the exhaust manifold pipe. It goes through the exhaust manifold.' Ray now touched something that Justin assumed was the manifold. 'They put this shroud around it and ram air blows it in. The heaters don't work too well except in flight because it takes air to push the heat through and more air comes in while you're flying. Here, you see, you regulate it by opening and closing the valve.' He demonstrated. 'There's no thermostat.'

'So what, there was no heat and the guy froze to death or something?'

Ray shook his head. 'The danger with this kind of setup is if there's a leak in the exhaust system. When that happens, it lets in carbon monoxide.'

'Carbon monoxide poisoning? That's how people get killed in garages when they leave the car running.'

'Yeah, well, it doesn't just happen in cars or planes. It killed that tennis player, the guy with the long blond hair. You remember that?'

Justin nodded. 'Vitas Gerulaitis. It wasn't far from here.'

'Right in the guy's home. Faulty heating installation. Big lawsuit.'

'So you think that's what caused the crash? Bad heating system?'

'I'm certain of it. So's Frank. The mechanic.'

'So, Ray, what does the FAA care if it's pilot error or faulty valve installation? It's horrible, and maybe there'll be a lawsuit, but so what? It's an accident. Shoddy work. What's the big deal?'

'The big deal is that this plane's new,' Ray said. 'No more than a year old. See this manifold? That ain't new. Gotta be four, five years older than the plane. Maybe more.'

'Maybe there was something wrong with the new one.'

'Maybe there was. But nobody legit would have put this thing in as a replacement.'

'Are you saying that someone took out a new manifold and replaced it with one he *knew* would leak?'

'I can't say he knew for sure. But this manifold looks pretty bad. Anyone who knew enough to put it in would know that. Hard to think it wasn't deliberate,' Ray Lockhardt said. 'Which is just what the asshole at the FAA doesn't want me to say.'

'Yeah. And you want to know what the asshole at the FAA doesn't want *me* to say?' Justin banged his palm against the dented body of the plane. 'If you're right, I've got a murder on my hands.'

Back in Ray's small, glass-walled office, Justin closed the door and waved for the airport manager to sit down.

'When the guy in the Piper landed, did he have to check in? Sign anything?'

'He just had to pay me eight bucks as a landing fee. And that's what he did. He got a Dr Pepper from that machine there and gave me my eight bucks.'

'You talk to him at all?'

'Some. Enough to know he was dying of thirst. He downed the soda practically in one gulp. Same thing before he took off two days ago. That guy loved his Dr Pepper.'

'Anyone flying with him?'

'Yeah. But I didn't really see him. He didn't come through the terminal, just unloaded some stuff from the plane and went to a car.'

'Rental?'

'Don't think so. Someone picked them both up.'

'Any idea who?'

Lockhardt shook his head. 'I wasn't really paying attention. I didn't get a close-up look.'

'Get any other impressions of the Dr Pepper guy?'

'I can tell you one thing for sure. He was a *pilot*. He wasn't one of those newcomers, just took it up and thought it'd be fun to zoom around up there. He knew what he was doing.'

'How could you tell?'

'I've been doing this a long time. You get a feel.'

'Okay. You get any kind of a feel for Martin Heffernan?'

'Yeah. The guy's a dick.'

'He told me he was here doing ramp checks. What does that mean?'

'It means bullshit work, basically. He goes around, looks to see if we're parking the planes properly. Then he hassles whatever pilots he finds, checks to see if they got their P.O.H. – Pilot's Operating Handbook – and their airworthiness certificate. Checks your weight

44

and balance, your license . . .' Ray looked off into the distance, then came back to focus on Justin. 'You know, that makes this even weirder.'

'What does?'

'Well, when Heffernan went inside the Piper, he had to have seen the extra gas tank.'

'So?'

'So it's illegal. I mean, again, I can't say guaranteed that tank's not kosher, but I'd pretty much bet on it.'

'Why?'

'Anything that throws off a plane's weight and balance has to be approved.'

'By . . .?

'The FAA. Everything has to be recalculated if you add a huge tank like that. By a certified mechanic. Then you gotta get a form 337. That becomes a permanent record in the plane's log and part of the airworthiness certificate. That tank just don't look like it's got a 337. And Heffernan couldn't've missed it.'

'Hold on.' Justin's voice got slightly louder now, the only outward sign that he was getting excited. 'Do you mean Heffernan was inside the Piper *before* it took off?'

'Yeah. When he was doing his inspections.'

'And did he talk to the pilot?'

'Sure. I'm tellin' you, he inspected the plane.'

'And checked his license?'

'Had to have.'

'That son of a bitch!' He saw the confused look on Ray's face, decided there was no reason he shouldn't explain. 'The pilot? The one who was killed – he didn't have any ID on him.'

'You think Heffernan stole it?'

'I thought so before. Now I'm certain of it.'

'Why?'

All Justin could do was shrug. It was the most intelligent answer he could come up with.

'So you don't know who the guy is?'

'No, not yet. I was hoping you could tell me.'

'Nope. He never mentioned it.' Ray grabbed a tissue, blew his nose. 'I think I'm coming down with something. The change in temperature, you know? One day it's fifty, the next day it's thirty.' He blew his nose again. Then said, 'You wanna find out the pilot's name?'

Justin had to bite his tongue. But all he said, quite slowly, was, 'Yes, Ray, I do.'

'Well, I know how you can do that.'

'You do?'

'Sure. If he owned the plane I do.'

Now Ray led him back to the hangar. When they got close to the Piper, he pointed toward the plane's tail. On it were black painted letters and numbers reading: *NOV6909 Juliet*.

'That's the tail number,' Ray explained. 'All you gotta do is check it out with FAA records and it'll tell you the name of the owner. Anyone can do it. It's a public record.'

'Ray, you are a very good man.'

Pleased, Ray Lockhardt said, 'So can I ask you a question? Couldn't you just take the guy's fingerprints to find out who he is? That's what they always do on *Law & Order*. I mean, isn't that the procedure?' He looked happy using the word 'procedure' talking to a cop.

'Yes, that is the procedure. But it only works if his fingerprints are on file somewhere. In this case it doesn't matter because there were no fingerprints.'

'In the plane?'

'Anywhere.'

'Well, I know he's dead and all, but he still has fingers, doesn't he?'

'Trust me, Ray. There are no fingerprints to be had.'

There was a brief silence, then Ray Lockhardt's mouth spread into a big smile. 'I wouldn't be so sure, if I were you.'

Before Justin could move, Ray was out the door of the hangar. When he returned, he was carrying a small plastic garbage can.

'It's from behind the counter in the terminal. Place has been pretty empty the last couple of days. Since the bomb. And Pepe, the cleaning guy, he's been out with the flu.'

'You trying to tell me something?' Justin asked.

'Yeah. I'm tryin' to tell you all you gotta do is find the Dr Pepper can in here. I mean, if you want some fingerprints.'

Justin was almost out the door, carrying the garbage pail, when he heard Ray call out, 'Does this mean we're finally even?'

Without turning back, Justin answered over his shoulder, 'Let your conscience be your guide, Ray. Let your conscience be your guide.'

Justin was outside and nearly to his red 1989 BMW convertible by the time Ray Lockhardt muttered to himself, 'There ain't no bein' even with that guy. Who am I kidding?'

chapter 4

Justin decided against going back to the station. He'd had it for the day. Besides, he had a computer at home and the work he had to do could be done there.

He pulled into the pebbled driveway of his small 1880s Victorian house. When it was built it was meant to be low-income housing for workers at the local watch factory, about a mile down the road, closer to town. There was a twin house right next door to Justin's, although the owners had made additions so it was no longer identical. Justin liked his house. It was charming and quirky and it had a nice, private backyard, well protected from his neighbors by a fence and tall trees, cherry and oak. Justin particularly liked his house because it had a lot of its own personality, which meant he didn't have to bother to put much of his personality into it.

And he hadn't bothered. His furniture was minimal. A bed and one chest of drawers in each of the two bedrooms. A TV in his bedroom. A comfortable couch in the living room. A PC. He'd put in a good stereo system because music was important to him. He could lose himself in music, mostly rock, sometimes jazz. Lately he'd tried opera and, to his surprise, he found that he liked it. He'd been listening to Maria Callas late at night, sitting in the dark, a drink in his hand, her passion spoke to him. Her urgency. But, at heart, he was a rock and roller. And as he got out of his car and headed inside, onto the screened-in front porch and into the living room, all he wanted to do was have a shot of a good single malt, maybe eventually smoke a joint, and be overwhelmed by some Warren Zevon or Lou Reed or possibly even Fun Lovin' Criminals, a New York band he'd recently discovered. By the time he got to the CD player, he'd decided on something a little softer, more melancholy. An old Arlo Guthrie. *Hobos Lullaby.* It had been one of Alicia's favorites. He couldn't listen to it without thinking of her. As he pressed the play button, he could already hear the words in his head, the words he used to listen to over and over again after she died. It was a song about living too fast and too hard, about taking a look around and seeing what you'd become and feeling that your life was not your own.

That's the way he'd felt for years after Alicia was gone. That, somehow, he had to be stuck in someone else's life. It was only fairly recently that he'd felt as if he'd begun to return to his own existence, his own path. Now there was no denying it. Here he was. His house. His furniture. His job. His murder investigation. His missing victim. His life.

The question was: Where the hell did that life go from here and how much control could he have over it?

As the first cut began, he went to his Compaq, turned it on. He was anxious to take a look at the FAA site and see what he could dig up, but before he could even sit down he noticed that the message light on his phone machine was flashing.

Justin sighed. He disapproved of phone machines. He disapproved of anything that made him more accessible to the outside world. But his job required it. Somehow, his life required it, too, which he couldn't quite figure out, but there you had it. So he went to the machine, pressed play, and heard the voices of two people he didn't want to talk to.

The first message was from Marjorie Leggett, Jimmy's wife. No —
widow. He immediately made the mental correction. 'Jay, it's
Marge,' she began. Then there was a pause, as if maybe she should
give her last name. Which she did. 'Marge Leggett.' There was
another silence, a brief one. Justin could all but see her timidity, her
confusion at having to do something for the first time without her
husband's guidance. Then she found her resolve and continued
speaking. 'I'm just calling to see if you've . . . done anything . . . after
our conversation. Please call me. I need to know. Thank you.'

Justin's face softened at her final instinctive politeness. Then he
thought about her message. He had promised her he'd find out
what Jimmy was doing in the restaurant. Why he'd died such an
ignominious death. But he hadn't done a thing. He'd been a little
busy. He had a murder case on his hands. A murder case that no one
knew was actually murder.

And now he had to add something else to the list of things that
belonged in his life: his promises.

How much control would he have over them?

The second message was from Leona Krill, the mayor of East End
Harbor. She wanted him to call the moment he got her message. It
was urgent.

He erased both messages. Decided he'd wait an hour or so to call
Marge back. So he could figure out what he could actually say to
her. Decided he wouldn't call the mayor back at all.

Justin went back to sit at his computer, began to go online, then
the phone rang. He got back up, answered it.

'Justin, it's Leona Krill.'

'Hello, Leona.'

'I'm assuming you got my message and didn't call me back.
Everybody I talked to said that's exactly what you'd do. So I'm
calling again.'

'I just walked in the door. Got the message ten seconds ago. And who'd you talk to who said that?'

'Were you going to call me back?'

'Eventually.'

'I need to see you right away. At my office, please.'

'Can't this wait until tomorrow?'

'No, I'm afraid it can't.' When he didn't respond, the mayor said, 'Justin, this conversation isn't about anything bad. It is urgent, but it's not going to make you unhappy.'

'Leona, almost all conversations make me unhappy.'

'Can you be here in fifteen minutes?'

He told her he could and hung up the phone. Then he reluctantly flicked off Arlo Guthrie and went back outside, wondering what he was going to hear that she thought he wasn't going to hate hearing – and wondering exactly how much he was going to hate hearing it.

The mayor's office was in the oldest building on Main Street, a town house built in 1839. It was four stores down from Deena's yoga studio and five stores away from her apartment above Norm's Contemporary General Store. Justin parked right in front of the studio, walked by the plate glass window that let passersby look in on classes of people stretching and contorting themselves into odd positions. He automatically sucked in his belly, which wasn't nearly as large as it had been a year ago, but was a little larger than it had been three months ago. He'd stopped taking his yoga lessons the same time he and Deena had stopped seeing each other. He also realized it had been a couple of weeks since he'd been to the gym. Maybe three weeks. Shit, he thought. A month.

He glanced into the yoga class as he passed by. Deena happened to be looking his way, saw him and smiled. He gave a half wave and thought about stopping in, seeing if he could take Kendall, Deena's nine-year-old daughter, out to dinner. Maybe a movie. Then he thought better of it – his stomach was suddenly pierced with a familiar ache when he spotted Deena; the uncomfortable pang that comes from dissipated love – and just kept walking.

Leona Krill greeted him warmly. Justin thought that she was probably looking for a friend. She needed one. Leona was gay and had just gotten married, quite publicly, to her longtime girlfriend. The weekenders who inhabited East End Harbor were fairly liberal by nature. But the full-time residents – the voters – tended to be blue-collar and more conservative. The mayor's wedding had caused quite a stir. A lot of people thought it would cost her when the next election rolled around. Personally, Justin didn't care who she slept with or who she married. His idea of a good mayor was anyone who was reasonably honest, didn't screw up too much, and left him alone. Leona had scored well on all three points up to now. Now the third part of the equation was up in the air.

They spent thirty seconds asking how they each were, then she said, 'Let me get right to the point, Jay. People do call you Jay, don't they?' He admitted that some did, and was impressed that she'd done some homework in the few minutes it had taken him to arrive at her office. 'I'm sure this has occurred to you, and I know it might seem a bit indelicate to bring it up so soon after Jimmy's death, but we need another chief of police.'

It actually *hadn't* occurred to Justin. Things had been moving too quickly. And everything at the station was proceeding smoothly. But he nodded, as if he'd done nothing but think about such a need.

'Well, I'd like you to take the job,' Leona Krill said.

'Excuse me?'

'I'm appointing you the new chief of police. On a temporary

basis. I'm hoping you'll agree on six months. That seems fair. And at that point, we can review the situation and, I hope, mutually agree on whether you should continue or not. It makes perfect sense. You have the background, the experience, people seem to respect you – in a strange sort of way. There'll be a nice pay raise, of course.'

Justin realized he was standing there, probably looking dumbfounded. It shouldn't have been such a shock, it was the logical move for her to make. If he accepted, it made her life easy. No outside search, no unknown quantity. But every voice inside him was screeching for him not to do it. He didn't want the responsibility. Or the pay raise. He didn't want the bureaucratic dealings. Didn't want people working for him. He didn't want the extra ties to the community. Didn't want to attend the social events or the town meetings or see any public-spirited liaison who would want to talk to him about whatever public-spirited people talked about. He didn't want anything about this job. Nothing at all.

'Okay,' he said. 'I'll do it.'

She thanked him profusely, told him how glad she was, thanked him again. She set up a meeting with him for two days hence, on Friday, so they could discuss various details. She even kissed him on the cheek before he left.

Walking back down Main Street toward his car, Justin wondered what the hell he'd just done.

He thought, *My life. My choices.*

Shaking his head, he got in the car, drove home, called Marjorie Leggett, told her he was working on keeping his promise. Then he made a second call, this one to Billy DiPezio, the Providence, Rhode Island, police chief. Billy was the reason Justin had become a cop. And he'd been Justin's boss for several years. Billy was also the most crooked honest man Justin had ever met. Or maybe he was the most honest crook. Billy was a cop who walked a fine line between right and wrong, sometimes crossing over, not always knowing when he did. And rarely caring.

'I'm calling to get your permission for something,' Justin said when he got Billy on the phone. Billy was, as usual, not at the station or at home with his wife. He was in a bar somewhere, probably sharing a booth with someone he shouldn't be sharing it with.

'Well, that's a first,' Billy said.

'I'm trying to do a favor for a friend and I need to do a little research.'

'There's a new thing,' Billy said. 'It's called the Internet. It's amazing, I'm told. You can look stuff up, just like it's a real library. In fact, they probably have a whole library building in that weird little beach town you live in. The Billy Joel Library or something, isn't it?'

'It's not that kind of research. I need the human kind.'

'And you're calling me, Jay? I'm flattered.'

'Don't be too flattered. I want to talk to Chuck Billings.'

Justin could sense Billy's demeanor – jaunty, unconcerned – shift slightly. Nothing major, Billy was too good an actor to be obvious. But his tone changed a bit, and there was a split second more thought before he began to banter.

'Local cop decides to get involved in terrorist bombing, Jay?'

'I'm not getting involved,' Justin said. And he quickly told Billy the truth about Jimmy and Marjorie Leggett. 'If Chuck's still your bomb guy, all I want is to pick his brain a bit. I just want to understand what really happened so I can tell Marge. Maybe it'll help.'

'Of course he's still my bomb guy. Probably the best bomb squad captain in the country.'

'So can I talk to him?'

'It'll be easier than you think,' Billy told him. 'The Feds called him in as a consultant, to take a look at the restaurant.'

'Harper's?'

'I told you he's good.'

'Is he here already?'

'Right in your neighborhood,' Billy said. 'Staying at some motel, Chuck said not the classiest place in town. Something about fish . . . the Fish Bowl . . . the Fish Net . . .?'

'The Fisherman?'

'Sounds right. He got in this morning.'

'Thanks, Billy.'

'Buy him a good dinner, that's all I ask. You can afford it and he can't, not on what I pay him.'

'Done.'

'You coming up anytime soon?'

'I'll be up,' Justin said.

'You can also take *me* out to dinner.'

'Billy, you haven't paid for a meal in twenty years. What the hell do you need me for?'

'I'm hanging up on you now. Make sure you send my regards to your very rich parents.'

'I'll quote you exactly.'

Justin hung up, immediately dialed the Fisherman Motel. Billings wasn't in his room so Justin left a message on voice mail. He took a deep breath, looked around his house, happy to be alone and isolated from the world for at least one more night, then he rolled a big fat illegal joint, got as stoned as he'd been in several months, and fell asleep listening to R.E.M. blaring from his speakers.

It seemed as good a way as any to spend his first night as police chief.

chapter 5

Justin Westwood had experienced many disturbing dreams in his thirty-eight years. Particularly since Alicia and Lili had died. Dreams that floated through his consciousness. Dreams that were filled with violence and inflicted waves of guilt and regret. Dreams that made him twist and turn and hurt and wake up drenched in sweat and dread. But very few of his dreams were as disturbing as what he was watching on television at eight o'clock the next morning, soon after he'd awakened and made himself four cups of very strong drip coffee.

He was halfway through his second cup, black, when he turned on one of the morning shows on TV and was greeted with images of the aftermath of the explosion at Harper's. It was all very frantic and ragged. Some tourist had been making a video document of his trip to the Hamptons and had been half a block away when the bomb went off. He had the actual explosion on camera. It was from a skewed angle, but there it was and it was terrifying. Even on this nervously shot amateur tape, the force and devastation were apparent. The tourist had kept taping but it hadn't taken long before he was no longer allowed in the thick of things. Then the news coverage took over. This footage was at least as disturbing. Viewers were able to see things they never wanted to see. The blood, the mutilation, the bodies. The tape ran for a good ten minutes, with occasional voice-over narration and explanations given by the show's host. When it ended, the attorney general of the United States, Jeffrey Stuller, was on camera, appearing from Washington, D.C., speaking to the normally perky – but now extremely somber – host.

'While there will continue to be a more detailed investigation, we have concluded the initial stage of our investigation into the devastating bombing of Harper's Restaurant in East Hampton, New York,' Stuller was saying. 'And I'm not going to mince words. All indications are that this was a terrorist suicide bombing. It is the kind of incident that has, tragically, become far too common in Israel and Iraq and other locations around the world. And now it has reached American shores. This is something we have dreaded for quite some time, ever since the events of September eleventh, but I want to assure the American public that it is not something that has been unexpected. Nor is it something we are unprepared for. Most important, it is not something that will go unpunished.

'No one has claimed responsibility yet for this heinous act. But, as the president said in his speech last night, we know the evildoers who are responsible. They are the same evildoers we have been battling and battling successfully. We have, ever since 9/11, been winning the war on terrorism. We defeated the Taliban and we defeated Saddam Hussein. We have been beating back and defeating those who place no value on human life and who, misguidedly, use their God to promote hate, destruction, and the deaths of innocent, good, and truly God-loving people.'

'Mr Attorney General,' the host said. 'If you know who is responsible for this latest act, what will the government's next step be?'

'I have already met early this morning with the president, the vice president, the heads of the FBI and CIA, and my own deputy attorney general, Ted Ackland. Many details of that conversation must remain confidential for national security reasons. But I can assure every single person in our strong and resilient country that those responsible will be caught and punished very quickly.'

'Mr Stuller,' the host said, but the attorney general cut her off.

'I'd like to make one other point, if I may,' he said. 'Then I'll be happy to take one or two questions. And I can't stress this point strongly enough. We are at war. We have been at war for several years now, whether certain people in this country want to acknowledge that or not. And in times of war, security must become a priority and strong measures must be taken. Measures that some members of Congress and the Senate, as well as some members of the media, have questioned. I've said this before and I'm going to say it again: Such questioning can only do this country harm at this point in time. Quite possibly irreparable harm. Terrorism must not be politicized for personal or political gain. I can assure everyone listening that no innocent people, no law-abiding American citizens, have anything to fear from their government. No rights will be abridged for those who deserve and value those rights. But I want to make this absolutely clear: Those responsible for this act . . . those who support this act . . . those who support any groups whose desire is to harm or destroy the United States of America . . . those people have much to fear. Those people will find that we will stop at nothing to make this world safe from the evils of terrorism and the ruin that would result from such lawlessness and godlessness. I know the American people support us in such a proclamation and in such a goal. And we will not let those people down.'

'Mr Attorney General, may I turn to something a bit more personal?' When Jeffrey Stuller nodded, the host continued. 'The names of the victims of the recent bombing are being released as their identities are confirmed. I know that you and the vice president lost a very dear friend in the tragedy. Bradford Collins . . .'

Stuller didn't wait for the question to be asked. 'Brad Collins was one of my closest friends. And Vice President Dandridge would, I know, say the same. Our personal loss will not, of course, influence any decisions when it comes to our actions or retaliations. But, at the same time, being human, there is no question that when justice is served in this instance, it will be all the more satisfying. Brad Collins was a great businessman, a great family man, a great man. Speaking for the vice president, I'd like to use this opportunity to send my condolences to his wife and children and all his friends and colleagues. It's an extraordinary loss for them, for all of us, and for this country as a whole.'

'You and the vice president were more than friends with Mr Collins, sir. You were both on the board of his company, EGenco. Would you care to comment on the burgeoning scandals that have recently enveloped that company? And do you think your involvement might cause a problem with your campaign against terrorism? With the vice president the almost certain presidential candidate next year—'

'No, Katie, I would not care to comment. And I find that question reprehensibly tasteless and inappropriate at this moment. A human being was murdered. Many human beings were murdered. Don't desecrate their memories by trying to ask ridiculous, ratings-motivated questions about insignificant matters.'

'Mr Stuller—'

'That's the end of this interview. Thank you and God bless everyone.

As the attorney general stood and walked off camera, Justin pressed the power button on his remote control and clicked the TV off. Strange. He suddenly realized that he hadn't allowed himself to focus on the wider-ranging implications of the bombing. Since it had happened he'd been concentrating solely on the immediate impact, on his personal involvement – Jimmy's death and its ramifications – and then he'd been distracted by the plane crash and the beginning of that investigation. He suspected that much of the country had had the same lack of focus. Understandable. What he'd just seen on tape was not something one wanted to think about and focus on. If this were indeed a suicide bombing, then daily life was, unquestionably, about to change. And change drastically. People had said that post-9/11 the country was going to be altered forever. But Justin found that the alteration had lasted only about three months. For that period of time, there was a cautiousness in the air. And, oddly enough, a certain gentility and politeness. People were more aware of their own mortality. Then, human resiliency – or denial; it could be called either way – took hold and things returned to normal. No one talked about Afghanistan's future. Bin Laden was the subject of comedians' jokes. Other enemies, like Saddam Hussein, leapt to the forefront and were either dispatched with ease and trumpets of patriotic fervor or ignored. Airport security lines moved much faster as impatience won out over fear. Anthrax disappeared. Irony didn't disappear. The urge to live for the moment subsided. And even as our troops kept dying over in the Middle East, corporate greed, devastating bankruptcies, and the plummeting economy once again dominated conversations. And people started hating New York again, just like in the good old days.

Normal.

Justin knew from his work as a cop that people spent much of their lives being frightened. Fear, too, was normal. But this: Suicide bombers. Destruction on a small, intimate scale. This was a different kind of fear. Fear that would come when anyone suspicious sat at a counter in a coffee shop. When starting a car. Or going to a club.

Fear that would grip people in their homes, watching television, having dinner.

That wasn't normal.

But it just might be the way of the world.

Making the world a lot crazier and a more dangerous place.

He opened the morning paper now. Glanced quickly at the front page of the *Times*. Five men with suspected links to terrorist cells had been arrested in New Jersey. They were being shipped to Guantanamo Bay – where Al Qaeda prisoners and other suspected terrorists were still being held – for questioning. Since the World Trade Center attack and the wars in Afghanistan and Iraq, over a hundred prisoners had been released from Guantanamo, almost all of them returned or deported to the Middle East. But there were still over five hundred men being detained. Some of them had been there for three years. Despite a Supreme Court ruling that proclaimed the practice unconstitutional, many of the detainees in the Guantanamo camp were still being denied any right to counsel. This was true of the five new suspects who'd just been arrested. The wife of one of the men said that her husband had been spirited away in the middle of the night, along with his brother. The woman was frantic. She said that no one in the family and none of their friends had any ties to any terrorists, they were completely innocent victims, just like the poor people killed in the restaurant bombing. The woman had hired a lawyer who'd already held a press conference. The lawyer, Shirley Greene, had announced that she was suing the government for the right to see the suspects. She said the case could take years before it made its way through the stacked court system, years before she might be able to speak to her clients. The president's press secretary claimed that many of the detainees did not qualify for legal rights under the Supreme Court's ruling. Those who did could retain the right to counsel. Those who didn't would not. He said they had enough proof to label many of the prisoners 'enemy combatants'. The press secretary also said that the president would soon be proposing a new law to Congress that would deal with the issue in a way that would satisfy the courts.

The text of President Anderson's speech was also reprinted in its entirety. It was basically an extended version of what Justin had just heard Stuller say on TV. We were winning the war. The evildoers would be punished. Goodness would rule. The American people must trust and support their leaders.

Justin wondered if he was capable of trusting and supporting anyone he didn't know. Lawyers, presidents, or innocent victims. He decided he wasn't.

Marjorie Leggett had probably watched Attorney General Stuller's appearance or seen the president's speech, which was why she'd be calling him again soon. Justin thought about his promise to Jimmy's widow. He had no illusions that he could out-investigate the FBI. But he knew a few people, had a few contacts. Perhaps he could learn enough to tell Marjorie what she wanted to know: some semblance of the truth.

He thought about how this would look on his 'to-do' list: buy groceries, order new Loudon Wainwright CD, solve crime of the century.

Justin looked at his watch, decided he'd better get going. He skimmed the rest of the paper, saw that the stock market had dropped 140 points, the main accounting firm connected to EGenco was being investigated for accounting irregularities, President Anderson's approval ratings had gone up twelve percent since the bombing, and the Knicks had lost again. Then he drained his fourth cup of coffee and went to work.

At the East End police station, Justin stood at his desk, fumbled with some papers for a few moments, cleared his throat and asked

Gary, Mike, and Dennis, the three young officers on duty that morning, if they would mind listening to him for a minute. When they looked up, he hemmed and hawed and finally told them about his conversation with Mayor Krill. Told them that he was the new acting chief of police. His announcement got nods of approval and quiet murmurs of congratulations. It was all he expected. This was not a time to celebrate a promotion. Jimmy Leggett's loss was still an open wound. It would be a while before it began to heal. But, in the meantime, his authority was now established, and that was all he wanted to accomplish.

A few minutes later, Mike and Dennis went off on their appointed rounds – Mike to pound the Main Street pavement and ward off parking violators; Dennis to cruise the side streets and look for speeders and kids playing their boom boxes too loud. But Gary lingered in the doorway after they had left. When Justin raised his eyes in a questioning look, Gary said, 'I'm glad for you. It's a good thing. If you need any help, anything at all . . .'

'Thanks,' Justin said. 'I was already counting on that.'

Gary now looked toward Jimmy's office. The door was half open. 'You gonna move in there?'

'I don't think so,' Justin said. 'Not yet.'

'Wouldn't feel right, would it?'

'No.'

'Well, it'll feel right sometime.'

'I know it will.'

Gary smiled, touched his forehead with two fingers, meant to be a salute, and headed outside. As soon as he was gone, Justin went to work on his computer.

The first thing Justin did was go onto Google and type in 'FAA.' A list of possible sites came up and the first one he clicked on was 'Aviation Standards National Field Office'. At the top of the screen it gave a post office box in Oklahoma City, and a phone number. Underneath that was, 'Where can I learn about an aircraft accident or obtain results of an accident investigation?' That's what he clicked on, but it wasn't much help. The instructions said to provide the exact date, location of accident, and either the name of the airline or the aircraft identification number to Public Inquiry Section AD 46. Justin typed in the precise information, waited for a response.

There was no record of any private plane crash involving the tail number NOV 6909 Juliet.

After playing around with a few more sites, and going down a few more false paths, he returned to the initial listing of different sites and realized he'd been signing on to peripheral organizations rather than the main FAA Web page. In typical government fashion, they couldn't even lead someone to the right agency with any ease. He finally hit on what he needed: the FAA link to 'Aircraft Registration.' He clicked on that, checked the tail number again as he prepared to type it in, but then the following information came up on his screen:

GENERAL INFORMATION REGISTRATION INFORMATION

NOTICE: Due to increased security requirements, access to the public documents room by the general public has been suspended.

Aircraft registration information may be found at the <u>interactive inquiry site.</u> Copies of aircraft records may be ordered by <u>letter, fax, telephone,</u> or online at *http://diy.dot.gov.*

He clicked on 'Telephone' and got the number for the Public Document Room in Oklahoma City. He decided that a little human contact couldn't hurt.

The phone rang five times before an answering machine clicked on. Listening to the message, Justin swore under his breath – he'd forgotten about the time difference. The office wasn't open yet. He almost hung up, but at the last second decided to leave word. He gave his name – gave it as Chief of Police Justin Westwood; every little bit helps, he decided – and asked if someone could give him a call, that he was in the middle of an investigation and needed some assistance.

Within seconds of his hanging up, the phone rang. He was impressed: they got in early in Oklahoma City. Except the call wasn't from Oklahoma. It was from the Southampton police station, perhaps seven miles away. The call was about the Dr Pepper can he'd sent over. They had not been able to access any records that matched fingerprints to the ones on the can.

'How wide was the database?' Justin asked.

'We went pretty extensive. Started statewide, went national, and used the Feebies.'

Justin sighed. 'Thanks for trying,' he said. 'I appreciate it.'

'You're taking it better than I thought you would,' the Southampton cop said. 'A guy with your rep. It pissed me off, I gotta tell you.'

'What can you do? If there are no records, there are no records.'

'I didn't say the records don't exist. I just said we were blocked from getting them.'

'I don't understand.'

The officer on the other end of the phone sighed as if talking to an idiot. 'When we ran the prints through our friends in the FBI we were told we couldn't access that information.'

'What does that mean?'

'Don't know. Maybe it means whoever you're looking for is out of our league.'

The cop hung up before Justin could ask any more questions. And Justin had plenty more questions, although he doubted the Southampton Police Department could help with any of them.

Information not available.

Public access suspended.

Access denied.

Here was question number one: Who *was* this guy?

And question number two: What the hell was going on?

Now that he thought about it, maybe there was a third question. Fear was in the air. Fear made people do strange things. When you boiled it right down, fear was the cause of almost all murders: fear of betrayal, fear of being left alone, fear of poverty. So if this mysterious pilot had indeed been murdered, the answer to the third question might be the most important of them all:

The people who'd murdered him – what exactly were they afraid of?

chapter 6

Wanda Chinkle was the assistant director of the FBI responsible for the New England bureau. She'd been in charge for a little over two years now. She'd gone up there to work when Justin Westwood was still on the Providence police force, and they'd joined together on a case. She still felt a little guilty that she'd been unable to protect his family in the mob attack that ultimately took their lives, which is why, when their paths had crossed a year ago, when he'd gotten caught up in the middle of the hunt to stop Douglas Kransten and his Aphrodite experiment, she'd helped Justin out. That helping hand had greatly jeopardized her standing with her bosses. But Justin had managed to repay the favor and dig her out of the jam. She liked Justin. He could be charming as hell. He could also be cold as steel and just as hard. She hadn't known him all that well before his daughter was killed and she sometimes wondered if he'd been any softer before that. Something told her that wasn't the case. Wanda's experience was that people didn't really change. The older they got – the more life they experienced – they just tapped into what was already there. What was just waiting for an excuse to come out.

As soon as she heard Justin's voice on the phone, Wanda knew he wanted something. That was okay. Very few people talked to Wanda unless they wanted something. It didn't bother her. She was tough enough and smart enough to handle most things. Even Justin Westwood.

'It's good to hear from you, Jay. How are things there? You're not far from the bombing, are you? At the restaurant.'

'Maybe five or six miles away.'

'Jesus. You okay?'

'I'm fine. I was nowhere near it. But my boss wasn't so lucky. He was there.'

'Was he . . .?'

'Yeah. He was.'

'I'm sorry.'

'Me too. But that doesn't have anything to do with why I'm calling. I need a favor.'

'Well, we're a little busy right now, considering what's going on. Full antiterrorist mode. Did you see Stuller's speech?'

'I saw it. And I appreciate what you're going through. But this won't take much time.'

'What kind of trouble are you in now?'

'No trouble. I swear. I just have a question.'

'I know your questions. They usually lead to trouble.'

'Wanda, I'm just trying to get to the bottom of something. Something that shouldn't be that complicated. But I keep hitting a wall.'

'All right, let's hear it.'

He told her about the plane crash. She'd heard some of the details; a memo had been e-mailed with an update saying that any connection to the nearby bombing had been ruled out. Justin didn't respond to that, just explained to her about Martin Heffernan's behavior at the crash site. He told her about being denied access to the fingerprint records. He left out the part about the exhaust manifold that had been tampered with. Better to keep some things in reserve.

'That is definitely strange,' she said. 'But, you know, the finger-print thing – there might simply be nothing there. Some kind of snafu. Maybe because of the proximity to Harper's. It could have been a precautionary restriction.'

'That's probably right, but . . .'

'But you're curious.'

'I'm definitely curious.' When she stayed silent on the other end, Justin said, 'Funny that none of your guys came to talk to me about the crash, don't you think?'

'They've got other things on their minds, Jay.'

'Still, you'd think they'd want to check this out.'

'Sounds like the FAA already checked it out. They got word to us about the pilot error, end of story. No need to put in the extra hours if we already know it's pointless. It doesn't seem like a big deal.' She thought for a moment, then said, 'Of course, with you just about everything's a big deal, isn't it?'

'I just like to be thorough,' he said. 'If it wasn't for me, what would you do for aggravation?'

She sighed. 'All right. Get me a set of the prints. I can't see any reason not to check 'em out.'

'I sent them already. They're probably in your computer.'

'Pretty sure of yourself, aren't you, Jay?' She was certain he was smiling smugly on the other end of the phone line.

'I'm just sure who my friends are, Wanda, that's all.' She didn't say anything. So he said, 'Call me when you've got something, okay?' And when she still didn't say anything, he figured it was okay to hang up.

Forty-five minutes after Justin spoke to Wanda Chinkle, the call came in from Oklahoma City.

The woman who called was named Cherry Flynn. He asked her to repeat it, but she just said, 'You heard it right. Cherry, like the little red fruit.'

'Thanks for calling back . . . um . . . Cherry.'

'My pleasure. What can I do for you?'

'Well, I went online looking for some information,' Justin told her. 'But I couldn't log into the public records.'

'That's right. In the last month or so, we had to eliminate access for the general public. Security reasons.'

'Then maybe you should change the name.'

'What?'

'You shouldn't call them public records if the public isn't allowed to see them anymore.'

'Oh, I see what you mean.'

'So, listen, Cherry. Here's what I need. I'm investigating a murder case . . .'

'Oh my.'

'Right. I've got the tail number of a plane that I think belongs to the victim. I need to know how to trace the number back to the owner.'

'Well, that's what we do.'

'Good. So if I just give you the number . . .'

'Well, I'll need some sort of authorization. Otherwise we might just as well let anyone still go online. If you see what I mean.'

'Okay, fair enough,' Justin said. 'What kind of authorization?'

'Well, you said you're from the police?'

'That's right. I'm the chief of police for East End Harbor.'

'Where's that?'

'Long Island. New York. Right near where the restaurant was bombed the other day.'

'Oh my. Does this have anything to do with that?'

70

For the briefest of moments, Justin thought about lying, thought it might help his cause. Then he realized the possible ramifications, so he quickly said, 'No. It's something completely separate.'

'Oh. Well . . . why don't you fax me something on your official police stationery. And include your badge number. I'll get verification and approval, and then I can call you back with the information.'

'Do you know approximately how long all that might take?'

'I'm afraid I don't. It'll take as long as it takes.'

'Right. That was always one of my favorite axioms.'

'Excuse me?'

'Nothing.'

'Would you like the fax number?'

He said that he would and then he copied it down. He told her he'd get the request to her momentarily. She said she'd respond as soon as she could. Justin hung up and realized he'd now spent the morning accomplishing absolutely nothing thus far. He'd been stymied using official police channels, the Internet, and the phone. He'd talked to one suspicious friend who was reluctantly trying to help him with something that probably wouldn't pan out, and one near-idiot woman who might never call him back. He hoped the afternoon would be slightly more productive.

It wasn't.

Cherry Flynn called back around 3 P.M. Her voice was not nearly as friendly and open as it had been six hours earlier.

'I'm afraid we can't grant your request, Mr Westwood. I mean, Chief Westwood.'

'Can't grant it because you don't have the info? Or won't grant it because you don't want to give it to me?'

This threw her for a major loop. She was not used to any response that didn't retreat in the face of authority. The stammering –

intermixed with long silences – went on for so long that even Justin finally felt sorry for her.

'Cherry, may I ask you a couple of simple questions? Nothing that can possibly get you in trouble, I promise.'

'Well, okay. I guess.'

'I understand that you can't give me the information I want. But just tell me if you have it. This way, I won't have to bother you anymore and I can go to your supervisor and try to get it. If you don't even have it, then I won't pursue it.'

'We don't have it.'

She was lying. He was absolutely positive. He hadn't counted on that. He'd thought she wasn't smart enough to lie.

'Are you sure about that?' he said.

'Well.' Her voice broke the word into two, maybe three syllables. And she waited a long time before uttering her next sentence. 'Could you ask another question?'

'What?'

'Ask another question. On that same subject.'

'What kind of question should I ask?'

'Oh gosh, I don't know how to say it. I shouldn't really help you too much, should I? But this doesn't seem very fair.'

'You want me to ask you a question that'll help you give me a better answer? Is that what you're saying?'

'I don't think I should say anything else,' Cherry decided. 'Even if this is a murder investigation.'

'All right, all right, hold it.' Justin closed his eyes. She said she didn't have the information on the tail number. But she wanted him to ask more about it. *What more is there to know? Something similar? A number close to the one I gave her? No, what good would that do? She has it or she doesn't have it, right? What's another alternative. You have it, you don't have it . . . Bingo!* 'You *had* the information. You had the file. But you don't have it anymore, is that right?'

'That's very possible,' she breathed. 'Uh-huh.'

'Who took it?'

'Well, it's not really paper anymore, you know. So you can't just take it . . .'

'Okay. Cherry, who transferred it? Or erased it?'

'I don't think I can really tell you that.'

Justin bit down on his lip until it turned white. *She wants to help. She's trying to help. Think think, think.* 'How about this?' he asked. 'Who has the authority to remove a file from the computer system? Not *this* file. Not the file for tail number NOV 6909 Juliet. I don't want to know who has that file. But who can remove *any* file? Can you?'

'Oh no,' Cherry said. 'I could get in a lot of trouble for that. I can only do that when someone tells me to.'

'So your boss can tell you to do that?'

'Well, not really,' she said now, and her words were very breathy now, as if she were starting to realize that she was getting in too deep. 'I mean, he *could*, I guess, but he would get in trouble, too. We're not allowed just to alter or delete a file. I think it's against the law.'

'Well, how about *his* boss, then?'

'Oh, his boss could do that. She's probably allowed to take any file she wants out. She sure *should* be, anyway.'

'And who's your boss's boss, Cherry? Can you tell me who that is?'

'Well, sure. There's nothing wrong with saying who the chain of command is, is there?'

'No, there isn't.' He waited. Silence. 'So who is your boss's boss, Cherry?'

'Martha Peck.'

'Uh-huh. And what's her job exactly?'

'You don't know Martha Peck?' Cherry was astonished.

'I'm afraid not.'

'She's the head of the FAA.'

'In Oklahoma City?'

'No. Uh-uh. She's all the way in Washington, D.C.'

Justin let this sink in for a moment. 'Someone in Washington told you to get rid of the file?'

'I never said that, did I?' Cherry sounded extremely worried. 'I never said we got rid of that file!'

'No, you didn't,' Justin reassured her. 'You absolutely didn't.' He could feel her relax. 'I just have one more question, Cherry. That's it. Then you can go back to work.'

'What is it?'

'The file you weren't told to remove. When was that?'

'Four days ago.' He could hear her bang something, presumably with her fist. 'That was a trick question!' she said. 'That wasn't fair!'

Four days ago.

Someone got rid of the pilots file the day before *his plane crashed.*

Somebody knew what was going to happen.

No. More than that. Somebody with clout *knew what was going to happen.*

'Thank you very much, Cherry. I appreciate all your help.'

'Damn it!' she said. 'And have a nice day.'

chapter 7

Around six that evening, Justin left his third or fourth message, he couldn't remember which, for Chuck Billings at the Fisherman Motel. Soon after that, all five members of the East End police force appeared at the station. Gary Jenkins said that they'd decided they should take Justin out for a drink. Maybe even dinner if he was free.

'Not to celebrate exactly,' Gary said. ' 'Cause, you know . . . But to kind of celebrate.'

'I wouldn't mind a kind of celebration,' Justin said. 'But I'll do the treating. My first official act.'

Nobody argued, and within fifteen minutes they were a block down from the police station at Duffy's Tavern. Justin liked Duffy's because it was the last remaining place in East End or anywhere in the Hamptons as near as he could tell – that hadn't gone upscale. For that matter, it seemed not to have changed at all in twenty years. It was a no-frills bar. If you wanted to eat there, you got a tuna fish sandwich wrapped in plastic and a bag of potato chips. Their wine list had two listings: red and white. But Donnie, the bartender, made sensational martinis, and he didn't stint on the shots of liquor. Duffy's was dark and quiet. There was often a sports event playing on the TV over the bar. There was a dartboard and some strange game where you tried to swing a piece of string with a metal loop attached to it onto a nail embedded in a wooden beam. That's what passed for serious entertainment at Duffy's.

By 8 P.M. that night, the place was crowded. And the entire East End police force was reasonably bombed.

They weren't rowdy, the way they usually were. Duffy's as a whole was subdued, had been since the bombing. The guys on the force were doing the same thing everyone else in the place was: slowly sipping beer or tequila or scotch or bourbon, talking about life and death and the present and the future, while half listening to Charles Barkley on TNT.

At some point, Mike Haversham said to Justin, 'I think that guy over there knows you.'

'Of course he knows me,' Justin said. He was feeling a little wobbly. 'I'm the police chief. What's he wanna do, buy me a drink?'

'I don't think so,' Haversham said. 'He just kinda seems to like starin' at you.'

Justin nodded, as if this made perfect sense, then shifted in his seat so he could turn around and look at his admirer. As soon as the man came into his line of sight, Justin's posture straightened, his eyes hardened, and his lips twisted into a small but distinct smile.

'You know him?' Gary Jenkins asked.

Justin nodded. 'Yes. I know him.'

'From around here?'

'No,' Justin said. 'He's from another life.'

He stared over at the man, then nodded. One firm nod. Taking his cue, the guy at the other table stood up and came over to the group of cops.

'Guys,' Justin said. 'Say hello to Bruno Pecozzi.'

There was a murmuring from the five cops and an easy wave in return from the man, who was still standing.

'You're a big motherfucker,' Thomas Fronde, the youngest, cock-iest, and drunkest cop at the table, said. 'What do you go, six-three?'

'Four,' Bruno Pecozzi said.

'Two-forty? Two-fifty?'

'Two-sixty-five. But I'm very sensitive about my weight, so I'd appreciate it if you wouldn't mention it again, please.'

There was something about the man's tone – it wasn't just the hoarseness of his voice, a rasping that made it seem as if someone had driven a knife into his vocal cords; it was also that he spoke so quietly you could barely hear him, and said the word 'please' like it wasn't really a request, more like an order – that made the cocky young cop sober up quickly and say, 'I'm sorry. It won't happen again.'

'Thank you,' Bruno Pecozzi said. Then, turning to Justin, 'Can I buy a round?'

Justin nodded again; Bruno caught the eye of the bartender and signaled for more drinks, then pulled up a chair, and wedged his huge frame in next to Justin.

'Good to see you, Jay. I was hopin' I'd bump into you.'

'What the hell are you doing here?' Justin asked.

'Me?' Bruno Pecozzi said. 'I'm shootin' a movie.'

'What?'

'Yeah. I'm in the fuckin' movie business now. Can you believe it?'

Justin couldn't believe it. But over several more rounds of drinks, Bruno explained his new job.

'Been doin' it for almost three years now. It's a great gig. It started with this picture, *Dead to Rights* . . .'

'Hey, I saw that,' Gary Jenkins said.

'Yeah, it was a good little picture,' Bruno said.

'What'd you do on it?'

'I was kind of a facilitator.'

'What does that mean?' Gary asked.

'It means,' Justin said, 'that Bruno knows a lot of people. He's very well connected.'

'Your boss is a smart guy,' Bruno said. 'You got it exactly right. We were shootin' in the city, mostly down in Little Italy. The producers or the director needed to get something done, something, you know, a little out of the ordinary, they'd call on me.'

'Like what?' That was from Thomas Fronde. It was the first time he'd spoken since Bruno mentioned the weight issue.

'Well . . . I'll tell ya. Here's a good example. The director wanted to shoot somethin' over by the East River around six o'clock. He wanted the sun to look a certain way, to be settin'. These directors, they're kinda crazy. Very artistic. Anyway, he had about an hour, hour and a half, to get his shot. Only these planes kept takin' off and landing at La Guardia and Kennedy, they kept screwin' up the shot. So he asked if I could do somethin' about it.'

'What'd you do?' Mike Haversham asked.

'Made a couple of calls. Got 'em to hold off on the flyin' for about an hour or so.

Gary looked at Bruno in amazement. 'You got them to stop taking off and landing at the airports?'

Bruno nodded and shrugged modestly.

'Who did you call?'

'Hey, if I told you that, you could get my job, you know what I mean?'

The cops all laughed. Justin started rubbing his eyes, partly in disbelief at the way Bruno had taken over and changed the mood of the entire table, partly because he was already beginning to anticipate the next day's hangover. Bruno slapped him on the back and immediately went into a story about the star of *Dead to Rights*, an actor who usually played tough guys. There was a scene where the actor had to crawl through a swamp and mud to get to the villain. He wouldn't agree to do it until the director found someone to warm the water – and the mud – to exactly seventy-eight degrees.

'Not seventy-seven, not seventy-nine. The guy actually checked the thermometer himself and wouldn't put a toe in until it read exactly seventy-eight.'

Bruno told stories of his movie experiences for the next hour, and had everyone at the table howling with laughter. He was so huge that his self-deprecating manner was irresistible. It was hard to know exactly how old he was, maybe mid-forties. He had a couple of scars around his eyes, and his nose looked liked it had been broken once or twice. Bruno looked like an ex-fighter, and he had that gentle demeanor that fighters sometimes have out of the ring. It was as if he knew he was scary-looking, so he went out of his way to soften whatever he could about himself – his voice, his eyes, his smile.

'So are you still a facilitator?' Gary asked, calling for one more round.

'Nah. Now I'm a technical consultant. I mean, I still do some facilitating if they ask me.'

'What's the movie they're shooting now?'

'It's a cop movie. *Blue Smoke.*'

'So what kind of technical stuff do you consult on?'

Bruno glanced over at Justin, rolled his eyes, as if to say, *What is it with these guys?* Justin shrugged in return.

'You know,' Bruno said. 'On whatever needs technicalizing. The language, some of the action, the behavior.'

'That is so cool,' Gary said. 'Your stories are unbelievable.'

Bruno smiled modestly.

'Tell them the story about Marty Braunheimer,' Justin said.

'Ahhh, I don't know if they'd really like that one,' Bruno answered.

'Yeah, yeah, come on,' Thomas said.

'Yeah,' Mike Haversham said. 'What's the story?'

They were like eager children waiting for their father to buy them toys. Bruno cocked his head to the side, closed one eye for a moment. 'Okay. This was a while ago. Up in Rhode Island. And this guy Marty Braunheimer, he was a gambler. Not a pro, you know, just some schmuck who liked to bet on the games. He couldn't pass up a big football game. And he liked basketball, pro and college. And he had a bad run. That's why they call it gambling, right? He was into this guy . . .'

'His bookie,' Thomas said, in case the other guys didn't get it.

'Right,' Bruno said. 'His bookie. He was into him for a lotta money. Over ten grand.'

'Jesus.'

'Yeah. It's some dough. Anyways, this bookie was kind of a tough guy. He didn't like nobody, you know, skippin' out on a payment. I knew both parties, the bookie and Marty, so I was asked to intervene. I went to Marty, told him he had a week to pay up or he could be in some trouble. Marty said he'd have the dough in three days, no problem. He said he'd meet my bookmaker friend at the track.' Bruno rubbed his nose with his two forefingers, took a sip of beer. 'So three days later, they're both at the track and, sure enough, Marty comes up to the bookie, gives him a hug, and pays him ten grand.'

The guys all nodded appreciatively. But Bruno said, 'There's more. The thing is, Marty was kind of a pickpocket. I mean, that's what he did for a living, you know? And when he hugged my bookie friend, he picked his pocket. That's why he wanted to meet at the track, he knew the guy'd be carrying a wad.'

'He paid the bookie back with his own money?' Gary said.

Bruno nodded and the cops all burst into laughter.

'Good story,' Thomas said.

Justin finished off his shot of scotch. 'It's still not over.'

'Ahh,' Bruno said. 'I don't think the rest is . . .'

'Tell 'em the end,' Justin said. 'I think they'll like it.'

Bruno shrugged his wide shoulders. 'Well, the thing is,' he said, 'when the bookie goes to the window to place his bet, he realizes what happened. He didn't get paid ten grand, he actually got picked for three.'

'Christ,' Thomas said. 'What'd he do?'

'You know,' Bruno decided, 'this part's not really too interesting.'

'Tell 'em what happened,' Justin said. His voice was flat but insistent.

'Yeah, what'd the bookie do?'

Bruno shrugged again. 'He got some guy to glue Marty's hands to a piece of cement. And then they tossed Marty in the river.'

Mike was still laughing. 'And then what happened?'

'Nothin' happened,' Bruno said. 'That's the end of the story.'

'I mean, what happened to Marty?'

'He died.'

'They *killed* him? They killed Marty?'

'Yeah.'

'Oh my God.' This was Thomas. 'Did they arrest the bookie?'

'Not really. See, he had an alibi. Pretty airtight.' He glanced over at Justin, whose expression was still neutral. 'And the cops never could find out who did the actual, you know . . . deed. Marty was kind of a scumbag, so I don't think they looked all that hard. That's my theory, anyway.'

'Geez,' Thomas said. 'The ending's not so funny as the beginning, is it?'

Bruno yawned and glanced at his watch. 'I got an early call tomorrow. Big scene comin' up.' He put his meaty hand on Justin's back. 'Can I buy you dinner tomorrow, Jay? We can do a little catchin' up. Maybe you'll actually do some talkin' so I don't have to listen to my big yap anymore.

Justin nodded. Bruno stuck his hand out and Justin shook it. They all watched as the big guy lumbered out of the bar, first tossing a hundred-dollar bill down on the table, saying, 'For my round.'

When he was out the door, all the cops started talking about what a great guy he was, what great stories he told.

'You good friends with him?' Mike asked Justin.

'We used to be pretty friendly. Haven't seen him for a while.'

'How do you know him?'

'From up in Providence.'

'Great guy. Really great guy.' Gary said. 'What'd he used to do? Before he was a technical adviser and facilitator?'

'The same thing he probably does now,' Justin said. 'In between his facilitating.' He finished the last of his mug of beer. 'Bruno's a hit man. For the mob. Last time I saw him he was at fifteen kills and counting. My guess is he's way over twenty by now.' He grabbed the check, Bruno's hundred, and stood up. 'He does tell great stories, though, doesn't he?'

chapter 8

Justin couldn't quite place the noise. Some kind of horrible bird? A fire alarm? Maybe a smoke detector. Whatever it was, it was awful and it seemed to be emanating from the middle of his hungover brain.

He opened his eyes – a big mistake – then rolled over in his bed. He waited for sunlight to come streaking through the window and put an end to his hazy darkness, but no light came. He realized it was still dark outside. And that damn noise kept hammering away at him.

It took another moment or two to realize the sound wasn't vibrating inside his head. It was coming from the end table next to his bed. From the general direction of the telephone. No, it was actually coming *from* the telephone. An evil invention, Justin decided. The world would be a lot better off with nice quiet tin cans and some string.

Justin sighed, regretted every shot and every beer he'd downed the night before, then he picked up the phone and heard:

'What the hell are you trying to do to me?!'

'Hello?' he croaked.

'You told me there was no trouble! You said it was just a favor! You almost got me goddamn fired a year ago and what, now you're trying to finish me off?! And you don't even return my calls?!'

'Wanda?'

'Of course it's Wanda. Who the hell else do you think it is? I left five goddamn messages for you!'

'I never check my machine. What time is it?'

'Well start checking! And it's six.'

'In the morning?'

'Wake up, Jay! I'm not kidding around here! Why the hell didn't you tell me what I was getting into?!'

He sat up – another mistake – and tried to rub his eyes to full awake position. He had a plastic bottle of Fiji Water next to his bed, which he grabbed and swigged down half the water in two gulps.

'Wanda, I swear to God, I don't know what you're talking about.'

'I spent half the night being interrogated about your goddamn fingerprints!'

Now he was awake. 'Tell me.'

'*I am* telling you, you asshole. I want *you* to tell *me*!'

'I get you're angry. But what happened?'

'You set me up, is what happened. I put through the prints and found the same thing – no clearance. So I called in a favor, trying to bypass the clearance. You got me curious, too, you bastard. And within five fucking minutes, I got a call.'

'From who?'

'It doesn't matter. But I spent the whole day and night in D.C. I didn't get home till after midnight.'

'You had to go to Washington?'

'Will you pay attention, please? You sent me to get you absolutely top-secret, classified information, you bastard! And I almost got my ass fried.'

'Wanda, I swear, what I told you is everything I know. I don't have a clue what's going on, I don't have any idea who this guy is. All I know is that somebody's getting away with murder.'

'Murder?'

He sighed. And told her about the airplane manifold and the conversation he'd had with Ray Lockhardt.

'Thanks for telling me before.'

'Look, it's probably a good thing I didn't tell you.'

'And why is that?'

'The people you were conversing with last night, did you tell them why you were looking for the info?'

'Of course I did.'

'Did you tell them about me?'

Her voice softened for the first time in the conversation. 'Yes. You didn't tell me there was anything to hide here.'

'It's not a problem. I didn't know there *was* anything to hide. But clearly there is. So it's better you didn't know the plane was sabotaged. Less for you to have told them.'

'What I should do is go tell them *now*.'

'Yeah. That is what you should do. Of course, it means they'll definitely come after me next. To find out if I know even more.' He gave her a few moments to mull it over. 'So *is* that what you're going to do?'

She didn't answer. They both stayed quiet for a while. Her breathing was a little softer and less rapid. He took another long swig of water.

'So, Wanda,' he said finally. 'Did you get the pilot's name?'

'You're an asshole, Jay,' she said. 'I can't tell you anything. Haven't you been listening to me?'

'Yeah. But there's something else I haven't told you. Something that happened after I spoke to you.' He gave her all the details of his bizarre conversation with Cherry Flynn in Oklahoma City. 'The guy's fingerprints have been removed and his FAA file is gone. Right now, we're the only two people who know he was murdered. Except for the people who killed him. Or ordered him killed. And whoever's covering the damn thing up.'

'You think it's this guy Heffernan?'

'I don't know if he did the mechanical work. But he's certainly involved. He knows what happened. But the guy's too low-level to pull the other strings. He didn't get the file pulled or the prints classified.'

'Jay, I don't think we should talk about this on the phone any-more.'

'Okay. Fair enough. How about if I come up there tomorrow night. We can have dinner.'

'Don't bother. I'm not getting sucked into this, Jay. I'm not getting involved in this one.'

'We could eat at my folks' house. They'll be happy to see you.'

'Jay . . .'

'You like duck? Their chef makes a superb duck.'

'Goddammit, Jay . . .'

'Let's say seven-thirty tomorrow night.'

'Let's not say anything!'

'Dress informal.'

'Make it eight, you asshole. Some of us work.'

Justin hung up the phone. Finished off the bottle of water. Decided he'd better gulp down about a dozen aspirin before he went to the station, so he swung his legs out of bed and went in search of the aspirin bottle. As he was fumbling to open the child-proof top, the phone rang again. Justin swore, wondered how the hell he'd gotten so popular, and, through his fog, made his way back to the phone.

'Don't yell at me again,' he said, expecting it to be Wanda. 'I think my head's going to fall off.'

'Then stay away from me,' a man's voice answered. 'I've seen enough headless bodies in the last twenty-four hours to last me a lifetime.'

It was Chuck Billings, the head of the Providence bomb squad. 'And here I thought I'd be waking you up and you'd be docile as hell.'

Justin apologized for his unfriendly greeting, then told Chuck why he'd been trying to get in touch with him.

'They're keeping me crazed busy,' Billings said. 'It's why it took me so long to get back to you. Genuinely nuts what's going on. And today's a really bad day. That's why I'm calling so early. I think the president might even be showing up here. Major photo op.'

'Can you give me any time at all, Chuck?'

'How about we get together tomorrow? Right before lunch. I can probably even get you into the site, show you a few things.'

Justin agreed, thanked him, then went back to trying to open the aspirin bottle. When the top popped off with relative ease, he took it as a good omen. After slipping three aspirin into his mouth, followed by another half bottle of Fiji Water, he decided things were definitely improving.

His eleven o'clock meeting with Mayor Leona Krill went relatively smoothly. Justin showed up on time, he was extremely polite, and he didn't have any particular problems with the specifics that she wanted to discuss. They agreed on the new salary. He listened quietly while she explained the parameters of his new job and the new responsibilities that came with it. They agreed to set up a bimonthly meeting, lunch if possible. Justin was ready to leave – he was already craving more aspirin, not just for his head but for his back, which was stiff and aching; he really had to start working out again – when she brought up the need for a new hire.

'We have room in the budget for another officer.' When he looked questioningly, she explained. 'In essence, you've replaced Jimmy. Now we need to replace you.'

'Okay. That makes sense. Good. We can use it.'

'I'd like you to hire a woman, Jay.'

He didn't answer for a moment. It wasn't an off-the-wall request. He had nothing against women police officers. But he was curious about the reason – there was always a reason with politicians, even small-time local ones – so, when he spoke, all he said was, 'Why?'

'Several reasons. One, it's time we had a woman in the department. It's the proper thing to do. Two, I think it'd be a good thing politically.'

'A lot of women voters in East End.'

'That's right.'

'What if a woman's not the best candidate?'

'Then I wouldn't ask you to hire her. But that's number three: someone's come very highly recommended.'

He raised an eyebrow. 'By whom?'

'Not one of my gay acquaintances, Jay, if that's what you're thinking. I don't live in quite that circumscribed a world.'

That is what he'd thought. 'Sorry. I didn't mean . . .'

'That's all right. I have no idea what this woman's sexual orientation is. But I'd like you to interview her. She has a superb reputation and it sounds like she'd be a good fit.'

'Okay.'

Mayor Leona Krill handed over a résumé and stuck out her hand for Justin to shake.

'No more kissing?' he asked.

'I just like to keep you off guard,' she answered.

'You're doing a good job so far,' he said. And headed back out to Main Street.

*

88

The rest of the day was spent on normal police department business. Justin was surprised how, after a day of talking on the phone to locals about various complaints, passing along instructions to the officers who now worked for him, paperwork, explaining to the head of the town council the pluses and minuses of a proposed roundabout near one end of town, and meeting with the head of the school board about the need for speed bumps on the road in front of the high school, when he looked up at the clock, it was nearly six-thirty in the evening.

At seven-thirty, he met Bruno Pecozzi at the restaurant in the Schooner Hotel on Main Street. Bruno was staying at the Schooner, probably the nicest place to stay, sit, eat, or drink on the entire east end of Long Island. The hotel was built in the late 1700s and it still reeked of colonial charm. The owner, who'd been married six times and, over the years, managed to lose just about everything but the hotel in his various divorce proceedings, kept one of the great wine lists in the country, maintained a superb humidor in the lobby, and always managed to lure top-notch chefs. He kept several tables for regulars and, by the front door, he always made sure there were three backgammon tables so anyone could come in, sit in a comfortable chair or sofa, have a relaxing drink, and play away for hours on end. During the summer, Justin thought the place was a hellhole of tourists and frantic singles. During the winter, it was one of the great places on the East Coast.

Justin shook his head when he saw where Bruno was sitting: the absolute, prime, A-number-one table in the front room. The so-called celebrity table. Bruno winked at him when Justin walked in, and motioned for him to come sit down.

Bruno said right up front that he was paying – it was on the movie studio – and he told Justin to pick the wine. Justin figured what the hell, and ordered an '82 Cheval Blanc. For his dinner, he ordered a Caesar salad and a pepper steak, medium rare. Bruno had exactly the same – except he asked for two steaks.

'Skip the extra side dishes,' he told the astonished waiter, 'but bring two slabs of meat.' When the waiter scurried away, he raised his wineglass toward Justin and said, 'Salut'.

They sipped the excellent wine and made small talk for a bit. Justin told Bruno that he was now the police chief, which got a laugh out of the big man. Bruno told Justin that he was screwing the female star of the movie he was working on – the married female star – which got an equal laugh in return. During the banter, Justin got the feeling that Bruno had something else on his mind. He waited, and, sure enough, Bruno soon held his hand up and said, 'You know, this is kind of hard for me, I'm not good at this stuff, but I wanna get this out in the open. I know I'm years too late, but I'm really sorry about what happened to Alicia. I didn't know your little girl but I'm sorry about her, too.'

'Thank you.'

'I wanted to come to the funeral, you know, but I didn't think it was appropriate.'

'I appreciate it, Bruno.'

'I want you to know something else. We told that shithead to stay away from you. We told him to leave them alone, too.'

Justin didn't need a name to know who Bruno was talking about. Louie Denbo. He was the thug Justin had arrested, had spent a year investigating, compiling enough information to send him to prison for the rest of his life. On the night before his trial was to begin, Denbo was the one who'd sent two men to Justin's house. The men who'd shot Justin four times. The men who'd killed his daughter and driven his wife to suicide.

After spending two years in prison, Louie Denbo had been

stabbed to death by a fellow inmate. The prison authorities never found the man responsible.

'Anyway,' Bruno said, 'I just thought you should know. We warned him. And he got his, the stupid prick.'

And now, for the first time, Justin realized what had happened. He knew what Bruno was telling him. It wasn't an accident – or even a prison brawl – that caused Denbo's death. It was a hired hit. Retaliation for crossing the line and disobeying orders.

Justin was surprised that this news didn't change anything inside him. There was no sudden gratification or sense of closure. The man who'd ruined his life was dead, had been for several years. It didn't matter to Justin how he'd died or who'd killed him. It didn't bring back the people he'd killed. So he just nodded at Bruno, acknowledging the info, and took another sip of the superb red wine.

The food came and they shifted the talk to more normal topics: cop and killer talking about movies and music – Bruno enthused about the new Roman Polanski movie and the live bootleg Phish CD of their farewell concert; he was a major Phish fan and until they'd broken up he'd followed their concert schedule whenever possible – and sports and politics. Eventually, the conversation got around to the bombing of Harper's.

'I saw the guy, you know,' Bruno said, polishing off the last of his side of broccoli rabe.

'What guy?'

'The bomber. The guy with the briefcase.'

'What do you mean, you saw him?'

'We were shootin' a couple of blocks from the restaurant. Second unit crew, buncha extras, couple of the actors. He walked right by.'

'How do you know it was him?'

'Well, I didn't know fuck-all when I saw him. But I been readin' about it. They traced the guy's path. So I know I seen some Arab guy with a briefcase walkin' past the shoot. I noticed him 'cause I saw him stop when he saw all the extras dressed as cops. It scared him. He must've thought they were real. I remember thinkin' he was a guy who was doin' something wrong somewhere or other. Some people look at stuff, know how much it's worth. That's their skill. Some people see things, tell you whether they're beautiful or not. Me, I know when people are scared. It's my talent. Useful in my line of business. And I noticed this guy 'cause he was scared. But I'll tell you somethin' else. Guys who do shit like this, I mean, ready to kill themselves for whatever, they don't get scared when they see a bunch of cops. They think, "Fuck them, they hassle me I'll take 'em with me." This guy was scared. Too scared to blow himself up.'

'You don't think he did it?' Justin sounded incredulous.

'I'm just saying there's more than meets the fucking eye, Jay. There usually fucking is.'

'You tell this to the police or . . .?'

'Oh sure. I waltzed in to the FBI and explained all my theories to them 'cause we're such good buddies.'

'Bruno, if you're convinced you're right, this is the kind of thing you have to tell somebody.'

'What? My hunch that the guy was too chickenshit to blow himself up? Anyway, I'm tellin' you. You pass it along. You're goin' up to see your FBI buddy tomorrow, ain't ya?'

Justin let his fork clatter down to his plate. 'How the hell do you know that?'

Bruno sat back in his chair, let an easy grin spread across his wide face. 'Gimme some credit, Jay. I know a lot of stuff.'

'What, do you have the Feebies' phones bugged up there?'

Bruno kept the grin on his face. 'Hey, they bug us, don't they? It'd only be fair if we did.'

Justin regained his composure enough to signal the waiter and ask for a double espresso.

'You eatin' dessert?' Bruno asked.

'I'm trying to watch my weight.'

'Yeah, me too.' Bruno turned to the waiter. 'So just bring me one piece of cheesecake instead of two, okay?'

chapter 9

Justin met Chuck Billings at eleven o'clock the next morning, two blocks from Harper's Restaurant.

'I'm just here as a consultant,' Billings said. 'I'm the only outside expert. Everyone else, at least everyone in my area of expertise, is from inside the Bureau.'

'Why you? I mean, other than your natural genius.'

'Signatures,' Billings told him, and when he saw Justin's puzzled expression he said, 'Not like handwriting. Bomb signatures. Things that tell us who's responsible. Let's say I'm kind of obsessed with that sort of thing.'

'How does one get obsessed with bomb signatures, exactly?'

'I'll explain when we're inside. I want to prepare you for what you're gonna see,' Chuck said. 'That's why I thought it'd be better if we walk a little bit first.'

'It's been cleaned up already, hasn't it?'

'Yeah, yeah. It's clean. Well . . . it's clean compared to what it was. You're not gonna see any body parts or anything. But it's still pretty disturbing.'

'Okay. I appreciate the preparation.'

'I want to prepare you for some other stuff, too.'

'Such as?'

Billings slowed down a bit. His walk turned into more of an amble. 'I've never been involved with anything like this. I mean, I've worked with the Feds before, I know the kind of assholes they can be, but this is something different.'

'Different how?'

'I can't explain it. I'm going against strict orders by bringing you into this restaurant, but one of the reasons I'm doing it is 'cause I hope *you* can explain it.'

'What is it I'm trying to explain, Chuck?'

'I don't want to say anything more. Let me just show you around, give you my impressions of what happened, then you tell me what you think. Fair enough?'

'More than fair. Anything you want to give me is fair. Like I told you, I'm just trying to get some info so I can help a friend sleep a little easier.'

'Good,' Chuck said. 'Maybe you'll wind up helping two friends.'

Chuck Billings had been right. He flashed his badge, told the two FBI agents at the front that Justin was with him, then they stepped inside. And despite the extensive cleanup, Justin almost burst into tears when he walked into the building that had, just a few days ago, been Harper's Restaurant. Justin had seen death and death didn't frighten him. But the bombed-out restaurant did frighten him. It sent a deep chill throughout his entire body and filled him up with sadness. This was much worse than being surrounded by death. It was as if the room they were standing in was filled with ghosts.

'Yeah,' Billings said, looking at Justin's expression. 'A bomb site can be pretty overwhelming.'

Justin took a deep breath, swiped at his eyes with the back of his hand, then nodded. 'Okay,' he said. 'What do you want to show me?'

'I don't know exactly what you're looking for,' Billings explained, 'so I'm just going to show you what happened, or what I can pretty much deduce happened. Things we've picked up from surviving witnesses, from people who saw the bomber on his way to the restaurant, from bomb fragments, a few other pieces of physical evidence.' He was all business now, he didn't even wait for Justin to respond. He launched into his recitation. And Justin thought it was just that: this was something Chuck Billings had been practicing.

'Okay,' Billings said. 'We believe the guy walked here from several blocks away. Maybe as many as eight or ten.'

'Where was he before that?'

'Let me go through this, Jay. Hold your questions until after I'm done. But remember 'em. You'll see why when I'm finished.' Justin nodded and Billings continued. 'What we know for sure is that our guy walked in the door carrying a briefcase. That was the bomb. He talked to the hostess, went to a specific table' – Billings walked to a spot in the restaurant, stood there as if trying to visualize the room intact – 'right about here. We narrowed it down to four possible tables. Our job is really to determine three things: the quality of the explosive, the type of explosive, and the location of the blast. So we got the location. This baby went off right here, give or take a couple of feet.'

Billings walked away from the spot, as if it were dangerous to stand on it for too long. 'Okay, we know he talks to someone at the table, leaves the briefcase on the floor next to the guy he's talking to. Takes a couple of steps away, like he's walking out of the restaurant, his cell phone rings.'

'His cell phone rang?'

'Yeah. Hold on. You got a pen and paper? Write down your questions if you have to, but lemme go through the whole thing.'

'Go ahead. I don't need a pen. I'll remember.'

'His cell phone rings,' Billings repeated. 'And then . . . boom.' The head of the Providence PD bomb squad shrugged his shoulders up to his ears, as if he were trying to block the sound of the explosion. 'You know anything about explosions?'

'Am I allowed to interrupt you with an answer?'

'Don't be a wiseass.'

'No,' Justin said. 'I don't know anything about explosions except they're loud and they kill people.'

'Look around you. You see this room?' When Justin nodded, Billings made a circle in the air with his left hand. 'All right,' he said, indicating the invisible circle. 'This is water. You smack your hand down right in the middle of it, you get a depression. Can you picture that?' Justin nodded again. 'Think of the water as the atmosphere. The atmosphere in this room. When a bomb goes off, the blast scatters the atmosphere the way your hand scatters the water when you smack it. It pushes it away. That's the initial effect of an explosion. It pushes everything away. Blows the windows into the street, sends tables flying, all that other shit. But nature abhors a vacuum, as we know from our sixth-grade science class, so there's a negative pressure that *replaces* the atmosphere. Right? You hit the water, it swirls, moves away, but then it comes back, fills up the vacuum. That's what happens with a bomb. This negative phase sucks things toward it. Lighter things like paper, clothing, debris are sucked back *toward* the explosion. It all happens instantly, it's why things get so surreal. All this pushing and sucking. It's why that table wasn't touched, the one next to it was pulverized. But the closer you are to the point of the explosion, the better chance you have of being pulverized. We call it a kill ratio. Within ten feet of a pound of a high explosive, like a grenade, you'll have a hundred percent kill ratio. With three pounds, it's approximately twenty feet. This bomb was about three pounds. You want to know about the actual explosion? I mean, what happened in here?'

'Yeah. I think my friend might want to know that.'

'It was a hell of a bomb. Like I said, about three pounds. They used Semtex. It's an ex-Soviet bloc explosive. They still make it. The Czechs still make it, too. Not so easy to smuggle in, but it can be done. It's basically the equivalent of our C4. Al Qaeda uses it. So do the Colombian cartels. Used to be big with the IRA, but I guess they've cleaned up their act. Anyway . . . the bomb went off right over there. Anything within twenty feet, forget it. The primary fragmentation on this was brutal.'

'Sorry, you have to explain that.'

'Primary fragmentation? That's pieces of the bomb that are intended to hurt. You read about it all the time when stuff goes off in the Middle East. If it's a pipe bomb, they'll stuff the pipe with rocks or glass or nails. The explosion drives those things outward, scatters them. They're like mini-missiles. They'll rip through just about anything – walls, flesh, bone.'

'Christ.'

'Yeah. Know what our genius used here?' Billings didn't wait for an answer. He walked over to the nearest wall and pointed to a small object embedded in it. When Justin squinted, not sure what he was looking at, Billings pulled the fragment out of the plaster and held it in the palm of his hand.'

'A jack?' Justin asked. 'A kid's toy?'

'Pretty fuckin' deadly kid's toy when it's packed into three pounds of explosives. It's the perfect thing. Doesn't matter which direction it's facing, there's a little spike on every surface. They're small enough, you can squeeze a shitload of them into the container, and the more there are, the more damage can be done. These things were flying at people at about two thousand feet per second.'

'Jesus, Chuck. Who the hell would think of that? Jacks . . .'

'Really pretty brilliant. In a sick kind of way. And if this isn't a one-time thing, he's gonna use 'em again, I guarantee you. It's what I started to tell you before. Bombers can't resist their little signatures on their work. Everybody's got a different one. When you know what they are, it's pretty much as defining as fingerprints. And this is one of the most distinctive signatures I've ever seen.'

'You ever seen it before?'

'Never even heard of anyone using jacks.'

'Would you?'

'Jay, I told you I was obsessed with this kind of thing, right? You know what the hell I do with my free time?'

'Do I want to know?'

'I'm on the weirdest fucking Internet bomb sites, shit you can't even imagine. I'm on crackpot blogs about explosives. Some psycho blows up a cat somewhere in Kansas, I'm looking into it, checking out the signature. It's why they called me in here.'

'All right. So you've got a signature: jacks. And they did a lot of damage. What's next?'

'Well, that's just the primary fragmentation. You've still got a secondary. Like all the window glass that was in this place. The glassware, silverware, all that stuff. That stuff was slicing the shit out of everything and everybody. The secondary fragmentation was devastating. What you have to remember is that it's not like in a movie. A bomb isn't static. There's a huge amount of bleeding. The lights are out, it's smoky, the noise is literally deafening, it's almost impossible to hear anything. Here, it was particularly bad because it was a restaurant. So it didn't just start a fire, there were live electrical lines that went down, there were gas and water leaks. When the fire hit the gas, that was worse than the initial explosion. It must have been a fucking nightmare. The only thing I can tell you that might help your friend . . . according to the seating charts, which we got off the computer, her husband was about eight feet from the blast. He wouldn't have felt a thing. Some comfort, huh?'

'I don't know what to say to all this, Chuck.'

'You want to indulge me a minute, Jay? Lemme guess the questions you've been storing up.'

'Go for it.'

'Okay,' Billings said. 'First has got to be about the bomber.'

'I've got a few about him,' Justin admitted.

'First is: Did we get a description? Yes, we did. A pretty decent one, from people who are pretty sure they saw him on the street before he arrived, and from a few survivors in the restaurant. We know at least a few of the blocks he covered to get here. I might have partial fingerprints, too, from recovered bomb fragments.'

'So—'

'So what's being done to track him down? Nothing.'

'Chuck . . .'

'I got your next question, too, Jay, 'cause I know you're a good cop. If it was a suicide bombing, why the hell was he moving *away* from the blast when it went off? Another few feet, he would have been out of range of the hundred percent kill ratio.'

'You're two for two.'

'How about the cell phone? You probably want to know about that, too.'

'Yeah,' Justin said. 'Like—'

'Can a phone be used to trigger a bomb? Yes. It's a delightful new technology. The tones can be programmed to set the thing off.'

'Okay, so—'

'So *was* it the trigger? I think it was. I'm pretty damn sure it was.'

'But—'

'But, then, does that mean it wasn't a suicide bombing? And if the phone *was* the detonator, what are we doing to find the guy who *made* the call?'

'You got the questions down cold, Chuck. Now, you got any answers?'

'No.'

Justin couldn't decide which was getting the best of him at the moment, his confusion or his anger. 'Why the hell not?'

'Jay . . . remember I told you I couldn't figure out the Feds on this one? Well, let me try out another question on you: Why wouldn't they want answers to all of the questions we just asked?'

'Because they don't want to know the answers,' Justin said. But even as he said it, he didn't believe his own words.

'Or?'

'Or' – and now Justin spoke very slowly, as if he wanted to hear exactly what he was saying, trying the words out to see if they could possibly make sense – 'they already know the answers. And they don't want anyone else to find out what they are.'

Billings stayed silent for a few moments. Then he said quietly, 'There are four or five guys working the bomb angle. I was partnered with a very good guy, a Feebie, Dorell Cole. We were making some headway, he knows a lot about signatures, too. As soon as we thought we might be getting somewhere, Dorell got yanked off. A new guy came in to oversee the whole thing, and believe me, this guy was a total asshole. He's the head of the New York bureau.'

'Fuck me. Was it Rollins? Agent Len Rollins?'

'No. This guy's name is Schrader. Hubbell Schrader. Who's this Rollins character?'

'Someone I had a run-in with, about a year ago. He was the New York bureau chief then.'

'A run-in, Jay?' Billings's left eyebrow rose, the first relaxed gesture Justin had seen since they met.

Justin shrugged. 'I told him if I ever saw him again I'd kill him.'

'That sounds like one of your run-ins.'

'What did this guy Schrader do?'

'Basically, just cut me off at the knees. Clearly doesn't want any input from anyone outside the Bureau. But he also dismissed everything that Cole had discovered or hypothesized. As near as I can tell, Schrader made his report, which was fast and inaccurate. Then President Anderson and Vice President Dandridge came swooping in, got their photo ops, declared the whole thing a suicide bombing, and went off wherever presidents and future presidents go when they're not acting tough or raising money.'

'But you don't think it is a suicide bombing, do you?'

'I can't prove it . . . but no, I don't.'

Justin sighed. 'It's not on this level, Chuck, but I'm having my own problems with the Feds. And it opens up a few questions, too.'

'Hey, as long as we're sharing . . .'

So Justin told him about the local plane crash. Billings said he had read about it in the East End newspaper but assumed it was an accident. As Justin gave him some of the details, Billings whistled in amazement.

'The weirdest thing is, I thought the Feds would be all over this thing. Just because of the proximity to Harper's. I mean, it's a long shot that there's a connection, even if the plane was tampered with, but still . . .'

'You'd think they'd want to see for themselves.'

'Yeah.' Justin shook his head. 'But nothing. No contact. They got their info from the FAA, and that info is . . . let's say skewed . . . at best.'

'And they're blocking the identity of the pilot?'

'It's what it looks like,' Justin said.

'Why?'

'Why the hell are they getting in your way? Because they can, because they're idiots, because they've got something to hide . . .'

'You know where the plane came from, Jay?'

Justin shook his head. 'The guy who runs the airport here, he thought it was a drug-running plane. Maybe up from Florida.'

Billings cocked his head and his eyes narrowed.

'That mean something?' Justin asked.

Billings shrugged. 'Could mean just about anything,' he said.

'Well, why don't you tell me *one* thing you think it might mean.'

'You know, my imagination seems to be running wild these days. I think I'm getting paranoid. And what I think doesn't really matter anymore. I'm outta here tonight.'

'You're leaving?'

'They don't want me. Said I did a great job, but my job's over. So I'm heading back to Providence tonight. Got a meeting tomorrow morning with your old pal Ms Chinkle. Gonna see if she's got any insight into what the hell's going on with her fellow federal employees.'

'You driving up?'

'The Feds are very generous. They let me rent a two-door Ford. Why, got a better suggestion?'

'Yeah. Dump the Ford. I'm going up tonight, too. Having dinner with Wanda. You can come with me and even join us tonight.'

'And your mode of transportation is . . .?'

'Chartered a plane. You can drop your car off at the airport.'

'I always forget you're filthy rich, Jay. I knew there was a reason people didn't like you.'

'Fly up with me. Plane's gonna leave at six sharp.'

'You know what? That's too good a deal to pass up. I got a meeting here, kind of a debriefing, total bullshit, then I'll go back to my motel, pick up my notes and files. I'll show some of it to you on the plane and we can talk a little more.'

'Deal.'

The two men shook hands.

'I'm looking forward to the flight, Chuck,' Justin said.

'Me too,' Chuck Billings said. 'But then, I look forward to anything I don't have to pay for.'

chapter 10

Justin was not in the mood to sit and interview someone to fill the vacancy in the East End PD. He wanted to blame his lack of interest on the frustration he was feeling over the stonewalling surrounding his investigation of the small plane crash and the information he'd learned from Chuck Billings – information he was still trying to absorb – but he realized that it wouldn't have mattered what he'd done or discovered over the last few days, he'd never be in the mood to sit and interview someone for a job. Unfortunately, he'd promised Leona Krill that he'd talk to this woman, Regina something, he couldn't even remember her name, but what the hell kind of first name was Regina? He sighed because . . . well . . . because everything that had happened over the past week made him sigh . . . but he'd made the appointment with this Regina woman and he knew he couldn't break it.

He didn't want to interview her at the station, it just didn't feel right with all the other guys around, so he'd told her to meet him at Duffy's. Not the classiest place in town but if she wanted to be a cop she might as well get used to cop hangouts. Also, unless you put away quite a few drinks, Duffy's was not a place to linger. He was hoping his choice of venue would keep the session short and sweet.

Their meeting was set up for two o'clock. Justin was hoping to be back at his desk by two-thirty.

He slid into one of the three booths in the bar, looked at his watch at one minute to two, decided if she didn't show up by five after, he was out of there, but the front door to Duffy's was pushed open just a few seconds later and Regina whatever-her-name-was walked in right on time. Justin knew it was her. She looked like a cop. She had that confident manner, the one that said no one was going to give her any trouble because there wasn't any trouble she couldn't handle. She glanced around the bar, took him in, immediately headed for his booth, no hesitation. He guessed he had that cop air, too.

Before she reached his table, he stood up and extended his hand.

'Justin Westwood,' he said as they shook.

'Regina Bokkenheuser,' she said.

'Nice name,' he told her. 'Trips right off the tongue.'

She slid out of her long coat, hung it neatly on a hook to the left of the booth. She was wearing a tapered jacket and a loose-fitting shirt underneath. Her skirt matched the jacket and came down to mid-thigh. Her legs were muscular and at least as tapered as her suit. Justin knew, even with much of her body hidden, that he was looking at a woman with a lot of muscle, physically and emotionally. He smiled, trying to put her at ease. She smiled back at him, probably doing the same thing. He relaxed, felt comfortable as she slid into the booth on the bench across from him, and he realized she was probably a lot better at this than he was.

'It's Danish,' she said. 'And if you think it sounds bad, wait till you hear people try to spell it.'

'That where you're from? Denmark?'

'My grandmother,' she said. 'I'm from Wisconsin. Madison.' She looked around the room and he was surprised to see that she didn't seem to disapprove. 'You think they'd have any form of fruit juice in this joint?'

'I doubt it,' Justin said. 'Maybe orange, but I guarantee you cranberry's out of the question.'

Donnie, the bartender, wandered over to their table and, lo and behold, he had both orange and grapefruit juice. She ordered grapefruit. Justin wanted a beer but settled for a club soda.

Before Donnie could even get back to the bar, Regina Bokkenheuser reached into her inside jacket pocket, pulled out a piece of paper neatly folded into thirds, and slid it across the table at him.

'My résumé,' she explained. 'Figured it would help answer a few questions and maybe spark a few others.'

Before looking at the paper, he did his best to study her face. Justin realized she was quite attractive. She reminded him of the dark-haired assistant DA on Law & Order, the one from the earlier days of the show, the one who quit because she married Richard Gere. Well, maybe Regina wasn't quite so perfect-looking as that, but the same type. Her hair was lighter than that actress's hair, somewhere between blonde and brown, layered and cut close around her face. He didn't let his gaze linger, but he took in the fact that her features weren't perfect, which somehow made her even more attractive. Her nose was a little too big and her smile a little lopsided. Good teeth, though. Straight and very white. And her neck was long and elegant. Her blue eyes were clear and curious, and he thought he detected just a touch of sadness in there. Those eyes didn't look away from him until they glanced down at her résumé, letting him know he'd been watching her just a little too long.

Justin unfolded the paper, scanned the information. Impressive. She'd been a cop for six years back in Milwaukee. Before that, college at the state university in Madison. Her educational background was in forensic science. Her age wasn't listed on the résumé, but he put her in her late twenties, maybe thirty.

'What made you become a cop?' he asked, looking up.

'I was about to ask you the same thing,' she said.

'I'm not actually all that experienced in this management position,' he said, 'but I'm pretty sure I'm the one who's supposed to ask the questions.'

'Oh, I'll happily answer,' she told him. 'I just thought your answer would be a lot more interesting than mine.' When he cocked his head slightly to the right, she continued. 'I don't like to come into something like this cold,' she said. 'I Googled you.' His head cocked farther to the right and she said, 'Not your normal mentions for a small-town police chief.'

'And what would I find if I Googled you?'

'Nothing comparable.' She smiled that lopsided smile. 'And nothing particularly interesting. If I even popped up, which I won't. Never been in the papers, never done anything exciting enough to be cited. My dad was a police officer for twenty-five years and I was always fascinated by it. Both my parents wanted me to go into something else. Business, law, teaching maybe. At least, my dad *said* he wanted that. I always got the feeling he was secretly happy when I decided to follow in his footsteps.'

'And why did you?'

'There's the million-dollar question. I'm sure there's some psychological baggage involved . . . father-daughter stuff . . . but my guess is neither one of us wants to go there. Mostly I think it's fairly uncomplicated. I just *like* the job. I like helping people. I like solving things. I know it's not really glamorous, but it *feels* glamorous to me. I like saying I'm a police officer. I enjoy the respect it brings, especially these days.'

'Next question: Why *here*?'

'Why did I leave Madison? Or why did I come to East End Harbor?'

'Both. This is not exactly a teeming hotbed of crime.' Well, not usually, he thought. But he decided to keep his thought to himself.

'Lifestyle,' she said. 'My father died a few months ago . . .'

'I'm sorry. In the line of duty?'

'No. Heart attack. On his way to the grocery store. Fifty-eight years old.' She hesitated a moment, it was still an emotional subject for her. She quickly got her voice under control and went on. 'He left me a little bit of money, so I decided it was time to get out of the Midwest. And I thought I wasn't quite ready for New York City. A friend from the Milwaukee force knew someone on the NYPD who knew Leona, yada yada yada, so I checked out the town and fell in love with it and . . .

'And here we are.'

'And here we are,' she echoed, flashing one more tilted smile. 'And my guess is you're not the kind of person who likes to be pressured, so you're figuring this meeting is just a courtesy. But I should tell you, I'm a really good cop and I know what I'm doing and I wish you'd at least check my references because they're going to be glowing. I don't think you could find anyone better than me.'

'Anything else?'

'Yes. As long as you're feeling pressure, I found a perfect little house and it's for rent and I told them I'd let them know in a day or two. So I don't just want you to hire me, I want you to hire me soon.'

She smiled, an acknowledgment of her brazenness, he relaxed enough to smile back, they both had a second drink – neither switched to alcohol – and they talked about some of the cases she'd worked on. Both police forces were reasonably small, so she'd covered a variety of crimes. She'd worked two homicides – not the lead

109

detective on either murder. One remained unsolved, the other – a fairly simple family squabble; a jealous husband stabbed his wife, tossed her body in a Dumpster seven miles from his house, and tried to claim she'd gone missing – resulted in a conviction. She'd done a lot of domestic intervention, had no aversion to paperwork, and even liked the idea of walking the East End beat. She was clearly good at her interpersonal relationships – he realized she was pretty much wrapping him around her little finger.

'You've got more and better experience than anyone on my force,' he said after the conversation hit the hour mark. 'I'd have to hire you as my second in command.'

'If your question is, will that intimidate me, the answer's no. I'm ready for that kind of position.'

'Not lacking confidence, huh?'

'No, sir. I have quite a few flaws, but that's not one of them.'

'Care to tell what some of them are?'

'My flaws?' When he nodded, she thought for a moment, chewing on her lower lip. Then she shrugged. 'I bite my nails and I spend too much money on clothes, particularly shoes, and I'm not always the most patient person in the world. I don't like bullshit, which I personally don't think of as a flaw, but it tends to get me in trouble sometimes, so maybe it is. I think I get that from my dad.'

Justin stared at her, just for a moment – she didn't back down from his gaze – then he polished off his second club soda. 'Glowing, huh?'

'What?'

'Your references are gonna be glowing.' He checked the résumé in his hand. 'From Captain Frank Quarry of the Milwaukee PD and Captain Harvey Rizzo in Madison.'

'I think they will, yes.'

He wasn't wearing a sport coat and his leather jacket was hanging over the back of a chair, so he held on to the résumé rather than jam it into his pants pocket. He folded it one extra time so it disappeared into his palm. 'I'll let you know as soon as I can,' he said. And then: 'Where's the house?'

'Excuse me?'

'The one you fell in love with. That's putting all this unbearable pressure on me. Where is it?'

'On Division Street. Just a few blocks out of town, still in the historical village, though. I could get it for a year. And for a very reasonable price.'

'Little Victorian job, yellow paint job, lots of charm?'

'You know it?'

'Yup,' Justin said. 'And I hope you're the friendly type, Regina. 'Cause if you get the job, we're gonna be neighbors.'

'Everybody calls me Reggie,' she said. And this time the smile was not quite so lopsided.

At ten minutes before six o'clock that evening, Justin called Chuck Billings's cell phone and got voice mail. After the tone, he left a message that he'd wait as long as he could before taking off and told Chuck to call him if he was lost and couldn't find the small airport. He left his own cell phone number and then hung up. Justin waited a few moments, then dialed the number for the Fisherman Motel. The desk clerk told him that Mr Billings had checked out earlier that afternoon, around one-thirty or two. Justin left his cell phone number with the clerk just in case Chuck returned there. Then he went to Ray Lockhardt's office. The airport manager flinched when he saw Justin but relaxed when he realized all he wanted him to do this time was keep an eye out for Billings, in case he arrived after Justin's chartered plane took off.

At six-fifteen, Justin boarded the plane. He convinced the pilot to wait on the ground another fifteen minutes. At six-thirty, when Billings was a full half hour late and still had not called, Justin gave the okay and the small plane left for Providence.

The flight was a quick one, about forty-five minutes. Justin didn't give too much thought to Chuck Billings. He figured the bomb expert had gotten caught up in some sort of FBI bullshit. He also figured he'd hear about it tomorrow or maybe even tonight from Wanda Chinkle. He hadn't pegged Chuck as the single most reliable guy he'd ever met. So instead, he thought about Reggie Bokkenheuser. Other than the name, he had to admit she was pretty close to perfect. He'd checked with both of her references and, if anything, 'glowing' was an understatement when describing their responses. They said she was smart, friendly, a terrific cop, had great growth potential, showed the potential for strong management skills, had an excellent investigative instinct, could get people to warm up to her, and, bottom line, he'd be crazy not to hire her.

He knew it would make Leona Krill very happy if Reggie was brought aboard. He suspected the rest of the guys at the station would not be thrilled, especially if she were brought in at the sergeant level and as their superior. He decided they'd get over it, though. If she were as good as he believed she might be.

Justin decided to sneak in a fifteen-minute nap on the plane. As his eyes closed, he realized there was something bothering him about Reggie. He couldn't decide what it was, though. Maybe it was that he found her attractive. Maybe it was that she'd be living two houses away from him. Maybe it was simply that he'd never hired anyone before and she was the first and only person he'd talked to, and it all seemed too easy and perfect. Maybe he was being lazy, he should look around, talk to a few more candidates. But as he fell

112

asleep, he knew that Reggie Bokkenheuser was going to become the newest sergeant on the East End police force.

He dozed for twelve minutes. When he woke up, he wasn't particularly refreshed. But he was back in his hometown of Providence, Rhode Island.

chapter 11

Returning to Providence always provoked mixed emotions in Justin Westwood. He genuinely loved the city. Found it beautiful and alive. He knew it well – and all sides of it. The comforting pomposity of its academia. The snobbish magnificence of its upper class. The small-town quality of its corruption. The New England backbone of its middle class. The violence and despair of its back alleys.

He was also afraid of the city. He had lost his wife and child there. Had endured excruciating pain there. Had gone through years of an unfriendly and hurtful separation from his parents.

Providence was not simple for him.

He had reconciled with Jonathan and Lizbeth Westwood about a year before, and that was a big step forward. It made him feel welcome again, not just in his childhood home but in his city. They had embraced him back into the family and he welcomed that embrace warmly. But both sides were still wary. Family ties were always capable of unraveling, he knew. For now, however, the bonds were strong. His mother and father were anxious to make amends and to try to heal old wounds. Justin suspected that some wounds could never completely heal but he was willing to play the comforted patient to help ease his parents' guilt. And he had to admit that

Jonathan and Lizbeth were capable of making things very comfortable.

He got a warm hug from his mother when he stepped inside the front door of the house. As always, he marveled at the splendor of the place in which he'd spent his youth. The cathedral-like ceilings, the enormous spiraling staircase, the exquisite detailing in the maple and cherry woodwork throughout the expansive mansion. Lizbeth followed him into the den, where his father gave him a warm pat on the back, the closest to a hug he could manage. They shared a glass of superb burgundy as they asked appropriate questions and revealed appropriate details about the past several months of their lives. His mother was saddened by the end of his relationship with Deena, but did no more than give a quick shake of her head when told it had ended for good. His father was mixed about the news of Justin's promotion: proud of the reward yet still bothered that he'd chosen police work as his profession instead of something more substantial – which, in his father's eyes, meant more profitable. Justin told them a little bit about why he was there, enough to pique their interest and get some valuable insight from his banker father. Jonathan Westwood said, when Justin had finished summarizing the stories of both the plane crash and Chuck Billings's observations of the bombing, 'Always look for the money.'

When Justin asked him what he meant, Jonathan cleared his throat and said, 'I've spent my whole life as a businessman. My whole life around wealthy, powerful people. And if that experience has taught me anything, it's that there are two reasons for all human behavior: passion and money. I don't know anything about your line of business, Jay, but I wouldn't imagine that criminal behavior is all that different from what I deal with in the business world. Somewhere, somehow, someone is making money. Find out who that is and you'll find out what's going on.'

'I don't know if everything in life can be made that simple,' Justin said.

'Life *is* simple,' his father told him, finishing his last sip of wine. 'It's what happens while you're living it that some people make so damn hard.' And then he said it again: 'Find the money.'

Wanda Chinkle arrived at eight o'clock and Justin was amused to see that she'd dressed for the occasion. It was usually hard to get Wanda into anything but a pair of pants and an open-neck shirt, but tonight she was wearing a dress and a short-sleeved cashmere sweater. With pearls. And stockings. Justin had never seen her in a pair of stockings before – in fact, he thought, he might never have actually seen her legs before – and she scowled when she saw him staring and grinning.

Wanda passed on the superb red wine, had a Diet Coke instead, much to Jonathan Westwood's horror, and then they sat down to a delicious dinner of rare roast beef, broiled new potatoes, and string beans, prepared by the Westwoods' longtime chef, Sidney. The dinner table talk veered between professional and personal, but nothing substantive was broached between Justin and Wanda until, after coffee and a dessert of key lime pie, they settled into the den, alone, and closed the door behind them.

'You don't seem quite as angry as you were over the phone,' Justin said.

'Don't let appearances deceive you,' Wanda responded. 'Just because I want to pistol-whip you doesn't mean I can't be polite in front of your parents.'

'Okay, as long as I know the affection's still there.'

'Let's skip the wiseass stuff, okay?' she said. 'I want to know what's going on.'

'A lot more stuff than the other day,' he said. And first he ran down everything he'd put together about the plane crash. He told her the circumstances of the crash and about Martin Heffernan's behavior at the crash site. He said he was fairly certain that the FAA representative stole the pilot's ID. He told her about the fake ambulance spiriting the body away and he told her, again, how he'd been denied access to the fingerprint identification. He recounted his session with the airport manager Ray Lockhardt, told her Ray's take on how the plane was tampered with and the pressure Ray was getting from Heffernan about the accident report, clearly an attempt to circumvent any investigation. Justin gave a blow-by-blow account of his conversation on the phone with the ditzy Cherry Flynn, trying to trace the ownership of the plane through the tail number. And then he told her he was convinced that someone at the FAA knew in advance that the plane would be sabotaged, because the files were pulled prior to the crash.

When he paused to take a deep breath, Wanda said, 'Are you done?'

'I'm done with the crash,' he told her.

'What else is there?' she asked.

'You have a meeting scheduled with Chuck Billings.'

She didn't exactly do a double take. But it was close. 'Jesus, does everybody know everything that goes on in my office?'

Thinking of Bruno Pecozzi, but deciding to keep Bruno's awareness of FBI activities quiet for the moment, Justin said, 'More than you might think.'

Wanda shook her head. 'I'm meeting with Chuck tomorrow morning.'

'Do you know what it's about?'

She stared at him, undecided about how to answer. Finally she decided to go with the truth. 'No. I mean, I assume it has something to do with the Harper's bombing. He was very mysterious, didn't want to talk on the phone. Just said it was urgent.'

'It is.'

'You know, it's starting to piss me off, Jay, that you know everything before I do.'

'I'm happy to share my info, Wanda. Although Chuck's going to have a lot more details than I have.'

'Let's hear what you got.'

So he told her about his disturbing conversation with Billings that morning. How Chuck felt that the FBI was not just hiding something, they were actively preventing any attempts to get to the truth behind the attack.

'It doesn't make sense,' she said when he was finished.

'I know. But he's very convincing.'

'What possible reason would we have for hurting the investigation?' When Justin shook his head, she furrowed her brow and rested her chin on the palm of her left hand and said, 'You think the two events are connected?'

'The plane crash and the bombing?' Justin threw his hands up. 'I don't see any connection. Nothing logical jumps out at me. But suddenly we have two . . . events . . . and we're not talkin' New York City here, East End Harbor is not exactly the center of international intrigue . . . and the FBI, along with God knows who else, seems to be doing their damnedest to make sure neither of them gets investigated properly.'

'Look, your crash is one thing. Who knows why they want this hushed up, but I could come up with reasons. Maybe the pilot's an ex-agent, maybe the guy's wife is best friends with the director's wife. Who knows? But Harper's . . . I don't believe it. It's fucking terrorists, for Christ's sake, Jay. This is what we live for. It doesn't jibe. I think Chuck's being paranoid.'

'Maybe. You're probably right.'

'Don't condescend to me, you asshole. I want to know what you really think.'

'I think,' Justin said, 'that I came up here to get some specific information to help me along in what I think is a murder investigation. And I think that's as involved as I want to be with anything. Why don't I just let you and Chuck handle this other matter. But I do think you should hear him out, although I'll be surprised if he shows up in the morning.'

'Why?'

'Because he was supposed to fly up with me and he stood me up. My guess is he's entangled in a whole lot of shit with your pals back in New York.'

'As long as you remember that they *are* my pals,' she said. 'That's who I work with. That's who I work *for*. I'm not here for the sole purpose of giving you or Chuck Billings inside information.'

'I know you're not,' Justin said. And then he said, 'So do you have the pilot's name?'

'Yes,' she said. 'I do.'

After another long silence, Justin just said, 'Wanda?'

She sighed. 'I don't know why the information's being blocked. But keeping it secret has been labeled top priority. Something nasty is going on here and I can't figure out what it is.'

'It's not your job to figure it out, is it?'

'No,' she said. 'But it is yours.'

He nodded.

'The pilot's name is . . . was . . . Hutchinson Cooke. People called him Hutch.'

'Anything else I should know?'

'No, no, please don't thank me for risking my job to give this to you.

119

'Thank you. *Is* there anything else I should know?'

'He was an Air Force pilot.'

'When he died? He was in the Air Force?'

'I'm not sure.'

'What does that mean?'

'He was definitely Air Force. And there's no record that he was discharged.'

'So he was still in.'

'There's also no record that he served anywhere. At least for the past eighteen months.'

'How do you know that?'

'Because we have access to records of all military personnel and where they're stationed. And he hasn't been stationed anywhere for the last year and a half. He just seems to have disappeared.'

'Was he still drawing a salary?'

'Air Force? Yes.'

'Okay, what aren't you telling me here?'

'Christ, Jay, don't you believe in doing any work on your own?'

'Wanda, I have a feeling there's going to be plenty of work to do here after you give me everything you can.'

She sighed. 'Two strange bits of info. He flew government officials.'

'What do you mean, government officials?'

'I couldn't get his log. It was frozen. All I can tell you is he didn't get as high as Air Force One. That log I could check. But that seems to have been his assignment for years, piloting whoever needed piloting to and from D.C. Other than that you're on your own.'

'All right. What's the second thing?'

'He was still receiving his Air Force salary, right? But he was also getting paid by someone else.'

'Who?'

'A company called Midas.'

'What the hell is that?'

'Don't know. I didn't have time to dig that deep. And to be perfectly honest, I didn't particularly want to.'

'It's not illegal to be getting a civilian salary while you're in the Air Force, is it? I mean, I imagine it happens all the time when rich guys go into the service. If any rich guys ever actually go into the service.'

'No. It's not illegal. It's just that . . . this guy was a lifer, Jay. That's what his records show. He wasn't rich. And he wasn't getting paid by Midas until eighteen months ago. Right at the time he seemed to disappear from the Air Force.' She cocked her head to the right and narrowed her eyes. 'What the hell is going on here, Jay?'

Before Justin could respond, there was a firm knock on the den door. Both Justin and Wanda jumped a bit at the noise.

'Jay,' Justin's mother called in. 'Billy's on the phone for you. He says it's important.'

'Billy DiPezio?' Wanda asked, and for some reason she asked it in a whisper.

Justin nodded, leaned over to the other side of the couch, and grabbed the phone. 'Billy,' he said. 'What's up? It's too late for a free dinner, if that's why you're calling.'

'That's not why I'm calling,' the Providence police chief said. 'I'm over at Chuck Billings's house.'

'Give him a message for me, please,' Justin said. 'Tell him he's an asshole. He'll understand.'

'I can't give him the message, Jay. I'm with his wife.'

'Well tell her to give him the message, please. I'd appreciate it.'

'Chuck's dead,' Billy DiPezio said.

'What?' Justin found himself stammering. 'When? . . . How ;'

'Late this afternoon. He was driving up here, got off the I-95 for

121

some reason, probably to find something to eat, and his car spun out of control, hit an oncoming car. Both cars were totaled.'

'What do you mean, he was driving up?'

'I mean he was driving from Long Island back home. He was supposed to get in tonight.'

'No, he wasn't. He—'

'Jay, what the hell's your problem with this? I spoke to him this morning, he was driving up. The local cops called me, said it looks like he fell asleep at the wheel. What the fuck are you arguing about this with me for?'

Justin heard Billy's muffled voice – he must have put his hand over the speaker in the phone – apologizing to Chuck Billings's wife for his language.

'Jay,' Billy said, quieter and calmer, 'I'm calling you because when I spoke to him, Chuck said he was going to see you this morning. It means you were the last one to see him alive. The last one of *us*. I thought you might want to come see Katy, that's Chuck's wife. Thought there might be something you could tell her about your conversation.'

'Of course,' Justin said. 'I don't have much to report, but I'll come in the morning. I'll do whatever I can.'

He took down Katy Billings's address, told Billy he'd talk to him in a few days, and hung up the phone.

He turned to Wanda Chinkle, told her about the conversation he'd just had with Billy. He realized his own nails were digging hard into his palm, causing the skin to turn a blotchy red and white. 'It doesn't look like Chuck was being paranoid.'

'Billy said it was an accident,' Wanda said slowly. 'Don't go off half-cocked, Jay.'

'He wasn't going to drive. He was flying up with me.'

'Maybe he changed his mind.'

'Or somebody changed it for him.'

'Jay . . .'

'Be careful, Wanda,' he said.

'Careful of what?'

'I'm not sure,' Justin Westwood said. 'But right now, just to be on the safe side, be careful of everything.'

chapter 12

Muaffak Abbas was not afraid. He was, however, angry.

He felt that the man who had paid him so much money didn't really trust him. Wouldn't let him do the job he was being paid to do. Abbas felt some shame in this fact. And dishonor. But by the time he reached his destination, he realized that shame and dishonor in this world were of no importance. Soon he would be covered in glory. He would never feel worthless again for he would be meeting his God and spending eternity bathed in His light.

The feeling made him lightheaded. He felt as if God were already nearby, gently pulling him toward His eternal reward.

Thinking about his place in heaven, even Muaffak's anger dissipated. When he walked into the small Italian restaurant on West 22nd Street in the evil city of New York, in the sinful borough of Manhattan, he felt nothing but peace.

His mother had received the money. Fifty thousand dollars. Money that would be spent feeding the poor and caring for the sick. The money was nice. But he was not doing this for money. Neither he nor his mother cared about physical rewards. They cared about their people. And the purity of their own souls.

She was proud of him, he knew. Proud that he was about to

become a martyr for Allah. A martyr to help rid the world of sin and evil and Jews and Americans. How could a mother not be proud?

Muaffak Abbas looked at his watch, waited for the second hand to tick off thirty more seconds, then he walked into the restaurant. Went straight past the hostess without so much as a nod or acknowledgment of her existence. He did not acknowledge insignificant, godless insects. He walked right up to the man at the table, the man whose picture he had studied. The man who sat alone at a table for two, waiting for his luncheon partner. Waiting for someone who would never arrive.

Abbas stood in front of the man, who looked up, confused. The man's eyes narrowed when Abbas threw his hands out, a grand gesture to God, welcoming Him as he would soon be welcomed in return.

He screamed out the words, realized that he was in America, that these people would not know what he was saying, and he wanted them to know, wanted them to understand. A final moment of vanity. So he screamed the words out again, this time in English: 'I am ready!'

It took another few seconds. Abbas stood there, arms outstretched, the man at the table staring up at him, the restaurant silent.

He wished they had let him do this himself. He wished they had trusted his strength. And then he wished for nothing more.

Because that's when his cell phone rang.

And Muaffak Abbas was, at last, bathed in light and glory.

And flesh and blood and bone and devastation and death.

He had received his reward.

Somewhere his mother was smiling and her heart was glad.

chapter 13

The morning after his dinner with Wanda Chinkle, Justin's chartered plane left the Providence airport at nine-thirty. At eight o'clock, he'd gone to pay his respects to Katy Billings and tell her of his final conversation with her husband. He didn't feel as if he was much comfort. He told her that he and Chuck had spoken about work, about the bomb at Harper's. He recounted the gist of the conversation – she did not seem very interested in the details – and then he told a small lie. He said that Chuck told him he was happy he was leaving East End Harbor earlier than expected because he'd be so happy to see his wife. He couldn't tell if Katy believed him. He hoped so. By the time he left, he was certain that she did. If there was one thing he knew from his years talking to witnesses and to victims, it was that people ultimately believed what they wanted to be true.

When he touched down at the East End airport, he went straight to his house. The first thing he did was call Reggie Bokkenheuser and tell her she had the job. She tried to play it cool but couldn't. She was too excited. When he hung up the phone, she was still telling him how he'd never regret this. He told her he didn't expect to regret it. And he told her to report to work the next day.

Justin walked to the station after that. He needed the three-quarters of a mile or so of fresh air. The conversation with Katy

Billings and the flight in the small plane had felt stifling and confining, emotionally and physically claustrophobic. It felt good to be out in the cold; it refreshed him to see his breath billow out in front of him as he walked. By the time he got to the station it was twelve-fifteen, his hands and face were turning red, and he felt both awake and alive.

When he got settled, he motioned for Gary and Thomas to come over to his desk. He gave them the name Hutchinson Cooke, told them to find out where the man lived. When they stared at him, baffled, he told them it was the name of the pilot who'd crashed in the small plane, the Piper, told them he needed as much background material as they could provide, and then he realized they weren't staring because they wanted more information about the assignment, but because they simply didn't know where to begin. So he said to start in Washington, D.C., check the city and every suburb within thirty miles for an address and phone number. He told them to use the Internet, to check Air Force bases around the country, any Air Force records they could get their hands on, anything it took to find out where he lived and anything else about him, no matter how much time they had to devote to it. They nodded, took one step away, then Justin cleared his throat, which meant they were supposed to stop and pay attention. When they stopped and paid attention, he said, 'I hired someone. A new cop.'

'Cool,' Gary said. 'Who is he?'

'He's a she.' They gave that same confused stare and Justin said, 'Her name's Regina. Reggie. Reggie Bokkenheuser.' And then, for some reason, he said, 'That's Danish.' They nodded, satisfied, turned to walk away again, and Justin said, 'She's got a lot of experience. She's going to be second in command here.'

This time the two young cops didn't just look confused, they registered some hurt. Justin said, again, 'She's got a lot of experience.'

127

Neither Gary nor Thomas said a word. They just nodded one more time, went back to their desks, and began working the phones and the Net.

Justin thought, *Hey, that went pretty well.* As he started to go through the mail, mostly junk or crank mail that came in to the police chief – unsigned notes complaining about barking dogs, angry letters decrying the mess left by the weekend tourists – he decided, *Maybe this management things not as bad as I thought.*

The smug feeling didn't last very long. In fact, it lasted less than a minute, because that's when Justin looked up and saw the man in the dark gray suit standing in the front door of the station house. The guy was wearing a dark overcoat, unbuttoned, so it flapped open. He was in his late forties to mid-fifties, hard to tell exactly because his hair was light and cut too short to reveal much gray, and dark sunglasses hid his eyes. He was tall, a little over six feet, and lean; he didn't look as if he could have weighed more than one-seventy, one-seventy-five. The muscles on his neck were taut, and Justin had a feeling the rest of him was probably just as taut. A Fed, Justin thought. And after that he thought, *I already don't like him.*

The man didn't hesitate, walked over to Justin's desk and stood over it.

'Justin Westwood?' he asked. And when Justin nodded, the man said, 'Hubbell Schrader, FBI.'

'You guys should think about neon,' Justin said. 'It'd be a little less obvious.'

Hubbell Schrader grinned. 'It's in the handbook,' he said. 'We have to look like this.'

Justin had to return the grin. 'What can I do for you?'

'I'm not exactly sure,' Schrader said. 'I thought I should check in with you, though.'

'About what?'

'For one thing, Chuck Billings. I was dealing with him and he was a good guy, damn good at his job.'

'So this is a sympathy call?'

'I know all local cops are supposed to hate us Feds, but maybe you can give it a rest for a while. I don't have any hidden agenda here and I'm not looking to bust your balls.'

Justin's warning light came on. He remembered what Billings had said about this guy: an asshole. And worse, an asshole who didn't want to get to the meat of the case. He'd basically told the bomb experts what to think and what to say. The warning light glowed only brighter at the words 'I don't have any hidden agenda.' That meant that Special Agent Schrader was out for blood. He was a magician masquerading as a cop: anything that was revealed was going to be fake; anything he placed in plain sight was not going to be real.

Justin looked up at Schrader and bit his lip, his expression as full of regret as he could muster. The guy wanted to throw around the bullshit, Justin could toss it with the best of them. 'You're right,' he said. 'Sorry. What can I do for you?'

'Is there an office or someplace a little more private?'

Justin hesitated, then stood and led Schrader back to Jimmy Leggett's office. He flicked the light switch and the fluorescent light flickered on for the first time since Jimmy had been killed.

The two men sat – Justin a bit uncomfortably behind Jimmy's desk – and the FBI agent said, 'I've been one of the men in charge of investigating the Harper's explosion. One of the reasons I'm here is that I know Billings took you there, gave you a little look-see.' When Justin didn't say anything, Schrader went on quickly. 'I said I'm not looking to bust your balls and I'm not. I don't know why he took you there and I don't really care. I assume he had his reasons. What I want to know is if he might have told you something that could in any way be useful.'

129

Justin hesitated, then said, 'He didn't really tell me anything.'

'So can I ask why you were there?'

Justin made a show of shrugging, as if apologizing for what he was about to say. 'My boss, the guy whose office we're in, was killed in the explosion.'

'Jimmy Leggett. I know. I'm sorry.'

'Yeah, well, the thing is, I made a promise to his wife. She was kind of hysterical and asked me to find out why he was killed. I asked Chuck to show me the site, no reason really, just so I could tell her I saw it. I mean, there's not much I'm going to be able to tell her – what the hell can I really do or find out? – but I at least wanted to make it look good.'

'So was it helpful?'

'No. Mostly it was just depressing as hell.'

'Did Billings give you any of his theories on what happened?'

'He tried. Not in any great depth or anything. I have to say, I wasn't able to understand most of what he was talking about. It was a lot of technical bomb stuff, and that's hardly my area.'

'Kind of a self-effacing guy, aren't you?'

Justin shrugged again. 'Just telling you what happened.'

'Did Chuck discuss with you anything about a notebook?'

'What kind of notebook?'

'His notes on the case. Anything he might have written down about his investigation.'

'No. I don't think he was carrying anything when he gave me the tour. I hate to use that word, but you know what I mean.'

'He didn't have a casebook with him?'

'No. But we weren't really there on official business. He was just showing me the site as a favor. I wasn't really picking his brains and he certainly wasn't picking mine.'

It was now a little after twelve-thirty, and Justin glanced up from the desk because Stanton 'Don't call me Stan, my name's Stanton' Carman from the East End post office was tapping his thin, nervous fingers on the doorframe. Stanton, a small, wiry guy with a thin mustache that looked like it had been penciled on, had worked in the post office for fourteen years. He liked to think he was both tough and cool, although he was far from either. In keeping with his self-image, he flirted with every single woman who mailed a letter or picked up a package, and on his lunch breaks he often stopped in at the police station to chat, annoying the hell out of everyone. He was harmless, and sometimes he'd take mail from them, saving a trip and a wait on line, so the cops all tolerated him. He always came in with a little swagger – the closer he got to the police station, the more he swaggered – and even lounging in the doorway his body language was self-important. Justin's eyes were raised but he didn't speak, because any opening for conversation was an invitation for Stanton to talk your head off, so the post office clerk just dropped a large manila envelope on the desk.

'Came for you this morning, Chief,' Stanton said. 'You in this office now?'

Justin looked up at him. Usually they were on a first-name basis. This 'Chief' thing was new. He shook his head, a silent answer to Stanton's question, and did his best to look as if Stanton should get the hell out now.

'Looked like it might be important, so I thought I'd drop it by.'

Justin nodded again. He knew if he said a word, he'd be stuck for the next ten minutes. Maybe longer. Even with Hubbell Schrader in the room. Stanton never seemed to care if he was interrupting even the most important business conversation.

'Expecting something?' Schrader asked.

Justin wasn't. He rarely got anything besides bills and the occasional postcard from Deena's young daughter, Kendall, when she went away on a short trip. But without thinking he answered, 'Yeah.' With a smile, as if there were something sentimental inside. 'From my dad.'

'Well . . . see ya,' Stanton said, and Justin waited until he was out the door before casually dropping the envelope on the desk and saying to the FBI agent, 'Anything else?'

'Maybe,' Schrader said. 'The plane crash a few days ago. Got anything on that?'

'I was wondering if you guys were going to get around to that. You interested?' Justin did his best to register genuine surprise.

'It hasn't been a top priority because our info is that it was an accident. But I'm interested in anything out of the ordinary right now. And that sure as hell qualifies as out of the ordinary.'

'You know, it's weird,' Justin said. 'I don't have a goddamn thing. Maybe you can help me out. Might be to your benefit, too. The pilot didn't have a shred of ID on him. I managed to get a fingerprint but it doesn't seem to be on record anywhere.' He thought about his next sentence, whether or not to toss it in, decided he'd go for it. 'I even called a friend of mine in the FBI. The agent who runs the New England bureau. I know her from Providence, that's where I'm from.'

'Chinkle or something like that, right?'

'Wanda Chinkle. Exactly.'

'She help you out?'

'Nope. Said she tried and got the same answer – nothing on record.'

'I'm sorry about that,' Schrader said. 'We restricted access.'

'But you know the pilot's identity?'

Schrader nodded.

'You gonna share it?' Justin asked.

'I don't want to be difficult,' the agent said. 'In fact, I'm under orders to try to be as cooperative as possible. But I'm also under orders not to reveal his name.'

'Why?'

'We've been looking into it,' Schrader said. 'We don't have any answers yet, but we're investigating. Like I said, we're looking at anything out of the ordinary. We got burned pretty bad on 9/11, didn't connect a lot of the dots we should've connected. We can't ignore anything that might relate to this bombing.'

'And does it?'

'It's unlikely, but we don't know for sure yet. That's why we're not releasing any information. I know it's frustrating, but if local cops get involved, even someone as competent as you seem to be, it can only muddle things even further.'

'Thanks for the compliment,' Justin said. 'That's the first time anyone from your organization admitted I might even be competent.' He grinned easily. 'So do you have a hunch? I mean, about the pilot's connection to the bombing?'

The agent hesitated, furrowed his brow thoughtfully, then shook his head. 'I think the plane crash is just a coincidence. Pilot error, accidental malfunction, something like that. Screwy . . . but screwier things happen all the time.'

'That's what I figured,' Justin said. And he did his best to furrow his own brow, before adding, 'Except . . . the pilot's body disappeared.'

'Yes, we know.'

'Have a hunch about that?'

'More than a hunch,' Schrader said easily. 'We've talked to Southampton Hospital and several other facilities within fifty miles of this place. They've had so many bodies, living and dead, after the explosion, they're sure this one just got misplaced. Put in with all the others.' He shook his head at the tragedy of it all.

'There didn't seem to be a record of any ambulance being dispatched to pick up this particular body,' Justin said.

'That also got lost in the confusion. But it's been found now. I think if you get in touch with Southampton Hospital, they'll corroborate what I'm telling you.'

'I'm sure they will,' Justin said.

Schrader stood up. 'Well,' he said. 'I just thought we should touch base. I'm sorry I can't be more helpful, but I wanted to fill you in.'

'I appreciate it. If there's anything I can do for you while you're around, just ask.'

'Same here,' Schrader said. And smiled.

Justin watched him go, but the agent didn't leave the station. He stopped at Gary Jenkins's desk, started up a casual conversation. Justin knew that Gary was smart enough not to reveal anything he shouldn't. At some point, Schrader looked up and caught Justin's eye. Justin flashed him a big smile and, staring straight at him, began opening the envelope that Stanton had dropped off. It was addressed only to Justin Westwood, East End Harbor Police Department. No street number. And no return address or name of sender.

Inside was a thick three-ring binder. Justin flipped it open to find pages filled with notes, diagrams, and hand-scribbled drawings. It took him a moment to realize what he was holding on to, and when he did, he involuntarily slammed the notebook shut. He glanced up, but Schrader wasn't watching him now. The FBI agent was heading toward the door, on his way outside. That's when Justin saw that there was a note taped to the cloth front of the book. It was handwritten and said, 'Jay: Just for safekeeping. If I've already told you to FedEx this baby up to me, you can have a good laugh at my expense. If you're surprised to get it, then it meant I did the right thing. Get the bastards.'

The note was from Chuck Billings.

He was holding all the information Billings had compiled on the bombing at Harper's Restaurant.

Justin licked his lips because his mouth had suddenly gone dry. But before he could open the book up again, it was 12:40 P.M., and Stanton came racing back into the police station, yelling for them to turn on the TV or the goddamn radio. Special Agent Hubbell Schrader came racing in, too, as Stanton began screaming that the fuckers had done it again, the goddamn fucking shitheads had just blown up another restaurant, this time in New York City.

Justin shoved the notebook into a desk drawer, came racing out of the small office. Mike Haversham was the closest to the small TV they kept in the main room and he punched at the on button and, sure enough, Stanton was right. On the TV screen there was smoke and sirens and cops and firemen. There seemed to be blood everywhere and you could hear the hysteria that was happening in Manhattan. And as Justin looked up, saw Agent Schrader staring at the TV just like the rest of them, he thought two things.

One: when Schrader had come into the police station, he'd walked right up to Justin's desk. He didn't hesitate, walked right up as if he knew who he was, as if he'd seen him before. As if he'd been briefed.

But that wasn't nearly as odd as the second thing Justin was thinking.

Watching Hubbell Schrader now, standing amid the cops, all of them staring in disbelief at the TV screen, Justin was thinking, *This guy doesn't look surprised.*

He looks as if he'd been expecting it.

chapter 14

Speech delivered at 6:07 P.M. on November 13, by Thomas Wilton Anderson, the president of the United States

My fellow Americans,

This afternoon, evil struck again, trying to insinuate itself into the very fabric of American life. Today, at 12:34 P.M., a suicide bomber detonated a bomb in New York City, in a Manhattan restaurant, La Cucina, killing twenty-eight people, including himself, and injuring nearly fifty more.

Some people, in what I believe is an unfortunate and dangerous attempt to politicize today's tragedy as well as the tragic bombing of Harper's Restaurant nine days ago, are already saying that these evildoers have succeeded in infiltrating our everyday lives, that they are successfully destroying the things that make America great. I say they have *not* succeeded . . . that they will *never* succeed. Not under my watch. No one will ever be able to successfully attack the core of our greatness. Because that core comes from strengths that are almost unimaginable in the world in which our attackers live. Our strength comes from faith, faith not only in a wise and just God, but in wise and just people. In the American people. Our strength also comes from our freedom, from our many freedoms. And right now

I'm declaring another freedom – one we've always had, one this country was founded on, one that we must exercise yet again, not happily but proudly: the freedom to fight back. And I mean more than simply strike back. I mean strike first. Strike hardest. I'm talking about the freedom to seize control of our own lives. The freedom to make other people pay – and pay big-time – when they try to take away our freedom.

My administration has been working very closely with the FBI and the CIA since the bombing at Harper's. I must commend our intelligence agencies, for they have moved swiftly, decisively, and effectively, which is not easy when dealing with the kinds of shadowy networks we're dealing with. As a result of their actions we now know the identity of the first terror suspect, the madman who blew himself up in Harper's, killing so many people. His name is Bashar Shabaan. He was an Iraqi citizen, with links to Al Qaeda and other terrorist groups, and he had been living here, in the United States, for three years. We not only know Bashar Shabaan's identity, we know other members of his terrorist cell and we know the members of his family who provided aid in his evil scheme. Many of those cell members and family members have been arrested and the remaining ones are about to be picked up and arrested. They will be questioned, and, believe me, when we are done, we will have all the answers we need to have. And they will receive all the punishment they deserve to receive.

We also know the identity of *today*'s bomber: Muaffak Abbas. He was a Saudi, also with links to Al Qaeda and other terrorist groups, and we have already rounded up family members and supporters for interrogation. We are looking for any and all links between these two villains, and if those links exist, we will find them. And we will find anyone else, any individuals, any groups, connected to them as well. I should add that the Saudi government has been extraordinarily supportive and helpful and wants to make it clear to all Americans that they abhor any and all acts of terrorism and will continue to do their best to rid their country and the world of such evildoers.

As you can tell from these results, we have moved swiftly, we will continue to move swiftly, and we will get results.

Standing beside me are Vice President Phillip Dandridge; the attorney general of the United States, Jeffrey Stuller; and the assistant attorney general, Ted Ackland. I have spent the last several hours with Phil and Jeff and with Teddy, along with some other key advisers. The vice president has been put in charge of the task force investigating the recent attacks and our enemies responsible for them. He is reporting directly to me. At first, I was going to step aside and let the vice president and the attorney general tell you about some of the decisions and plans that were made today. But then I decided no, I want to speak directly to you myself. Partly because, as everyone knows, next year is an election year and I will be stepping down after two terms, and I in no way want to politicize these proceedings, just as I hope no politician, from either party, tries to politicize these tragedies. But mostly I'm speaking to you because these are things I believe in so deeply and so passionately. These are things upon which hang the future of America, the future of the world as we know it. And I want to make it clear that I expect *support* for our vision of the future. Not my vision, not the vice president's vision, but *our* vision – America's vision. I expect bilateral support from the Senate and the Congress, support from the media by having fair and accurate reporting, support from judges who will stop their activist agenda so we can do what is right for the country, and military and political support from our allies around the rest of the world. There used to be a saying: You are either part of the solution or you are part of the problem. I'll say this: If you are part of the problem, get the hell out of our way or we will sweep you out of our way, because right now I am only interested in solutions.

To that end, I am going to ask Congress to pass what we are calling the Triumph of Freedom Act. And I am asking that it be passed unanimously to show our support not just for the dead, for those who died in these two horrible attacks, but for the living, those who care about protecting our future.

What is the Triumph of Freedom Act? It's many things. Mostly it will guarantee that terrorists and terrorism will never get a foothold in our country. We will wipe them out with several bold strokes – and the first stroke will start now, with this Act.

The Triumph of Freedom Act means that we will be able to put any terror suspect's DNA in a national data bank. This will be an enormous benefit to everyone, to all agencies fighting this sort of horrific crime.

We will be able to clamp down on and seize any assets found in Arab *hawala* transactions. *Hawala* is where cash is exchanged and funneled to terrorists.

We will be able to get business records without a court order in all terrorism probes.

We will be able to track wireless communications with a roving warrant.

We will be able to revoke U.S. citizenship of anyone we suspect of militant extremism.

We will be using volunteer civilian groups, trained and armed civilian groups, as terrorist deterrents.

We will be imposing a mandatory death penalty on all known terrorists and anyone known to aid terrorists.

Terrorists and known terror suspects will no longer have the same rights as the American citizens they are trying to destroy. We will no longer tolerate government policies that protect the very people who are threatening to dismantle our government.

Many more details will emerge over the next forty-eight hours. But what I would like to make clear to our friends and to our enemies is this: if we are struck, we will strike back and our strikes will be far more forceful, harder than anything you can possibly imagine. If we believe we are going to be struck, we will strike before you, and those strikes will be just as forceful. I believe this to be my mission as president of the United States: not merely to eradicate terrorists and terrorism but to eradicate the *idea* of terrorism.

This is a sad and tragic day. But it may also, sometime soon, be seen as a day of hope, optimism, and renewal because it is the day when we declare to people around the world that we are a free nation, under God, and that we will remain so long after our enemies have disappeared.

Thank you and God bless you all.

Justin Westwood spent that evening the same way most of the country did: watching the president's speech and the omnipresent media coverage that followed it. There was disturbing and intimate film of the bombing – or rather its immediate aftermath – and, partly due to the excessive commentary, it was like watching a gruesome instant replay of the destruction at Harper's. Interspersed with the painful footage were responses and declarations by various public officials. Senators and congressmen from both major parties were backing the president one hundred percent. The support of the American public was nearly as strong: instant polls were taken immediately after the speech and Anderson's words received a ninety-two percent favorable rating. Despite the president's stated intent not to politicize his actions, the political ramifications were huge and immediate. Within

140

an hour after the president's speech, a record sixty-eight percent of Americans said they would be voting for Dandridge in the next election no matter who he ran against. Everyone in the government – from both parties – assured the nation that the Triumph of Freedom Act would pass handily. Everyone promised that this was a fight we would not lose.

The most forceful and impressive performance came from Ted Ackland, the assistant attorney general of the United States, who, according to political rumormongers, was very much in the running to be Phil Dandridge's vice presidential running mate. Ackland was a handsome man, in his mid-forties, Clark Kent-looking with his horn-rimmed glasses and conservative suit and his lean, clearly chiseled body. Ackland was the most eloquent member of the administration, soft-spoken yet commanding, and when he elaborated on the T.O.F. Act – pronounced 'tough' – as it was already being labeled, he was both convincing and reassuring. It was hard to dislike Ackland. He did not have the hard edges – or the controversial background – of Attorney General Stuller. Jeff Stuller made people ill at ease, sometimes even frightened them, including members of his own party. He was a man of stern religious upbringing and never wavered in his moral convictions, of which he had many. Pornographers were akin to murderers in Stuller's book. Foul language was a violation of freedom of speech equal to words of treason. He was famous for never having danced, even with his wife, for dancing was not embraced by his Pentecostal religion, as it was considered frivolous and overtly sensual. The joke, often repeated in the print media, was that Stuller did not believe in sex – because it led to dancing. He was a stern man, with steely eyes and a steelier demeanor. His politics – as a two-term governor of Wisconsin and a one-term senator from the same state – were just as unwavering. He had, at various times in his political career, been branded as

141

racist, anti-Semitic, and anti-civil rights. Stuller rarely responded to such criticism. He didn't seem to even care about anything his detractors said. When Jeffrey Stuller spoke, it was clear that he did not believe he had ever been wrong or ever would be wrong.

Ackland was the perfect counterpoint to his boss. He was not linked to the religious right. He had never held an elected office and so had no traceable history of controversial votes or preferences. The speeches he'd made that had been on the record, as well as his performance as a Second Circuit judge, were considered moderate and reasonable. That combination of attributes – even his detractors sometimes referred to him as Ted 'Tough but Fair' Ackland – made him a rising political star. There was talk that, if he wasn't put on the national ticket, he might run for senator in his home state. But the smart money was on the assistant attorney general to get the vice presidential nomination. Dandridge, hard-nosed and humorless, was much in need of someone like the more congenial Ackland if he was to continue the Anderson legacy for another four years.

As the evening progressed, and as responses to the latest attack and to President Anderson's speech came from around the country, Ted Ackland's star began to burn even brighter. He spoke in a voice that was unafraid but not hell-bent on revenge. A voice fervently defending the new Triumph of Freedom bill, but also cognizant of its flaws. A voice that was strong but compassionate. In a world gone seemingly mad, his was a reassuring voice of sanity.

And more than anything, that was what the country was demanding right now: sanity.

In his living room, Justin Westwood was finding anything but sanity.

The TV was on – it was impossible to turn off; the violent replays and the constant commentary were a necessary link to the real world – but for Justin, the bulk of his attention was focused elsewhere. When he'd had his fill of sound bites and tough political talk, he'd begun to read through Chuck Billings's notes. He wasn't sure why Chuck had gotten them to him. Maybe just for safekeeping, as his cryptic cover letter had stated, but Justin suspected it was more than that. A lot more. There was something he wanted Justin to know. And judging from Justin's visit from Special Agent Schrader this afternoon, something the FBI *didn't* want him to know. So Justin figured he'd better plow through the scrawls. At first it was tough going. The beginning was rife with technical jargon, hypothesizing about various ways the bomb was built and detonated. Justin recognized several phrases from the conversation he'd had with Billings and was able to piece together enough to understand the makeup of the explosive device. There were several pages under the heading 'Signature'. Justin couldn't follow it all but he got the gist. Billings was analyzing the bomb's quirks, the 'tells,' as he called them in the notes. Chuck discussed the primary fragmentation and explained the importance of the use of jacks in that capacity. There were other tells, too, but none as important as the jacks. He stressed the uniqueness of that as a killing tool, noted that if they were used again in another attack, it meant, with great probability, that there would be a specific person in charge. Someone separate from the bomb carrier.

In his scribblings under the 'Signature' section, it was clear that Chuck's biggest desire was to know the exact tone transmitted by the cell phone that set the bomb off. But that was unknowable information. It was also crystal clear that Billings believed that the poor bastard who'd carried the device into Harper's Restaurant was not the person who'd set the thing off. Chuck seemed convinced that the incoming call was what had set off the detonation. Which was exactly the opposite of what the president of the United States and all his appointed spokespeople were saying after the first attack. The official word was suicide bombing. One man, one fanatic, random havoc.

After that came a section on Semtex, which was what Chuck believed the explosive to have been. He had various pages on the different terrorist and criminal organizations known to favor the material – sometimes with names of specific members and their level of expertise. He detailed various signatures in this section, too, but none of them matched up to the bits of information he had about the bomb that went off in Harper's. Chuck knew manufacturers of Semtex as well as known couriers. He even had various maps – some standard and slipped into the book, some hand-drawn – to show the various ways Semtex was brought into the country. He had put a red asterisk at the top of a subheading labeled 'Colombia,' and by the asterisk had scribbled the letters 'JW-Piper', with several exclamation marks after it. This was connected to a map with a thick red line drawn along it, tracing a route from Colombia to Florida, then to Long Island. It took Justin a few moments to decide there was a pretty good chance that 'JW' stood for 'Justin Westwood,' and that Billings was making a connection between the explosive used to destroy Harper's and the plane that had crashed in the middle of East End Harbor. Justin knew enough about the way that Billings's mind worked – or at least the way it was working in this investigation – to begin to make his own connections.

If the guy with the briefcase – the president had revealed his name, Bath-something Shabaan, something like that – wasn't the one who set off the bomb, if he was only the messenger boy, then it was likely he hadn't been expecting to be blown to smithereens. That was backed up by the witnesses who said he was on his way toward the front of the restaurant when the cell phone rang and the bomb went off. Shabaan had expected to survive. But the men who detonated the bomb wanted him dead. One less connection to the real source.

If the Piper that crashed in East End Harbor had carried the explosives up from South America, it was also tied to the bombing. Ray Lockhardt had speculated that the plane was carrying drugs. It could just as easily have been carrying Semtex. If that were true, it also made sense that the pilot was murdered. Yet another connection eliminated.

But a connection to what?

A connection to whom?

Justin put the notes down. He was breathing heavily and realized there was a reasonable chance his imagination was running away with him. He was getting spooked. Or just as paranoid as Wanda had accused Chuck Billings of being.

There were too many ifs. Too many broken links in the chain. It was safe to assume that the two bombings were connected, even the government spokespeople were acknowledging that. They had revealed the possible existence of a terrorist cell connected to both events, but they weren't revealing any direct link between the attack at Harper's and the one in the city. Without a direct link, it would be almost impossible to find the person or persons responsible for both attacks. Not the two suicide bombers, the person *controlling* the bombers. It was that link that Chuck thought the Feds were doing their best to hide. It was that link that Justin decided he needed to find.

He wished he could talk to Chuck right now. He didn't know enough about signatures. Hell, he didn't know enough about anything. All he had, all he could really tell from the notes, was that he needed to find out if jacks were used as the primary fragmentation for the second explosive. If there were, he'd have the link he needed.

He wasn't sure what the hell good it would do him, but at least he'd have something concrete. But it was highly unlikely he could get far enough inside the investigation to pursue that any further. And the only person he knew who had been inside the investigation – and questioned it – had been killed.

Justin shook his head. What the hell was going on inside his brain? Signatures? Jacks? Connections? International terrorism?

No, he decided. This was nuts. He was way overthinking this one. The world had turned into a crazy place where things rarely made sense. Where patterns weren't always logical and where motives no longer came from jealousy or rage but from God or the latest messiah with a message of hate or a desire to find a spaceship to take his followers into outer space. Nope. There was no point in following Chuck Billings's thought processes. He was looking for something he'd never find. Something that wasn't there.

One good way to put a stop to *that* problem, he decided.

Justin went to the kitchen, opened the fridge, and pulled out a cold beer. A bottle of Pete's Wicked Ale. He leaned against the door of the refrigerator and downed the brew in three large gulps. It made him feel more settled, so he reached for a second bottle, took one long swig from that, and carried it back into the living room. He stared at Billings's notebook for a moment, listened to the drone from the television commentators. He did his best to resist. It was pointless to keep reading. He'd already decided that. He thought about turning the TV off, putting some good hard rock and roll on his CD player – maybe some Stones, *Sticky Fingers*, or some Kinks – but his mind wouldn't stop racing, it just didn't feel right, and if he'd learned anything at all it was that things had to feel right, so he went back to Billings's book, flipped it open again, skipped ahead to a page that was covered with circles and numbers. He realized it was a hand-drawn view of the table arrangements at Harper's.

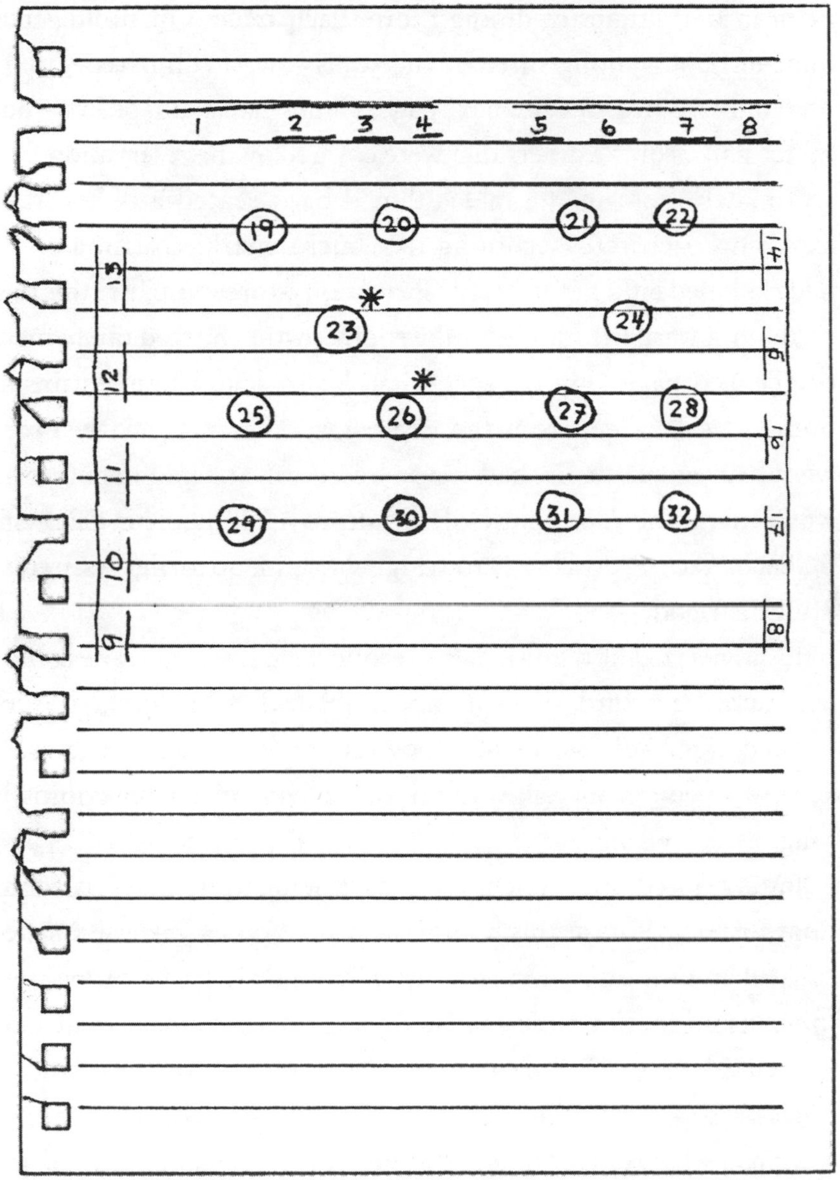
1 2 3 4 5 6 7 8
19 20 21 22
13
14
23
24
12
15
25 26 27 28
16
11
29 30 31 32
10
17
9
18

Chuck had drawn circles to represent each table and its placement in the restaurant dining room. Each table – including the built-in booths along three of the walls – was numbered, from one to thirty-two. On the next page, Chuck had managed to line up the names of the diners that were covered by the reservation list and match them to the tables they'd been seated at when the explosion occurred. According to Chuck's markings, the bomb had exploded either at table number twenty-three or table twenty-six, both toward the middle of the room. Justin checked the names on the next page. Jimmy Leggett had been eating at table thirty-one, just a few feet from the explosion. At table twenty-three were two names Justin had never heard of. At table twenty-six was a name he *had* heard of: Bradford Collins. The CEO of EGenco. Vice President Dandridge's friend. Attorney General Stuller's friend.

Justin realized he'd finished the second beer. He decided he could definitely use a third, so went back to the fridge. In fact, he pretty much decided at least one of the two six-packs on the refrigerator shelf was a goner, but halfway back to his living room, his doorbell rang.

Justin glanced at his watch. Ten o'clock at night. He wasn't used to unexpected visitors at this hour. He wasn't used to *any* visitors, he realized. In the nearly seven years he'd lived in East End Harbor, not more than a dozen people – including the exterminator and the kid who cut his grass – had been inside his house.

He headed for the door. Through the shaded glass panel he saw a woman's figure. He pulled the door open, cocked his head in surprise.

'I'm sorry,' Reggie Bokkenheuser said. He saw that she'd been crying. He must have been staring because she wiped at her cheek with her fingers, brushing away the moisture. 'I just couldn't stand being alone anymore and I don't really know anybody else.' She waved in the direction of his television, which was still tuned to CNN. 'I can't stand watching it, but I can't stop. I'm sorry, I just needed some company. If you want me to—'

'No, no,' he said. 'Come on in.'

She hesitated, standing on the scraggly straw welcome mat on his screened-in porch. He gently took her by the elbow and guided her inside.

'It just got to me,' she said. 'The images, all the blood, the god-damn talk about war and—'

He handed her his untouched bottle of beer. She looked surprised, but when he nodded, she raised it to her lips and took a long swallow.

'I didn't want to drink alone,' she said. 'I didn't know if I should drink at all. I didn't know what the hell to do. Every time I thought of something that'd take my mind off all this, I felt like such a coward. Do you know what I mean?'

'No idea,' he told her. 'I was just about to get blind drunk.'

She did her best to smile, almost succeeded, wiped at her cheek again and sniffled back a potential tear.

'You moved in already?' he asked.

'This morning. I didn't have much. And I rented it furnished. All I really had to do was unpack.' They were still standing near the front door. 'Look,' she said, 'I really am sorry. I didn't mean to come barging in here.'

'It's okay. It got to me, too. I'm sure it's getting to everybody.' He did his best to look reassuring, realized that wasn't one of his best things. 'Did you eat dinner?'

'No. I couldn't bring myself to eat.'

'How about now? A cheese omelet goes extremely well with beer. And I hope that appeals to you, because the only things I've got in the house are eggs and cheese and maybe a frozen steak that'll take half a day to defrost.'

She used her shirtsleeve to dab at her eyes and nodded. 'I'm starving all of a sudden. Craving a cheese omelet.'

So he went inside and made a six-egg omelet, mixed in some strong Epoisse cheese, cooked it until it was firm and nicely browned. She watched him cook, didn't say a word. Occasionally he would glance up at her. Once, her eyes were unfocused and she was drifting off into her own thoughts. He noticed that she was wearing low-cut jeans, and scuffed black boots that added a couple of inches to her height. And a shirt that was too small, fashionably so, revealing some skin around her midriff. She was not a small girl, he realized. She was a little bit fleshy but it was sensual and sexy. She did not look very much like a cop at the moment, he thought, but then their eyes met, and she was jarred back into the present, so he stopped looking at her and concentrated on the omelet, which was almost ready.

He got them each another bottle of beer and they went into the living room to eat. She gobbled her eggs down in what seemed like three bites. He liked the way she ate. There was no pretense to it, no attempt at being dainty. She was hungry and she attacked the food. After her last bite, she ran a finger around the rim of the plate, soaking up the olive oil, then put the finger in her mouth. When she was finished she said, 'I guess eating was a good idea.'

'I can make you another one if you want. You practically inhaled that.'

'No, no, that was perfect. But yeah, I kind of like to eat. I'm not exactly the Gwyneth Paltrow/Calista Flockhart type.'

'That's probably a good thing. I don't think they'd make such good cops.'

She managed a real smile this time, like something had just

loosened up inside of her, and she offered to go to the fridge to get this round of beer. When she returned they sipped slowly from their bottles, in no rush to finish. She talked a little bit more about the bombing, kept trying to change the subject, kept returning to the violence and the shock. Her legs and feet were tucked under her as she sat on the couch. Her boots were still on and for some reason he liked the fact that she knew he wouldn't care if the leather rested on the couch. At some point, she pointed over to Chuck Billings's notebook, asked what it was, but he just shook his head and said, 'Work.' She asked if it was anything she should know about and he said no. He waited a few moments, then went over and closed the book. He couldn't help himself. She didn't seem to mind.

It got to be midnight and they were still talking and the talk had not gotten any less gruesome. She was asking him about the violent things he'd seen and experienced. He told her about one case in Providence. Over a period of six months they'd found the bodies of three women whose eyes had been gouged from their sockets. The ME said that the gouging had come when each woman was still alive. When they caught the guy who did it, they found him living with his blind eighty-year-old mother. He was fifty-six years old, a CPA with a good job, well-liked at the office, but he'd never left home. He couldn't break away. All he could do instead was leave work at the end of the day and go blind other women, torture them the way he wanted to torture his dear old mom.

Reggie was interested, kept asking questions, so then he told her about a domestic disturbance call. A woman had swung a meat cleaver at her husband and it lodged in his neck. Justin answered the call, said he'd never seen so much blood. The neck was practically severed, but the guy was alive and talking. Kept talking about how his wife thought he'd been cheating on her but he wasn't. Kept saying how much he loved his wife. Justin called for an ambulance. They took the guy to the hospital while Justin took the wife to the station. The guy died before they reached the hospital. The EMW said that the guy was talking up until the moment he died, still saying how much he loved his wife and how he was sorry he made her so jealous.

Reggie asked him how he dealt with that kind of thing – didn't it turn his stomach, didn't it make him hard and insensitive? Justin said that yes, it turned his stomach, but you deal with it. You ignore the horror and do what you have to do until it's all over. Then the horror returns, inside your own head, and you have to deal with that. And yes, he said, it does make you hard. It makes it difficult to feel anyone else's pain because you spend your whole life having to put that pain out of your head so you can do your job.

Then she asked him about his own pain.

He knew that she knew. She'd said at lunch that she'd Googled him, had seen the stories about his past. They'd been in the Providence papers when it had all happened, and was rehashed in the media after the Aphrodite thing broke. So he told her about Alicia and Lili, about their deaths, about his helplessness and guilt. He hadn't talked about it with many people, no more than a handful, didn't know why he was talking about it now except that the bombings seemed to have turned the whole world upside down and, for the first time, his own loss seemed connected to a greater loss, even seemed connected to the woman sitting on his couch with her scuffed black boots tucked under her.

And she talked about the losses she'd suffered, too. She was hesitant to reveal too much of herself, would start to say something, stop, give a quick, hard shake of her head as if reminding herself of her own vulnerability, and then she'd bite her lip, stopping the flow of words in midsentence. But she did tell him a bit more about her father, how devastated she was by his sudden death. How alone she felt and how afraid she was to ever be so dependent on one person for a sense of family, for a feeling of love and safety. Her mother had died when she was very young, twelve years old. She'd slipped and fallen from a balcony. Killed instantly.

When she told that story, his eyes moved slightly and she caught the motion.

'Yes, I know,' she said.

'Know what?'

' "Slipped." I always accepted that because it's what I was told. I was too young to ever think anything but that. But when I became a cop, I guess it's the way we think, it occurred to me for the first time that maybe it wasn't just an accident.'

'Is there something that made you think that?'

'She drank. I don't know how happy she was. It could have been a suicide. I loved my father but he couldn't have been easy to be married to. He didn't talk much. Didn't show much.'

'It doesn't much matter, does it? Accident or . . . no accident. It doesn't change you or what you are. Or what's happened since.'

'No. It definitely doesn't change me.' She gave a half smile. 'I am what I am.'

At one o'clock in the morning, he bobbed and weaved his way to the kitchen and the refrigerator, came back and said he was out of beer. Reggie said she didn't care. She also made no move to leave. When he sat down on the couch, the first time he'd been next to her all night, his hand grazed against her thigh. He pulled it away quickly but she reached out and grabbed his wrist and pulled him closer to her.

'This is really awkward,' she said. 'But . . .'

'But you don't want to be alone tonight.' When she nodded, he said, 'Neither do I.'

The next few words came out slowly, and she kept shaking her head and stopping herself as she spoke, as if nothing that came out of her mouth was what she really wanted to say. 'I can't . . . I mean, I don't think . . . what I want . . .'

'You can have my room. It's the most comfortable bed.'

'Jay, I feel like an idiot. I mean . . .'

'I know. Feels a little like high school.' She nodded again, looked down as if afraid to speak. 'Get into bed,' he said. 'I'll sit with you until you fall asleep.'

She smiled, thankful.

'I don't have a spare toothbrush,' he said. And then he added, 'I don't have a spare anything.'

'I'll live,' she told him. And then she went upstairs.

He waited a few minutes, then he slowly climbed up to his room. He saw her clothes tossed over an old red felt-covered piano bench in the corner of the room. She hadn't folded them. One leg of her jeans was inside out. One boot was upright, the other toppled on its side. He looked over at the bed and Reggie was in it, under the sheets, the thick blue quilt pulled up to her chin. She was already half asleep. Her eyes were almost closed and she looked peaceful. He could see her chest moving gently up and down under the covers.

Justin gently eased himself down on the bed. She murmured something incoherent, it wasn't even meant to be a word, just an acknowledgment of his presence. He stroked her hair slowly and softly and she sighed quietly and contentedly. He stayed there, just like that, for five more minutes until he knew she was asleep, and then he stayed several minutes more, his hand not moving, just resting on top of her head, slightly tangled in the strands of her hair. He pushed himself up off the bed, almost in slow motion, careful not to disturb her, and the moment he stood he was overcome with exhaustion. It hit him like a wave of heat, making him dizzy.

He didn't go to the tiny second bedroom at the top of the stairs. Instead he went back down to the living room. First he sat on the couch, then slowly stretched out. His body was too long to fit perfectly, so he curled his knees up, felt his side sink deeply into the cushion.

He stayed awake for several minutes, listening to the quiet hum of the television, which he'd never turned off, not looking at the screen, instead watching the light emanating from it flicker and reflect off a window.

Justin thought of the woman upstairs. About the smell of her shampoo that still lingered on his hand. About the way the day's violence had frightened her. Changed her.

He thought about the hundreds of thousands – the millions – of others who were also frightened, who were also changed.

And before he finally fell asleep, he thought about himself. And wondered if he could ever truly be frightened again.

Or changed.

Some part of him hoped it was possible.

But he didn't really believe it.

chapter 15

Justin awoke at 7 A.M. He instantly twisted his stiff neck and heard it crack. His lower back was tight and when he stretched his body he felt an ache up and down his spine. His mouth was dry and fuzzy and his head hurt. Another day in paradise, he thought, and managed to sit up.

The television was still on, still showing images of the latest bombing. He cleared his throat, trying to get rid of the stale taste of beer, and stood up. He took a few steps toward the TV, swiped at the power button and watched the picture fade. He slowly made his way upstairs, still twisting his neck and stretching his back. He pushed open the door to his bedroom. Reggie was sound asleep. He gently shook her, but she was in a deep sleep. He decided he could let her be, then he suddenly remembered the alarm, quickly reached out over her and hit the off switch on the radio before the Mark Knopfler CD he'd put in began to blare. He headed for his closet, walking as softly as he was capable of, pulled out a clean shirt. He then made it to the one chest of drawers, pulled out a pair of socks and underwear.

He was on his way to the shower, but he stopped before leaving the bedroom, stood in the doorway and looked down at the woman in his bed. The blanket was only pulled up to the middle of her back. She slept on her left side and he could see most of her right breast and a tattoo on her right shoulder. A purple, black, and red butterfly. Her skin was remarkably smooth and soft. His gaze moved down her arm, which was perfectly proportioned, toned and muscular but not too thin. Just the right amount of flesh. It was an arm you wanted to touch. To stroke. Looking closer, he saw that she had elegant fingers. Long and perfectly manicured. In sleep they were relaxed. When she'd been awake last night, he realized her hands had been clenched much of the time.

Justin couldn't take his eyes off her, pleased by her loveliness, touched by the soundness of her sleep. Finally, he forced himself to turn away, went into the bathroom, brushed his teeth, felt the stubble on his chin and cheeks, decided against shaving, then stepped into the shower stall and let the heavy stream of hot water do its best to cleanse him.

When he was dry and dressed he almost felt like a new man – something he knew could only be an improvement. He went back downstairs to the front door to pick up the various newspapers he had delivered every morning. Before opening them, he headed into the kitchen and made a large pot of coffee. He had a feeling Reggie Bokkenheuser would match him cup for cup and he didn't like to leave the house without having at least four large mugs of very strong, black French roast.

He couldn't face the real news, not right away, so he went immediately for the *Daily News* sports pages. It was a slow sports period. Justin searched for some good news about the Knicks, saw that Houston was hurt again. Near the beginning of the season, second leg injury. He read *Doonesbury* and *Dilbert*, then glanced at the front section. There was little about the bombing that he hadn't picked up from CNN. The lunatic, Muaffak Abbas, had come into the restaurant in Manhattan and strode up to a table on the left side of the room. Several survivors said it looked as if he'd gone to a specific spot, as if it had been choreographed. There was no mention anywhere that anyone had heard a cell phone ring this time. But that didn't mean one hadn't rung. It was the kind of detail that could easily be overlooked. One survivor said that Abbas yelled out the words 'I am ready,' and the device went off. End of story.

Justin wondered why Abbas had picked the specific spot he'd chosen in the restaurant to unleash the explosive. He remembered Billings telling him about the kill ratio – the range in which a bomb is certain to destroy whatever is in its path. If that were the rationale, then Abbas would have chosen the center of the restaurant, wouldn't he? That's where the damage would be sure to be greatest. It didn't make sense.

Hell, Justin thought. Nothing made sense. Not anymore.

He turned to the *Times* front page, began to read through their coverage. At the jump, on page eighteen, there was a box that listed, in alphabetical order, the victims of the La Cucina explosion. His eyes quickly ran down the list. It was habit. Cops always looked for the dead.

About a third of the way through he stopped scanning and froze, staring at one name. For a moment he thought he was rattled and disoriented because he'd just discovered the death of a friend. But although he recognized the name, he quickly realized that this man who'd been killed in the La Cucina explosion was no friend.

Martin Heffernan.

That was the name on the victim list.

The FAA agent. The guy who'd boarded the downed plane in East End Harbor, stolen the pilot's identification and wiped his fingerprints clean. The man who told Ray Lockhardt the result of the FAA investigation – before any investigating had begun.

Justin ran his fingers through his hair, rubbed his eyes, trying to ease away the headache he could feel starting to swell up inside. What the hell was going on? A coincidence? A cruel twist of fate? This asshole does his best to sabotage a murder investigation and he winds up randomly blown to bits?

Or was it something else?

Justin's father had said that what things boiled down to, always, every time, was money. Follow the money, he'd said, and everything will fall into place.

Okay, Justin thought. *To follow the money, you have to know the players. There ain't no stakes if nobody sits down at the table.* In his mind, he ran down the list of names that seemed to be in play.

Bradford Collins. The CEO of EGenco.

Hutchinson Cooke, the pilot of the small plane.

Chuck Billings, the FBI agent investigating the first bombing.

And now Martin Heffernan.

Justin felt a stream of bile rise up through his throat. What was the connection between those four men? Other than the fact that they were all dead. *Was* there a connection?

Yes. Now he was fairly sure that there was. Cop instinct: what he wasn't sure about was whether or not he wanted to know what that connection was.

Justin walked into the kitchen, poured himself a mug of coffee. He sipped it slowly, letting the too-hot liquid quickly scald his lip, then slide down his throat. He wanted a whiskey instead of black coffee. He wanted another shower, to have jets of hot water wash away the slime that suddenly seemed to be building up all around him. He wanted to get into his bed and stroke the smooth neck and warm, naked back of the woman still lying there, wanted to kiss the tattoo on her shoulder blade, watch her eyes open, see her smile when she saw him. He wanted to touch her, kiss her, make love to her.

He wanted a lot of things.

And not one of them was the thing he was about to do.

Justin forced himself to walk calmly over to the phone, dial a number, and wait until a sleepy Gary Jenkins answered on the fourth ring.

'Gary.'

'Whazzit,' the young cop mumbled.

'Your little brother, is he still hacking away?'

'Jay?' He cleared his throat. 'I mean, Chief?'

'Yeah, yeah, it's me. Listen, I want to hire your brother. What the hell's his name? Ken?'

'Ben.'

'Tell Ben he can name his price, same as last time, but he's got to do this thing for me *now*. Can you reach him?'

Gary cleared his throat again, came awake. 'Yeah, sure. I mean, I guess. He probably hasn't left for school yet. I'll call him right away.'

'Write him a note for his teacher if you have to. If he's already left, go get him and take him out of class. And if need be, let him use a computer at the station. But I want it done now, got it?'

'Got it. What do you want him to do?'

'I want him to see if he can hack into the computer setup that stores the reservations at La Cucina.'

'The place that got blown up? What do you—'

'I don't have time to explain. The FBI found similar information in the Harper's computer. I need to know if someone named Martin Heffernan had a reservation. And if he did, I need to know what table he was sitting at. If the kid can get me a seating chart showing me where all the tables are, I'd particularly like that, too.'

'I'll call you right back.'

Justin hung up the phone, exhaled for what seemed like the first time in minutes. He needed some more coffee.

'What's going on?'

He looked up, surprised. Reggie was standing on the bottom stair, still half asleep, peering into the living room. She was wearing one of his long-sleeved shirts. That's all she was wearing. Her bare legs curled to lean in against the railing.

'I thought women only did that in the movies,' Justin said. 'Put on the guy's shirt and look so sexy.'

She smiled. 'I thought about just putting on your pants, but it didn't seem quite right. Thought you might not be able to handle it.' She shook her head, trying to wake herself up a bit more. 'What's happening? Are you working?'

'It's probably nothing,' he told her, making himself sound unconcerned. 'I might be turning into one of those conspiracy nuts.'

'Is there a conspiracy against getting a cup of coffee?'

'It's made. I'll get it.'

But before he could move, the phone rang and he jumped for it. He waved in the direction of the kitchen, pointing her toward her own cup of coffee.

'Yeah,' Justin said into the phone.

'Okay, I talked to Ben,' Gary said. 'He's sure he can do it if the info exists. Or if the restaurant computer wasn't damaged.'

'The one it was entered into probably was. But if it's like the Harper's setup, it was probably fed into a second computer somewhere else. That one might be okay.'

'He wants an iPod. The little mini one. He says it's non-negotiable.'

'Okay. When I get the info, he'll get an iPod.'

'The mini one.'

'He wants mini, he's got mini.'

'I'll call him back.'

Justin watched as Reggie walked back into the living room. She

161

didn't slink or slither. She walked. Kind of heavily. He liked it. The way it was so unaffected and unselfconscious. She started to ask him if he wanted more coffee, but he quickly put his finger to his lips.

'Thanks, Gary. I'll be at the station in about half an hour.'

'Ben said he'd have the info in about five minutes. If he can get it at all.'

'Jesus.'

'Yeah, he's good.'

'If he doesn't go to prison by the time he's sixteen, he's definitely got a future ahead of him.'

'I'll give him your number, tell him to call you directly. Is that okay?'

'It's perfect,' Justin said. 'I'll see you in a little while.'

He went and finally poured himself that second cup. In the living room, he sat down next to Reggie. As soon as he was settled in, he realized the close proximity made her uncomfortable. She didn't move but he could feel her tense up. He waited a few seconds, stretched as if his back was stiff, stood and stepped over to the chair a few feet away. He could see her instantly relax.

'I'll get going in a minute,' she said. 'I just need a little more coffee.'

'Do you want to talk about last night?'

She shrugged, tried to keep it casual, but her body stiffened as if he'd brought up a taboo subject. 'Is there something to talk about?'

'Not really. Nothing happened. I just don't want it to be awkward.'

'It won't be,' she said. 'I know how to behave professionally. Last night . . . We were both vulnerable, but nothing happened.'

Her tone was surprisingly distant and cool. There was no vulnerability today. Last night she'd been inviting. This morning there was a wall around her. A brick wall. He suddenly felt like a teenager, unsure of himself and off balance. The phone rang, letting him escape from his discomfort.

'Yeah,' Justin said into the receiver.

'It's Ben,' the voice on the other end said. 'Gary's brother.'

'You got anything for me, Ben?'

'Do I really get my iPod?'

'It's practically in the mail.'

'Okay, I got everything you wanted. You have a fax in your house?'

'Yeah,' Justin said. 'Do you?'

'No. But I can fax it straight from my computer. I'll do it right now 'cause I gotta get to school. My mom's already ready to kill me.'

'Tell her I'll write you the world's greatest letter of recommendation when you're ready for college. That'll calm her down.'

'I don't think anything can calm my mom down when she's like this. What's your fax number?'

Justin gave it to him and a few seconds later his fax machine rang. Moments after that, Justin was holding a sheet of paper with a well-designed layout of La Cucina restaurant, not dissimilar from the table layout of Harper's in Chuck Billings's notebook. A second piece of paper had the names of everyone who had a lunch reservation from the day before, the day of the bombing, and the tables where they were to be seated.

Justin checked the list of names first. Martin Heffernan had a reservation. For two people. The restaurant had put him at table seventeen.

Justin went back to the page with the table layout. Table seventeen was to the left of the room after you came in. It was in the exact area to which Muaffak Abbas made a beeline with his bomb.

Justin Westwood forgot that Reggie Bokkenheuser was even in the room. He raced back to the phone, dialed a number in Providence.

'Wanda,' he said, when the FBI agent answered her phone. 'Don't say my name out loud.' There was silence from the other end. 'Do you know who this is?'

'Yes,' she said.

'Can you call me back on a secure line? I'm at home.'

'You do know you're starting to piss me off,' she said.

'Secure line. As fast as you can.' And he hung up.

'Well, I must say.' Reggie was looking at him now, her legs once again tucked under her. 'You've piqued my curiosity.'

'I'll explain later,' he said. 'I think you'd better get out of here. Get to the station.'

She saw the look on his face, decided to skip any further banter. Reggie just got up and went upstairs to put her clothes on. The phone rang before she came down.

'Okay,' Wanda Chinkle said. 'Now what?'

'Do you have any vacation time coming?'

'What the hell are you talking about?'

'Listen,' Justin said. 'These bombings. Harper's and La Cucina. They're not what they appear to be.'

'More of your paranoia?'

'No.' He told her about Martin Heffernan and the location of Abbas's bomb. He told her about Bradford Collins and the location of Bashar Shabaan's explosive.

'You got all this just since you were up here?'

'These weren't random terrorist bombs, Wanda. We're talking about victim-specific attacks here.'

'It's a stretch, Jay. It's a huge stretch.'

'I don't think so. Chuck was onto something. He said that Shabaan's bomb wasn't a suicide device. That it was set off from somewhere else. *By* someone else. And he told somebody. I'm pretty sure that same somebody killed him. Or got him killed. And I'm also pretty sure that the somebody works for the goddamn FBI.'

'Jay—'

'Listen to the rest of it. Heffernan knew that plane crash wasn't an accident. My guess is he's the guy who rigged the manifold. But at some point, he also must have known it was tied into the Harper's bombing. He probably figured it out on his own. And maybe he opened his mouth. He had a big one. So they had to kill him, too.'

'Jay, you're starting to sound—'

'Yeah, I know how I sound. But guess what, Wanda? The FBI are the only ones, other than me, who knew Chuck had started to figure out something was wrong. They probably knew Heffernan's role, too. And they're both dead.'

'What does this have to do with my taking a vacation?'

'They know about you. You were asking about the pilot's fingerprints. And you had an appointment with Chuck. Knowing you, your date was on the record, right there in your appointment book.'

'I'm listening.'

'You're connected to both of them. So it won't take long for somebody to figure it out. Disappear, Wanda. Take a paid vacation starting now. Or just get the hell out of there. But disappear.'

'Jay, I just can't leave—'

'They've killed a lot of people already. Two people are dead, Chuck and this guy Heffernan, just because they knew something about the Harper's bombing and the plane crash.'

'Okay, Jay, let's look at this logically. Who killed them?'

'I don't know. Have you ever run across an FBI agent named Hubbell Schrader?'

'He's the head of the New York bureau . . . For God's sake, Jay! You're not saying he's responsible for—'

'No. I'm not. I said I don't know. But I just met Schrader and I didn't like him.'

'You don't like anyone.'

165

'Well, I particularly didn't like him.'

'All right. Well, what about the other two guys? Collins and Cooke. Who killed them? Or better yet, why were they killed?'

'I don't know that either. I just know that the four of them are dead. Don't be the fifth.'

'I—'

'You're what? You want me to tell you what you are? You're the only other person they can connect to those two things.'

'What about you?'

'I don't think they can tie me to it. Not for sure. I was just doing my job at the beginning, trying to get the pilot's fingerprints. They don't know what I have or don't have. *You* gave me Cooke's name and they don't know that. Or do they?'

'No,' she said. 'At least they don't know it from me.'

'Well, Schrader was asking. I protected the both of us, at least the best I could. I don't think they've got anything other than circumstance to connect me to Billings. There was no reason for him to mention me. I wasn't talking to him about anything official. I told that to Schrader, too, and he seemed to buy it.'

'Let me think about it, Jay.'

'Wanda . . .'

'I said I'll think about it. I'm not ignoring what you're saying. I just need to decide what to do about it.'

'Where are you calling from?'

'My neighbor's. The apartment next door. She's making me a nice hot cup of tea, which I'm going to drink and figure out whether you're crazy or not.'

'Well, when you figure it out, lemme know.'

He hung up the phone just as Reggie came back downstairs. She was back in her jeans and boots.

'I'll go get changed,' she said. 'I can be at the station in about twenty minutes.' He didn't respond to her, his mouth had opened a bit and his eyes were closed. 'Is that okay?'

'Shit,' he said. And now his head was thrown back. 'Shit shit shit shit!' He opened his eyes and, as she backed her way toward the front door, he snapped his fingers at her. 'Hold on. Don't go anywhere.' Justin grabbed for the phone again and dialed. 'Gary,' he barked into the mouthpiece. 'Call Thomas and Dennis. Tell them to find out where the hell Ray Lockhardt lives and tell them to get over there as fast as they can.'

'The guy from the airport?'

'Yeah. The manager. Get 'em to his house ASAP. If he's there, tell them to make sure he stays there. And make sure they stay with him.' Justin slammed the phone down. He turned back to Reggie. 'Come on,' he said.

'Like this?' She pointed down to her noncoplike clothes.

'Yeah,' he said. 'Just like that.'

Justin stopped only to grab the gun that he kept locked in his desk drawer. He didn't brush against Reggie on the way out or grab her by the hand. He looked at her the way he'd look at any other cop and just said, 'There's another one, goddammit! There's already a goddamn fifth person.'

He knew it. As soon as he realized that Ray Lockhardt was in the picture, that Ray had also known that the plane that Hutchinson Cooke crashed had not gone down by accident, he knew he was going to be too late. And he was.

There was very little traffic this early at the East End airport. Ray's office was dark and locked. Justin told Reggie to wait there and then he moved slowly, a defeated gait to his walk, to the nearer of the two private charter services. The guy working the counter was named Don and Justin asked if he'd seen Ray Lockhardt yet this morning.

'No,' Don said. 'He's usually in by now, checkin' up on things, but I ain't seen him.'

Justin went back to Lockhardt's office.

'You know how to pick a lock?' Reggie asked.

'Sure,' Justin said, and took his gun out of its holster, used the butt to smash the beveled glass panel above the doorknob, then reached inside and opened the door. He didn't wait for Reggie, he stepped quickly inside the office, flicked the light on.

Ray Lockhardt was sitting in his chair, behind his desk. Everything looked fairly normal. Except for the blood splattered on the back wall of the office. And the bullet that had shredded most of the right side of Ray's face.

Justin rubbed his eyes. The headache was coming on big-time.

Dr Morgan Davidson walked into the East End Harbor police station. He nodded at the usual bunch of cops, all of whom he knew. And he smiled at the sexy young woman sitting at one of the policemen's desks. Dr Davidson had an eye for the ladies. And they were usually pretty good about eyeing him back.

'If there's anything you need,' he said to the woman with a wink, 'let me know. If they're not doing what they should for you. I know these guys pretty well.' She nodded. 'Morgan Davidson,' he said. '*Doctor* Davidson.'

'Reggie Bokkenheuser,' the woman said. '*Sergeant* Bokkenheuser. If you're here to see Chief Westwood, he's in the office back there.' As the flustered physician bobbed his head up and down nervously, then headed for the office, she added, 'And thanks for the tip, Doc. I'll let you know if I need you.' Then she winked.

168

Inside the small office, Davidson closed the door behind him. 'New officer?" he asked.

'You mind if we skip the small talk just now, Morgan? I've got a lot on my mind.'

The doctor shrugged, put his report on the desk in front of Justin. 'Lockhardt's been dead about twelve hours. Which means he was probably killed around seven or eight last night. No surprise, it was the bullet that did all the damage. Probably a .38, shot from very close range. That's about all I can give you right now.' When Justin didn't answer, Davidson said, 'You all right?'

'Oh yeah,' Justin said. 'I'm just great.'

When the doctor left, Justin sat on the edge of the desk for a good minute.

Bradford Collins, Hutchinson Cooke, Chuck Billings, Martin Heffernan, and now Ray Lockhardt. Not to mention Jimmy Leggett and nearly seventy other innocent victims.

He picked up the phone, called Wanda Chinkle, once again insisted she call him back on a secure line. When she returned the call, he told her that Lockhardt was dead.

'You still want to think about what you're going to do?' he asked. When she didn't answer, he took a deep breath, exhaled slowly. 'Wanda,' he said. 'What do you think it is that makes a good cop? I don't mean just cop, I mean investigator, FBI, whatever.'

'Lots of things,' she said.

'Like what?'

'Doggedness. Determination. The ability not to panic under pressure.'

'Yeah. All that's true.'

'But that's not what you're looking for.'

'No. You know what makes a good investigator?'

'What?'

'The ability to see things.'

'What kind of things, Jay?'

'Patterns. Why people do things. *How* they do things. But mostly a good cop sees something that happens over here, then connects it to something that happens over there. You agree?'

'Sure,' she said. 'I'll go along with that.'

'Well, there's a connection, I mean a real connection, between what happened at Harper's and what happened at La Cucina. Not just a connection, a lead. A way to find out who's behind all this. Only your guys are ignoring it. Because they don't *want* to find out who's behind it.'

'I can't believe that, Jay.'

'How about if I make you believe me?'

'And how are you going to do that?'

'I'll catch the guy who did it.'

'Excuse me?'

'I'll catch the guy who blew up the two restaurants. The guy the lying scumbags you work with don't want caught.'

'You're a good cop, Jay. And you can make all the connections you want. But you're a crazy son of a bitch if you even think about getting in the middle of this.'

'I *am* a crazy son of a bitch, Wanda. That's why you've gotta find something out for me. Just one thing. If you can do it without getting yourself killed.'

'What do you want to know?'

'Jacks,' he told her.'

'What?'

'Jacks. The little kid's game. The little pointy things.'

'Whatever you might think, I'm still a girl. I know what jacks are. What about them?'

'I want to know if your boys found any in La Cucina. After the bombing. But be careful. I'm not screwing around here. Don't go anywhere without other people. Other people you know and trust. Don't get caught alone. And especially watch out for anyone official who's involved in this investigation.'

She paused again. Then: 'While I'm being careful . . . and while, as usual, I'm spending my life trying to give you something you need to know . . . what exactly are *you* going to do?'

'I'm the new chief of police,' Justin Westwood said. 'I'm gonna do my fucking job.'

part two

chapter 16

Special Agent Hubbell Schrader had never thought of himself as a violent man.

He had never struck his wife, or any other woman, no matter the provocation, nor had he so much as spanked any of his three children when they were still of spanking age.

He rarely raised his voice, he did not grind his teeth, he had never experienced even the remotest form of road rage, he did not have a residue of anger that he carried around with him, as so many law enforcement officers he knew carried with them, and as best as he could remember, going all the way back to childhood, he had never even been in a fistfight.

Which is why he was so surprised when he woke up several mornings ago to realize that he had, in his life, killed six people.

He had no regrets about any of the first five deaths. They had all come in the line of duty and all of them had been fully investigated and validated. Three of the killings were, in fact, viewed so positively he could trace his latest promotion – Special Agent in Charge of the New York office of the Federal Bureau of Investigation – directly back to them. They had occurred at the end of a kidnapping case; the six-year-old daughter of the U.S. senator from Oregon had been taken, part of a protest against the senator's stand in favor of gay

175

marriage. At least that's what the kidnappers had said. Schrader knew that was bullshit. Kidnappings were never political. Kidnappings were only and always about one of two things. They were either personal – someone couldn't have a child but wanted one; someone hated the parent and wanted to deprive him or her of a most beloved possession – or they were about money. Nothing in between. The senator's daughter was about money. But the people who snatched the kid weren't bright enough to pull it off. They left a trail so traceable they might as well have scattered breadcrumbs leading to their doorway. Schrader had broken the case easily but the endgame got messy. Three of the kidnappers – two men, one woman – used the little girl as a hostage. There was a shootout. One agent serving under Schrader took a bullet in the leg, had his kneecap shattered, and was now on permanent disability. Schrader took out all three perps. The little girl was saved, Schrader was proclaimed a hero – got his fifteen minutes of fame on the front page of the *New York Post* and even had some movie producer give him thirty-five thousand dollars as option for his 'life rights,' although nothing ever came of it other than his wife got a long weekend in Bermuda and his kids' college funds got padded. Within a few weeks of the rescue, he was put in charge of the New York office.

Schrader had been surprised at the fuss. He did not think what he'd done had been anything special. It was part of the job. It was what he was paid to do. Find a problem. Solve the problem. That's how he always described himself: a problem solver. Whatever it takes. He always figured that if he had a card with a motto on it, that's what would be printed in neat little letters underneath his name.

Whatever it takes.

The other two killings had not been nearly so productive or celebrated. The first one had come at a raid of a militia camp in

Montana. Some idiot came running straight at him, gun pointed, as if it were some kind of cowboys and Indians movie. Schrader calmly fired twice, both bullets found their target, and the idiot went down. The next killing came while preventing a terrorist attack on Dulles Airport. Or a supposed terrorist attack. One man was detained by airport employees when he refused to have his carry-on bag searched. The man shot and wounded a security guard, then escaped and, luggage in hand, ran to the boarding area. The FBI was summoned and the guy was quickly surrounded. He was given an order to drop the bag and step away. Instead, he frantically went to open the overnight luggage and the agents, including Schrader, opened fire. The lunatic died instantly and Schrader received credit for the kill. When the bag was later searched, nothing was found. No bombs, no weapons, nothing that could remotely be considered dangerous. No drugs, even. Schrader never found out the cause of the man's panic and he never had a burning desire to discover it. He'd done what he had to do. That was the way Hubbell Schrader saw not just his job but life: You do what you have to do.

Whatever it takes.

After Schrader killed the guy at the militia camp, the Bureau sent him to a shrink. He had four sessions and they talked about his sleep habits and his relationship with his wife and kids and any anxieties he might have. He told the shrink he was sleeping fine, his relationships were good, and he didn't have any anxieties. After the fourth session, she said she believed him and he was returned to active duty. He went through the same thing after the event at the airport, only this time it took only two sessions. They didn't bother to head-shrink him after the shooting of the kidnappers. They just promoted him. He had no guilt, no remorse whatsoever, felt no questioning about his motives or his actions over any of those five deaths.

The sixth victim was different.

Schrader didn't exactly feel bad . . . but he felt *something*.

It wasn't the same as the others. Yes, it was in the line of duty. But still, things weren't as clear-cut. It wasn't a life-or-death situation. There was no immediate danger to another person. This one was a lot more complicated. He'd killed someone because he'd been *told* to kill someone. Because the target was a potential threat.

The question was: to whom? Schrader had been told that he was a threat to the security of the United States. But he wasn't totally convinced of that. He had doubts.

Maybe that was it. Maybe that's why he was feeling edgy. Hubbell Schrader had never had doubts before. But this was definitely different. He hadn't killed a rabid militiaman or a kidnapper or someone he thought was going to blow up an airport waiting room.

He'd killed a cop. A bomb squad cop.

Chuck Billings. Not a bad guy. Smart.

Too smart.

Still . . .

And then there was the airport manager. Lockhardt.

He couldn't claim credit for that one. He hadn't actually pulled the trigger. But he'd sanctioned it. And Lockhardt wasn't part of the game. Lockhardt was a civilian. He'd just gotten caught up in the shit. He'd been a threat to talk. And this was a new world. A brand-new world where threats had to be taken as seriously as deeds.

Preemptive action. That's what the new world was about.

Even so . . .

Doubts.

Son of a bitch.

There was one other thing Hubbell had never experienced. Both shrinks, when he'd been ordered to visit them, had noted this, too, and passed the information on to his superior: Schrader didn't seem to have any fear.

He had to admit, that was pretty much true. He was not afraid of getting hurt or, for that matter, of dying. If either thing occurred, so be it. It was part of the job description. When you do what you have to do you also have to suffer the consequences.

Because Schrader had never specifically experienced fear, he wasn't really familiar with its symptoms or its warning signals. That's why he felt so uncomfortable now. The man whose office he was standing in made him feel strange in a way he'd never felt around anyone or anything else. The man made the hair on the back of Schrader's neck stand on end, and he caused a slight shiver to creep its way down along Schrader's spine.

Schrader wasn't sure if this was fear – whether he was, in fact, afraid of this man.

But he thought it was a possibility.

And that in itself was quite something. More than enough for Schrader to pay very close attention to everything the man was saying.

'What about the woman in Rhode Island?'

'She's being watched,' Schrader said.

'What does that mean?'

'It means we're making sure she doesn't do anything she shouldn't be doing.'

'Phones tapped?'

'Yes.'

'Surveillance?'

'Yes,' Schrader said. He rolled his eyes just slightly.

'You like your job? Running the New York bureau?' the man across the desk asked.

'Yes, sir.'

'Then let's can the attitude. 'Cause you're a phone call away from losing it. Got it?'

'Yes, sir,' Schrader said.

'How about our . . .' The man waved his arms, searching for a description.

'Our guest from overseas?' Schrader made sure his facial expression didn't change one bit.

'Yes.'

'He's well taken care of.'

'What do people call you? Is Hubbell short to anything?' The man smiled now, doing his best to be warm and friendly. 'Do people call you Hub?'

'My wife calls me Hubie. Like the basketball coach. Most people just call me by my name, sir.'

'Hubie . . . I like that. It's an uncommon name. It's fitting. You're an uncommon person.'

'Thank you, sir.'

'Hubie . . . I know that certain elements of this job are distasteful to you. As they are to me. But these are distasteful times. People don't always know what's best for them. In the long run. People don't look at the big picture, they don't always understand it.'

Schrader just nodded. Stone-faced.

'I realize it's difficult for you . . . keeping an eye on our guest, as you so accurately dubbed him. But he's serving a valuable function. More valuable than even you can realize. In the long run . . . in the big picture . . . he may be saving this nation.'

'Yes, sir.'

'And when he stops serving his purpose . . . and that will happen fairly soon, Hubie . . . then we'll be able to dispose of him the way we all would probably like to dispose of him.'

'I think I understand, sir.'

'You think?'

'Yes, sir. But to be perfectly honest, it doesn't really matter whether I understand or not, does it? As long as I do my job.'

'So you're fine with everything that's going on?'

'I am, sir.'

'Good.' The man leaned back in his chair, gave a relaxed smile, as if everything was now okay, as if all the cares of the world had just been lifted. 'Now, what about the cop?'

Hubbell Schrader took a long breath before answering.

'Justin Westwood, you mean?'

'Is that his name?'

'Yes, sir. The cop from Long Island.'

'So what about him?'

'He's kind of a wild card, sir.'

'You care to explain that?'

'The Bureau has crossed paths with him before. He's good at his job.'

'Meaning you're not sure you can control him.'

'I can control him, sir.'

The man across the desk leaned forward now. The cares of the world seemed to have descended a bit.

'Agent Schrader,' he said. 'I don't give a damn if you *can* control him. I just want to know that he is controlled.'

'He is, sir.'

'You understand the resources that are at your disposal.'

'I do, sir.'

'Our people are in place?'

'They're in place.'

'If there are any doubts, if we need to know anything from him, anything at all, you understand what's available to you.'

'Yes, sir, I do. I've been in contact with the appropriate people. Just in case.'

'Good. And I want to make sure you understand one more thing. Because it's very important, Hubie.'

'What's that, sir?'

'We're talking about the future of this country. The future of the United States of America, Hubie. Think about that for a moment. Are you thinking?'

'Yes, sir. The future.'

'Good. So if, even for a moment, one single solitary moment, you think you might be losing control? Or if our other alternative is not effective?'

'Yes, sir?'

'Then you're to take more extreme measures. The *most* extreme measure.'

The man leaned back again, and the smile returned to his face.

'Is there anything else we need to discuss, Hubie?'

'No, sir.'

'Good.'

Hubbell Schrader understood that the conversation was over, so he nodded, left the office, and went back to do whatever it was going to take to keep things under control.

chapter 17

Justin was a big fan of lists.

Police work was about details and thoroughness and all sorts of other things. But mostly, he thought, it was about lists. Things to do. Things already done. Things that couldn't get done. Things to tell other people to do. Things to follow up on. Things to learn. Things to forget.

He had spent four years at Princeton studying business and almost two years in Harvard Medical School. If things had turned out differently – if he'd become a banker or a doctor as he'd originally planned, as had been expected of him his entire life – he wondered if he'd be doing the same things he was doing now. Entering columns of numbers or potential stock buys into his computer. Or putting together strings of ailments and symptoms. He thought that would probably have been the case. No matter how complicated or high-powered the job, it was all about information, knowledge; it was all about who made the right connections between otherwise unconnected things. Which meant it all came down to lists. So by the early afternoon he was sitting in what had recently been Jimmy Leggett's office – so much for sentiment; space requirements took precedence – working away.

There were five people who might have a connection to each other, each of whom was now dead. Justin made one column of names. One of dates. And one of facts: anything he could think of that might be relevant to the investigation. The fourth column was for questions, for things he didn't know but needed to find out.

The names in the left-hand column were Bradford Collins, Hutchinson Cooke, Chuck Billings, Martin Heffernan, and Ray Lockhardt. He began – because it was the only way to begin – with the premise that each of the men had been specifically and personally targeted. Lockhardt and Cooke had definitely been murdered; Justin was satisfied with the evidence he had in hand. Was it *possible* that Collins was an accidental death – just another innocent person caught in the Harper's bombing? Yes. Absolutely. The same with Heffernan; it *could* be coincidence that he was eating at La Cucina when that bomb went off. Even Billings. There was no concrete proof that he'd been murdered. It was conceivable that the bomb squad cop had changed his mind about flying with Justin, that he had, as the official report declared, driven home and fallen asleep at the wheel. But Justin hadn't become a banker or a doctor, he was a cop. A dogged and oddly fanatical cop. So he didn't much believe in accidents or coincidences. He didn't have that luxury. He had to go with the premise that they were all murder victims. And if there was a link between them, between any or all of them, he was sure as hell going to find it. By learning whatever he could and seeing where all that information led to and where the different elements crisscrossed. It would all be done logically and dispassionately.

With lists.

He began with the first man killed – Bradford Collins. To the right of his name, Justin put the date of his death, the date of the Harper's bombing. Next to that, Justin began to list all the scraps of information he had about Collins. He was the CEO of the Texas energy company EGenco. Justin realized he had only a vague idea of what EGenco did – it was in the oil and energy business – and that what he mostly knew was that the company was immersed in a burgeoning scandal rivaling that of Enron. So he skipped over to the right and wrote in, 'Understand EGenco'. Beneath that he added, 'Details of corporate scandal'. And underneath that, he added, 'Follow the money'. He underlined that last phrase for emphasis. Going back to the third column, Justin quickly scribbled everything else he knew: that Collins was a friend of the vice president of the United States, Phil Dandridge, and of the attorney general, Jeffrey Stuller; that Collins was sitting at or very near to the detonation point of the Harper's explosion; that it was possible that the briefcase that contained the explosives had been given to Collins or someone else having lunch at his table. That reminded him of something else he needed to check, and he added this question: 'Who was Collins having lunch with at Harper's?' He stared at his own handwriting for a moment, not the worst he'd ever seen but not the most legible either, and finally he added two more questions: 'Who the hell is Bradford Collins?' and 'Why would anyone want him dead?'

He decided to stick with chronological order, so next on his list was Hutchinson Cooke. Justin put down the date the small plane crashed, November 7 – the day of Jimmy Leggett's funeral – and added the following information: the make of the plane, a Piper Saratoga, and its tail number: NOV 6909 Juliet. He scribbled in a few comments about his conversation with the ditzy Cherry Flynn – the name she'd given him, Martha Peck, the head of the FAA, and the fact that Cooke's files had been removed prior to the crash, indicating that someone knew the crash was going to happen. He added the info that Wanda Chinkle had given him, about Cooke's Air Force background, that he flew government officials, that for the previous eighteen months he seemed to have disappeared from the Air Force and had been collecting a salary from a company called Midas Ltd. Justin's pen hovered over his yellow legal pad as he hesitated about making a first but very tenuous link: victim number one was a friend of Vice President Dandridge; victim number two had piloted government officials. To get a private pilot, one had to be fairly high up in the government – but as high up as the vice president? Justin added a new page to his list, with the heading 'Connections'. And he added that one – followed by quite a few question marks. Even if the link was a legitimate one, he didn't know what it could mean. But he left it on the page.

Chuck Billings was next and Justin had to put his emotions aside. He needed to be objective here, and the fact that Chuck had been his friend was irrelevant to the investigation. So he narrowed his known information about Chuck to this: the head of the Providence bomb squad had a meeting with someone from the FBI the day he was killed. He had anticipated danger because he'd sent Justin all his notes on the Harper's bombing for safekeeping. Chuck suspected that the first bombing wasn't a suicide bombing – and the key information was the sound of the cell phone ringing. Chuck believed the FBI was covering up the truth. He had a meeting scheduled with Wanda Chinkle for the day after he died. Justin closed his eyes, reached into his brain to see if he could come up with anything else of importance, but he didn't think there were any more key facts. So, in the far right column, for the things he needed to know, he wrote:

'Who did Chuck meet with the day he died?'
and
'Read his notebook again.'
and

'If not suicide bombing, who made the cell phone call to detonate the bomb?'

and

'Sound of cell phone at La Cucina?'

and

'Jacks – were they found at the La Cucina bombing? How can signature be used to identify suspect?'

There were two names left. First was Martin Heffernan. Known info: 'Works for FAA. Probably responsible for murdering Hutch Cooke.' Under 'Need to Know,' Justin wrote, 'Who was his direct boss? Who gave him the order to kill Cooke? Why was he killed – to stop him from talking?'

The final name was Ray Lockhardt. Justin kept his notes brief for Ray. What he knew was: 'Shot at point-blank range. Threatened by Heffernan in name of FAA. Knew that Cooke was murdered by rigging plane.' In the far right column, he wrote, 'Who killed him?' then 'Why was he killed?' After that, he hesitated, held his pen in the air, frozen, and finally wrote, 'Because I fucked up.'

Justin put the pen down on the desk, went to the computer, and began tapping at the keyboard to enter his list. He didn't do this just because he liked things neat and clean – although he did; his life might be chaotic and raw but he preferred his investigations to have all their edges rounded off and smooth – but rather because he found that when he transferred his notes, when he typed, he usually found something new to add to the equation. Just one more step in the thinking process. He'd been doing it long enough, and successfully enough, that he knew the process wasn't always rational. Subliminal thoughts crept in, and, while he didn't always know what they meant or why he was asking the questions he asked, he trusted those instincts. And he trusted his questions. It was a lot like doing a crossword puzzle, Justin always thought. You could stare and stare at a clue and draw a total blank on the answer. Then you could put the puzzle aside, take a nap, do anything to keep from thinking about the specifics, and you'd pick it back up again later, look at the same clue, and the answer would be right there. It was hard to stop the brain from working once it latched onto something. He knew that well. It was why he drank so much and kept a nice little cache of grass at all times. Sometimes he needed his brain to stop working. Sometimes he *had* to stop it from working.

Sure enough, his ritualized process was successful again. Sitting at Jimmy's old desk, Justin wound up typing in several new entries. By Ray Lockhardt's name, he added that he'd been shot with a .38. He also added a notation: 'Killed between 7 and 8 P.M., same night as La Cucina bombing.' When he put in the information about Bradford Collins, he realized that people murdered other people for three basic reasons: passion, money, and protection. With Collins, it was fairly safe to rule out the first category – a jilted lover might shoot someone, but blow up a roomful of strangers? – but the last two could be valid. So he added: 'Money?' and then: 'What did he know? What could he tell? Who could he hurt?' For Cooke, he typed in: 'Where was he going? Where had he come from?' And then: 'Passenger?' and 'Cargo?' and, thinking back to Chuck Billings's notes, 'Connection to Semtex?'

He ran the cursor back over to Bradford Collins's name, let it linger there for a moment, waiting for the thought he knew was going to emerge. It did and he threw his hands up, wondering why he hadn't thought of this before. He quickly went online, went to the *New York Times* website, because he knew they'd kept a running track of the bombing victims, and ran down the list of all those known to be killed at Harper's. There were a few names he recognized, Jimmy Leggett's among them. When he came to Jimmy's listing he almost did a double take. Jimmy's death already seemed disconnected from what he was investigating, and for a moment Justin was actually surprised to see it there, but then he realized that he was only making this list because Marjorie had asked him to find out what had happened to her husband. He shivered involuntarily, yet again surprised at the brain's ability to make wounds that seem so raw recede into the background, then he kept scrolling through the names. He didn't know what he'd expected to find, but whatever it was wasn't there. He saw the name of a local contractor he knew, a big guy with a bad temper who once, while installing storm windows in Justin's East End house, had taken a swing at Justin after listening to a complaint about some of the workmanship. Justin hadn't taken kindly to the contractor's attempt to remove his head from his neck. While the guy was off balance after Justin ducked his punch, Justin grabbed a lamp and used it in one swift and compact motion to break the contractor's nose. There was a lot of blood and a lot of swearing, neither of which had particularly bothered Justin. Nor did it bother him to find out the guy was now dead. Justin was not big on grudges. But on the other hand, he found no real reason to grieve over assholes.

Going through the rest of the names, Justin saw an array of businessmen and -women who had died that day, none of whom seemed overtly connected to Bradford Collins in any relevant way. There was a writer whom Justin had heard of but had never read, a literary agent who'd been visiting from London, the comptroller for the City of New York, whom the *Times* praised lavishly, a yoga teacher, a gourmet caterer, busboys, waiters, hostesses. A lot of innocent people who'd been in the wrong place at the wrong time. But there was no one who jumped out at Justin as useful to his investigation. So he went offline, switched back to the word processing program and his list, and under 'Need to Know' he wrote, 'Who was Brad Collins having lunch with?' And that sparked one more thing, so he scrolled down to Martin Heffernan's name and wrote the same thing: 'Who was he meeting at La Cucina?'

He'd had it. He could tell his brain was turning off, so he clicked on the print option, heard the quiet whirr of the printer preparing to do its work, and he sat at what was now his desk, his hands cupped together, his head resting on the edges of his fingers. As the two-page document printed, Justin breathed deeply, letting his mind go blank, allowing his instincts to tell him where to start, what to do first. When he decided, he nodded a firm, crisp nod, pleased with the decision, and as he reached over to pick up his notes he was surprised to find that Reggie Bokkenheuser was standing in front of his desk, looking at him with the faintest curl of a smile on her lips.

'Trying to see into the future?' she said.

'The past,' he told her. 'With cops it's always the past.'

She nodded, as if he'd just revealed something valuable. There was a moment of silence that hung thickly in the air, then she said, 'Is there anything I can help you with?' When he didn't answer right away, she sat down in the chair across the desk from him. 'I don't know exactly what's going on, or what exactly you're trying to figure out, but I know there's a lot of shit going down. Maybe you shouldn't be trying to do it all by yourself.' He still didn't respond, so she said, 'If not me, then some of those guys.' She waved her hand in the direction of the cops in the main station room.

'I have two of them working on something.'

She waited but he didn't say anything further, so she stood back up and said, 'I'll go back to my parking tickets.'

Reggie turned around, took a step toward the door, but Justin said her name out loud and she stopped.

'Ray Lockhardt,' he said.

'What about him?'

'I want you to handle the investigation.' Her eyes widened a bit. He thought she looked pleased. He'd definitely managed to surprise her.

'Um . . .' she said, 'what are you going to be doing while I'm looking into only the second murder in this town in twenty-six years.' Now it was his turn to look surprised, and she said, 'I do my homework.'

'Time to graduate from homework,' Justin told her. 'It's the real world now.'

'I'm ready for it,' she said.

'I know you are.'

'But you still didn't answer my question. What are you going to be doing?'

'There are a lot of pieces to this thing. I think you're better off not knowing what all of them are. At least for now. But you'll be working on one piece. Gary and Tom working on another one.'

'And you'll be working on another one.'

'Yup.'

'And putting all the pieces together so they make a nice, coherent whole?'

'See?' he said, nodding. 'You're already putting your crack investigative skills to work.'

He told her to sit back down, then he spent a few minutes going over the details of Ray Lockhardt's murder and pointing Reggie in several right directions. He told her to begin by looking for anyone with a registered .38 on the east end of Long Island. If that didn't lead anywhere, find out if any registered .38s had been reported stolen. Said she should track Ray's movements for the day he died, and to check with airport employees and pilots to find out if anyone saw anything suspicious. Told her the results from fingerprinting Ray's office should be back momentarily and gave her the name of the officer on the Southampton force she should contact to get them. That would be enough to keep her busy for a while. Then he told her to report in at the end of every day or anytime something interesting occurred, day or night. He saw her eyes flicker when he said the word 'night,' and he almost said something, something like, 'Come on, sex is one thing, a murder investigation's something else, cut the crap,' but the flicker wasn't really that blatant and it seemed better to leave the whole thing alone. Besides, he'd felt the change in his voice when he said the same phrase. It wasn't much of a change, he doubted she'd even heard it. But he had.

When Reggie left the office, he hesitated for just a moment, then picked up the phone and dialed.

He gave his name to the secretary who answered the phone, and she immediately put him through to her boss. When the man came on the line, Justin took a deep breath and said, 'Dad?' Then he explained to his father what he needed and what he wanted and when his father said, 'Okay,' Justin said, 'See you Saturday.' Before he could even hang up the phone, Gary and Thomas burst into his office. They looked like little schoolkids who couldn't wait to show the teacher they had the right answer to a tough question.

'We found him,' Gary said.

'Hutchinson Cooke,' Thomas added.

'Yeah.' This was Gary. Justin wondered if they'd actually rehearsed who would get to tell him what information. 'We have his home address and the name of his commanding officer at Andrews Air Force Base.'

Thomas stepped in now. 'That's where he was based.'

'Where's the house?' Justin asked.

'In Silver Spring, Maryland. It's right outside of D.C.'

'And it's up for sale,' Gary said. He couldn't resist a slight boast. 'I spoke to the Realtor.'

'Who's selling it?' Justin wanted to know.

'Cooke's wife.' That was Thomas. 'They were married for sixteen years. Her name's Theresa. They have two kids.'

Gary shot his fellow cop a sharp look. Justin wondered if it was Gary who was supposed to spill the news about the kids. 'The oldest one's Reysa. She's twelve. And the younger one's Hannah. Nine.'

'Here,' Thomas said, handing over a piece of paper. 'That's got all the info on it.'

'Thank you,' Justin said. 'Good work.'

'There's one other thing that's weird,' Gary said. Justin could see that there'd been an internal struggle about whether or not to reveal this last chunk of info. 'This guy Cooke was pulling down two paychecks. We finally found him using IRS records, that's how come we know about it.'

Justin couldn't help himself. 'He was getting paid by a company called Midas, right?'

Both of the faces of the young cops fell nearly to the floor. Justin felt guilty. But, hell, they deserved it. They'd been just a little too eager to show off. Still, he could have been a little less show-offy himself.

'Did you get any information on Midas? I didn't come up with a thing,' Justin said.

His ignorance on that score didn't seem to make them feel any better. Gary looked down at his shoes and said, 'No. We didn't find nothing either. It's weird. It's kind of like the company doesn't exist.'

'Well, keep working on it, would you? It might be nothing, it might be important. But see what you can find out, okay?'

They nodded, turned to go back to the main room.

'And I mean it, guys. That was good work. Thank you.'

They shrugged but were still pleased by the compliment. As soon as they were gone, Justin hunched forward and looked at his calendar for the next day, saw that other than a meeting with Leona Krill, he had a blank slate. He decided he could cancel Leona. He was sure she'd understand. So he made two quick calls. One to the travel agent at the end of Main Street, right on the pier. She booked him the round-trip flight he requested. The second call was to Leona. He got her secretary, told the woman to reschedule the next day's meeting. When she asked for a time to reschedule, he said he'd get back to her, and hung up. He'd barely gotten his hand away from the receiver when his intercom buzzed. When he answered it, Dennis said, 'Mayor Krill's on the one-three-six-four line.' Justin nodded to himself, tapped down on the right button and said, 'Leona, what can I do for you?'

'You cannot cancel your meeting with me just because you don't feel like meeting. Not when we've got a murder investigation in this town. That's what you can do for me.'

'I canceled it because of the investigation,' he said. 'I have to go out of town. On business.'

'What time are you leaving?'

'Early,' he told her. 'A nine A.M. plane, so I have to leave here around seven.'

'I'll meet you at six-thirty,' she said. 'I'll even make it easy on you. We can meet at your place.' When he didn't answer, she said, 'Six-thirty tomorrow morning at your place, okay, Jay?'

'How do you like your coffee?' he said.

'Skim milk, no sugar.'

As he put the phone down, Justin sat back in his chair. He looked through his large plate glass window into the front room of the station house. Thomas had left to patrol the town. Gary was working on his computer. Reggie was putting on her coat and was on her way out. She glanced into his office on her way to the front door, saw that he was watching her. He was expecting a smile but it didn't come. Their eyes met, but no smile. Then she was gone.

Still leaning back, Justin wondered if he really knew what the hell he was doing. He decided, as usual, that he didn't, but he was damn sure going to go ahead and do it anyway.

chapter 18

The doorbell rang at exactly 6:30 A.M. Justin knew that Leona would be prompt; he'd planned on opening the door with a flourish seconds before she was due to arrive. But his timing was off. He chalked it up to a combination of the early hour, the icy chill that permeated his house, and the half a bottle of scotch he had consumed the night before. He hadn't been able to sleep. He chalked that up to the phone conversation he'd had with Marjorie Leggett, in which he'd told her not to worry, that he'd tell her everything she wanted to know real soon; to the fact that he spent much of the night trying to force himself not to call Reggie Bokkenheuser, whose house he could see from one of his living room windows; and to the scotch. At some point he'd had the choice of sleeping or drinking. Sleep wasn't nearly as delicious as the single malt.

'You look like hell,' Leona said as she stepped inside.

'It's not my best time of day.'

'What is your best time of day, Jay?'

'Good point.' He shrugged. 'I guess I don't really have one.'

Leona Krill stood by his couch but didn't sit. 'Where are you going?' she asked.

'Are you going to want every detail of what I'm doing? 'Cause I don't really work too well that way.'

'The town's paying for this trip, I assume. Don't you think that gives me the right to ask?'

'I'll submit my expenses. If you don't want to pay them, I'll pay myself.'

'You're an arrogant bastard sometimes, aren't you?'

'I'm an arrogant bastard most of the time, Leona. It just comes out more when I have to get up before dawn. Plus I've got a few things on my mind.'

She shook her head. 'Did you make coffee?'

'And bought skim milk.'

He disappeared into the kitchen, came back a moment later with a mug. Steam curled out of the top.

Leona thanked him, took a sip of the coffee, and said, 'I don't know anything about murder investigations, Jay.'

'No reason you should.'

'But I'm the mayor. And whatever happens, I'm going to be responsible.'

'Feel free to shift the blame to me. If that's why you're here, I give you my permission.'

'I'm here because I want to make sure that *you* know how to handle a murder investigation. Because if you don't, I can get help.'

He held back the laugh that wanted to come out. But he couldn't hold it back entirely. 'Leona, I don't think you're going to find anyone who's gonna be much help on this one.'

'Do you want to tell me what's going on?'

'No.'

'Why not?'

'Because there's a lot more going on than you should know about. I wasn't really kidding about taking the blame. If I'm right, this is gonna get messy and dangerous. If I'm wrong, at least you can say you didn't know anything about it.'

'And you don't think maybe you could use some support? Some help?'

'Probably. But I'm not asking for any.'

'You know, I was meeting with Jimmy once and I asked him about you.'

'Was this before you decided to switch teams?'

'I was asking about you professionally, not personally. You want to know what he said?' When Justin shrugged, she took another sip of coffee and said, 'Jimmy was a fairly solid guy. Nice, he cared about things, not exactly a philosopher. But what he said struck me as smart, not the kind of thing I ever would have thought of. He told me he thought you were the most trustworthy person he'd ever met. I said that was quite a compliment, and he said he didn't really mean it that way. So I asked him what he meant and he said that most people were honest because they thought they'd get caught if they weren't. If someone found a suitcase full of cash, and no one was around, he'd usually keep it. But if someone else was there, if someone was watching and could tell on him, he'd do the right thing and turn it in. Because he'd be afraid of what might happen to him if he didn't. But Jimmy said that you didn't care if anyone was watching. You'd do what you thought was right no matter the situation. If you thought it was right to keep it, you would. If you thought it was right to give it back, that's what you'd do.' She took one more long sip of coffee. 'He said the reason was you didn't care about getting caught. He said you didn't care at all about what happened to you. That's why he said he trusted you. Because you'd tell him what you were going to do with that suitcase, and he knew you'd be telling the truth. Because you didn't care. Interesting, don't you think?'

'Well, like you said, Jimmy was a pretty good guy. He wasn't a genius, though.'

Leona started to put the mug down, looked for a coaster, couldn't find one, so she got up and took it to the kitchen sink. From there she went straight to the front door, stopping only to say, 'Thank you for hiring Regina. I appreciate it.'

'I hired her because she's good, not because you asked me to.'

'Okay, then I don't appreciate it. Check in with me when you get back.'

'Yes, boss,' he said.

'Don't forget it,' she told him.

Justin tried to pay attention. But it was almost impossible. For one thing, he was thinking about what Leona had told him, what Jimmy had said about him. For another, the woman across the desk from him would not stop talking.

She was not unattractive, although she did her best to downplay any hint of a feminine side. She was probably in her early forties, her skin was clear and smooth, her dark brown hair drably cut, absolutely straight with no faddish layering. She wore a Nancy Reaganish red wool business suit – jacket buttoned nearly up to her neck and a matching skirt that came down to mid-calf. Shiny, trim brown boots with a thin two-inch heel rose up to meet the hem of the skirt, leaving no room for even an inch of skin to show through. Underneath her jacket was a dark blue shirt. The only thing left open in her outfit was the top button of the shirt, which allowed perhaps two inches of her neck to be exposed. She wore delicate and tasteful pearl earrings; other than that her only jewelry was a simple gold watch clasped around her right wrist on an equally simple gold band. As a package, it added up to something that was very conservatively marketed, refusing to draw attention to itself, insisting that the viewer concentrate on the substance rather than the nonexistent glitz.

Her voice was another thing altogether.

It was nasal and too high-pitched and did nothing but draw attention to itself. It lacked confidence and firmness and was just a shade too quiet. Mostly it was empty. It belied her substantive appearance and did little more than timidly whisper that underneath the surface there was absolutely nothing.

Justin Westwood wondered which half of this woman was for real – the substance or the emptiness. If he had to bet, he knew which way he'd go. She was a bureaucrat. Bet empty.

Justin was not, for the most part, prone to self-analysis. He did not usually care to examine the reasons he acted the way he did, because, with rare exception, he had little interest in acting any other way. Jimmy had definitely been right in that regard. When Justin mourned, it was because he wanted to mourn and had no interest in overcoming his grief. When he retreated from the world – which he'd done, in his own way, for quite a few years after Alicia and Lili died – it was because there was no desire to come out of hiding. When he got drunk or stoned, it was because being high felt better than not being high. And when he was sober it was because it seemed right to be anchored to reality and any ensuing pain was worth the effort. He might not like what he was doing at any particular moment but whatever he was doing it was because he liked the alternatives even less.

He rarely questioned himself when he took a stand, and it was even less rare that he cared about pissing someone off. He probably could have handled the few relationships he'd had after Alicia a lot better than he had, but even that didn't worry him much. If he'd wanted them to last – *really* wanted them to last, not just superficially – then he knew he *would* have handled them better.

He did not put much stock in other people's morals or values, only his own, because it was his morals that he trusted. Jimmy had been absolutely right about that. Justin knew that he did not even hold the law particularly sacred, even though he'd become a cop. He was much more interested in justice than the law. And justice, he understood, came from within. It was a belief, not a prescription for how to behave.

But as Justin sat across the desk from Martha Peck, in her impersonal, glass-encased Washington, D.C., Federal Aviation Administration office overlooking 1st Street NW, he was seriously questioning himself. As she droned on, he was wondering why it was he so detested bureaucrats. He could have a calm conversation face-to-face with a serial killer but one phone call with an employee of the phone company could drive him straight over the edge. There was no problem staying calm when some drunk in a bar was furiously trying to rearrange his face, but trying to convince a bank manager to change the mailing address on a tax form was enough to bring forth visions of the apocalypse. It was that bureaucratic condescension. That awareness that you needed them, that there was no place else to go. Maybe that was it – Justin liked alternatives. He *believed* in alternatives. For bureaucrats, choice was nonexistent. There was one way and one way only – the system. As the nasal voice went on and on, Justin felt himself relaxing. The simple act of understanding his disdain calmed him down. And he understood that, when dealing with an implacable system, anger was self-defeating. So he sat quietly, pushing any traces of ire away, and forced himself to listen to the administrator of the FAA as she told him that it was not possible that anyone in her area could possibly have done anything wrong. Certainly not willingly.

Justin had three people to see during the twelve hours he was planning to spend in the D.C. area. He'd thought that Martha Peck would be the easiest to deal with and probably the most productive.

Based on the conversation so far, he sure as hell hoped he was wrong about that.

'Ms Peck,' Justin interrupted. 'Let's forget the question of wrong or right, for the moment, okay?'

'As a police officer, I would have thought that was your most important question.'

'What I really need to know is why you removed Hutchinson Cooke's file from your Oklahoma City office two days before his plane crashed.'

The woman behind the desk chewed on her lower lip for a moment, her subtle shade of red lipstick rubbed off on her front teeth. 'I was told that if you came here I wasn't to talk to you.'

'I'm sure you were.'

Her eyes widened just a bit. 'That doesn't surprise you?'

'The same person – or at least someone from the same organization – came to my station and told me not to pursue this.'

'So why are you?'

'Because someone was murdered in my town. And whatever else is involved, my job is to find the son of a bitch who did it.'

'You're not afraid of the FBI?'

'Hell, Ms Peck, I'm even afraid of you. But I'm not going to stop asking questions. And I don't get frightened off my cases, no matter who's doing the blustering.'

Now she used her tongue to wipe the lipstick off of her teeth. She hadn't looked in the mirror so Justin wasn't sure how she knew it was there. Maybe it was just a nervous habit. 'What makes you think Hutchinson Cooke's file was removed?' Martha Peck asked.

'Because it's missing. It was electronically removed. Everything about Cooke and the plane he was flying is gone.'

'Files do go missing all the time. I sincerely doubt there was any intent to mislead or obstruct any kind of investigation.'

'Fine. If you didn't do it, just tell me who else has the authority to remove a file. I'm happy to talk to him or her.' When Martha Peck didn't answer, just began nibbling around the edges of a very red fingernail, Justin said, 'Ms Peck, I'm sure you can make my job extremely difficult. You and your bosses can hire lawyers and block subpoenas and all sorts of things you government people are really good at. But here's the thing: I need to know who took the file and why it was taken. If you want me to guess, I'd say someone from the FBI came to you or someone else here and you or whoever it was buckled in the face of a badge and a few words about national security. If that's the case, I don't blame you. I probably would have done the same and I'm not looking to nail you, not at all. But I need to know who owned the plane that Hutchinson Cooke was flying the day he crashed. And, on top of that, I'd like to know who in your office had direct contact with Martin Heffernan. I'll get that info somehow. Believe me. I will. I'm one of those annoying cops who sinks his teeth in and won't let go. You'd be a lot better off telling me the truth and getting me out of your hair.'

'That's the first thing you've said that makes any sense to me.'

'Good. Then you'll give me what I need?'

'I mean the annoying part.' She straightened up the few pieces of paper on her desktop, which was already tidy and clean. 'Do you truly think that someone in the FAA is involved in a crime?'

'Most likely murder.'

'I just don't believe it.'

'At the very least, whoever took that file is guilty of covering up a murder. It's still good for serious jail time. Unless I get some co-operation.'

'Martin Heffernan certainly didn't take it. He was a mid-level management person. The equivalent of an insurance salesman. He was harmless.'

Justin sensed that she was weakening. She clearly hadn't liked being bullied by the FBI any more than he had. He'd been hoping to fly under the radar for a while longer, but what the hell, he knew that was a pipe dream, so he shook his head and bit the bullet. 'He stole the dead man's identification,' he told her. 'And wiped the plane clean of fingerprints, trying to make sure I wouldn't find out Cooke's identity.'

'Oh my God. Are you absolutely certain of that?'

'Everybody starts out harmless, Ms Peck. But it's amazing, somehow prisons still manage to fill right up.' When she didn't respond, he said, 'I don't think for a moment it starts and stops with Heffernan. Mid-level management guys don't make the kinds of decisions he made. Someone was making them for him. That's the person I want to find.'

'I wish I still smoked,' she said. 'This is a very disturbing conversation. Although it wouldn't do me any good, would it? This is one of those damn smokeless buildings.' She sighed. 'Do you have the tail number of the plane?'

He gave it to her, made sure she wrote it down correctly.

'If something was taken,' she said, 'someone might have had a perfectly good reason for taking it.'

'Will you give me the information?' he asked. 'I promise to let you know the minute I find any perfectly good reasons.'

'I'll look into it.'

'Right,' he said, and started to stand. 'Should I leave my card or should I just go fuck myself?'

She stared at him silently. And then, miracle of miracles, she smiled. Her lips – not as red as the nails but still a tad too red – parted. A little of the red had managed to scrape onto her teeth but it was a welcome sight because it was indeed a smile. She was human. He smiled back at her.

'You'd think I'd have dealt with a lot more policemen in my job. But I haven't. Not directly. I'm mostly involved with policy so I spend my day with committees and politicians.'

'So you spend more time with the criminal element.'

She smiled again. And this time she licked the lipstick smudge off her teeth. 'Do you really think Heffernan and this missing file are connected to your murder?'

'I know it,' he said.

'Then leave me your card,' she told him. 'But if you want to go fuck yourself, too, that'll be fine with me.'

Justin always thought that he was someone who'd had more opportunities than most to sample the various experiences that life had to offer. He had seen rich and he'd seen poor. He'd experienced the ultimate in pristine lifestyles and he'd been in the midst of unimaginable violence and depravity. He'd been in love, he'd lost love, he'd been loveless. He'd been both wildly undisciplined and fanatically ordered. There was little, he felt, that could surprise him. Or make him feel uncomfortable and out of place. But one thing he had no experience with whatsoever was military life. He'd never come close to combat, he'd known few soldiers, he'd never, in fact, been on any kind of military installation until he was ushered in to the office of Colonel Eugene T. Zanesworth. From the moment he'd driven past the armed guards who manned the gates to Andrews Air Force Base, he realized that this was a separate world. A world about which he knew nothing. And was likely to learn nothing.

For one thing, everyone he passed stood ramrod straight. There didn't seem to be an ounce of fat on anyone within the entire compound. Even sitting in his rented Grand Am, Justin did his best to sit upright and suck in his gut. It depressed him just a little to realize that there probably wasn't one person – man or woman – on the entire base that he could take in a fair fight. He cheered up slightly when he realized it didn't really matter, since he would never fight fair.

The resolute politeness with which everyone dealt with him also made him uncomfortable. It began just outside the main gate at the Visitor Control Center. The soldier at the reception desk in Building 1840 called him 'sir' four times as he phoned to verify Justin's appointment, took his driver's license and registration card for his rented Grand Am, and issued him a restricted area badge and vehicle sticker. At the gate, he was called 'sir' six times as his car was searched and he was patted down. After he parked on the base in his assigned spot, the person who escorted him to the colonel's office addressed him as 'sir' twice. The woman at Zanesworth's desk – Justin wasn't sure if a sergeant also was called a secretary – called him 'sir' three times. Everyone's voice was at the same modulated, calm level and delivered in the same brisk manner. Justin realized that he would never have made it as a soldier. Military life was all about restraint and learning to survive by taking and accepting orders. The idea was that at some point – when we were at war – everyone would know what to do and, more importantly, do it, even though the restraints were no longer in place. A well-trained soldier was supposed to equal a soldier who functioned well. Justin thought it was a little bit like taking an electric dog collar off a dog. As long as the collar was there, the dog would stop before leaving the grounds. Take the collar off, he might stop once or twice, still expecting the electric shock, but at some point, he'd realize the fence no longer existed – and he'd be chasing a squirrel with no thought to the dangers that might lie in waiting ahead of him.

At the same time, there was something uniquely moving about being on this military base, Justin thought. Actually, there were

206

many things that were moving. The youth he was surrounded by. The fact that everyone he saw might be called to battle. The fact that everywhere he looked was someone who was *willing* to go to battle for something he or she believed in.

Of course, everyone believed in his own side of a war. That's why wars were fought. To prove that your country was right or your God was right.

Justin decided he was lucky he had very few beliefs. His wars were private and personal. In the long run, a lot less dangerous than the wars facing these kids. And in the short run . . . well, maybe not as inspiring, but in some ways, more satisfying. He didn't have to take orders. He didn't have to operate under restraints. He didn't have to fight fair.

Of course, there was one serious drawback to his position. He was beginning to think that he might not have the opportunity to fight at all. Not after two entire minutes in Colonel Zanesworth's presence.

'I'm not sure I understand why you're here,' the colonel said when Justin was ushered into his office.

'I'm not a hundred percent sure either,' Justin said. He didn't know if he was supposed to call the older man 'Colonel' or not. Justin didn't put much stock in titles. He didn't call doctors 'Doctor.' And he never understood why sportscasters on TV called guys like Bob Knight 'Coach,' as if it were some anointed attachment to their names. But in this instance he figured it couldn't hurt. People were people – they liked to be shown respect. He wasn't there to make a point, he was there to get information. 'To be honest, Colonel, I'm conducting a bit of a fishing expedition.'

'What are you fishing for?'

'Information about someone who was stationed here for several years. Hutchinson Cooke.'

'I understood that much. That's why I pulled his file. I'm curious as to *why* you're fishing for it.'

'It's relevant to a murder investigation.'

'Hutch Cooke's murder?'

'That's right.'

'According to the reports I've seen, Captain Cooke wasn't murdered. They call it an accidental death.'

'I'd love to get a look at any paperwork you've seen, Colonel, but I'm not sure any of that's accurate. As far as I know, I'm the only person investigating and I haven't written any reports yet.'

'Anytime a serviceman is' – Zanesworth hesitated, not sure where to go with his phrasing – 'involved in anything of this nature, we immediately check things out.' The colonel tried a brief flicker of a smile. 'The military is all about reports, as I'm sure you know. They're standard and, in this instance, inconsequential.'

'I don't really know, Colonel. But even so, at the very least I'd like to talk to the person who prepared them.'

Zanesworth coughed into his hand. He looked unhappy. 'If what you're saying is true about Captain Cooke, of course we'll do everything we can to help. But I will be your contact here. I'm afraid it will be too disruptive to just . . . how shall I put it . . . let you loose on the base.'

'If anyone else has begun any kind of investigation, it would really be better if—'

'What information are you looking for?'

Justin knew he'd been effectively cut off. It was Zanesworth or nothing. At least for the moment. 'Okay. Let's begin with this: I'd like to know what Cooke was doing the past eighteen months.'

'You're going to have to be a lot more specific than that, son. Doing where? And in what capacity?'

'According to the reports *I've* seen, Captain Cooke was away from the base for that period of time. In fact, he didn't seem to be filling any official Air Force function.'

'Now *you've* got incorrect information. I was his commanding officer for that period. And I probably didn't write those reports you read.'

'So he was stationed here for the past year and a half?'

'Here and nowhere else.'

'Did you know he was drawing a salary from a private company during that same period? Something called Midas Ltd. You ever hear of them?'

'No. No, I didn't know he was getting paid by them, and no, I've never heard of them. But there's certainly nothing illegal or even suspicious, even if it's true.'

'He was stationed here the whole time?'

'He was in the Air Force, son. This was his home base.'

'And what were his responsibilities during the past eighteen months?'

'The same thing he was responsible for over the past eighteen years. Serving in the Air Force and serving proudly and well.'

'Can you be more specific, Colonel?'

'Captain Cooke was a member of the 89th Airlift Wing and, as such, he was part of SAM FOX.' When Justin shook his head blankly, Zanesworth went on. His words were in even more of a monotone than seemed usual, as if he'd offered this explanation thousands of times, which Justin realized he probably had. 'SAM FOX was originally used as an aircraft tail number; it formed a radio call sign to identify Air Force aircraft that were transporting high-ranking VIPs, usually on a foreign flight. SAM is Special Air Mission, FOX for Foreign.'

'That's what Cooke was doing? Piloting VIPs?'

'*Captain* Cooke. And yes. That's our primary mission at Andrews.

We transport the president of the United States and worldwide air-lift for the vice president, the president's cabinet, members of Congress, military leaders, and other dignitaries of the appropriate stature.'

'Do you keep flight logs for all your pilots?'

'Of course.'

'Could I see his? *Captain* Cooke's?'

'I'm afraid not. You don't have the clearance to see that kind of information.'

'And I suppose there's nothing I could do to get that kind of clearance?'

Zanesworth didn't bother to respond to that one. He just let his lips spread into the thinnest of smiles.

'Did you know him, Colonel? Captain Cooke?'

Zanesworth waited an appropriate length of time – two or three seconds – before nodding his head and saying, slowly, 'Of course I knew him. There's no one I don't meet under my command. But I didn't know him well, unfortunately. We had very little interpersonal contact.'

The man was lying. It was a strange lie to tell and there was no real reason for it. But Zanesworth stumbled over the words and his eyes shifted just slightly when he spoke. Up until now he'd been difficult and obviously resisting any kind of probe. But now he was definitely lying. Of that Justin was certain. He just had to try to figure out why.

'Funny. I'd think you'd make it a point of knowing the people who fly heads of state.'

'Captain Cooke wasn't flying heads of state. At least our head of state. And there are twenty thousand people living and working at Andrews. I wish I knew them all, but I don't.'

'So he never flew Air Force One?'

'No.'

'You know that without checking?'

'I know who flies the president. I know everyone who flies the president.'

'Did he ever fly the vice president?'

'It's possible. I'd have to look at his flight records over the years.'

'Would you mind doing that?'

'Yes, I would. I don't see the relevance.'

'There probably isn't any. It's just that, you know how it is, once you start snooping it's hard to stop.'

'I'm afraid I don't know how that is, Mr Westwood. But unless you can show me the relevance, I won't be revisiting the records.'

'Okay. Then let's try this one: When did you hear about Captain Cooke's death? What day was it?'

'I assume it was the day he died. Possibly the morning after.'

'Really? That soon? Because somebody went to a lot of trouble to hide his identity. I didn't know who he was the day he died. Or the morning after.'

'It was probably the day after that, now that I think about it. Or at least I assumed it was that close to his death. I certainly could be off by a few days.'

'Who called to tell you?'

'I . . . um . . . I'm not sure. One of my aides. The police must have called and he took the call.'

'The thing is, Colonel, I'm the police. For some reason, that doesn't seem to be getting through. But I'm the only one who could have called that soon. And I didn't.'

'Then maybe it wasn't the police who called. Maybe it was Captain Cooke's family. I'll talk to my aide and see what he says. He'll have all that information.'

'How about if I ask him?'

'He's not on base today. I'll talk to him when he's back and let you know his response.'

'Can I have his name?'

'I'll get back to you with all the information.'

Justin cleared his throat and twisted his neck to the right. It was stiff as a board. That was because since he'd set foot on Andrews Air Force Base he felt as if he were carrying around a thousand-pound weight on his shoulders. 'How long have you been on the base, Colonel?' he asked.

'What relevance does that have?'

Justin exhaled a deep breath. It wasn't a happy exhale and he made no attempt to hide his dismay. 'Have you ever conducted an investigation, sir?'

'On a small scale.'

'I'm not talking about stealing a quart of strawberries here. I mean something on the level of a multiple-murder investigation.'

'No, of course not.'

'Then let me give you a little lesson, just in case you ever find yourself in my position. You know . . . investigating. The first thing you have to keep in mind is that my questions don't necessarily have any implicit belief or disbelief to them. I'm just trying to get to the particular information I need to solve my problem. So, for instance, if you didn't know Hutchinson Cooke well, my question doesn't necessarily mean that I think you're lying. It could mean that I'm trying to find out if there's someone else I should be talking to. Your predecessor, for instance, who might have known him better. And had some interpersonal contact.'

'I've been base commander here for eleven years.'

'And Captain Cooke was here for . . .?'

'Eight years.'

'Huh. Out of those twenty thousand who live and work here,

how many are officers who serve under you?'

'We're here to talk about Captain Cooke, Mr Westwood. I'm not going to discuss anything about other men and women.'

'Chief.'

'What?'

'Chief Westwood. As long as we're doing the whole title thing. I'm the chief of police, actually. Of the town where Captain Cooke was murdered.'

'Are there any other questions, Chief Westwood?'

'What was Hutchinson Cooke doing in East End Harbor when his plane crashed? Why was he there?'

'He was on official leave. He had a few days off. I can't tell you what he did during his private time.'

'Was it his plane?'

'Again, private information. I don't have any idea whether or not he had his own plane.'

'Not curious?'

'The man's dead. It doesn't strike me as relevant whether he was flying his own plane or borrowing someone else's. The man was a pilot. He preferred being in the air to walking on the ground. As most of us do.'

'Any idea where he was coming from? Or flying to?'

'No.'

'Is there anyone who might, Colonel?'

'I'm afraid not.'

Justin made no attempt to hide his exasperation. 'What was he, a hermit? Eight years on this base and he didn't have any friends he might have talked to?'

'I've asked anyone here I thought might be helpful, in anticipation of your arrival. No one had answers to any of the questions you've asked.'

'So you already anticipated all my questions?'

'It doesn't exactly take Sherlock Holmes to come up with this list.'

'Would you mind if I asked them myself? To the people who didn't have any answers when you asked?'

'Yes, I would mind. I'm afraid that won't be allowed.' Colonel Zanesworth stood. A not very subtle sign that the interview was over. 'Is there anything else I can help you with?'

Justin nodded slowly. 'Here's one question I can't quite figure out the answer to,' he said. 'And you probably didn't anticipate this one because it wasn't on my list.' The colonel's expression didn't change. There was only the slightest flicker in his eyes to reveal his anger. He was better at covering up anger than he was at lying. 'One of your men died in a plane crash. An expert pilot, so I was told. And someone who worked for you . . . well, that's not the right term, but you know what I mean . . . for eight years. Suddenly, someone comes into your office and tells you this officer didn't die accidentally, that he might have been murdered . . .'

'So far I haven't heard a question in all of this.'

'The question is, Colonel: How come you don't seem to give a shit? How come you're not saying to me, "What makes you think what you're saying is true and how can I help?" That's my question. Well, I guess it's two questions, if you want to get technical.'

Zanesworth still showed no outward signs of anger or discomfort. He stared at Justin for a long time, as if he were used to winning such staring contests. 'I don't know who you are, *Chief* Westwood. I'm going to make a point of finding out, however. And when I do, my guess is that this is what I'll learn. That you're a smart-ass, small-town cop who's decided to cause trouble for God knows what reason. It's not that I don't give a shit about what happened to my officer, it's that I don't give a shit about you. I'm in the Air Force. That's where my loyalty lies, that's who I answer to. Not to an arrogant little turd like you. Does that answer your question? Or questions?'

'Not exactly. But I have a feeling that's as close as I'm going to get.'

'I'll have Lieutenant Grayson show you to your car.'

Justin stood up. Neither man made any attempt to shake hands. But before Justin moved, he pulled a piece of paper from his wallet, dropped it onto Zanesworth's desk. 'That's my card, Colonel. If you decide to go for the truth instead of all this bullshit about loyalty, feel free to give me a call.'

'How long have you been a police chief, son?'

'Why?' Justin asked. 'Think I need to work on my technique?'

Colonel Eugene T. Zanesworth's only answer was a quiet snort, followed by, 'I think you need to start looking for a whole new line of work.' Then he closed the door firmly behind Justin, who didn't say a word until he and the lieutenant escorting him reached the Grand Am and the lieutenant was holding the driver's door open.

'So did you know Captain Hutchinson Cooke?' Justin asked as he was climbing in behind the wheel of the car. 'Did you ever meet him?'

'Have a nice trip, sir,' the lieutenant said, closing the car door.

'Thank you. That's damn polite of you.'

'No,' Lieutenant Grayson said. 'Thank *you*, sir.'

When Justin pulled up to the gate, about to turn out of the complex, he glanced in his rearview mirror. In the reflection he could see the lieutenant, still standing in the same spot, seemingly at attention, unmoving, staring straight ahead. It wasn't until Justin was a couple of blocks away and picking up speed that he realized he was breathing normally and that his hands had unclenched. He took his cell phone out of his jacket pocket and called the station house. He heard Reggie's voice on the other end of the line say, 'East End Police.'

215

'Hey,' he said.

'How's it going?' she asked.

'Great. Couldn't be better.'

'You sound kind of funny. Are you okay?'

'Yeah,' he said. 'I just needed to talk to somebody normal.'

He heard her laugh and then say, 'Things must be tough if you're using me as the standard for normal.'

'You have no idea.'

'Where are you headed?'

'Silver Spring. Outside of D.C.'

'You need me to do anything?'

'I'm just going to go try to charm a woman and see if I can get her to talk to me. I should be able to manage on my own.'

'You sure? I've seen you turn on the charm. You probably could use the help.'

'You got anything for me on Lockhardt?' he said.

'Not a thing.' When he didn't respond, she said, 'I'm trying, Jay. But there's zip on the ballistics and nobody saw anything. The only possible lead that's come up at all is a car that was parked about a quarter of a mile away from the airport. Looks like it was parked there at the time of the murder and moved sometime not that long after. But the witness didn't see the driver. Just the car pulled off to the side of the road. And his ID on the car is pretty tenuous.'

'All right. Keep on it.'

'When are you coming back?'

'Tonight. Catch a seven or eight o'clock shuttle, I hope.'

'Well . . . if you're hungry . . . or something . . . feel like talking . . . you can knock on my door. I'm sure I'll be up.'

'What a good neighbor,' he said.

'You can even borrow a cup of sugar,' she told him.

They hung up and Justin headed for Silver Spring, Maryland,

blaring the Lou Reed CD, *Magic and Loss*, he'd brought with him. It was the perfect music for his mood. Quiet and harsh, and all about love and loss and bewildering, incomprehensible death.

Justin found the house without too much trouble. Sense of direction was not his best thing, so he made several wrong turns, went too far going one way, went too far again coming back, finally stopped and asked directions, made one more wrong turn, then he was there. Not too much trouble compared to his usual treks.

There was a car in the driveway and there seemed to be movement in the house, so he knocked on the front door. It was a decent-sized two-story colonial, and when no one answered, Justin figured it was possible that whoever was home had gone upstairs and hadn't heard him, so he knocked again, this time louder. He waited one full minute, knocked one more time, then forced himself to wait two more minutes, timing it to the second on his watch. He decided enough was enough, that something was wrong, so he tried turning the doorknob, confirmed that the door was locked, took two steps back, swayed his weight onto his back right foot, lowered his left shoulder, took one very deep breath . . . and then the door slowly swung open. Justin didn't move for what felt like a very long time, long enough for him to feel extremely foolish, hunched over, ready to try to ram the door open. He coughed awkwardly, stood up straight. There didn't seem to be anyone on the other side of the door so he stepped forward, gently pushed the door a few inches farther open with two fingers. He heard a quiet breath, then another, but didn't see anything until he lowered his gaze. That's when he saw them: two large brown eyes at about the level of his waist, peering up at him from behind the door. Justin let a little air seep out of him.

'You're Hannah, I bet,' he said. When the little girl nodded shyly, Justin asked, 'Is your mom home?'

The girl nodded a second time. 'She's in the bathroom.'

'Would you do me a big favor?' he asked.

'What?'

'Would you go tell her that I'm here?'

The little girl pondered the request quite seriously, then nodded again and went scurrying up the stairs. Justin stepped farther into the small foyer, peered into the living room. The house was spotlessly clean. Everything was obsessively dusted, waxed, and shiny and there was the pervasive odor of Lemon Pledge everywhere. Odd for a house with two kids. It was *too* clean. Seemed like there were very few personal possessions or touches, too. It was all rather barren and antiseptic. Like a movie set meant to parody a suburban, middle-class house.

Justin turned around when he heard footsteps on the stairs. The woman coming toward him was probably in her early fifties, tall and bony, with her dark hair pulled into a tight, severe bun. She looked stern, not particularly attractive, but as she got nearer he saw that she had probably been quite attractive. And she wasn't nearly as old as he'd thought. She could have been in her mid- to late thirties, but fear or worry or sadness had both aged and hardened her. As he took a few steps in her direction, he saw that she was shaking. Her cheek was twitching and the veins in her neck were taut. Her fingernails were bitten down to the quick, but that didn't stop her from chewing on her cuticles. As she walked, her fingers were in constant motion, and the only way she seemed to be able to keep them still was to pick and scratch at them. He saw that the areas around her nails were bleeding and that her fingertips were picked red and raw.

'Mrs Cooke?' he asked. 'Theresa Cooke?'

'That's right.' Her voice was as twitchy as the rest of her. He got the feeling that if she didn't bite off each word, keep each syllable short and terse, she'd just open her mouth and scream as loud as she could. Scream until she couldn't make another sound. 'What can I do for you?'

'I'm sorry to bother you,' Justin said. 'I'm a policeman. Police chief. Justin Westwood.'

'The police chief of Silver Spring?'

'No, ma'am. I'm from a town in Long Island, New York. East End Harbor.'

She practically wrapped her arms around her chest, as if she were now physically holding herself together. 'That's the town where my husband was killed.'

'Yes. That's why I'm here.'

She seemed to age several more years tight before his very eyes.

'What . . . what . . .' She had to lick her cracked, dry lips to get the words out. 'What is it you want?'

'I'm just looking for some information.'

'What kind of . . . of . . . information?'

Justin lowered his voice to a near whisper. He looked the woman directly in the eye and did his best to give her a gentle smile. 'Is there something you're afraid of, Theresa?' When she didn't answer, just stared back at him, he said in the same even tone, 'You can tell me. What are you so afraid of?' he asked.

'Afraid of?' she whispered back. And when he nodded, she said, 'I'm afraid of everything.'

'Then let me help you.'

A laugh escaped through her lips, but there was no humor in it. It was a harsh, crackling sound.

'Then help me,' Justin said. 'Help me find out who killed your husband.'

'They said it was an accident.'

219

'But you know it wasn't, don't you?'

She stared with her hard, almost lifeless eyes, and then she said, 'Yes. I know.'

From upstairs, the sound of the television filtered down. Justin heard frenzied, silly music. The girls must be watching cartoons.

'Do you mind,' Justin said very slowly, so carefully, 'if I just sit and have a cup of coffee?'

Another long silence. The woman's neck was stretched so taut he didn't think it was even possible for her to speak. Her fingers moved even faster, picking deeper into her own skin, and he could see her shiver. She was like a fragile piece of glass and he was afraid to speak; she'd flinched at his words as if each were a rock being hurled directly at her. But the silence ended when she turned back to the stairs and yelled, 'Reysa! Hannah! Stay upstairs and play! I need some quiet so I can talk to this man. Do you hear me? Stay upstairs!'

Justin heard two voices yell down, 'Yes, Momma,' and then Mrs Cooke spun on her heels and headed toward what he assumed was the kitchen. He waited a moment, watching the woman walk, her spindly legs looking as if they were going to snap after each step. When she disappeared around a corner, he emerged from his reverie and realized he should follow. It looked like he was about to get what he'd come for.

Justin sipped the hot black coffee, served in a delicate cup and saucer. He raised his eyebrow to let her know that it was good.

'I've lost twelve pounds since my husband died,' she said. 'I haven't been able to eat. Or sleep.'

'Have you been talking to anyone?'

She shook her head. It didn't move more than an inch in either direction.

'Is there anyone who's been coming in to help with the children?'

Now she recoiled as if slapped. 'You think I don't know my responsibilities?' she snapped. 'I know my responsibilities!'

'I'm sure you do. That's not what I meant. I was talking about making things a little easier on you, that's all. You're under a lot of strain. And you've suffered a loss. Everybody needs help in that kind of situation.'

'My husband! Hutch had responsibilities but he didn't care!'

'I'm sure that he did.'

'No! He didn't! And now my babies don't have a father!'

Justin kept his voice soft and soothing. 'What was he doing, Mrs Cooke? What was he doing that made someone rig his plane and cause a crash?'

She didn't seem to hear the question. She wrapped her arms even tighter around her chest. 'Where is he now?'

'I don't know.'

'They took him, didn't they? Those bastards! We don't even get a real funeral.'

Justin nodded. 'Do you know who "they" are?'

'No. Not really.'

'But you have an idea.'

'Maybe.'

That was as far as she was willing to go, at least for the moment. She tried drinking some coffee but she only managed one sip before putting the cup down.

'Theresa, do you know—'

'Terry. People call me Terry.'

'Okay. What was your husband doing over the past year or so, Terry?'

'Flying. Flying like always.'

'But not for the Air Force.'

221

'No. Special people.'

'What kind of special people?'

'Scary people.'

'Like who?'

She shook her head again. This time it might have swung two whole inches from side to side.

'People at Midas?'

He could see the fear run through her. It left her eyes and seemed to rip through her insides like an insidious, all-consuming disease.

'Can you give me the names of any people at Midas, Mrs Cooke?' When she didn't answer, he said, 'A phone number? An address?'

The fear was clamping her jaws shut. Justin waited until he knew she wouldn't – or couldn't – respond.

'I spoke to your husband's commanding officer,' he said finally.

The fear let go of her throat and allowed her to speak now. 'Zanesworth?'

Justin nodded and said, 'He told me your husband was stationed at Andrews the last eighteen months, that things were done just as they'd been done in the past.'

'That's not true.'

'Do you have any idea why he'd lie?'

'Because somebody told him to. Because he's scared, just like me. Or at least he should be.'

Justin wished he'd brought a flask with him. He'd sneak into the bathroom, have a long pull, and feel a lot better than he felt at this moment. But it was just wishful thinking. Something he didn't have much time for. 'Who did your husband fly when he was in the Air Force?' he asked, when he finally got away from the image of nice, warm alcohol flowing down his throat. 'What kind of passengers?'

'Everyone.'

'The president?'

'No. Everyone but him.'

'The vice president?'

'Sure.'

'He piloted the vice president? Vice President Dandridge?'

'Yes.'

'Who else?'

'Lots of them. Secretary of state. Defense secretary. Everyone had their territories. Hutch had the Middle East a lot. That was his route.'

'He never left the Air Force, did he?'

'No.'

'They just let him take time off from his duties to do something else.'

She nodded.

'The people he was working for, they must have been pretty important to arrange that.'

She nodded one more time. He was beginning to wonder if he'd hear her speak again.

'During the time off, did he fly some of the same people he was flying for the Air Force?'

Another nod. Then, 'I think so. Yes.'

'Was he still flying to the Middle East?'

'Yes. I mean, I was never sure where he was. He said it was usually better for me not to know. But he forgot sometimes, and told me things. They slipped out. Or else he'd give me hints. It was kind of like a game. Once he called me up from a hotel and I asked him how he was and he said, 'I fell down the tower,' and I didn't know what he meant but it sounded bad so I got all concerned, but he was just laughing and told me to think about it. After we hung up, I figured out what he meant. He was saying Eiffel Tower to let me know he was in Paris. I think he flew the secretary of state there for some secret conference. No, it was the vice president, because after that he flew him to Saudi Arabia. I remember because Hutch brought me back this little veil thing, like Arab women wear, and he said that Dandridge was making fun of him on the flight back. Whenever he had time, Hutch always tried to bring me back something from one of his trips.'

She laughed now, at the memory, then started to cry. She was starting to break down, so he asked her a question quickly, wanting to get her to focus again. 'Where else did he fly, Terry, while he was flying these special people? Over the past year and a half.'

'Florida.' Suddenly she jumped up, ran over to the kitchen counter, brought back a bottle. 'This was from his last trip there, that's how I know where he was.'

Justin looked at the bottle. The label said it was Havana Club rum, aged fourteen years.

'This is Cuban, Terry. Not from Florida.'

'I know. Hutch said they sold it in Florida 'cause there are so many Cubans there. Refugees.'

'Where else did Hutch fly?'

'Texas. A lot of times to Texas. I don't think I can keep talking,' she said. 'I think I'm going to start to cry again.'

'You're entitled to cry,' he told her. 'Can I just finish my coffee? I won't talk about Hutch anymore.'

She nodded. He took another sip. It was cold but he pretended not to notice.

'I heard that you're selling the house.'

'Yes.'

'How come?'

'Because they told me to.'

Justin put his coffee cup down. 'What? Who told you to?'

'The people who bought it for us.'

'Who was that?'

'The people Hutch was working for. That was one of the reasons why he did it. They said they'd buy him a house. This house. And they did. Now they told me to sell it. They said I could keep all the money. But they said to sell it and move away.'

'How did they tell you this?'

'On the phone.'

'When?'

'The day Hutch died. They called to say that his plane had crashed, that he was dead. They said I should sell the house, that I could keep all the money, they'd take care of it, not to worry about the mortgage. They said I should just take the money and use it to go somewhere else.'

'Who called you?'

'I can't tell you that.'

Justin closed his eyes for just a moment. When he opened them, he said, 'Terry. If you tell me who called you, then maybe I can find out who killed your husband.'

'And maybe, if I tell you what you want to know, they'll also kill me and my little girls. I think you better leave. I shouldn't have talked to you at all.'

Justin tried to think of something else to say, to prolong his stay, but no words came. He stood up, stretched his stiff back, and let Terry Cooke escort him to the door.

'I don't want any trouble,' she said. 'I just want to get out of here, forget everything that's happened.'

'Where are you going? I mean, when you sell the house.'

'My parents live in New Mexico. I thought we'd go out there. It'll be good for the girls. Maybe I'll be able to eat and sleep out there.'

'I bet you will.' He reached for the doorknob. 'Can I just ask you one thing? Did Hutch own his own plane?'

'No. He never needed one, really.'

'Whose plane was he flying?'

She didn't answer.

'Terry, why was he in East End Harbor? Why that airport? Why that town?'

'You think it's because of the bombing, don't you? The Harper's bombing.'

'Yes. That is what I think.'

'My husband was a pilot. All he did was pick people up and drop them off. He wasn't political. He didn't even like the Air Force all that much, they just let him fly. He was just a good guy who liked to fly.'

'Why East End Harbor, Terry?'

'Did you see him?'

'What?'

'Hutch. My husband. Did you see him . . . after the crash?'

'Yes.'

'Was it . . . was it bad?'

'I think it's always bad when someone dies who doesn't have to.'

She closed her eyes for a moment. With them still closed she said, 'He was going to stop, you know.'

'Hutch? Stop what?'

'He was going to stop working for these people. He didn't like what they were doing.'

'He told you that?'

She nodded. 'He just flew them. And it was exciting at first. Glamorous and fun. And he made a lot of money. But he said he thought he was working for the good guys. Only it turned out they were the bad guys. That's what he told me. So he was going to stop.' She sniffled, holding back another barrage of tears. 'Well . . . he did stop working for them, didn't he? He just stopped a little too late.'

'Why East End, Terry?'

'I don't know. I guess even bad guys have to live somewhere, don't they?' When he nodded tentatively, she took his hand. Not shaking it, just holding it for support. Or simply to have some human contact. 'I'm sorry,' she said. 'Things are just so muddy. That's what Hutch would have told you. Things are muddy. Do you understand?'

'I understand,' Justin said, then he gently released his hand, thanked her for talking to him, stepped outside. She closed the door behind him and he heard the click of the lock turning inside. He walked to his car that he'd parked in the thin gravel driveway. Muddy, he thought. A strange phrase but an accurate one. Things were definitely muddy. Thick, slimy, filthy, and muddy.

He got behind the wheel, started the ignition, glanced in his rearview mirror . . . and there were those eyes again. The big brown round saucer eyes that he'd seen peering out at him from behind the Cookes's front door.

'You know, it's dangerous to get into strangers' cars,' he told the little girl.

'You're not a stranger,' she said. 'You know my mom.'

'Hannah, right?'

'My sister's Reysa.'

'I have to go now, Hannah, so you'd better go inside. I don't want your mom to worry.'

'My mom's not worried. She's afraid.'

'I know she is. But you don't want her to worry, too, do you?'

'No.' But the little girl didn't make any move to leave. 'Can you help her stop being afraid?'

'I don't know. I'm going to try. But I don't know.'

'Sometimes she's too afraid to take us to McDonald's. Yesterday, Reysa cried because she wanted a Big Mac but Mommy wouldn't take us.

'Sometimes,' Justin told her, 'when people are afraid it makes

227

them not act like themselves. But you know what? It always changes. People change back to the way they were. And they act just like they used to. You and your sister have to try to be really nice to your mom while she's nervous and afraid. That's what she needs. And pretty soon she'll be just like she used to be.'

'And she'll take us to McDonald's?'

'I promise.'

Nine-year-old Hannah Cooke thought about this for a moment, then she decided to continue the conversation from the front seat. She pulled herself up over the top of the passenger seat and plopped alongside Justin. As she landed, something fell out of her hand. Something small and shiny.

'What's that?' Justin asked.

The girl reached down, picked it up with her right hand, then opened the palm of her left to show him what she had.

'Jacks,' he said quietly. 'Are you a good jacks player?'

'Uh-huh,' she told him. 'I play all the time. Are you good?'

'I haven't played in a long time.'

'I know. That's what happens to grown-ups. They stop playing.'

'Can I ask you something, honey?' She nodded, so he said, 'Do you know what your mom's so afraid of?'

'The men.'

'What men?'

'The men Daddy brought to the house.'

'Do you know who they were?'

Hannah shook her head. 'One was scary. I didn't like him.'

'Do you remember anything about him?'

'Uh-huh. He was a general.'

'A general? Like in the army?'

'I think he wasn't a real general. Just an assistant general.'

'An assistant general? Like a colonel?'

'No. He wasn't a colonel. He was an assistant general. And he was mean to my daddy.'

'How about the other man? Was he mean, too?'

'No. He was nice. I liked him.'

'What did you like about him?'

'He played with me. The general talked bad to my dad but the nice one played with me. For a long time.'

'Hannah,' Justin said, and suddenly the inside of the car seemed very quiet and still. 'Did he play jacks with you?'

'Yup,' the little girl said. 'And guess what?'

'What?'

'He was really, really, really good.'

He was back in his house by a few minutes before ten, happy to be in East End, happy to be away from soldiers and bureaucrats and widows. By ten, he was at his living room window, looking at the house across the street, catty-corner from his. Reggie's lights were on. She was awake. *Go on*, he told himself. *She told you to come over. So go. Go.* But he stayed, one knee on the couch, his arms leaning on the backrest, looking at the stillness of her front yard.

Justin's eyes slowly grew accustomed to the darkness outside his window. He could make out the edges of the telephone wires across the street. And the hedges that sat below them. He thought about the little girl's jacks, the way her soft hands curled around them, and it made his stomach hurt. He thought about Martha Peck, not knowing whether or not she'd come through as promised. And the colonel; his fierce and misplaced loyalty. Again, he could see Hannah Cooke's hand curl around the jack, and now he closed his eyes and he was back inside Harper's, walking through the bombed-out remains, and Chuck Billings was pulling a jack out of the wall. A tiny

229

children's toy, embedded in the wall. A toy stained with dried red-brown blood.

He opened his eyes. Saw – or maybe just felt – some kind of movement in Reggie's house. Maybe she'd noticed his car. Maybe she was coming over. He waited but there was no further movement. Just silence. And shadows.

Things are muddy, he thought. *Things are muddy.*

He looked at his watch. Ten-twenty.

He walked over to his computer, turned it on, waited for it to boot up. When it was ready, went to his 'Shared' folder, where he kept his downloaded music. He turned the volume on his computer all the way up, clicked on a Tim Curry song from the early '80s, 'I Do the Rock'. He let the music wash over him, its hard, staccato rhythm and its cynical obscure lyrics. In a crazy world, the only thing that still made any sense was to do the rock. Forget ideology. Forget growing old. Stay away from fame and politics and philosophy. Just do the rock. Justin agreed. It was about the only thing that still made sense to him, too. But his job was to make sense of things he didn't understand, so, music blaring, he went to the folder he'd cleverly labeled 'MI' for 'Murder Investigation' and began to update his list. The first column he went to was 'Connections'. There he found the link he'd initially marked as so tentative – Vice President Phillip Dandridge – between Bradford Collins and Hutchinson Cooke. He had typed in several question marks his first go-round. Now he deleted every one of them. He didn't know what it meant, but he had a firm connection. Dandridge definitely knew both men. Justin stared at the fact, couldn't make anything new of it, glad in a way that he couldn't because what the hell was he possibly going to do to the vice president of the United States if it ever came to that, so he began typing again, adding everything he'd learned in D.C. Not a hell of a lot, he realized as he typed. But small bits and pieces. In the space he'd allotted for Hutch Cooke, he added, 'Daughter plays with jacks,' and to the right of that he put in 'Connection to bomb?' – and then he typed in all the question marks he'd just removed from link number one. He also wrote down just about everything he could remember that had come out of the mouth of Theresa Cooke. He even wrote down, 'I fell down the tower – Eiffel Tower.' It seemed idiotic, but he'd learned never to dismiss anything. It meant that Cooke was a game player, he liked puzzles. Info that somehow might prove relevant since this was as complicated a puzzle as Justin could imagine. When he'd entered everything he could recall, he was about to shut down the computer, stopped, went back into the file, and added one more thing: 'Everything's muddy.' It seemed fitting.

Then he turned the computer off, took the half bottle of single-malt scotch left over from the night before, and went back to his lookout spot on the couch.

Reggie's windows were dark now. She'd gone to bed.

Justin decided he'd better do the same.

His visitors would be arriving at nine in the morning. It was going to be a long and interesting day. He had to stay sharp. He'd have to be alert because he was going to need to absorb a lot of information.

Yes, he decided. Definitely time for bed.

One last look across the street.

Nothing but darkness.

Everything's muddy.

He went to his computer, clicked on an illegally downloaded version of Eric Clapton's 'Cocaine,' and cranked it up. It was the perfect song.

A half a bottle of scotch and three-quarters of a thick, hand-rolled joint later, Justin Westwood was sound asleep.

chapter 19

Nuri Al-Bazaad liked driving American cars.

They were so quiet. When you rolled up the windows all the way, you couldn't hear a thing. It amazed him every time because it was like being in a small room shut off from the rest of the world. You could see what was going on in that world, you could sense the mayhem, the corruption, the evil all around you, but you couldn't hear any of it. And it couldn't touch you. You were sealed off and removed. Safe. Protected.

Everything was soft and spotless inside American cars, too. It must be very similar to being in heaven, Nuri decided. So clean, so far away from the pain of the world, so comfortable and relaxing. He couldn't wait to go to heaven. Nuri did not like it very much on earth where everything was so filthy and rough and corrupt. Where women exposed themselves and tried to be like men, and nobody had respect for anything or anyone, and everyone was in so much pain. So much awful, awful pain.

Nuri turned up the volume on the car radio now. Not too much, just a little. Just enough so the gentle strings washed over him like a soothing bath. The sound systems in these cars amazed him. It was like having an orchestra playing in the backseat. You could hear the resonance, the timbre in the music. Nuri thought there would have to be beautiful music in heaven, too. He couldn't imagine it more beautiful than the surround sound coming from the four speakers in the rented Buick.

Nuri was never bored sitting in a car like the one he waited in now. How could you ever get bored? he wondered. As the music played, he slid the front seat back and forth. It moved so easily forward and back, up and down. He was parked now, he had to wait for the people to come out of their house, and he was becoming a little anxious. Not because he was worried about what he was going to do but because he was anxious to drive again. He was very impressed with the smoothness of the ride, the way this car barely felt any bumps, the way it seemed to glide over any obstacle in its path. He had to give credit to the American roads, which were paved and solid and built to last. Not at all like the roads at home, which were hardly even roads; they were ruts for wagons. They were filthy and ragged and bumpy. They were not like the road that led to heaven. That road would be like an American highway: long and straight and smooth and beautiful.

More than anything else, Nuri liked the heating system that warmed the car. He would turn it all the way up and blast himself with hot air until he would be dripping with sweat on even the coldest day. He still had childhood memories of his cold desert home, of lying awake at night shivering, of thinking he would never be warm again, of his father beating him when he had the temerity to ask for a blanket. 'Men do not need blankets,' his father would say, and then *slap*, hard across the face. 'Men do not fear the cold.'

Nuri told his father that he wasn't afraid. But he was. He was very frightened of the cold. As a child, he thought it would freeze him in place, that it would make his blood a solid block of ice the way it did with water, and that he'd be unable to move. He told his father he didn't need a blanket and he never asked for one again, but he was always afraid that one day the cold would come and take him. It's why he kept moving. Why he was always running. He wanted to stay one step ahead of the cold.

It would be warm in heaven, he knew. Warm like a rented Buick, driving along strong, sturdy roads with beautiful surround sound music everywhere.

He slouched down behind the steering wheel now, lowering his chin to his neck, his shoulders hunching up tensely, his eyes peering over the top of the dashboard.

They were coming out of the house.

Moving to their car. All of them.

Holding hands and looking happy.

Yes, yes, they were leaving. They were finally leaving, all together.

Life was very good. The heat was blasting and the music was sweet and they were finally emerging from their home.

Nuri started the engine of his Buick, waited until the other car pulled out of the driveway, then he gently put his foot down on the gas pedal and drove carefully after them along the uncrowded street. He shifted into drive, pressed down harder on the accelerator, and stayed with them, always twenty feet or so behind. Always there but never seen.

As he made his way past the manicured lawns and the young boys playing basketball in their driveways and the occasional bundled-up jogger, Nuri Al-Bazaad was very pleased. He knew he'd be in heaven soon. He knew he'd be far away from the squalor and the misery that lurked behind these suburban doors. That lurked behind all doors everywhere. And as he adjusted the thick seat belt that went around his waist and swung over his chest and back, he knew, too, that soon everything would be warm. The explosion he was going to set off would blow warm breath all over him, blow hard enough to make sure his blood could never freeze, hard enough to make him rise into the air and carry him along the beautiful, straight, glimmering road.

All the way to heaven.

chapter 20

'So why don't you start to tell me about EGenco.'

Justin was anxious to get down to business. The first thirty minutes that his father had been inside his house made him feel as if he were sixteen years old again. Jonathan Westwood didn't say anything about Justin's East End house. Nothing complimentary, nothing derogatory. He looked around, took it all in, raised an eyebrow and said, 'How far away is the ocean?' When Justin told him it was a ten- or fifteen-minute drive over toward East Hampton and that the bay was just a five-minute walk in the other direction, his father went, 'Ahh.' Justin didn't offer to show the upstairs of the house and his father never asked to see it.

They spent half an hour in small talk. Justin said that he'd take him to the police station later in the day, if he wanted, and Jonathan nodded stiffly. Justin said he'd show off the town, they could go for a short drive, and Jonathan smiled noncommitally. Justin studied his father's clothes while they sat and had coffee. And his demeanor. Jonathan was dressed casually, beige pants and a light green sweater, and yet somehow gave the impression that he was wearing a three-piece suit. His posture was relaxed and confident and yet he never slouched, never looked awkward in any way. In comparison, Justin felt grubby. He knew he gave off the faint whiff of scotch. And he probably should have shaved. His jeans weren't pressed, his sweat-shirt was expensive but still a sweatshirt.

Yup. Sixteen years old.

Justin realized that a lot of things were making him feel sixteen again these days. The combination of Reggie Bokkenheuser and alcohol, for one. He quickly shoved that thought away. And he shoved hard. There was too much at stake to allow any distractions. Not parental, not sexual, not romantic.

A bit more self-insight, Justin thought. He definitely believed in alternatives. He just didn't believe in distractions. So he decided to get a big distraction out of the way as quickly and easily as he could.

'Look,' he said to his father. 'I know this is hard for you. It's different seeing me here than when I'm up in Providence. But this is the way I've chosen to live and this is what I do. I know it's not what you'd choose for me but the choice has been made. And it was made a long time ago.'

'I understand,' Jonathan Westwood said.

'I know you do. I just thought it needed saying. And I also want you to know I appreciate your coming here. I think it's going to turn out to be very important.'

'There's nothing to appreciate,' his father said. 'You asked and I came.'

It was as intimate an exchange as the two had had in years. And it was followed by an awkward silence that lasted until Justin turned to the third man in the room, a man who was blushing furiously and looking in every possible direction but at the two Westwood men, and said, 'Sorry, Roger. Family shit. But now it's out of the way. So why don't you start to tell me about EGenco.'

His father had flown in with Roger Mallone, at Justin's request. Mallone was one of the elder Westwood's key financial advisers and had been extremely helpful to Justin in the past. Roger wasn't a redhead but he looked as if he should be, with his ruddy complexion and tousled hair. He had the aura of someone who'd once been a terrific high school athlete but hadn't done much in the thirteen or fourteen years since other than pick up a tennis racket for an easy game of doubles. Softer than he should be, with a self-mocking demeanor that recognized his own lack of strength, Roger was no hero, he was a numbers man with superb connections in the business world, great insight into that world, and tremendous access to information. Right now, all of that was more important to Justin than heroism.

'The last time you were asking me for information,' Roger Mallone said, 'you were pointing a gun at me.'

'Slightly different circumstances,' Justin said.

'No one's trying to arrest you now, I assume.'

'That's right.'

'Or kill you either.' Mallone smiled. But the smile faded quickly when Justin didn't answer.

'Jay?' Roger said, looking to prompt an answer with a raised eyebrow. And when Justin just gave a little shrug, Mallone said, 'Shit,' and then, quietly and grimly, 'You lead a very interesting life.'

'Yes, interesting,' Jonathan said.

'I just hope I don't have to be around it too much longer,' Mallone muttered.

'EGenco,' Justin prompted. 'What can you give me?'

'I can give you days and days. You see the suitcase I brought? That ain't clothes, pal. It's filled with financial reports, corporate histories, Wall Street analyses, depositions, reports on various lawsuits. It'll help if you can narrow things down. The company's all over the globe and has twenty different divisions that are larger than most companies you've ever heard of.'

'Start simple. How about a general overview if you can? And remember, I've been out of the financial world a few years.'

Justin could see his father nod firmly at his last statement, as if to add some sort of emphasis.

'All right,' Roger said. 'Let's start with a little history. I'll work my way forward, and, at some point, if I go off track you lead me back so I can try to focus on the areas you need to understand.'

'Perfect.'

'EGenco was founded in 1922. The founder was a Texan named James Merriwell . . .'

The story Roger Mallone proceeded to tell was one of picture-perfect American capitalism. As he listened, Justin tried to relate the story to anything in his own experience, realized that was an impossibility. EGenco's past was one that paralleled and exemplified the country's history: it was a tale of dedication to constant and obsessive expansion. Justin's life was, he realized, the longer it went on, becoming one of gradual retraction. The boundaries of his existence had, for quite a few years, narrowed and gotten smaller. Something that could never be said of the business that started as an entrepreneurial Oklahoma-based company with the overly grand and self-important name of the Merriwell 20th Century Ultimate Oil Well Cementing Company. As the firm's reputation grew, it was referred to simply as Merriwell.

For the first thirty-five years or so, James Merriwell was content to carefully expand from building to buying wells and making investments in wildcatters. As his fortune rose, so did his ambitions – or, at least, so did the ambitions of his third, and much younger, wife, Laylene. She pushed her husband, as he was approaching his sixty-fifth birthday, to broaden his business interests, which in turn would broaden their social, cultural, and political circles. Merriwell was only too glad to appease the latest Mrs Merriwell, who could be rather sharp-tongued when she didn't get her way. So, in the mid-1950s, Merriwell – as the company was now officially named, and of which Laylene had been given a hefty piece – acquired Green & Duggin, an engineering and construction company. G&D, as it was called, had been formed in 1918. After its acquisition by Merriwell, it was renowned as a road construction company, a general contractor, and builder of the world's first offshore platform in 1947. In the mid-1970s, not long before James Merriwell's ninetieth birthday, Merriwell GD, as it was now called, bought Windmer Industries, a project management company for the oil industry. Windmer had also prospered during the first half of the century. The founder, an inventor named Horatio Windmer, began the company during the country's first oil boom at the end of the nineteenth century. In 1880, Windmer's position in the oilfield products manufacturing business had been launched when he patented a cylindrical packer that revolutionized the industry.

The three giants of this industry, Green, Duggin, and Windmer, were all dead by 1960. James Merriwell finally died in 1978, leaving Laylene as one of the richest women in America. Within two years of her husband's death, she had bought a professional football team, built an opera house in her small Montana hometown and paid Pavarotti a one-million-dollar fee to sing at the opening night ceremony, married a man thirty-two years her junior, with a prenup agreement that gave him thirty-five million dollars upon her death unless he didn't fulfill his end of the bargain, which was to fuck her a minimum of three times every week, and she'd taken Merriwell public, earning several hundred million dollars more, and changing its name to EGenco. The E was for energy. The Gen was for Genevieve, the daughter she'd had with old man James. Six months after the company went public Genny was killed in a car accident. Laylene was driving but was unhurt. Rumors were that she was drunk as a skunk, but this was Texas so money changed hands, lips were sealed, and no charges were ever brought.

Justin interrupted Roger at this point in the narration to ask him how the hell he knew all these little details. Particularly the one about Laylene's husband having to fornicate thrice weekly. Roger just raised one eyebrow and said, 'When I do an investigation for your father, I make sure I'm thorough.' Then he went back to telling his tale.

In the late eighties the new management team of EGenco took over a corporation called F.X. Springs, an acquisition that expanded them into petroleum refining and petrochemical processing. Francis Xavier Springs had begun his business in 1902. Initially they were pipe fabricators; eventually he created technology that altered petroleum refining and petrochemical processing and, with the money that rolled in after that, he built his own facilities based on those techniques. When they were merged into EGenco, they formed the next-to-last piece of what the corporate report called 'vertical and horizontal energy integration.' The final piece was a relatively new company called LecTro, a midsize utility company that was acquired in 1991. There were now five divisions that formed the base of EGenco's production attributes: Merriwell, Green & Duggin, Windmer, F.X. Springs, and LecTro. Together, they offered an enormous array of products, services, and integrated solutions for oil and gas exploration, development, and production. And when they officially outgrossed their biggest rival, Halliburton, the company was able to rightfully call themselves the largest and broadest unified oil and gas services company in the world.

By 1997, EGenco's worldwide revenues were somewhere around nineteen billion dollars. Then, according to Roger Mallone, they got greedy.

'Can we go back a minute?' Justin asked.

'We can do anything you want,' Roger said.

'A unified oil and gas services company. Put that in English.'

'It's simple. There is literally nothing in the finding, development, and processing of oil and gas that they don't have their hand in. They explore and develop, they produce, they handle maintenance for other producers, they convert and refine. They run plants and oil wells, build plants and wells, manufacture everything from drill bits to subsea pumps. And with LecTro, they actually even supply and sell electricity. So they literally are capable of controlling every aspect of the energy business.'

'Is that legal?'

'It's legal if the government decides it's legal. Would it have been twenty years ago? Well, let's say pre-Reagan? Probably not. Today? Well . . . would you want to be the government prosecutor that downsizes them and runs the risk of costing people tens of thousands of jobs?'

'The numbers are that big?'

'Sure. They probably employ a hundred thousand people, maybe even more, full-time.'

'Worldwide?'

'Christ yes, worldwide. They've got bases in a hundred and twenty, hundred and thirty countries. I'd be willing to bet they're in every country you can name and a hell of a lot you can't. Over the years they've expanded both internally and through major acquisition. They're sharks. They've bought engineering and construction companies, petrochemical processing plants, you name it and they've built it, managed it, or devoured it.'

'You said "the base of their production attributes." What other attributes are there?'

'This is where it gets a little complicated. And it's where they got

242

greedy, as I said. And my guess is, it's also the root of their current problem.'

'The government investigation.'

'Investigations, plural. Right.' He glanced at Jonathan Westwood. 'Do you agree with that?'

Jonathan nodded, so Roger went back to his dissertation.

'What happened is, about seven, maybe eight years ago, they were huge and successful. Particularly after they bought LecTro. And when they bought it, that company was a money machine. The energy business was being deregulated – the rate of returns, the caps – so cash was just flowing in. They decided to take advantage of that and began trading electricity.'

'Electricity trading? Is this remotely as complicated as NBA salary cap stuff?'

Jonathan Westwood groaned. Roger Mallone just shook his head and said, 'Actually, no. It's a lot simpler. Especially with deregulation. Think of electricity as something physical. A plant somewhere has excess supply and someone somewhere else doesn't have enough. They *need* electricity – California power plants, for instance, a few years ago. At first, our guys just sold. No problem. Then they saw the profit margin and began brokering. If they didn't have enough, they went elsewhere and acted as the agent. For both sides. They negotiated the selling *and* the buying price.'

'That can't be legal.'

'Welcome to the twenty-first century and a government that'll let big business do just about anything they want.' Roger snuck a glance at Jonathan Westwood and added, 'Thank God.'

'Keep going,' Justin said.

'Electricity is traded very actively – because it's unevenly used. So the geniuses over at EGenco decided they didn't want to just broker. They wanted more. So they decided to buy, not just represent. They

243

brought in a bunch of Masters of the Universe types who looked around and saw what was happening on Wall Street – remember, this is when the economy was at a record high – so they thought they couldn't lose. And now what they were doing was buying from plants, holding on to the electricity, and then selling what they owned to other plants. The problem was they bought high. *Very* high. They bought everything at the top, and suddenly, as things began to turn, they were selling all of it at huge losses.'

'How huge?'

'EGenco probably wasn't going to go under, if that's what you're asking. They had too many other assets. But from what I hear – and, again, all this is conjecture – LecTro was a fiasco. If I'm right, we're talking billions of dollars of losses. If that's true, I suppose it's possible it might have sunk the whole thing.'

'So what happened?'

'Well, that's the question. That's what's being investigated.'

'What do *you* think happened?'

'Look – at a certain level, you get so big, you have so many fixed assets, it's almost impossible for anyone to know exactly what you're doing. Again, if the losses are as great as I suspect, my guess is that EGenco management decided to hide a huge amount of debt. In essence, keep the stock high, fool the public and Wall Street, and hope they could keep things hidden until they figured out a way to right the sinking ship.'

'How?'

'How'd they cover up? Again, this is just a guess, but I'd say they've been screwing around with retirement funds, IRAs, and pension plans, a lot like Enron did. If that's true, there are going to be a lot of angry, broke people. It'll make the Enron thing look like small potatoes. I've also been hearing rumors about SPEs gone wild.'

Justin forced himself to think back to his business school days.

SPE . . . Special Something Something . . . Special Purpose . . . Entities! That was it. A way for corporations to hide money. They'd create a company within a company, make someone the CEO with signing power, and, like magic, you had a financial structure that could work outside of any corporate rules. That CEO could authorize salaries – including his own – and designate payments for board members. Without anyone else even knowing about it. Big business was a world where rules were something to be bent or broken. Another reason why Justin liked being a cop: you could play around with the rules but ultimately there were limits. Once you exceeded those, you had to pay the price.

'Special Purpose Entities?' Justin said now. 'Good way to make sure someone's taking out a lot of cash if the company's going down the drain.'

Jonathan spoke up, a touch of relief in his voice. 'I'm glad to see that Princeton wasn't a total waste of time and money.'

'SPEs are a great way to hide a lot of crooked things,' Mallone said. 'And to buy a lot of favors, which EGenco has certainly done. I mean, look at their presence in Iraq and other parts of the Middle East. They don't get there unless they're paying a lot of people a lot of money. It doesn't just happen that they get no-bid government contracts for billions of bucks to reconstruct an entire country.'

'You said something about lawsuits,' Justin said. 'What's that all about?'

Mallone tapped the suitcase. 'You'll have your reading cut out for you. There are several hundred pages of those babies in here. The two most interesting ones are from STE and New York.'

'Okay, you've lost me.'

'STE – Save the Earth. The ecological group. They had the suit that the Supreme Court just rejected.'

'Oh, right. About the energy policy, right?'

'About the meeting that set the energy policy. It got a ton of publicity and it's all in the suitcase.'

'What'd you mean about New York being the other interesting suit?'

'I'm not a legal expert. You're better off reading the filings. I also downloaded a bunch of articles off the Net that'll help give everything some perspective. The thing you have to understand is that this country's so politically divided, it's hard to know what's valid or not. I mean, half the people hate our vice president so much, they'll do anything to harass him. And the other half will do anything to validate his actions. I can't say if these suits are valid or if they're politically motivated.'

'When was Dandridge involved with EGenco?'

'Involved? He was more than involved, Jay. He was their CEO from . . . ohhh . . . I'd say for about eight years, right up until he ran for VP. When he got the nomination, he resigned.'

'And ended his connection?'

'Hardly. I can't tell you how much stock he still owns, but I guarantee it's a hell of a lot.'

'It's all in a blind trust,' Jonathan Westwood added. 'Common practice for elected officials."

'That's his financial connection. And he certainly didn't end his personal connections. Or his political connections, for that matter. Brad Collins probably raised more money for Anderson and Dandridge than anyone in the country. EGenco loaned them their private jets during the campaign, supplied a fortune to PAC groups under the guise of organizing nonprofit organizations, whatever they could do.'

'All this stuff . . . the things that are being investigated . . . the business irregularities . . . happened under Dandridge's watch.'

'That's the question. Very little has been made public.'

'And the lawsuit about the energy policy . . .'

'Same answer. These guys are so damn secretive. And no one's been able to force Dandridge to reveal a thing. Thus the lawsuits.'

'But what's being thrown around as an accusation . . .'

'What's being thrown around is that Dandridge, soon after he and Anderson were elected, called a meeting of some of the top energy experts in the country. And that's where they set the administration's energy policies. Which were, obviously, extraordinarily favorable to the energy industry. The only irregularity, the only bump in the policy, was when they shocked everyone and went against the oil companies to protect that land up in Alaska.'

'The National Petroleum Reserve,' Jonathan put in. 'It's several million acres.'

'Yeah,' Justin said. 'I read about that. Why do you think they did that?'

'Why do they do anything?' Jonathan's dad answered. 'Political expediency. They feel confident they've got big business and energy support no matter what they do. So I assume this was a nod to environmentalists, a way to stave off criticism that they're in anyone's pockets. Pretty effective, too.'

'So who was at the big energy policy meeting?' Justin asked.

Mallone shrugged. 'No one knows. That's part of what they're refusing to release. All I've got are rumors.'

Now Jonathan Westwood shook his head and said, 'Christ, everyone knows who was there. It was Dandridge's cronies from EGenco and a few of the Saudis.'

'Why would they include the Saudis?' Justin asked his father.

'Why would they tell the Saudis about attacking Iraq before they tell their own secretary of state? Because the relationships between Dandridge and Anderson and the Saudis go way beyond anything political. They've all made each other rich. The Saudis don't

247

do anything that'll piss us off – at least not when it comes to oil supplies and prices – and we don't do anything to piss them off. We keep them in power – we've got military forces over there to make sure no one rises up against them – and they make guys like Dandridge and Anderson even richer. And you wonder why no one trusts politicians.'

Justin took a deep breath. What the hell was he doing? He was supposed to be investigating a rigged plane crash. Now he was talking about Saudi royalty and the vice president of the United States and oil prices and SPEs. He wanted a nice little shot glass of scotch. Maybe even two. Or, now that he thought about it, three. Instead, he gulped from a plastic bottle of Fiji Water and listened as his father took over the conversation, explaining what he knew – either personally or secondhand – about the past and present personalities that ran EGenco. Justin absorbed a crash course in big-money backroom political relationships and financial kickbacks and government contracts and the cost of money. And he'd never been so glad in his entire life to hear a knock at his front door because his head was spinning and he was overwhelmed at how all he'd meant to do was open a door just a crack and what he'd really done was let in a cyclone.

He had to smile when he opened his front door for real. The cyclone analogy was not a terrible one, because standing there was Bruno Pecozzi and a woman Justin thought might be the most beautiful woman he'd ever seen.

'Thought you might like to have some lunch,' Bruno said. 'This is Connie Martin. She's the star of the movie I'm working on. We're hungry and I told her about you so she thought maybe you'd want to get a sandwich.'

'Nice to meet you,' Justin said to the actress. To Bruno he said, 'How'd you find the house?'

'Very difficult," Bruno told him. 'But you know I have, how shall I put this? – contacts. So I made a few calls and asked around and then, 'cause I'm kind of a nut, I looked you up in the fuckin' phone book. You gonna ask us in or what?'

Justin stepped aside and waved them forward. 'We were in the middle of a business meeting, but I think we can use a break.'

'Mr Westwood.' Bruno recognized Justin's father, took a step toward Jonathan. 'Pleased to meet you.'

'Bruno Pecozzi,' Justin said, as his father's eyes narrowed and he moved his hand in Bruno's direction so it could be shaken. 'And Connie Martin.'

Justin turned to see that Roger Mallone's mouth was agape and his jaw had dropped, cartoon-like, as far as a human jaw could stretch. At first Justin thought it was a not uncalled-for response to Connie Martin's presence. Then he realized that Roger wasn't paying the slightest bit of attention to the blonde woman in jeans and a midriff-baring T-shirt. He was staring at the huge man who was dominating Justin's living room.

'Hey,' Bruno said, turning slowly to Mallone, 'I know you.'

Roger didn't say anything or make a motion to shake hands. He just swallowed deeply, and then Bruno said, 'Where do I know you from?' When Roger still said nothing, Bruno snapped his fingers and said, 'You were on the jury.' He turned to Connie. 'Talk about your small world. I was on trial for somethin' . . . not a big deal . . . and this guy was on the jury.' Turning back to Roger, he said, 'Right? I never forget the face of a juror.'

'That's right,' Mallone said. He spoke as if the words were physically stuck in his throat.

Turning to Connie Martin, Justin added, 'It was a little bit more of a deal than Bruno's making it out to be. He was on trial for loan sharking and extortion, if I recall.'

249

'Yeah, somethin' like that,' Bruno said.

'He got off because one juror refused to convict. Seems to me there was a decent amount of talk about jury tampering.'

'You musta been one of the ones voting guilty, huh?' Bruno said to Roger.

The financial adviser, as white as Justin had ever seen him, nodded stiffly.

'Don't worry about it,' Bruno said. 'I don't hold a grudge. And the whole thing had a happy ending anyway, right? So forget about it.'

Bruno stuck out his hand and, with one more gulp, Roger shook it.

'So we gonna have lunch or what?' Bruno said. 'My treat.'

chapter 21

Nuri Al-Bazaad sat in his Buick, in the parking lot of the fast-food restaurant, and used the cell phone he'd been given to make the call he'd been instructed to make. When the voice on the other end answered, all it said was, 'How long?' Nuri had already calculated the time it would take to get out of his car, walk into the restaurant, and find what he needed to find.

'Two minutes and twenty seconds,' he said into the phone.

The voice said, 'You have three minutes. Starting . . . now.'

Nuri was already moving when he hung up the phone. Out the door, across the lot, past the five or six big American cars parked there. Through the heavy glass door. Step inside. He looked around, as he'd done during his test run, but things had changed. They had moved. No. Just two of them had moved. The third one was right where she'd been.

Nuri had to make a decision. He went for the two. They were standing in front of a small counter that held ketchup and mustard and napkins and plastic forks and spoons. He went up to the person he was supposed to go up to. They had said not to talk, just to stand there, but he wanted to speak, wanted to say something that might be comforting. So he walked right to her, leaned forward, and spoke into her ear.

'You're very lucky,' he said.

She backed away from him and he saw a look of fear cross her face.

'You're lucky,' he said again. 'Soon there will be music everywhere. Like surround sound. And there will be great warmth. You will all be protected and happy.'

The woman looked at him like he was mad. Then she turned back to the table, back to the second child, who was smiling. The child waved to her mother.

The mother began to scream.

And then Nuri's cell phone rang.

chapter 22

They got a table at Art's Deco Diner, a casual place in the middle of town, decorated in black and white and chrome. It was on Main Street, tucked between the 1950s-style movie theater that usually showed artsy foreign films, and an equally old-fashioned five-and-dime. Art had owned the restaurant for years, periodically changing its identity so it didn't become as stuck in the past as his neighbors on either side. At various times he'd had a small art gallery, a Zen temple, a resting room for pets, and a video arcade at the front of the restaurant; for the past year he'd converted the space into a bookstore with a short rack of magazines and international newspapers. Art was in his early fifties and knew his way around a kitchen. Anytime anyone mentioned to him that he was a terrific chef, he always said the same thing: 'Cook. Not chef. I'm a cook. Big difference.'

Bruno Pecozzi didn't care about the difference. He loved the food at the Deco Diner, and to prove it, after everyone had given their orders to the waiter, Bruno ordered two complete pork chop lunches, including two orders of mashed potatoes, two mixed green salads, and two orders of spinach. While they were waiting for the food to arrive, he began to regale them with stories about life on the movie set. Justin couldn't help notice that while he talked, one of Connie Martin's hands was firmly planted on Bruno's thigh.

Midway through the lunch, the front door opened and three of Justin's police officers sauntered in – Mike Haversham, Gary Jenkins, and Reggie Bokkenheuser. As they headed for their booth, they all saw Justin, hesitated, unsure exactly what the social protocol called for, then continued on. As they passed by, Gary and Mike mumbled, 'Hey, Chief,' and gave a half wave, but didn't slow down. Reggie stopped to say hello, realized that Mike and Gary had left her behind, so she flushed red and started to hurry to join them. But Justin reached her, touched her wrist, so she slowed again, then stopped, taking a step back so she could face the table. Justin introduced her around. He saw the surprise on her face when he told her the older man at the table was his father, and she showed no reaction when he gave her Bruno's name, except for her eyes, which couldn't help but scan his bulk and widen a bit in awe. She smiled at Connie Martin and said that she was a big fan. Connie smiled graciously in return, then Reggie moved on to join her coworkers.

'Cops are definitely gettin' better-lookin',' Bruno said.

Justin shrugged off the comment, but he could see the way his father and Bruno were looking at him. Bruno's gaze shifted from Justin over to Reggie, then back to Justin. He didn't say another word about it, just nodded as if he'd confirmed something in his own mind.

The lunch went on, Justin's father a bit amazed at Bruno's stories, Roger Mallone finally regaining some color in his face, and then the phone at the bar rang and, as part of the background, he heard Art answer the phone, say, louder than normal, 'What?! Jesus Christ!' Justin turned around, saw Art hurriedly slam the phone down, go to the television that hung in the corner of the bar, and use the remote control to click it on. Art switched to CNN and Justin saw several customers get up and rush to stand in front of the TV. He heard the solemn tone of the commentator, then without saying anything, he too stood and moved to the bar. He found himself standing next to Reggie, and he realized the entire restaurant had surged forward. They were all circling the television, and there was total silence except for the newscaster's voice, saying, 'Again, this just breaking story coming to us from outside Washington, D.C. Edwin McElvy is standing by outside the McDonald's in Silver Spring, Maryland, the site of what is apparently the latest suicide terrorist bombing here on American soil. Edwin?'

The scene on the television shifted to an African American reporter standing across the street from a McDonald's. In the background, firemen were working fervently to put out the flames that enveloped the boxlike structure. The building was basically a shell, with smoke clouding whatever was left standing. The odd thing was that the golden arches in front of the building – the ultimate corporate symbol – had been untouched. The smoke seemed to give them a divine glow as they loomed above and behind the newscaster.

'Thank you, Al. Another tragic bombing has occurred, the third on American soil in the past several weeks, this time shattering this quiet D.C. suburb and striking at perhaps the ultimate symbol of American culture. The bomber, who was killed in the explosion, apparently strolled into the fast-food restaurant at approximately one-thirty this afternoon, a little over half an hour ago. According to one of the two survivors, a young woman who worked behind the counter, a Middle Eastern-looking man came in, walked up to a customer, a woman in her forties, who was there with two young children, and said something to her. The witness, a young woman named Dinitia Ogilvie, did not hear what was said, but she reports

255

that the woman began to scream uncontrollably. Mere moments later, the bomb went off. Approximately fifteen customers were killed, along with the entire McDonald's staff, with the exception of Ms Ogilvie.'

'Edwin, excuse me for interrupting.' This was from the first newscaster, Al something, back in the studio. 'Were there any survivors other than Ms Ogilvie?'

'One little girl survived, Al. I don't have any of the details, or any identification. The only information I've got is that she seemed to be around eight or nine years old and she was hurt quite badly. She's been taken to St Joseph's Hospital in Washington where the medics were not sanguine about her chances, but, of course, right now the whole world is hoping and praying for her and we'll keep everyone apprised of her condition. It's somewhat of a miracle she's made it this far.'

'Thank you. Is there any information at all about the bomber himself or about the reason for this particular target?'

'Right now, Al, we don't know anything about the bomber. The FBI has not been able to even enter the building so far. As you can see, firemen are still battling to put out the blaze. So anything I reported would be merely conjecture or rumor, and that's not what the situation calls for.'

'No, that's absolutely right. Thank you, Edwin McElvy. A very good job under very difficult and traumatic circumstances. We'll be back to you as events develop.'

The newscaster began a rehash of recent events – the explosions at Harper's and La Cucina – and Justin turned away. He was overcome by something he hadn't felt in a long time. Rage. He could feel the blood rushing to his head and he looked down to find his hands clenched. The customers at Art's had broken their silence now but Justin couldn't understand anything they were saying. It was a cacophony of noise and, as he started to sway at the bar, he felt the rush of conversation turn into something physical and stifling and he realized he had to get out of there fast. He was going to burst and he knew what could happen, what he was capable of, when things burst inside of him. So he began pushing his way through the crowd. Head down, he made a path for the front door, vaguely aware that his father was watching him curiously, that Bruno saw what was happening, that someone was in his way but then Bruno was there and the guy was gone, lifted out of Justin's path, then Justin was outside, on Main Street, in the cold. He'd left his jacket inside the restaurant but he was sweating as he stood on the street. His breath was coming hard and quick. He forced himself to slow it down. He remembered what Deena had taught him during her yoga lessons: breathe deeply, breathe through the nose, let the breath go all the way through, feel it in your face and your neck, your chest, all the way down and out . . .

He was feeling better. The world was coming back into focus. The red and yellow lights that were flashing behind his eyes had gone away. And then he felt someone come out from behind him, step out from the restaurant to join him on the street. He turned. It was Reggie. She'd left her coat behind, too, and as she stepped to be beside him, her arms went wrapped around her torso and she shivered. They stood together, saying nothing, until she spoke quietly and gently.

'You all right?'

He liked the way she said it. Not condescending, not even too curious about what had set him off. Just concerned and letting him know that's the way she felt, no judgment involved.

He nodded. 'Better,' he said.

'It just got to you, huh? I mean, another explosion.'

This time he shook his head and she looked surprised. 'So what?' she asked.

'It was the target. The people who got killed there.' He swallowed deeply. Took another slow yoga breath.

'What target?' When he didn't answer, she said, 'You mean specific people?' This time, when he gave a quick, curt nod, she said, 'But they don't know who was in the place. They don't know the identity of the victims yet.'

'I do,' Justin said.

'How can—'

'Where was I yesterday?' he asked. And when her eyes just narrowed, he said, 'Silver Spring.'

'You're talking about the pilot's family.'

'Yeah.'

'But just 'cause you were there, that doesn't mean—'

'Yes it does.'

She kept quiet, stared at him intently as if trying to figure out which one he was: smart or crazy.

'The little girl I talked to. She said she and her sister wanted to go to McDonald's but their mother was too afraid to take them out. I told her she'd get to go soon, that she should help her mother get over her fear.' He exhaled an icy breath. 'I guess she felt a little safer after I left. Or else she didn't care anymore.'

'Jay, you don't really know it was them.'

'A little nine-year-old girl. Hannah. They said the guy, the bomber, went up to a woman with two kids. The one that's still alive, barely, they said she was eight or nine. A mother and two kids, same age, it's not a coincidence. I went and talked to them and now they're dead. Or might as well be.'

'Why?' she breathed. 'Why would they kill a mother and two little girls?'

'I don't know,' he said. And shaking his head, he said it again. 'I don't know. But I'm going to find out. I'm going to find out why and I'm going to find out who.'

She kept quiet now, which was the right thing to do. They stood out there together, maybe ten more minutes, until Bruno came out, alone.

'You want me to take your dad and that other guy to the airport?' he asked Justin.

Justin nodded.

'You gonna need me for anything after that?'

'No. Thank you.'

'I don't like this shit either, Jay. So if you need my particular skill sets, whenever that might be, I'm offerin'.'

Justin raised his eyes wearily, an acceptance of Bruno's offer. Then Bruno went inside, returned a few moments later with Jonathan Westwood, Roger Mallone, and Connie Martin. The actress looked concerned. Mallone looked frightened. Justin's father was impassive. He said nothing to his son, but he did reach out and gently squeeze his arm.

'Bruno,' Justin said. 'Check with the pilot. Make sure no one, and I mean no one, had any physical contact with the plane. If anyone did, make sure it's checked out before it takes off.'

'I don't think that'll be necessary,' Jonathan said. 'It's my usual pilot. He couldn't be more trustworthy.'

'But these aren't the usual circumstances,' Justin told him. To Bruno he said, 'Check out every little detail.'

'If you need anything, let me know,' his father told him.

'Hopefully, you've given me enough. But I will. Thank you.'

'Jay,' his father said, then stopped. His lips were pursed as if the words were stuck inside.

'Go ahead and say whatever you want to say.'

'The thing is, I don't think I have anything to say. I feel like I should give you some advice, but I doubt there's anything I could tell you that you don't already know.'

'I guess we'll see soon enough,' Justin said.

Jonathan nodded crisply and Bruno led his group down Main Street to where his SUV was parked. Justin couldn't help himself; he held his breath when the engine started up. As the car pulled onto the road, he relaxed.

'The big guy. Bruno,' Reggie said. 'What *are* his particular skill sets?'

'Pretty much what you think they are.'

'Must be nice to have so many people who want to help you out.'

'I guess it is.'

'You need any more help?' she asked.

'Yeah,' he said. 'I think I'm gonna need all the help I can get.'

chapter 23

Associated Press story, circulated on America Online

Updated: 03:37 PM EDT
President Anderson Approval Rating
Carries VP Dandridge to Top of Polls
By DEB REYNOSO, AP
November 21

Concerns About Civil Liberties
Dismissed by Attorney General
Priority Given to War on Terror

Washington, D.C. – According to the latest Gallup Poll, the recent spate of terrorist activity within the United States has propelled President Thomas Anderson from the lowest to the highest approval rating he has achieved in the three years of his presidency. In the wake of those positive numbers, Vice President Phillip Dandridge now has an unprecedented lead over any possible opposition in next year's presidential race.

Prior to the suicide bombing of Harper's Restaurant in East Hampton, New York, on November 4 of this year, the percentage of

Americans who approved of President Anderson's performance stood at 42%. The poll has a margin of error of plus/minus 4%. According to those questioned in September of this past year, the President's numbers were down because the majority of people disapproved of the way he was handling the economy as well as the ongoing military situation in Iraq, the various human rights scandals that have emerged there, and what Secretary of State Clayton Bendix calls 'The Path to Peace' in the Middle East. As a result of such negative reaction, Vice President Dandridge's poll ratings were dragged down as well. The Vice President lagged well behind his two likely opponents for next year's election. The poll now shows, however, that an overwhelming 91% of the American people approve of the job President Anderson is doing. A nearly equal amount, 88%, support the Triumph of Freedom Act the President is currently attempting to pass through Congress. The legislation is the centerpiece of the administration's self-declared war on terrorism.

Carried by President Anderson's newfound popularity and support, Vice President Dandridge's numbers have surged. He is now viewed favorably by 78% of the American population – up nearly 30% from the previous poll – and 67% of registered voters now say they will support him in the next presidential election.

There has been muted criticism from political opponents that the President and, in particular, Vice President Dandridge and Attorney General Jeffrey Stuller, are using the Triumph of Freedom Act to greatly limit civil liberties, as well as to cement their political standings, but the public does not seem to agree. The Vice President stated yesterday, 'No one wants to erode or abridge anyone's civil rights, especially the President and myself. However, as President Anderson and Attorney General Stuller have said repeatedly, what people must understand is that we are at war.

And during wartime, priorities must sometimes shift away from the idealistic and toward reality. Right now, the reality is that we must and will do everything possible to protect our country and our country's citizens from further attacks. That is the President's priority, and it is, he believes, the country's priority. To that end, his hands must not be tied and he must be able to deal with these unprecedented attacks.'

According to the Gallup Poll, President Anderson and his likely successor have correctly assessed the desires of the American people and the Congress. The Triumph of Freedom Act is expected to unanimously pass through both the House and the Senate within a matter of days. During the same period of time, the Supreme Court is due to make a ruling on the treatment of prisoners being held as suspected terrorists at Guantanamo Bay. The President has drawn a line in the sand, openly declaring that any and all prisoners seized during combat with Afghanistan and Iraq, or as suspects connected with any act of terrorism, shall be considered 'enemy combatants' and thus not subject to the rules of the Geneva Conventions. If the court rules in the administration's favor as it is expected to do, and if the Triumph of Freedom Act passes, terrorist suspects will be able to be detained and questioned for an indeterminate length and with no right to legal counsel.

At a press conference, Shirley Greene, the lawyer for five men living in upstate New York recently accused of being members of a terrorist cell and currently being detained at the U.S. military base at Gitmo, as it is often called, said, 'No one is denying the horror of the acts [such as yesterday's McDonald's suicide bombing] being committed. And no one wants an end to such acts more than I do. But the ramifications of what the President and Attorney General Stuller are trying to do are at least as terrifying as the terrorist acts themselves. Mr Stuller wants us to understand that we are at war.

Well, even during wartime, people have rights. The reason we're fighting this war is to preserve the very rights that Attorney General Stuller is trying to take away from us.'

Mr Stuller did not respond directly to Ms Greene's criticism, but at a separate press conference, he did say, 'This is not the time for anyone to be questioning our government's commitment to freedom or to give any encouragement to an enemy bent on destroying everything this country has stood for and fought for since its inception. I will not dignify such criticism with a response other than to say that those critics will also be protected from terrorist activities by our actions and our policies.'

President Anderson issued a statement saying that he fully supported Mr Stuller and his handling of the terrorist attacks. 'We have done a remarkable job gathering information,' the statement said, 'under the supervision and leadership of Attorney General Stuller. I expect that the whole country will soon realize, when new facts come to light and this terrorist cell that's attacking our country is destroyed once and for all, what an extraordinary job he's doing. It will not be long before the siege we have experienced is over and the evildoers responsible for it are brought to swift and final justice.'

The only voice of caution within the government has been from Assistant Attorney General Ted Ackland, who is often mentioned as a possible vice presidential running mate for Mr Dandridge. Mr Ackland said that he supported the steps taken by the administration to curtail terrorist activity but he acknowledged the dangers that come with such steps.

'I understand the concerns that citizens have about the potential for the abuse of the rights of individuals,' he said. 'I share them. Most thinking, caring people do. But those concerns must, at least momentarily, be weighed against the concerns for the greater good. If we should ever lose the war on terrorism, such rights would be nonexistent. My belief is that we should put a time limit on this proposed legislation, see how the government handles its newfound power, and then reexamine the situation. Wartime is no time to panic or to make irrevocable decisions. It's a time to lead decisively but thoughtfully. It's also a time to constantly examine one's decisions so errors can be corrected and we can move into the future with a clear sight and sound mind.'

Attorney General Stuller had no comment on Mr Ackland's comments but he did stress that he agreed with the President's position that the Triumph of Freedom Act should be passed as a permanent fixture of this and future governments.

CNN Moneyline *story, circulated on America Online*

Oil Prices Percolate Close
To Record Levels
November 21

London – World oil prices bubbled to record highs today as OPEC's top official said producers were powerless to manage a spike driven by factors outside its control.

U.S. crude futures by 1600 GMT were up 8 cents at $55.25 a barrel, surpassing Friday's $53.92, to reach an all-time high in the 21-year history of the New York Mercantile Exchange contract.

Crude rebounded strongly on Wednesday from a reversal early in the week that raised hopes among consumer nations that the worst might be over for an oil price scare threatening to blunt global economic growth.

Struggling to cope with growth in fuel demand fired by world economic expansion, OPEC says it can do little to douse prices now up more than 25 percent this year.

Cartel President Parnum Yasianto of Indonesia blamed hedge fund speculators, who have bet heavily on oil markets this year, and refinery bottlenecks in the United States.

'While the oil market still holds above $50 a barrel . . . that is due to factors beyond OPEC's scope,' Parnum told a press conference in London.

Analysts agree that low stocks of gasoline in the United States are leading prices now.

But they say OPEC has helped create the conditions for an overheated market by restraining supplies so tightly that crude stocks are failing to rebuild as normal during the third and fourth quarters.

Gasoline Record

In the United States gasoline inventories rose slightly in the week to November 14 but remain four percent lower than a year ago, a substantial deficit when demand is running three percent higher year-on-year.

'There is a short-run situation that is very much associated with the problems of the U.S. gasoline market; problems that OPEC can do very little about,' said Dan Gross of Barnum Capital. 'The U.S. gasoline inventory situation remains highly precarious.'

U.S. gasoline futures traded on Thursday at a new record of $2.368 a gallon.

A firm decision on output is not expected until a full OPEC meeting in Beirut on January 3, by which time $50 oil and above could be more firmly established.

Spare cartel capacity is estimated at about 2.5 million bpd, limited mostly to Saudi Arabia. Real extra volumes might need to be added to change market psychology and prevent prices rising further later in the year, analysts say.

chapter 24

The coffee was cold, had been for a good twenty minutes, but Justin took another sip, peered down into the dregs of the paper cup, tilted his head back and drained the dark, bitter liquid. There was still a bit of black ooze clinging to the side, so he swirled it onto his finger and licked it off. It didn't make him feel any more awake.

It was now ten-fifteen in the morning. Things should be happening pretty soon. At least he hoped so. Justin had been sitting in the car since 7:30 A.M. He'd flown into D.C. the night before, the ten o'clock shuttle, checked into some crummy hotel near Dulles Airport, paid cash, just in case anyone tried to trace him, and set the alarm for five-thirty. In the two hours he'd been awake he'd driven back and forth over the route he expected to be using later, familiarizing himself as much as possible with the streets, looking for the right spot to do what he'd decided he was going to do. He was exhausted. Getting up that morning was about as difficult as anything he could remember doing in a long time. Maybe the second most difficult. First was leaving Reggie Bokkenheuser the night before.

She'd said, 'Do you need any more help?' and then they'd gone back to his place. He saw the way she was watching him, hungry, as if something had changed between them and she couldn't wait to comfort him. Or devour him. He wasn't sure which. He probably would have let her. No, that wasn't right. He was as hungry as she was, maybe even hungrier. He wouldn't have just *let* her, he would have gone right at her. But he was sitting by his desk and he began flipping through his mail, just for something to do, just so he didn't have to look her in the eye quite yet, and stuck in with his bills was a letter-size manila envelope, no return address on it. He ignored the rest of the mail, carefully tore the envelope open. Inside was a small piece of paper, memo pad size. The message on the paper was typed:

> *You don't call, you don't write, you don't e-mail. But who's complaining?*
>
> *My phones are tapped and I'm under surveillance. If you want to get in touch with me, call Bruce's Gym. Ask for Leyla. She'll give me any message.*
>
> *You were right.*
>
> *Jacks were found at La Cucina. A whole bunch of 'em.*
>
> *You always were a smart boy.*
>
> *—W*

That was the end of his hunger. At least the hunger for Reggie. The note from Wanda Chinkle made his throat tighten and his stomach roil with pain. The last time he'd felt this way he'd killed four people and beaten another one close to death. So he looked up at Reggie and told her the kind of help he wanted her to give him now. She didn't say a word, just nodded and smiled. A smile that said they both knew what additional kind of help would be waiting when he wanted it. Then he made a call. To Colonel Eugene T. Zanesworth. He wasn't put through at first, but he stressed how urgent it was, and finally Zanesworth got on the phone. Chilly at first. No. Icy. Justin told him he had crucial information about Hutchinson Cooke's murder, and when the colonel still resisted, Justin said he knew what had happened and they needed to talk. He wouldn't go to Andrews, he insisted they meet someplace neutral, someplace, he said, where he'd be sure to be safe. He wanted a restaurant, he told Zanesworth, someplace with a lot of people, very public. The colonel scoffed, said, 'Are you saying you don't trust me?' and Justin, knowing he had to play this just right, knowing he had to appear smart but not too smart, said, 'That's exactly what I'm saying, Colonel. Try not to take it personally. Right now I don't trust anyone. And I want a suit-and-tie kind of place. Calm and fancy, so if there's a disturbance it'll be obvious.' So Zanesworth picked a place, Justin agreed, said he'd fly out in the morning, would get to the restaurant by twelve-thirty.

And that's when he said good-bye to Reggie, because he had no intention of leaving in the morning. He was, he hoped, a lot smarter than that. He threw a toothbrush, a shirt, a pair of socks, and some underwear into a gym bag, then he drove straight to La Guardia, caught the 10 P.M. shuttle to D.C., checked into the hotel. Justin knew that as soon as they'd arranged their meeting, Zanesworth would call someone, FBI or private cops, whoever had been talking to him up until now. And he knew the cops would immediately make a precise and detailed plan. He figured they'd want Zanesworth to get to the restaurant an hour and a half early, maybe even two hours, hoping to set up before Justin could. But he didn't believe in taking any chances whatsoever, so he'd prepared for as many alternatives as he could, and was in position several hours before he expected Zanesworth to move. There could be no mistakes.

Of course, while he waited, he did nothing but think of all the things that could go wrong.

He'd mapped out the route from Andrews to the restaurant Zanesworth had chosen, and driven it, round trip, seven times before he felt comfortable. He knew it only made sense for the colonel's car to make a right turn coming out of the Air Force base. And he was certain Zanesworth would come to the base in the morning – he was a business-as-usual kind of guy. That's why Justin had made the meet for lunch, so the officer wouldn't just take the first part of the day off. And Justin knew the way cops handled this sort of thing – they'd be at the meeting place, have it staked out from hell to high water, expecting Justin to show up there early if he were trying to be clever. He had it all figured out, absolutely. Unless Zanesworth knew a shortcut and made a left or the colonel decided to stay home until the big meal or unless these cops were different and smarter and came with Zanesworth, picked him up from the departure point rather than at the meet.

No. He had to try to put all that out of his mind. This would work. would definitely work. Wouldn't it?

Yes.

It was working.

At least so far.

Ten-twenty-two and there was Zanesworth's car. He had a driver, which Justin had figured on, probably the young officer who'd escorted Justin to his parking space the time he'd come to meet the colonel. Justin started up the engine of his rental car. Waited. Let them get half a block ahead. There didn't seem to be any cars accompanying the colonel. It was definitely working.

About five blocks from the base, they reached one of the streets that Justin had decided would suffice – it was quiet but not too quiet; he wanted a few people around so things didn't appear suspicious right from the start – and then he stuck the baseball cap he'd brought along on his head, and sped up. When Colonel

Zanesworth's driver stopped at the stop sign, Justin didn't slow down. He rammed straight into the back of the officer's car. Without hesitating, Justin hopped out of his car, sauntered up to the car with the smashed-in back fender. He knew the colonel was expecting him to be in a suit and tie – as Justin had specified over the phone – so he figured he had an extra few moments before he was recognized in his jeans and baseball cap. He went to the driver's window, saw that Zanesworth's chauffeur was indeed the same officer escort Justin had already met, but it was the back door that opened a few inches. The colonel stuck his head outside and started his sentence with, 'We're involved in government business right now, we can't—' but he stopped speaking when the muzzle of Justin's gun was placed firmly up against his left eye.

'Shove over, Colonel,' he said. And when the officer hesitated, Justin added, 'I probably won't shoot you in the head but I sure as shit'll put one right in your knee or someplace that'll hurt like hell. So just do what I say and it'll be fine.' And as he slid inside the car to sit next to Zanesworth, Justin said to the driver, 'Keep both hands on the wheel until I tell you different. If one finger so much as comes loose, I'll cripple your colonel for life. You got that?'

The young officer said, 'Yes, sir,' and Justin closed the door behind him.

'Make a right turn,' he told the driver. 'Go slow, as if you're just pulling away from the accident so you don't block traffic. Then go two blocks and make another right.'

The colonel started to talk but Justin tapped him with the gun – not as lightly as he might have, he wanted it to hurt. 'Shut up,' he said, and he was almost embarrassed how satisfying it was to speak those words. He then did a quick frisk, took a pistol out of Zanesworth's shoulder holster.

The driver had now made the second right. Justin told him to go one more block and make a left. They went about ten blocks farther, turning a few more times. Justin saw that no one was following them, so he told the driver to stop and pull over. They were in a business area near a strip mall and a few small stores.

'Colonel,' Justin said, 'get down on the floor, facedown, hands interlaced behind your back. Once you're there, if I see you move, I'll shoot you.'

Justin opened the car door on his side, stepped outside, and watched Zanesworth settle into his position. Then he tapped the driver on the back of the head with his gun, said, 'Okay, Junior, I'm going to open your door. Keep your hands completely visible at all times and get out of the car.'

They managed that maneuver. Justin took a pistol off the driver, made sure he had no other weapons, then he said, 'Step behind the car here and get undressed.'

'What?'

'Give me the keys to the car first, then take your clothes off.'

'Why?'

'Here's the way it works in the real world. Say another word and I'll beat you senseless. Now get out of your clothes. Fast.'

The officer clamped his mouth shut, kicked off his shoes and removed his shirt and pants.

'Underwear and socks, too,' Justin told him.

The young officer glared but said nothing. And then he was completely naked.

'Okay,' Justin said. 'Crouch down behind the car, here on the curb side.'

The young officer followed instructions. Then Justin went around to the street side, opened the door, reached inside the car, and grabbed Zanesworth by the neck. He pulled the colonel roughly out

273

onto the street, then quickly shoved him back into the passenger seat in the front.

Justin strode quickly back to the driver's side, got in, and started up the engine. 'Have a nice day,' he said to the naked officer, and drove away.

Half a block later, Zanesworth said, quietly, 'There was no need to humiliate the lieutenant like that.'

'Sure there was,' Justin said. 'I'm hoping I don't need you for long, Colonel, I just need one piece of information. And it's going to take a naked guy with no ID at least fifteen or twenty minutes to get anyone to pay attention to *anything* he says. Hopefully you'll be heading home long before then.'

When Zanesworth didn't respond, Justin said, 'Thinking of all kinds of threats to make? Hard to think of any that don't sound really clichéd, isn't it?'

'You can't possibly get away with this,' Zanesworth answered.

'See what I mean?'

'You're as good as dead.'

'Colonel, I've been as good as dead for a pretty long time, so that doesn't exactly get me shaking in my boots.'

'I'm not giving you any information.'

'We'll see.'

'Son, I don't know what the hell you're thinking—'

'I'll tell you what I'm thinking, Colonel. I'm thinking that you're an arrogant, egotistical, pompous asshole who's boxed himself into a corner. You've spent so many years giving orders and taking orders that you don't know your ass from your elbow. I also don't think you're all that smart. How am I doing so far?'

Zanesworth didn't answer. Justin shrugged and went on. 'But you're a military lifer, right? So I do think you're smart enough to know when it's time to retreat. And it's time, Colonel. You picked the wrong side. I don't think you even knew you were picking a side, that's how well you were played. Somebody called you about eighteen months ago, said they needed a pilot. That it was business but it was patriotic business. Whoever it was sold you a pretty good case that this was a matter of national security. Must have been someone pretty high up, who could get your attention. You want to hear more?'

'I'm listening,' Zanesworth said.

'Maybe it was someone who Captain Cooke had flown, someone who was comfortable with Cooke. And who Cooke trusted. Shit,' Justin said, 'I think I just answered my first question. No wonder you paid attention.'

'I'm not confirming anything,' Zanesworth told him.

'And I'm not done talking.' Justin told him about Hutchinson Cooke now, about the rigged manifold in his plane, about going to talk to Cooke's wife and how, a day later, they were the targets of the McDonald's suicide bomber. When he heard about the timing of the bomb, Colonel Eugene Zanesworth's whole body seemed to collapse into the seat.

'You want me to tell you about the other bombs, Colonel? About how they aren't what you're being told they are? How the first one was used to murder Bradford Collins and the second one to kill a nasty little guy who worked for the FAA?'

Zanesworth was white as a ghost. 'Martin Heffernan?'

'Is he the one who called to tell you that Cooke was dead?'

Zanesworth was staring straight ahead. Justin could tell he was considering his options.

'I can't prove it, Colonel, but I'm reasonably sure that Heffernan's the one who killed your captain.' And over the next silence, 'If you're in on it, I promise you I'll bring you down. If you were just a dupe, which is what I think, I'll do my best to leave you out of it. But I need the pieces. Now. It's a big, dangerous puzzle and I'm missing too many pieces to solve it. So first tell me who arranged for Cooke to go to work for Midas.' Then quietly, 'Was it the vice president, Colonel? Was it Phil Dandridge?'

'Yes. Yes it was.'

'And who called you to say that Cooke was dead?'

'Heffernan.'

Justin nodded, instantly pulled out his cell phone and dialed. 'Hey,' he said when Gary Jenkins answered the phone at the East End police station. 'Your brother in school?'

'Chief?'

'Let's skip the formalities, okay? Is your brother in school?'

'Well . . . sure . . . I guess.'

'I want you to get him out of class.'

'Now?'

'Not just now. Five minutes ago. The school's what, five blocks from the station?'

I guess.

'Well I don't want you to walk. I want you to drive. And I want you to use your siren. Go ninety. Then get him out of class, take him to the station, and tell him I want him to hack into New York phone company records. He's done it for me before.'

'Sure. Okay. What do you want him to get?'

'I want the records for all calls coming in and out of Martin Heffernan's apartment on November sixth, seventh and eighth. I'm particularly interested in any calls he made to Washington, D.C., on those dates. You got it?'

'Yeah, sure . . . uh . . .'

'Gary, stop talking and get in the fuckin' car. You got my cell number?'

'Yeah.'

'Well call me as soon as he has the info. If I know Ben he'll have it in about ten minutes.' He hung up.

Zanesworth was staring at Justin as if he were a madman. 'A schoolboy,' he said. 'That's who you've got on *your* side?'

'You'd be surprised,' Justin said, 'what the youth of America is capable of.'

It took thirteen minutes for Gary Jenkins to call back.

'Ben did it,' he said. 'But he—'

'Yeah, I know. Whatever he wants is fine.'

'TiVo. The one that tapes eighty hours.'

'Okay. As soon as I get back.'

'He wants the lifetime guarantee, too.'

'Just give me the information, Gary.'

'Okay, okay. There are two calls to D.C.' He read off the first number. 'That one was called in the afternoon of the seventh.'

'What's your phone number?' Justin said to Colonel Zanesworth. 'Your office number.'

Zanesworth told him and Justin impatiently said into the phone, 'Okay, that one's confirmed. What's the next one?' He listened as Gary rattled off the next number. Justin asked him to repeat it one more time. As soon as he heard it again, he hung up without even saying thank you, and immediately dialed.

He heard the voice answer on the other end of the phone, just one word, uttered in that bureaucratic monotone, then three more words, a little bit of life put into those, and Justin didn't answer. The voice on the other end of the line waited a moment, when there was no response said, 'Hello?' and Justin flicked his cell phone shut.

'You better get a story ready for where you've been this morning, Colonel.'

'Who answered the phone?'

'Things have just gotten even more complicated. So here's my

277

suggestion. The lieutenant had some kind of breakdown. You'll have plenty of witnesses for that. Just say he got out of the car and ran, maybe he threw the keys away and it took you twenty minutes to find them before you could go looking for him.'

'Who answered the phone, son?'

'The Justice Department,' Justin said quietly. 'The attorney general's office."

'Son of a bitch,' the colonel whispered.

And Justin, in much the same whisper, said, 'Yeah. I think that pretty much sums things up nicely.'

chapter 25

He didn't like being back at the house. For one thing, he wanted to get the hell out of Washington and back to East End Harbor. Not that East End would be any safer. But at least it was smaller. Here he felt like he was swimming around in a large fish tank, the only non-shark in the water. And all around him were people watching, just waiting for him to be eaten.

For another thing, being here felt too much like violating the dead.

Justin didn't believe in ghosts, but sitting in his rental car, staring out at the slightly overgrown lawn with its wintery patches of brown, looking at the silent white two-story house, the suburban lot felt haunted. Justin felt haunted. Right now the whole world felt haunted.

But he knew he didn't have much time. The place would be cleaned out soon, and Theresa Cooke was beyond caring about anything as trivial as breaking and entering, so Justin forced himself to open the car door and step out into the quiet street. Not breaking stride, determined to look as if he belonged there – as if he weren't an intruder; as if he weren't the reason the house was empty and silent and dead – he went up the walk to the front door. It didn't take him long to break in. Then, inside the foyer, he closed the door behind him and stood still, just listening. All he heard was the silence.

He went upstairs. There were three bedrooms, one master and two for the girls. He was momentarily stymied; he'd only been expecting one extra room, but he figured out which one was Hannah's – he checked the bookshelves; Reysa, the twelve-year-old, had a higher reading level – and he began his search. It didn't take long. He tried not to disturb her things. It didn't make sense, someone would be disturbing them soon enough, packing them up, giving them away, saving them, tossing them into the garbage, whatever, but Justin wanted no part of it. After a few minutes of combing through the dolls and toys, he shifted a large pink stuffed dog off to the side, away from the drawer it was blocking, and inside the drawer he saw what he was looking for.

He'd brought a manila envelope in his gym bag, along with a small piece of bubble wrap, and soon the envelope had a bulge in it. He'd put several dollars' worth of stamps on it before he left home, figuring that would be plenty. Justin sealed the envelope, and left the little girl's room, closing the door behind him. Then he was downstairs and out the front door, not bothering to lock it behind him – it made no difference now whether it was open or shut – and he walked back to the car.

Twenty minutes later, he noticed a mailbox on the street, in front of the entrance to a minimall. He pulled the car over, hopped out, and shoved the envelope into the box. He pulled into the mall when he saw a cell phone store. It took him less than fifteen minutes to buy and pay for a new phone with prepaid minutes. He didn't want to be traced, not for this call, anyway. Using the new phone, he got the number for Bruce's Gym in Boston. When a woman answered at the other end, Justin said, 'Leyla?'

'Hold on, I'll get her,' the voice said. And momentarily, another female voice was on, saying, 'Yup?'

'I need to speak to Wanda Chinkle,' he said. 'This is—'

'Bup-bup-bup-bup-bup . . . no need to gimme your name,' Leyla told him. 'You the troublemaker?'

'Yeah,' Justin said. 'That's me.'

'I ain't seen Wanda lately.'

'But you know how to get in touch with her.'

'Not so much. Not for the last forty-eight hours or so.'

'Why not?'

' 'Cause she ain't where she said she'd be. And I don't know where else she'd be goin'.'

Justin didn't say anything for quite a while, started to hang up, remembered that this woman Leyla was still holding on at the other end, so he just said, 'Thanks,' very softly and clicked the red off button on the phone.

She ain't where she said she'd be.

Wanda was missing.

He took a deep breath, felt a sharp pain rattle his chest – realized it was pain that stemmed from fear – and exhaled, hoping the pain would go away. It didn't. But he decided to ignore it. Decided to ignore the news about Wanda, too, because it was the only thing he could do right now. And thirty minutes after that he was at St Joseph's Hospital, which is where he knew he had to be, Wanda or no Wanda, because the news had reported that this was where the girl was being cared for.

At the front desk, Justin asked for the doctor who was in charge of Hannah Cooke. The nurse at the reception desk looked him over carefully, then lifted a phone and spoke into the receiver. It only took a few minutes after that for a youngish doctor to approach him, introduce himself as Dr Graham, and say that he was looking after Hannah. Justin asked if there was a place where they might have a couple of minutes of privacy, and Dr Graham took him into a nearby office.

Justin didn't bother to sit down, he just said, 'I want to make sure the girl gets the best care possible, and I'll pay for it.'

'Are you a relative?' Dr Graham asked.

'No.'

'A family friend?'

'I've met her,' Justin told him. 'It doesn't matter what my relationship is, does it, as long as I'm willing to pay?'

'I suppose not. But Hannah was badly injured. Parts of her body were badly burned and there's some disfigurement—'

'Is she going to survive?'

'I don't know yet. Not for certain. But I believe so.'

'I want her to have whatever reconstructive surgery is necessary. When this is over, if she lives, I'd like her to be as close to normal as possible.'

'The bills are going to be—'

'I don't care what they're going to be.' Justin handed over a credit card. 'Run this through. If you reach any kind of a limit, which I don't think you will, just let me know and I'll provide more.'

'Mr' – the doctor looked down the card – 'Westwood, this is fairly irregular. It would help if I had a little more information.'

'Well, you're not going to get any. I want to be out of here in five minutes. All I want to do is make sure this little girl gets as well as she possibly can get. And I want no publicity whatsoever. This stays strictly between you and me and whatever hospital administrators you have to deal with.'

'Do you want to see her?'

'Is she conscious?'

'In and out. Not really.'

'I'd like her to have twenty-four-hour nursing. I don't want her to be alone.'

'I understand.' The doctor kept silent for a moment, they both did, then Graham said, 'So do you want to see her?'

Justin nodded, just the smallest of nods, and the doctor escorted him down the hall and down the elevator to the intensive care unit and down another hallway until he was standing not far from a bed, on it the small form of a young girl. Her face was bandaged, her head shaved, a seemingly endless maze of tubes running to and from her body. Her chest was rising and falling in short, rhythmic bursts, the only sign that inside the bandages was a living thing.

'You can talk to her,' the doctor said. 'I'm a believer in that. Even if they can't respond, sometimes they know when we talk to them. And even if they don't know, sometimes it just makes us feel better.'

'When it's over,' Justin said.

'When what's over?' the doctor said.

But he didn't get an answer. Justin was already heading back down the hall.

Graham was about to call after him, decided against it, instead he let the guy turn toward the elevator and disappear. *Strange,* the doctor thought. *Strange guy all around. He seemed so . . . tormented. So determined.*

Graham decided part of the strangeness was that he couldn't figure out exactly what this guy Justin was so determined to do.

Oh well, he thought. *Don't look a gift horse in the mouth. Better get back on my rounds.*

But as he walked off down the hall, smiling at two nurses hurrying past him, he realized he couldn't quite get Hannah Cooke's new benefactor out of his mind. And, turning into a patient's room – he checked his chart to make sure he got the name right; a Mrs Isadora Sashaman – he thought, *I wonder what he meant by 'over'.*

chapter 26

When Justin stepped into his living room at five-thirty that afternoon, it looked like a hurricane had swept through the house. Papers were scattered everywhere. As were beer cans and two pint containers of Ben and Jerry's Chunky Monkey ice cream.

'Make yourself at home, why don't you?' he said to Reggie Bokkenheuser.

'You can't have it both ways,' Reggie said. 'You want neatness or you want results?'

She was in jeans and a T-shirt, on the couch, her black boots curled under her. He smiled at how natural she looked, and how earnest. Her hair was kind of a mess, one lock kept falling over her eye and she kept blowing it away.

'Any calls for me? Any word from someone named Wanda?'

'No calls, no women named Wanda banging down your door. Sorry.'

'Okay, what have you got for me?' Justin said.

'I haven't moved in, like, eight hours. How about a 'thank you' or 'how are you' or something good for morale like that?'

'Thank you. How are you?'

'Fine. Thanks for your sincerity.'

'What have you got for me?'

She blew out a breath. 'A lot.'

He gave her a 'gimme' sign with his hands and her response was to lift her right hand to her mouth and mime drinking from a bottle. he went to the kitchen, came back with two bottles of beer. She nodded a thank-you, and then she began to roll off what she'd learned from reading through Roger Mallone's suitcase full of material.

She told him that there was some financial material she just wasn't capable of understanding, but she'd tried to note anything of relevance, even if she couldn't quite follow it. Mostly, she said, she had tried to follow his instructions and trace connections between people and organizations. Three hours later, she was still reading from her notes and interpreting and he was still inputting info into his computer, dizzy from the information he was trying to absorb and translate into workable patterns.

He tried to organize everything into his preexisting lists and some things fit nicely into the categories he'd already set up. Other pieces of information required their own separate organization. Reggie had done a superb job of sifting through Mallone's research. She provided him with charts detailing Phil Dandridge's long relation-ship with EGenco – as well as the company's ties to other government officials. She also provided a kind of political family tree for him, with Dandridge the head of the family. The intercon-nection between EGenco and the vice president stretched all the way back to his days at Yale University. Yale was the breeding ground and seemingly the genesis for the political and economic ties that appeared to be at the core of everything that was now going on around them. Dandridge had been at the college at the same time as Bradford Collins, the EGenco CEO who'd been killed in the blast at Harper's. Dandridge and Collins had both been members of the tight-knit and secretive campus organization Skull and Bones.

Jeffrey Stuller, the attorney general, had also attended Yale during those years, but was not a Bonesman. Stephanie Ingles, the current administrator of the Environmental Protection Agency, was also a Yalie from those days, and although Justin could not see any relevance she might have to his investigation, he entered the connection into his computer. He would worry about information overload later.

He'd asked Reggie to scrutinize the main lawsuits that had been filed over the past three years against EGenco and she'd provided background on three of them. He now had six pages of facts, figures, and names relating to the environmental group Save the Earth and its suit against Dandridge. EGenco was only a peripheral part of that legal action, but their connection was substantial. STE was suing Dandridge to provide a list of the attendees and the input given by those attendees at the Conference on Energy the vice president had organized at the beginning of his second term in office. The suit had taken nearly two and a half years to get to the Supreme Court, where it was quickly dismissed. Dandridge fought to the bitter end to keep all information about that conference secret and confidential. And he won.

As a kind of subset of that suit, Justin had asked Reggie to put together information on the Saudi royal family. His dad had practically blown a gasket talking about the Saudi role in U.S. energy policy, and Justin knew enough to know that Saudis were never far away when it came to any kind of terrorist acts. He didn't know if those connections would apply now, but the links couldn't be ignored. If they were there, he wanted to know what the possibilities were. In Reggie's list of information about the Save the Earth suit, she'd included the fact that there was a specific request to subpoena Mishari al Rahman, a Saudi royal, as someone who might have information about Dandridge's conference. Mishari, a longtime friend and business associate of Dandridge, was supposed to be representing the entire royal Saudi clan. In particular, the suit was claiming that the White House, in conjunction with the Saudis, was manipulating oil prices. The intent, the suit said, was to bring the cost way down before the next presidential election, using the ensuing economic advantage as a further boon to Phillip Dandridge's campaign. The main argument against this allegation was that oil prices *weren't* going down. They were rising like crazy, and until the bombing attacks, that fact had unquestionably been hurting Dandridge's campaign.

There were several pages related to the lawsuit New York City had filed against EGenco. The suit was complicated and detailed and Reggie had done her best to simplify things, but there were gaps that Justin wasn't quite able to bridge. The gist of the suit was that New York had pension fund money – firemen's and police pension money in addition to that of many other city employees – invested in EGenco. The suit charged that EGenco was violating federal law by doing business with countries that supported state-sponsored terrorism. Justin couldn't follow every step, but the suit traced over a trail of shell companies that existed only to launder money and circumvent the law. The suit emphasized the fact that post-9/11, the city couldn't allow its money to be invested in countries and businesses that were responsible or supportive of that attack.

The third major area that Reggie had done her best to condense was the Justice Department's investigation into EGenco's business practices, stemming from the financial improprieties that Roger Mallone had explained.

By eight-thirty that night, the living room was even messier, Reggie was chomping on her third piece of pizza from the pie she'd gone out to pick up at the Italian place on Main Street, and Justin had to turn away from his computer screen and say to her, 'Okay, enough. I have to stop.'

'What have you put together?' Reggie asked.

He shook his head. 'In some ways too much, in some ways not enough.'

'You want to talk it out?'

'I don't know if I can even make sense of it. I can see the threads, see some of the corruption, I can even see where people are making a shitload of money they shouldn't be making, but Christ, tying it in to the bombings and the plane crash . . . it's inconceivable.'

'The bombings, Jay? I thought you were just looking at the crash.'

'It's all tied together, Reggie. I can't prove it, but I know it.'

'Maybe the McDonald's thing, I know you think it was all meant to kill the Cooke woman, but come on, Harper's and La Cucina?'

'I know. I *know*. It's crazy. But . . .'

'Talk.'

'Okay, look. Bradford Collins is the head of EGenco. The company's under investigation by the Justice Department for huge, mind-boggling financial misconduct.'

'The misconduct hasn't been proven yet.'

'A lot of things haven't been proven yet. But let's go with it for a minute. Let's just say it's justified, that they're heavily in debt and they tried to hide it, that they screwed around with pension funds. Let's just say they're Enron. I heard a good case made for that. Plus, in a separate suit, they're being sued for illegal dealings with terrorist-supporting countries.'

'Nice company.'

'Yeah, they're sweethearts. But it's not hard to see why someone wanted Collins dead.'

'Why?'

'Because he was going to talk.'

'To who?'

'To the Feds . . . Wait, hold on a second.' He went back to his computer, called up his file on the case. He didn't find what he was looking for, went on the Net, back to the *New York Times* site. He went to a story in their files that he'd looked up before, one that had had the names of the people killed in the Harper's bombing. He scanned the list and the brief bios that went along with them. 'Damn!' he said, when he came to what he was looking for. 'He wasn't just going to talk to Justice. He was going to talk to Elliot Brown.'

'Who's that?'

'The New York City comptroller. He was killed in the explosion, too. I'll bet the house he was one of the people at Collins's table that day.'

'All right, so he was going to talk. Who'd want to stop him? I mean, stop him badly enough to kill him.'

'The Justice Department.'

'Jay, I'm not following. I thought you said he was *talking to* the Justice Department.'

'Yeah. But he was talking to the lower levels. The investigators. It's a higher level that wanted him to keep quiet.' She waited for him to say more. Finally, he sighed and said, 'He was going to blow the whistle on the attorney general. On Stuller.'

'For what?'

'I don't know. I just know he's involved. Stuller and Dandridge both.'

'Jesus, Jay.'

'Yeah.'

She got up, went to the kitchen, came back with two more beers. When she offered him one, Justin shook his head. 'How 'bout we split it?' she said, and he nodded. She took a long sip, offered him the bottle. He took a quick hit and passed it back to her.

'I just want to get this straight. You think the vice president and the attorney general of the United States have something to do with the three terrorist attacks this month?'

'Yeah, I do. I don't know whether they're involved or they're covering something up. But they're connected.'

'Jay—'

'It's why Hutch Cooke was killed. It's why his plane was rigged. Because he could link things to Dandridge.'

'You think he knew what was going on?'

'I don't know. But even if he didn't, he could've figured it out at some point. If I had to guess, I'd say he already did. But either way, he was a loose end. And these guys definitely don't like to leave anything loose laying around.'

'What was Cooke doing? He didn't fly Collins or Elliot Brown here, did he?'

'No.'

'So what's his connection?'

'I think he flew whoever's responsible for the Harper's bombing.'

'The guy who killed himself?'

'No. The guy *behind* the guy who killed himself.'

She took this in, stayed quiet while she mulled it over. 'Why here?' is what she asked finally. 'Why East Hampton or East End Harbor?'

Justin shook his head. 'There has to be a reason. I just can't connect it. But here's what I think: that someone from Justice set the meeting up with Collins and Brown and that same person specified the place. Hutch Cooke flew somebody into town and either he made the connection, after the explosion, that he'd flown in the bomber, or whoever he was working for realized that he *might* figure it out. Once that was in the air, they couldn't risk having him around anymore.' He stood up, paced back and forth across the living room with quick, hard strides. 'I'm close,' he said. 'It's so close, but I can't put it together.'

'But you will.'

His eyes closed with fatigue, he nodded, and murmured, 'Yes. I will.'

When he opened his eyes, Reggie said, 'I'll be right back.'

'What?'

'I'd like to go home and get something. Will you wait here?'

'Where am I gonna go? And what the hell are you going to get?'

'Something that'll make you feel better.'

'Hard drugs?'

'Better,' she said.

He smiled, plunked himself down on the couch. On her way to the door her hand brushed his arm. It was a friendly gesture, a touch of support, but it also sent a sexual charge up and down his spine. That charge kept him frozen where he was for the few minutes it took her to cross the street to her house and then back to his. She didn't knock when she returned, just opened the door and stood in the doorframe. She didn't seem to have anything with her and he looked puzzled.

He could hear the exhaustion in his own voice when he said, 'I thought you were bringing something.'

'I did. Two things, actually.'

He waited. She reached into her pocket. Pulled out a toothbrush.

Then she reached into her other pocket. Pulled out a pair of handcuffs.

Reggie cocked her head and shrugged. He remembered the hunger in her eyes that he'd seen the day before. It was there again, even deeper and more rapacious. Without saying another word or even glancing down at him, she walked past him and headed up the stairs.

Justin stayed behind for just a moment. He felt the exhaustion rise and leave his body.

It was replaced by his own hunger, one as powerful as the one he recognized in Reggie. It had been there for quite a while, he knew, but now he realized it had to be sated. And when he realized that, he stood up slowly and, led by the hunger, followed Reggie Bokkenheuser upstairs.

She was already on the bed when he moved into the bedroom, and she asked him to undress her. She slowly put her arms up into the air and let him pull her shirt up over her head and hands. She had full breasts that seemed to explode out from the restraint of her clothing. She leaned forward and kissed him. Her tongue was thick and filled his mouth. He started to pull away but she didn't let him. Her tongue stayed inside him, and she slowly pushed him down, climbing on top of him, straddling him, letting her breasts graze over his chest. He reached up and undid her belt buckle, unsnapped her jeans, slowly slid them down her legs. They were firm legs, and shapely. They shifted and he went to pull her boots off, but she shook her head, she wanted to leave them on, so he slid her pants down and over her two-inch heels.

She turned over, stretched luxuriously across the bed, her movements slow and easy, and he saw that she had a small tattoo of a butterfly on her back, right below her right shoulder, and one of a bird in the small of her back, stretching down to the top of her buttocks. She turned back to him now, the carnivorous expression had spread to her lips, and she wrapped herself around him, enveloping him, practically smothering him, as if they were longtime lovers who'd been apart for months. Her body seemed instantly familiar to him. They fit together well. They couldn't stop kissing, their tongues exploring, but more than that, also linking and connecting them together.

Their faces were close together, she was staring straight into his eyes, and she nodded, a sign that he somehow understood. Their lovemaking turned wild and passionate and rough. Rapacious. It was as if the violence that had surrounded them was suddenly brought into their bed. She scratched his back and, in a whisper, told him to pull her hair. She bit down into his shoulder until he had to yank his arm away. She stretched her hands out above her head, running them up the headboard, and he realized she wanted him to grab them, to hold her and pin her as if she were restrained. He hesitated, but she nodded her head and her eyes urgently pleaded with him, so he grabbed both of her wrists with one hand and held tight. She moved her head from side to side and finally he realized she wanted the handcuffs. He was caught up in it now, it was out of his control, he was too excited, so he reached over and cuffed her to the bedpost. She thrashed beneath him but couldn't escape and he saw the excitement in her eyes. When he entered her, she moaned, and when she came she screamed. And then she shuddered, some kind of cross between agony and ecstasy, and she tried to throw him off her, but he hadn't come yet, so he moved faster, and faster still, and she was screaming now, and struggling against him, almost as if, suddenly, it didn't matter who was there with her, she just wanted it over, then he came and she screamed louder, and sobbed, a wracking sob, and then he was off her, exhausted, spent, and she lay, hands stretched back to the headboard, absolutely still, except for her chest, which was heaving up and down, and her eyes, which fluttered open and shut, until they slowly closed and stay closed, unseeing, while her breathing slowed and the violence that had possessed her body quietly disappeared.

He thought he might have hurt her or overpowered her, and he wasn't sure what to do or say, but then her eyes opened and she smiled at him, a slow, almost shy smile which he found somehow touching after the wildness he'd just seen and felt in her. She lifted one leg up into the air, almost in slow motion, and now he finally unzipped one boot, then the other, and pulled them both off. Her calves were thick, he ran his hand over the right one. She told him dreamily that she didn't like her calves, she thought she had football player legs, but he told her that her legs were lovely. He told her her calves were beautiful.

He went to uncuff her; in the stillness after their lovemaking he felt embarrassed that she was restrained, but she shook her head. He freed her from the bedpost but kept her wrists bound together, and she lifted her arms up over his head and around his back, drawing him to her, forcing him so close he could feel her heart beating against his chest. She was asleep instantly, drained by the outburst of passion and the emotion she'd let loose. He lay there, sweaty, breathing hard, watching her sleep, staring at her smooth, white skin. She had a small mole on her back and he gently touched it. He was glad for the mole because he thought otherwise she'd be perfect.

He reached up and softly put his palm on Reggie's neck, leaned over and kissed the top of her head. Then Justin, too, closed his eyes, his arm curled across her back, her face buried into his chest. He drifted into sleep to the rhythm of her soft breaths warming his heart, and he didn't wake up until he heard a stirring, a footstep on the floorboard, and when his eyes opened, there were four men, expressionless, all with short hair and all with weapons. For a moment he thought it was a dream, a 4 A.M. nightmare, but he could smell their sweat, he could feel their presence, and he began to move, only he couldn't, because he was tangled together with Reggie, her cuffed hands wrapped around him.

Her eyes opened then, and when she stirred she saw the men.

Justin saw the fear in her eyes, the panic, and she tried to claw herself away from him, but it was no good. One of the men leaned down and hit her. Justin heard the crack of fist against jaw and he saw her go slack. He still couldn't move, not freely, but now he knew it didn't make any difference. He was one and he was naked, and they were four and they had guns.

So all Justin could do was watch in horror and then resignation as one man raised his pistol and shot Reggie Bokkenheuser in the chest. As she toppled sideways, Justin realized he knew one of the men, recognized him, he'd been in Justin's office. Hubbell Schrader. And it was Schrader who now looked at him, said something in that monotone they all had, all these guys. Justin didn't hear everything that Schrader said. He just heard the words 'FBI' and 'enemy combatant,' and Justin started to go, 'What the fuck? Enemy combatant?' but the words didn't come out because he couldn't speak when he got a look at Reggie, on her side, deadly still, and then Hubbell Schrader turned his gun on Justin, held it at point-blank range, and pulled the trigger.

All Justin could do was feel the darkness, the shadows that fell over him, then he rolled over, consciousness fading, and something happened that he'd wanted for a long time, for years, ever since Alicia had died, but not now, he thought, he didn't want it now, not now, not now. But whatever he thought didn't matter because it had finally happened: he slipped away into the blackness and felt and saw and heard nothing.

part three

chapter 27

The air smelled stale.

The foul odor wafted up his nostrils, slid down his throat, and his stomach turned over. He began to gag. That's when he understood that he was alive. In a cramped place, facedown on a floor, his face shoved down into some grungy carpet-like thing, unable to move much. But alive. His first response was surprise. Then confusion. And then Justin Westwood realized that he didn't feel elated or even relieved. As his head slowly cleared, as his eyes began to focus, he realized that he felt resigned. Resigned that things hadn't come to an end. Resigned to the throbbing in his temple and the empty feeling that had long ago replaced his soul. Resigned to the fact that life was going to go on. At least for a little while longer.

He struggled to turn over on his side, felt his face brush up against something. A new smell overwhelmed him. Leather. He coughed and the force from the movement made his eyes fly open. The smell of leather was coming from a shoe, just inches from his face. He heard the rustling of cloth. His vision was wavy, his senses jumbled, but it seemed like a pant leg moving. Then he heard a drone, a harsh, steady buzz. The light – it seemed to be streaming in from a window – was making him wince, but his eyes stayed open, and Justin thought, *I'm on a plane.*

It felt familiar. Looked familiar. His head twisted and he saw something, his brain couldn't quite take it in, then it clicked: a large fuel tank, like the one he'd seen in the small plane that Hutchinson Cooke had died in. His head turned again and he saw the shoe move. A quick sudden movement. He anticipated the blow a moment before it happened but there was nothing he could do about it. The kick came and the pain in the side of his head was sudden and overwhelming. He had another brief wave of nausea, then there were no more smells, no more sensations, and his eyes were shut and there was only darkness again.

When Justin woke up again, the drone of the plane had disappeared. So had the stale air, replaced by the smell of dirt and humidity and sweat. His head ached, behind the eyes from whatever drug had been used to put him out, and in his right temple, where he'd been kicked. His mouth felt dry and dusty, his tongue was coated with crust, his throat constricted. Things were quiet; he ascertained no movement around him. The sense of elation was still missing and the deep crush of resignation was overwhelming.

It was life as usual, Justin decided.

He slowly stood up, was overcome by dizziness, looked for some-place to sit back down and realized there was nothing to sit on. Only floor. He took a step toward the wall, leaned heavily against it, surveyed the room he was in. It was small, the size of a cell. The wall he was leaning against was made of stucco and he assumed the other three were the same. The front wall had a wooden door that he didn't even bother trying. He knew it would be locked. The door had a small slat in it. The slat was shut now but Justin figured it could be opened from the outside. A way to peer in. When closed, no way to peer out. On the opposite wall, maybe eight or nine feet off the ground, was a small window. It let in just a sliver of air and sunlight, and as best as Justin could tell, there were bars across it. He looked down now. The floor was dirt. Nothing fancy about it, just hard-packed dirt.

He felt a dull pain in his chest, opened his shirt and looked down to see an ugly purplish bruise immediately below his heart. It's where they'd shot him, using some kind of tranquilizing bullet or dart. Some sort of stun gun. He hoped it's what they had used on Reggie. He told himself that it had to have been. It was too painful to think otherwise. He had to drive the picture of her – sprawled on the bed, turned on her side, her head thrown back, twisted in fear – out of his mind. He wondered if she were alive. If she were there or if they'd only taken him.

He turned suddenly, lurching at a noise that came in through the tiny window. A bird maybe. Or wind. Or a branch rustling against the roof. The movement made his chest hurt like hell but Justin ignored the pain. He decided that pain was the least of his worries. What bothered him the most was that he didn't have a clue what the *most* of his worries was.

All he could do was wait.

He tried jumping up to look out the one window but his head and his chest felt like they'd explode, and it didn't matter anyway because he couldn't see a thing. The slit was too narrow and there was nothing to hold on to to keep him eye level with the opening for more than a moment. He could hear sounds wafting in. Nothing specific, but he took the noise to be other human voices. He wondered if there were other prisoners there. Probably not, he decided. More likely workers. Or people who had absolutely nothing to do with this and were oblivious to his circumstances. Briefly, he wondered where the hell he was, but he cut off that line of thinking when he realized it was pointless. He could be absolutely anywhere.

At least anywhere warm. That was all he could ascertain: the breath of air that managed to find its way in through the sliver of a window was hot for November. So he took a guess: Florida. That was the best he could do.

He waited for what he figured to be an hour. Maybe even two. He was still not alert yet, although the fog caused by the tranquilizer was beginning to lift. But he waited, not letting the solitude bother him, until it had been long enough that he thought, *Where are they? Why hasn't anyone come?* And then maybe another hour passed and still nothing.

Absolutely nothing.

Justin was hungry now. And thirsty. He didn't know how long it had been since he'd eaten. Hell, he didn't have any idea what time it was. Or how long he'd been unconscious. He assumed it was the same day, the day he'd been taken, but he couldn't even swear to that.

He'd tried to keep his brain clear. Knowing that, at some point, someone was going to come in and question him, he wanted to be as loose as possible. He didn't know how far his interrogator might go, but he didn't want to make it easy on him. He didn't want any names or facts right at the front of his brain, nothing that would roll quickly out of his mouth.

Less noise was filtering in from outside, but Justin was still certain that what he did hear was human voices. No specific words were understandable, though. He had only the vague sense of a current of conversation.

He tried counting to keep some estimated track of the time. Each time he reached sixty, he'd make a little mark in the dirt. When he reached five full counts of sixty, he'd make a larger mark and erase the smaller ones. At some point, after about ninety minutes by his clock in the dirt, exhaustion overcame him. He had done nothing but count, occasionally pacing the length and width of the room, but still he was tired. The fatigue was stronger than his hunger. He lay back down on the floor, made himself as comfortable as he possibly could, although comfort wasn't a priority; he was so tired it didn't matter what position he was in. His eyes closed and, within moments, he was asleep.

The next thing he knew, he was jarred awake by a stabbing pain in his back.

His head jerked up and his eyes opened. A man in military fatigues was standing over him, holding a rifle. The man slammed the butt of the rifle into Justin's back, in the same spot he'd obviously just hit to jab him awake.

Justin sat up, the pain fully registering now, hot and searing. The soldier jabbed at him again with the butt, this time clipping Justin in the chin, knocking him flat. Justin rolled onto his side, used the motion to propel himself to his feet. He took a wobbly step toward the soldier, stopped short when he saw there was a second man in the room. That man was holding a pistol, pointing it at Justin. Standing now, Justin let his arms drop to his sides. The first soldier stepped forward, expressionless. His right hand moved quickly, too fast for Justin to react, slapping him across the face. The crack resonated throughout the room and Justin could feel his cheek redden. He swayed backward but didn't lose his balance. The room fell silent again and all movement stopped.

'Where am I?' Justin asked.

The man's hand moved a second time, just as quickly. Justin felt the slap again and staggered several steps back this time.

'What the fuck do you want?' he said. 'Or is that too tough a question for you?'

This time, when the man's right hand flew toward his face, Justin was ready for it. His own right hand intercepted it, but he was weak,

303

his resistance was low. The soldier was strong enough to push Justin backward, and he lost his footing. As Justin's hands went to his side, trying to give himself some balance, the man in fatigues threw a hard right to the gut and Justin went down. He sat on the floor, gasping for air.

When he could speak, he said, 'Just tell me what the hell you want from me.'

Neither man answered. They glanced at each other, the man with the pistol nodded, then they both spun on their heels and left the room. Justin could hear the door bolt behind them.

Sprawled on the floor, he fought back the strong feeling of panic that was rising from his stomach like the bitter taste of bile. He sat there for perhaps another hour, but it was getting harder and harder for him to count off the minutes in his head. All he really knew was that at some point his eyes began to close again, and he was once more overcome by exhaustion.

He could not have been asleep for more than thirty seconds before the door burst open again. Justin didn't need to be hit, he awakened at the sound of the two men thundering through the door and instinctively curled into a protective position to help shield the blows he was certain would follow. But he felt nothing. There was just silence. When he slowly turned his head, the same two men were standing above him. One of them had a bucket, and as soon as Justin moved, the soldier dumped its contents – ice-cold water – on top of his head, drenching him.

Both men turned with military precision and headed for the door. Not a word had been spoken. Justin hurtled himself into the air and lunged for one of them, managing to grab him around his knees. He was able to do no more damage than slow the soldier down for one moment, because the other man was on him like a flash. The rifle butt crashed into the side of Justin's head, then a thick, heavy boot thudded into his side, and Justin lost his hold. He slid helplessly to the dirt floor and made no further attempt to move until the two men had marched out the door.

Justin lay on the dirt, wet and cold and aching and remembering how quickly strength can disappear. When Alicia died, so did his foundation. Faith and hope and optimism and joy all deserted him. He had thought he was not going to be able to go on, but it turned out he was left with something at his core that helped him survive. It took him years to understand that what was there was a certain toughness, a stubbornness, a meanness really, that wouldn't let him give in to the agony that had become his life. To the unpleasant thing that, as he saw it, had become life itself. He had felt his strength fade then, and he remembered the feeling when he knew it was back. It was the moment he knew he was not going to join his wife and daughter in whatever world they'd gone to. Now, confined in the sweaty, foul-smelling cell, he felt that strength fading again, replaced by fear and uncertainty. But as he shivered, he thought, *No, no, I won't let it go that fast; this time they can't take my life so quickly.* So he shook off his exhaustion and the aches and pains and he climbed to his feet and stood at the door and, breathing heavily, just stared straight ahead, in case, somehow, they could see him, showing them that they had done their best and that he could take it.

They were not going to take his strength away.

Others had tried. The world had tried. No one had succeeded yet. And neither would they.

Ten days later, Justin wasn't so sure.

That's how long the torture had gone on. He'd had no sleep. It was the same routine: anytime his eyes closed, two men would jump into the cell. He'd be kicked or slapped or beaten. Ice water would be thrown on him. Sometimes there were electric shocks. Justin couldn't tell exactly how they were being administered. There was some kind of box, he could feel clamps on his arms or on his feet, one time something clamped over his head. His body twitched and quivered when the waves swept through him. Once the shock was so bad, he could feel himself jerk and flop upwards off the ground and into the air. Once he smelled something burning and realized it was his flesh.

Twice a day someone would come in to feed him. Never a real meal. Some bread. A piece of ham or some indeterminate piece of meat. And one small paper cup of water.

Once, one of the men in fatigues spit in the cup before handing it to Justin. Justin drank it anyway.

There was no toilet in the room. Justin picked out a corner closest to the door to shit and piss in. He had no way to clean himself off. At the beginning, he felt some revulsion and shame at his uncleanliness. But at some point, neither the smell nor the self-disgust nor the helplessness bothered him.

For several days, he tried to resist. He forced himself to do sit-ups and push-ups and walk around the tiny room. But as the beatings went on and as his hunger grew and as he began to be dehydrated, he lost any desire to resist. He just wanted to tell them whatever they wanted to know. Anything they wanted to know.

Only no one seemed to want to know anything.

Justin was not frightened by the isolation or even, strangely enough, the beatings. What was beginning to terrify him was the lack of boundaries, the fact that there seemed to be no limit to the torture. No one had spoken to him, no one had asked him a question, no one seemed remotely interested in ending the process. It was the endlessness that was getting to him. The fact that he was beginning to think it might *never* end.

It was the endlessness that was taking his strength away.

At one point – he didn't know if it was day or night; with no sleep, it made no difference anyway – two soldiers entered. He'd seen one of them before but not the other. One of them had a thick piece of rope. In front of Justin the soldier tied one end into a noose and, using a stepladder he'd brought into the room, attached it to a rusty metal hook that had long ago been driven into the wall.

The second soldier looped the noose around Justin's neck and led him up the ladder. The noose pulled taut – and then the first soldier kicked the ladder out from under Justin's feet. He felt the rope tighten and he thought he was dead, really dead, but the rope broke and Justin tumbled to the ground, more or less unhurt, the noose still tight around his neck. Still, his captors said nothing. When the two men left the room, Justin removed the noose, felt the rope at the point where it had fallen apart, and realized it had been cut. Their intention had not been to hang him. It had been to terrify him.

It had worked.

Justin cared deeply about staying alive now. He didn't know if he could but he suddenly had a deep and desperate thirst for life. He wanted – no, needed – to find out who was doing this to him. Find out who it was, find out where they were, and stay alive until he could kill them.

Holding the rope strands, he smiled through cracked lips. Life suddenly seemed good again. He had a reason to live.

They hadn't taken his strength yet.

Some time after the mock hanging – Justin had no idea when; it could have been hours, it could have been days – another man in fatigues came through the door and into Justin's cell. It was the first time someone had come in alone. Justin waited for the backup but no one else came. Just this one guy. His light brown hair was slightly longer than the others, not a buzz cut. His skin wasn't as tan as most of the other men who'd come in. His clothes seemed crisper, as if they were newer or had been recently starched.

Justin was sprawled on the floor and made no attempt to stand. The man had his back to the wall with the door and he leaned casually against it. Watching him, Justin realized he was going to hear the first words he'd heard since he'd been there. This soldier wasn't just a thug. Justin made a silent bet with himself that this was an officer. And that this was his interrogator.

'The explosion at Harper's Restaurant,' the soldier said. His voice was calm. Whatever anger lurked behind them wasn't detectable. Nor was it visible in his eyes, which were slate gray and as blank as eyes could be. 'Tell me what happened.'

Justin didn't answer. He had no response that could remotely be seen as satisfying.

'How long have I been here?' he said instead, and was surprised to hear his own voice – harsh and dry and cracked. It hurt his throat to expel the words and he didn't know if the man would even understand the words.

'Not long enough,' the man answered. 'You should try answering the questions that I ask.'

Justin tried licking his lips before speaking this time. It didn't do much good. He couldn't conjure up any moisture.

'How much longer?'

'Tell me what you know about the Harper's bombing.'

'How much longer . . . will I be here?'

'You'll be here until you tell us what you know.'

'And then?'

'It depends on what you tell us.'

'Where?'

'Are you asking where you are?' And when Justin nodded, because he was almost out of energy and that was the best he could do, the man in fatigues said, 'You're in hell, pal.'

Justin knew he'd lost the guy, that he was going to turn and leave the tiny cell, so he quickly spit out the word, 'Why?' And when the officer hesitated, didn't leave, just stared at Justin, a look of disbelief on his face, Justin said it again quickly, as loud as he could: 'Why?'

'You're being held as an enemy combatant.'

Justin raised his head. He hoped his eyes were registering the disbelief he felt. 'You think I'm a terrorist?'

'We know you have knowledge of terrorist activities. And that you may be aiding and abetting the enemy.'

'Fucking crazy.'

'I couldn't understand that. You're not speaking clearly.'

Justin coughed out some of the hurt in his throat and forced the words out: 'You're fucking crazy.'

The man didn't answer. This time he just turned and headed for the door.

'Wait,' Justin said. And when the man turned back, Justin, doing his best to be understood, added, 'Want to call a lawyer.'

The man actually smiled. A thin, cruel, delighted smile. 'You don't have the right,' he said.

'Bullshit.' It was the clearest word Justin had yet uttered.

The man took two steps forward now, leaned down to get closer to him. Justin could see the man recoil slightly at the smell. The proximity to this kind of filth seemed to finally anger him. The grin was gone, as was the calm civility. Both were replaced only by cruelty. 'Listen, you little fuck. You don't have the right to an attorney, you don't have the right to remain silent, you don't have the right to shit. Not anymore. Guys like me, we can finally do our fucking jobs. I can keep you here for the rest of your natural fucking life and no one can do a fucking thing about it, do you understand that?'

When Justin didn't answer, the man kicked him. Hard. Justin didn't feel any real pain but he realized he must have blacked out, because suddenly his eyes were open and he'd missed some time, and the man was standing over him.

'What do you want to know?' Justin said.

'Right now, all I want to know is if you understand what the fuck I just told you. 'Cause the stink in here is making me sick and I don't want to have to spend one second more than I have to talking to scum like you.'

'I understand what you told me.'

'Good. Now you think about it until I come back. That might be tomorrow, it might be a few months from now, it might be never. You think about that, too.'

Justin felt the panic rising up again. The idea of going back into the endless isolation, no conversation, no communication, more beatings, it was the feeling he imagined would come with being buried alive. The feeling he had when he dreamed about Alicia and Lili. The fear was suffocating but he refused to show it, did his best to keep his breath smooth and steady. The man turned and left.

Justin Westwood curled up on the floor. He didn't know if he could stay awake, exhaustion had consumed his entire body. But he didn't think he could fall asleep, so deep was his dread of being beaten and humiliated, his usual punishment for drifting away from consciousness. So he lay there, doing his best to keep his thoughts coherent and his fear too deeply embedded to emerge.

They didn't have his strength. They hadn't taken it away. That's what he told himself over and over and over again.

And then he began to weep.

chapter 28

The beatings and sleep deprivation resumed soon afterward. Justin estimated they went on for three more days, although he knew his sense of time had little proportion to it. That was as close as he could get and it was preferable to no guideline at all.

On what he thought was the fourth day, the man – the only one who had thus far spoken to him – returned. He offered a small paper cup full of water, which Justin grabbed and downed in one gulp. The cold liquid hurt his throat; the coldness was jarring enough that it made him drop the cup on the floor. He watched sadly as a tiny stream of water dropped onto the dirt and formed a moist bubble of a puddle.

'Tell me about the bombing at Harper's,' the man asked. No lead-in, no attempt at banter or good cop tactics. Just, 'Tell me about the bombing at Harper's.'

Justin nodded slowly. 'What do you want to know?'

'Tell me about the bombing at La Cucina.'

'I don't know anything about it.'

The man's voice didn't change. 'Tell me about the McDonald's bombing.'

'I'll tell you anything I know. Ask me questions I can answer.'

'Tell me about Midas.'

'Midas?' Justin was surprised. 'I don't know anything about Midas. All I know is they paid Hutchinson Cooke to work for them.'

'Tell me what you know about Midas.'

Speaking was still difficult and his throat was so raw it felt as if it had been scraped to the bone with a sharp blade. 'It's a company.'

'What kind of a company?'

'I don't know. The kind you should be fucking investigating instead of talking to me, you fucking asshole.'

Justin had no memory of the blow. He also had no idea how long he was out. All he knew is that when he came to, the man was gone and he was, as usual, all alone in his cell.

The next time the man came, Justin estimated it was two days later. 'Tell me about the bombings,' the man said.

'I need some real food,' Justin said. 'And my gums won't stop bleeding.'

'The bombings. Start with Harper's.'

'Just tell me what you want to know. I swear to God, I'll tell you.'

'What happened at Harper's?'

'I don't know.'

'You were there.'

'What? What do you mean?'

'Afterwards,' the man in fatigues said. 'An FBI agent brought you there.'

'Right,' Justin nodded. 'He showed me what happened.'

'Why?'

'I asked him to.'

'Why?'

'I know someone who was killed there. In the explosion. I wanted to see.'

'What was the agent's name?'

'Billings. Chuck Billings.'

'Did you kill him?'

'No.'

'But you think someone did.'

'I don't know. Maybe.'

'What about Hutchinson Cooke?'

'He's dead, too.'

'Who killed *him*?'

'I don't know.' Justin's voice was just about gone now. His throat felt like it was going to close up.

'Why are you looking into his death?'

'I'm a fucking policeman, you fucking moron.'

When Justin woke up, he decided he must have been hit in the mouth this time. One of his front teeth was loose.

Justin saw no one, after that, for what he estimated to be two full days. Sometime during the third day, the door to his cell opened. Justin didn't respond because he'd learned that response was meaningless. He got no points for being passive, nor was there an advantage to any resistance. So he just lay still. He'd taken to estimating the time of day and he decided it was the middle of the night.

When the door opened, only one man stepped through. Through his half-closed eyes, Justin saw that the man looked Middle Eastern. He had dark skin and deep-set, equally dark eyes. His hair was black and, though cut very short, was very straight. He walked slowly over to Justin's prone body. When Justin stirred, the man jumped back, startled. He looked frightened. More frightened than Justin.

'It smells terrible in here,' the man said in a whisper. When Justin didn't respond, he raised his voice just slightly to say, 'Can you hear me?'

Justin tried speaking but no words came out. So he nodded.

'I am not going to hurt you,' the man said, and Justin could definitely hear the Middle Eastern accent. 'I'm just here to tell you something.'

Justin nodded again.

'I am not a guard, I am not a soldier. I am a prisoner here, like you.

Justin held up his hand for the man to stop. He tried to speak, but only a cough-like croak came out. He hoped the words sounded like what they were supposed to be: 'Why . . . here?'

The Middle Eastern man patted him gently on the arm, a sign that Justin didn't have to speak.

'I'm here because a guard was bribed,' he said. And when Justin's eyes narrowed questioningly, the man continued, 'No, not by me. I am just the messenger.'

'Who . . .?' Justin's voice was still raspy. But it definitely sounded like a word this time.

'The message is from someone named Pecozzi.'

Justin's eyes widened. 'Bruno . . .'

'Yes. Bruno Pecozzi. Please, let me speak. I don't know how much time we will have.'

Justin nodded. The man's whisper continued.

'The message is, 'We know where you are. They know that we know. So they won't kill you.' Does that make sense?'

'More?' Justin breathed.

'The woman is okay. I was told to say that, also.'

'Which woman?'

'The one who was with you.'

Justin closed his eyes, a moment of thanks. The weight that had been pressing down his chest, suffocating him whenever he thought of Reggie, shot, lying on the bed, disappeared. No word about Wanda, though, and the weight was replaced with another sensation, a tightening around his heart. 'Whole . . . message?' he rasped again.

'Yes. It is very hard to communicate, so that is all. But it makes sense?'

Justin closed his eyes. Bruno had let him know that Reggie was alive. That was to provide comfort and satisfaction. But Bruno was also telling him that whatever they did to him down here, however brutal it got, he didn't have to be afraid. They wouldn't kill him. Justin wasn't sure how Bruno could know that, but this was an area in which he trusted the big man completely. So all he had to do was tolerate the pain. Torture only worked when there was the thought of no end in sight – or an end that no one would ever want. That was not going to be the case. So Justin opened his eyes and nodded. It made sense.

'How?' he now asked the man crouching down next to him. 'How . . .'

'I will tell you everything I know. I don't know who this man Pecozzi is, or how he was able to do this, but I have a lawyer. I believe she once represented him.'

'Lawyer . . .?' Justin managed to say.

'A very good woman. Shirley Greene.'

'Read . . . about . . . her. Terrorists.'

'She represents Arabs. And people think all Arabs are terrorists.'

'You . . .?'

'I am not a terrorist. And my brothers are not terrorists. But we are being treated as such. And I believe we will be deported as such. If we live to be deported.' He hesitated and shook his head sadly. 'We are not being treated as terribly as you. We are not in isolations. This is very bad.'

'Where . . . am I?'

'You don't know?'

Justin shook his head.

'Guantanamo Bay,' the man said.

Justin managed a long exhale. 'You . . .' he said, '. . . how long . . .?'

'My brothers and I have been here for several weeks. Many weeks. I don't know exactly. Some men have been here for two, three years.'

The slit in the cell's door slid open and a quick, quiet whistle came from the other side.

'I would have brought you water if I had known. I'm sorry.'

Another whistle.

'I've got to go,' the man said. 'If I can, I will come again.'

'Thank you,' Justin whispered.

'Go with God,' the man answered.

And as he left, Justin closed his eyes. *Better to go with the devil*, he thought. *Much more useful when you're in hell.*

chapter 29

No one showed up in the cell after that for some time. Justin had several hours of relative peace. During that time, he made a decision. Bruno's message had had its desired effect. All they could do was hurt him, and he could survive that. There was no way to fight back, not in these circumstances, not in the condition he was in. There was only one thing he could do that would help him survive, or at least help keep him from going crazy.

He could use his brain. He could spend every moment sifting through information and putting the pieces together. He remembered Billy DiPezio, his onetime mentor in Providence, talking about the power brokers up there, saying, 'You can only take what they give you.' Well, they were only giving him one thing: time.

So Justin decided he'd take it. And use it to try to figure out the puzzle.

He began by placing his finger in the dirt he was sitting on and slowly scratching out a series of names. To the left he put the dead men: Collins, Cooke, Heffernan, Billings, and Lockhardt. Below them, he dug out the name Theresa Cooke and under that wrote 'Reysa' and 'Hannah.' Hannah was still alive, but she more than counted as a victim. He moved his finger slowly, somehow drawing some importance from the texture of the visual in the dirt. To the right, he began tracing the names of the people he believed were connected to the deaths. Stuller and Dandridge.

To their right he put a new column. Justin listed every name he could think of in conjunction with the case. First, he tried to remember every person he'd spoken to: Martha Peck, Colonel Zanesworth, Hubbell Schrader, the son of a bitch. He hoped that someday he'd get a chance to get his hands on Schrader. Justin forced himself to stop thinking of revenge, then he calmly drew all those last names in the dirt. Then he added one more column. He tried to visualize all the names he'd come across in Roger Mallone's reports and lawsuits, some of which he'd read, some of which Reggie had encapsulated for him. He did better than he thought: writing down the last names of the Yale attendees: President Thomas Anderson; the head of the EPA, Stephanie Ingles; Stuller and Dandridge again. He added Elliot Brown, the New York City comptroller. And he tried to think of the name of the Saudi, the one who was so connected to EGenco, but he could only recall the first name: Mishari. He remembered that it was followed by 'al' something . . . but he couldn't come up with it. He knew he had all the time in the world, let himself relax, trying to visualize the name on Mallone's report, but it wouldn't come. So he just scratched out 'Mishari' in the dirt. He was reasonably sure that Arabs didn't go by their last names anyway, it was the first name that mattered, so he decided that was good enough.

And then he added one more word. They seemed so concerned with Midas. It was definitely worth adding. He gave it its own separate column.

He looked at the hastily drawn names as he'd laid them out:

Collins	Peck	Stuller	Anderson	Brown	MIDAS
Cooke	Zanesworth	Dandridge	Ingles	Mishari	
Heffernan	Schrader		Stuller		
Billings			Dandridge		
Lockhardt					
T. Cooke					
Reysa					
Hannah					

He stared at them, not trying to make sense of anything, not trying to form any patterns, just memorizing them. Putting them into groupings inside his head so he could call them up at will. In his current state, it had taken him over an hour just to put the list together. He wanted to be able to do it in seconds, without having to think. So he burned them into his memory, until he felt himself falling asleep again, and before he conked out, he ran his hands through all the names, erasing them, leaving no trace, and then he fell asleep. Immediately the door burst open, two men came rushing in, and the torture began again.

Justin thought it was three days later, but it could have been two. Or four. Or even five. But to keep himself sane, he called it as three and decided that's what it was, no matter what. Three days later – absolutely, three days, final, done deal.

That's when he began to figure it out.

He started going meticulously, step by step, as he'd done many times by now, and each step focused him, kept his mind off the pain and the fear. Each step, each piece, bringing him closer to the puzzle's solution. He turned every angle over in his mind. There was no limit to the amount of time he spent on any one aspect of the puzzle. Time was what he had. The longer the better. Every minute he spent thinking about the case was every minute he wasn't going to go crazy.

Each exhaustive thought process began with an event. Then he tried to explain to himself the reality behind the event: exactly why it had occurred. Then he listed questions raised by each event and tried to formulate a coherent and structured line of reasoning to propel himself toward the most logical answers. With each answer, he felt as if he'd reached a level plateau after having climbed one small segment of a mountain. He viewed each plateau as a rest stop at which he then catalogued and isolated each one of the answers, keeping them separate in his mind, making them part of the next process, which would take him further up the mountain to the next plateau. At some point, the goal was to reach the peak. There at the top would be all the facts, neatly laid out, and all the names he needed to put the entire puzzle together. To that end, for every question he answered to his own satisfaction – at each new plateau – he tried to link a name to it, using the list of names he'd originally drawn with his fingers on the dirt floor. Every day, while he was thinking, he would redraw the list, sometimes in the original configuration, sometimes in different columns and rows. Whenever he moved the names around, he could find new ways to connect certain people to other people, and connect the right names to the right facts.

He understood that there was a chance it was all gibberish, that his mind was not functioning properly after his weeks of imprisonment. But he also understood that his only choice was to keep going. He often thought of the words uttered by Theresa Cooke: *Everything's muddy.*

More than muddy, he decided quite a few times during the days and nights. Muddy, dirty, smelly, and painful.

Right. And on that note he had decided to begin.

Step One: An Iraqi walks into Harper's Restaurant and detonates – or is used to detonate – a bomb, killing dozens of people, including himself.

Theory: The dozens of innocent people were decoys. The purpose of the explosion was to kill *one* person: Bradford Collins, CEO of EGenco. *Maybe* two. Elliot Brown, New York City comptroller, might have been a primary target, might have just been gravy. Or even an innocent lure to get Collins into the restaurant.

Theory: It was not a suicide bombing, as the FBI claimed. The Iraqi was a dupe. He did not expect to die (proof: he was moving away from the intended target when the bomb went off). The bomb was activated by someone outside the restaurant. Cell phone-activated.

Question: Why kill Collins?

Thought Process: Because he was going to talk. *About what?* About EGenco's illegal business practices. *And that's worth killing over?* At this level, yes. *What would he talk about?* The lawsuit brought against EGenco by the City of New York. He'd reveal the shell game and the dummy companies used so they could do business with terrorist-supporting nations. *And?* And he'd talk about the illegal deals EGenco has made with members of the administration. *Why would he talk?* To make a deal with the federal prosecutors and either cut or eliminate jail time. *Okay. Makes sense. Definitely makes sense. But who would want to keep him quiet? Who would want to kill him?* Anyone he implicated in the upcoming scandals. Anyone who had something big to lose.

Question: Why make the murder so elaborate? Why the devastation to kill one person?

Thought Process: Everything has a reason. We know the entire process, so work backwards . . . *What was the result of the Harper's bombing?* There were so many deaths that they hid the real purpose, which was to kill Collins. *What else?* Mass hysteria. General fear. *Was that just an unplanned-for side effect or was that part of the intention?* I don't know. I just don't know. *Well, lets say it was deliberate. Who did it benefit?* Terrorists. It planted the seed that they were winning the war. *Who else?* To be cynical about it, certain politicians. The administration. The people in power. *Why?* Because the explosions created nationwide fear. And people don't like change when they're afraid. *Who benefits from lack of change?* The president. The vice president. The attorney general. *Why?*

That was a hell of a question. Justin figured the Triumph of Freedom Act had passed in Congress while he'd been incarcerated. It was on the verge of passing, and if it had, it made sense that he hadn't been allowed to contact a lawyer or be in touch with the outside world. He had no rights whatsoever now – that's what the T.O.F. Act was meant to accomplish. It was like the RICO laws put in place to stop the mob. There was no recourse.

So back to the question: *Why did those three benefit?* Because the government could do whatever it wanted now. If Anderson passes the Triumph of Freedom Act, it becomes his legacy, his holy grail of legislation. And it sets up his party as the one to turn to in times of fear and danger. There's an even greater benefit for VP Dandridge: He's running for president. He was losing – now he's a shoo-in. Attorney General Stuller reaps the same benefit. The Triumph of Freedom Act gives him extraordinary power. Lots to gain for all three of them, particularly the last two. Lots to gain . . .

But how can this be? The heads of the U.S. government perpetrating terrorist acts on their own people? It can't be. It doesn't make sense. It can't make sense. There's something wrong, there's got to be a gap in the logic.

And yet . . . Why the cover-ups? Why the misinformation? Why else would there be so much resistance to and so much obstruction in the way of the truth?

Okay. Let's go with it for the moment. As crazy as it seems, say it's real. It still doesn't solve the second part of the Harper's equation: Who's masterminding the bombing? Who was on the other end of the cell phone? That's the key because even assuming the crazy assumption that Anderson, Dandridge, and Stuller – or any combination of the three – are involved, they couldn't possibly be hands-on. They'd have to be many times removed from the physical reality of the plan. The FBI? Hard to imagine. Even someone as bloodless as that guy Schrader . . . no. Just can't see it. They might cover up the investigation under orders, but to actually perpetrate a terrorist act. Uh-uh . . .

Hold it. Take a break. Getting ahead of yourself. Getting too complicated. Keep things simple. One step at a time. Time to see where we are . . .

First Plateau: The explosion at Harper's Restaurant was designed specifically to kill Bradford Collins. Collins was murdered to stop him from talking about EGenco's illegal business dealings. His revelations would have implicated people who could not afford to be implicated – the list possibly goes as high as the attorney general, the vice president, and the president of the United States.

Unanswered Questions: Who was actually behind the bombing? Who made the cell phone call? And what was the specific information that Collins had that was so dangerous to such important people?

Okay, go to the next step. It's related. It'll help pull you up the mountain.

Step Two: . . .

The door to the room opened, Justin was so absorbed in his thought process that he didn't hear the initial sound, but when he realized that someone was coming in, before he even looked up, he stretched out casually on the floor, obliterating his scribblings in the dirt. As he slowly stood, he dragged his foot over the same area, further obscuring any trace that he'd been doing something other than staring blankly off into space

His interrogator stood just inside the doorway. He was still wearing fatigues. They'd been washed and newly pressed.

'Tell me about Hutchinson Cooke,' he said.

Justin nodded accommodatingly. 'What do you want to know?'

'Why were you talking to Martha Peck?'

'Looking for information.'

'What information?'

'Cooke was killed in my town. I was trying to solve the case.'

'Who killed him?'

He thought about his answer, decided to go with the truth. He had nothing to gain by lying. Not now. 'I'm not positive. I didn't get far enough. But I think it was someone who worked for Martha Peck. Someone named Martin Heffernan. He either rigged the plane or knew who did it and decided to cover it up, I don't know which.'

'Did you kill Hutchinson Cooke?'

'For Christ's sake.' He would have screamed but his throat was still too raw. Then he just nodded and said, 'Yeah. I killed Hutch Cooke, and to throw everyone off the track, I decided to spend the rest of my life pretending to find out who did it. I arranged for myself to get thrown in here 'cause I knew that would really confuse the hell out of everybody.'

Justin waited for the attack, but it didn't come. The man in the fatigues didn't change his expression, just waited a moment or two, then said, 'Tell me everything you know about Midas.'

For a moment, Justin thought he might burst into tears. Forget the pain and the horrendous conditions. He was being driven mad by the idiotic repetition, the boredom. 'Look,' he said, 'I'd like to tell you about Midas. I'd really like to tell you about Midas. But I don't know what it is, where it is, or who it is. All I know is they paid Hutch Cooke's salary. That's it. I swear to God.'

'Who runs Midas?'

'I don't know.'

'Who owns it?'

'I don't know.'

'Where does their money come from?'

Justin shook his head slowly. 'I don't know.'

'Tell me about Theresa Cooke.'

Justin closed his eyes for a moment. He opened them before answering. 'Some stupid bastard killed her because he thought she told me something. That's all I know about her.'

'What did she tell you?'

'Nothing.'

'What did Theresa Cooke tell you?'

'She didn't tell me a goddamn thing.'

'You'd tell me, wouldn't you? If you knew something, you'd tell me.'

'Yes.'

'Because you want to get out of here.'

'Yes.'

'You don't want to be beaten anymore, do you?'

'No,' Justin said quietly. 'I don't.'

'And you'd like to be clean. And have a good meal.'

'Yes,' he breathed. 'I would like that very much.'

'Then just tell me what you know.'

Justin took a deep, long breath. The air that came in through his mouth and his nostrils felt particularly tropical. Warm and wet. 'I don't know anything,' he said. 'I don't know a thing.'

The man in the crisp, starched fatigues looked at Justin, who'd stayed standing during the entire conversation, and said, 'I almost believe you.'

Then he left Justin alone again. From the world outside his tiny window, Justin thought he heard a bird screeching. It was a

325

high-pitched noise, piercing and mournful. When the sound came again, Justin wasn't quite so sure of its source. It was piercing enough to be a bird. But it was also mournful enough to be a human being.

He scribbled all the names into the floor again. He'd done it so often by now, he didn't have to think or pause while pushing his finger through the dirt. As he'd done each time, he rearranged them in a slightly different order than the previous time. Looking for patterns and connections. To the left he kept the victims in one column. For the first time, he added Elliot Brown's name to that column. Next he organized any of the names connected to either the military or the FBI – anyone with a connection to the government's investigation of terrorism. To the right of that column he listed all government officials. In a column all by itself, he listed the Saudi connection and, after a bit of hesitation, added a final column: Midas. At first he left it blank under the company name, then he added Cooke, who worked for them, and then he remembered that Colonel Zanesworth had told him that it was the vice president, Dandridge, who had made the call asking Cooke to be assigned to Midas as a pilot, so he put Dandridge's name under that column, too.

Collins	Zanesworth	Stuller	Mishari	Midas
Cooke	Schrader	Dandridge		Cooke
Brown	Stuller	Anderson		Dandridge
Heffernan	Cooke	Peck		
Billings		Ingles		
Lockhardt		Heffernan		
T. Cooke				
R. Cooke				
H. Cooke				

He stared at the columns, saw no new connections to be made. Took a deep breath – almost reveling in the horrible smell; he'd seen how repulsed Mr Starched Fatigues had been this last time and somehow it gave him a kind of strength to know he was used to it, was no longer overpowered by it – and he went back to the puzzle . . .

Step Two: Hutchinson Cooke's plane is rigged and he is murdered.

Theory: Cooke was on non-Air Force business. He was working for a company called Midas. Cooke flew into East End airport before the Harper's explosion. Cooke was killed because he'd made a connection between his cargo on the plane and the explosion. He was killed so he couldn't make that connection public.

Thought Process: What was the cargo? Two choices: the explosives used to destroy the restaurant or the man who used the explosives – the man who made the cell phone call. Or perhaps both.

Where was Cooke flying from? Unknown. Find that out and it should help to know who or what he was carrying.

Why was Cooke killed? Again, find out exactly who or what he was carrying and find out exactly why he was killed. Best bet: Cooke had been suckered into the flight – he didn't realize quite what he was doing; when he realized the connection between his cargo and Harper's, he panicked, maybe threatened to expose his bosses – the people who ran Midas? – and so he was killed.

Who killed Cooke? Heffernan either killed him or covered up the killing.

Justin looked at the list he'd drawn into the dirt. He'd put Heffernan down as a government official. True – he worked for the FAA. That counted. One more government connection. One more signal that this whole thing had to be government-connected . . . and high up in the government to reach this level of manipulation.

Okay. Time to take a breath.

Plateau Two: Cooke was killed because he was a link to Collins's murder and to the explosion at Harper's. The link is the cargo. The key questions: Who or what was Cooke flying into East End Harbor? And *for* whom? If he was flying for Midas, what is Midas and who is behind it?

Time to start climbing again . . .

Step Three: Martin Heffernan is killed in the explosion at La Cucina restaurant.

Theory One: Same as Harper's. The explosion is an elaborate and deadly cover-up to mask the murder of one man: Heffernan.

Question: What did Heffernan know that got him killed?

Thought Process: He knew about Hutchinson Cooke. If Cooke was the link to Midas – and had to be eliminated to remove the link – then Heffernan was the link to the government. Heffernan had called the Justice Department to pass along information about Cooke's death. But Heffernan didn't work for Justice – his boss was Martha Peck, FAA. She didn't seem to be tied in to this. Although . . . she was a link to the murderer or murderers. Despite Martha's protestation, she knew who removed Heffernan's file from the FAA office in Oklahoma City. She had to know. She had probably removed the file herself at the person's request. Find that person, find a closer connection to the murderer.

Justin went through the next deaths quickly. Chuck Billings was clear-cut. He'd been brought in through official channels and, because of his expertise, he found out exactly what those officials didn't want him to find out. He'd been lured to his death, most likely by the same bureaucrats he'd so distrusted. Justin would put money on Hubbell Schrader as Chuck Billings's killer.

Lockhardt was also simple. He was killed because he was a final loose end in the murder of Hutchinson Cooke. He knew about

Heffernan's connection and that was enough to seal his death warrant. Justin mentally penciled Schrader into the blank space next to the question, *Who killed Lockhardt?*

Theresa Cooke was killed because she, too, knew something about her husband's murder. Or, more likely, about her husband's job. Theresa was dead, Justin was certain, because she knew something about Midas . . .

Justin took another look at his markings in the dirt floor and decided to draw in a new column: Organizations.

So at the far right of his scribblings, he added:

Midas
U.S. government
Yale
Saudi government

He decided to go one subset further:

Midas
U.S. government
   Executive
   Justice
   FAA
Yale
Saudi government

He went back and, remembering Stephanie Ingles and her Yale connection to Dandridge and Stuller, added 'EPA' under his 'U.S. government' heading. And then suddenly he decided to add another organization. A business that seemed to be at the center of all of this. EGenco.

He began scribbling separate columns for each listing:

Midas	Exec	Justice	EPA	FAA	Yale	Saudi	EGenco
Cooke	Anderson	Stuller	Ingles	Heffernan	Ingles	Mishari	Dandridge
Dandridge	Dandridge			Peck	Dandridge		Cooke
					Stuller		
					Anderson		

What jumped out at him was Dandridge. He popped up every-where. Justin twisted around so he'd have a clear space on the dirt floor – he'd begun to think of it as a giant blackboard – and he wrote the name Dandridge, and under that, every possible connection to the vice president that was relevant to the puzzle.

DANDRIDGE
Midas
EGenco
Cooke
Anderson
Stuller
Ingles
Mishari

He erased that list, rubbed it out quickly with the heel of his right hand. Then split the list into two – people and companies.

Cooke	Midas
Anderson	EGenco
Stuller	
Ingles	
Mishari	

330

In his mind he went over the connections one more time:

Dandridge had made the call to Zanesworth to get the colonel to release Cooke from his Air Force duties so he could pilot for Midas.

Dandridge had been CEO of EGenco.

He'd been piloted by Cooke as vice president. He'd made the call to Zanesworth to get Cooke to come to work for Midas.

He was Anderson's vice president. They'd known each other since their Yale days.

He knew Stuller from Yale. Stuller was reporting to Dandridge as point man in the government's search for the suicide bombers.

Dandridge knew Ingles from Yale.

As CEO of EGenco, Dandridge had to have a close relationship with Mishari. EGenco did too much business with the Saudis for that relationship not to exist.

Dandridge was a connection between EGenco and Midas. Dandridge was a connection between Midas and the government.

Justin studied the names on the list. Rearranged them several times. Stephanie Ingles still seemed to be the weakest point: he couldn't see any connection between the terrorism, the conspiracy he was convinced existed, and the head of the EPA. There just didn't seem to be any political link between her area of expertise and the events of the past two months. So he erased her from his list and mentally shoved her off to the side.

After the third time he'd put the names in different order, something began to gnaw at him. Something was trying to burst through. He tried to empty his head so whatever was in the back of his brain could make its way forward. It felt close. Very close . . .

But something else struck him now, rushed at him with a burst of clarity. As he saw the list of names, he realized there was a new piece to the puzzle that suddenly fit in. He'd been wondering one thing since he'd been brought to this godforsaken place: *Why?* Why had they done it? Whoever had given the order to take him couldn't possibly want him to give damaging information to his interrogator. They didn't *want* anyone to know what he knew. They wanted him silenced. So why question someone if you don't want to know the answers?

Because, he thought, *they don't want to know what you know. They want to know what you* don't *know.*

So what *didn't* he know?

What were the questions the starched little prick kept asking him: *What was Midas? Who runs Midas?*

They weren't looking for those answers! Whoever was behind the questioning *knew* the answers! They wanted to make sure that he *didn't* know.

So what the hell was Midas? *Who* the hell was Midas?

Goddammit, he was close. He could feel it coming. He was so close his brain felt like it was exploding. Information was rushing at him – the reports he'd read, the background on the lawsuits, the history that Roger Mallone had thrown out to him. It was there. It really was. It was all inside his head . . .

He heard the familiar noise at the door, immediately ran his hands over the dirt, obscuring everything he'd written, and as he did he felt the bubble burst.

He felt his brain shutting down, the pieces of the puzzle dissolving into nothingness.

He sagged with disappointment.

That's when the door swung open. Two soldiers stood in the doorway, both holding rifles. They didn't seem to care about the obscured swirls on the floor or why Justin was on his hands and knees. Behind them was the man in starched fatigues. He didn't seem to care either. And when the man spoke, Justin didn't particularly care about them either.

'Clean him up,' the man in the starched fatigues said to the two guards. 'He's going home.'

chapter 30

He was thrown into an outdoor shower stall that was big enough for ten men.

The sun at first burned his skin and scorched his eyes, but the fresh air enveloped him like a lovely ocean wave. As he was propelled to the shower area, he was vaguely aware of steel mesh pens that looked like animal cages. It took him a few moments to realize that they were for humans. These were the human voices he'd heard drifting into his cell.

The cleansing water made him aware of the sores on his legs and the bruises on his arms and chest and face. But they didn't really hurt. Or if they did, the pain seemed unimportant. He let the warm shower water stream into his mouth and drop down his chin and thick beard. He scrubbed himself with soap, scraping off feces and layers of dirt and dead skin, and used some shampoo provided for him to wash his hair three times. He'd been handed a toothbrush, too, already slathered with toothpaste, and he ran the brush across his teeth over and over again until the paste was long gone, periodically spitting water and foam and blood from his mouth in the direction of the drain. The minty taste of the toothpaste tasted like fine wine. It was as if the sun and water were breathing life back into him.

They let him stay in there maybe fifteen minutes. At some point, he was too weak to stand under the hard and steady water flow, but he didn't want it to end, so he just sat down and let the shower pelt down on him. A guard came to help him stand, and when he dried himself off, he was presented with new clothes. A crisp and clean blue work shirt, an equally fresh pair of chinos, thick white sweat socks, and a pair of sneakers.

He ran his fingers through his long hair, relishing the fact that it was no longer matted and gnarled. He kept grasping his beard with his fingertips; what felt normal in the isolation of his cell now felt coarse and strange and unnecessary. He wanted to rip the thick, bushy growth right out of his chin, and he started to pull it, hard, until he forced himself to close his eyes and relax, told himself that it was over, that he was going home, that he could deintensify his reactions and wait until he was in his own bathroom with a can of shaving cream and a razor. It was just a beard, he told himself, not a symbol of all he'd been through. It was something that could easily be removed when the time was right.

He could see other prisoners in their mesh pens. Justin looked for the man who'd come to see him in his cell, but was unable to pick him out of the crowd.

Two guards came and escorted him – half carried him because his legs were not working all that well – to a tin building that was set up as an office. It struck him as plush and rather luxurious. Justin was told to sit on a folding chair, which he did. The guards stood watching him for several minutes, but he knew that even if they left him alone, he didn't have the energy to snoop or pry. He sat still until Starched Fatigues strode in and dismissed the guards. In daylight, in these surroundings, the man looked slightly older than Justin had believed him to be. And a bit smaller. Justin studied his face as the man sat behind a desk. The hair was visibly graying on the sides. His eyes had developed lines around them. His face, which was doing its best to look boyish, was beginning to reveal its age, as well as the pressures and traumas that lived inside it.

'You've been cleared of any wrongdoing,' he said, looking past Justin rather than at him.

Justin didn't say anything. There was nothing he thought needed saying.

'You'll be flown home today. I'll be your military escort.'

Justin still didn't respond. A slight tilt of the head was all.

'There is a very strong feeling that you were not acting in the best interests of your country, Mr Westwood. You were moving into a very dangerous and suspicious territory. But we accept the fact that you were doing what you believed to be your job and didn't understand the direction your investigation was taking you.'

Justin's head tilted the other way now.

'I'm sure you'll also want to know,' Starched Fatigues said, 'that the terrorists responsible for the various attacks on our country have been eliminated. The immediate threat is over. We accept the fact that you were not in any way tied to this group.'

Justin couldn't stay quiet any longer. 'They were caught?'

'They were found. They resisted and were killed in a gun battle.'

'Who are they? Who were they?'

'It was a terrorist cell. Five of them were Iraq-connected. They hooked up with three suspected members of Al Qaeda who we'd been tracking for months. That's how we found them.'

'How many were there?'

'Eight.'

'And they were *all* killed?'

'That's correct.' Starched Fatigues shifted uncomfortably for a moment. 'We'll allow you to ask some questions if they relate to your investigation. We believe you deserve that much after the ordeal you've been put through.'

'Who's "we"?' Justin asked.

'*I'll* allow you.'

'May I ask where the eight men were found?'

'They'd been moving around the country. We stopped them in Delaware.'

'Was anyone from our side killed in the gun battle?'

'Is there a reason for that question? Or an implication behind it?'

'I'm a cop. I like to know all sides of an equation.'

'Well, you're not going to be allowed to know the different sides of this equation. Stick to your investigation. Or no more questions.'

Justin tried to focus. He knew he wouldn't get a lot of leeway. 'What was Hutchinson Cooke's involvement?'

'Before I go into this, understand that this entire conversation is confidential. We will share information with you because we feel you're entitled to it. But it cannot be shared outside this room.'

'If it is?'

'You've got some political clout behind you, Mr Westwood.'

'That's news to me.'

'Maybe. But you do. It's one of the reasons you're being released. That and the fact that many of the loose ends surrounding the bombings have been tied up. But if you ever talk about anything that you learn here or that happened to you here, you would be violating the security of the United States and a return visit could very well be justified.'

'That's a good argument for confidentiality,' Justin said quietly.

Starched Fatigues gave what Justin thought was the closest he could come to a quick smile. 'Captain Hutchinson Cooke was a traitor.'

'Can I get any elaboration?'

'We've interviewed many people who knew him at Andrews Air Force Base, including his commanding officer. Cooke apparently had become wildly political. Been studying the Koran. He'd spent many years flying to the Middle East. He made a lot of friends there and obviously was easily influenced. He'd become convinced that the government here was his enemy.'

Justin had enough energy to squint dubiously and say, 'He wasn't Arab.'

'Neither was the young man in northern California who went to Afghanistan and joined the Taliban. Just tragically misguided.'

'Cooke was working for a company called Midas.'

'That's right. A Saudi-formed company, based in Iraq. They had an American branch, trying to do business here.'

'What kind of business?'

'Oil.'

'And *were* they doing business here?'

'Not really. They'd made contacts. It's easy to make contacts in that business when you're from the Middle East. But it seemed to basically be a shell. A terrorist front.'

'And . . .?'

'And it's been closed down. The people responsible for it have been arrested. They're being dealt with.'

'How did Cooke pull off the doubleheader? How'd he work for Midas the same time he was supposed to be flying for the Air Force?'

'He was AWOL. It's what led us to him in the first place. We'd been looking for him ever since his commanding officer made it official.'

Justin thought his head might burst. They had answers for everything. It was all getting tied up in a neat and seamless package. 'Who killed Cooke?' he asked.

'We believe the crash could have been an accident. Although it's possible it was suicide. Cooke flew Bashar Shabaan, the man who blew himself up at Harper's, into the area. It's possible he felt remorse when he realized the consequences of his support. Or fear because he realized he'd be caught.'

'And his wife?'

'Also involved with the cell. Our people believe she became unhinged after the Harper's incident. When Cooke died, she blamed America and our government. She was clearly deranged or she couldn't have done what she did.'

Justin spoke very slowly and carefully. 'You're saying she was involved in the McDonald's bombing?'

'Yes.'

'She blew up her own children?'

'These are very sick, evil people we're dealing with.'

'Yeah,' Justin said. 'They sure are.'

'We're not going to be revealing to the public what I just told you. It wouldn't do us any good to announce that a U.S. military man had switched sides, and ultimately it's not really relevant to the story.'

'But you're telling me.'

'As I said, your investigation of Captain Cooke is what led you here. We believe you deserve to know the truth.'

'What about Martin Heffernan?'

'Heffernan did us a favor. He happened to be on the spot, saw Cooke's ID, and called Cooke's commanding officer. Zanesworth had been alerted that Cooke was under investigation and he immediately contacted us.'

'"Us" meaning . . .'

'Meaning those of us directly involved in the war on terrorism.'

'So you guys told Heffernan to wipe the plane clean, take any ID . . .'

'We made the connection immediately. As I said, we'd been suspicious of Cooke and his wife for some time. We made an immediate decision to keep their involvement quiet. You can question that decision, it was not made easily, but it's the one that was made and it's one we're not deviating from.'

'Why didn't you question Theresa? After her husband died, she could have been a valuable source.'

'Who says we didn't question her?'

'Well . . .' Justin hesitated. 'She did.'

'Was she nervous when you spoke to her? Jumpy? Frightened?'

'Yes.'

'That's because we were putting the screws on her. She gave up valuable information right away but we didn't let up. It's largely through the information we gathered from her interrogation that we found the cell in Delaware. She was guilty as hell, that woman.'

Justin stayed silent, trying to poke holes in the story he was hearing. But he wasn't sharp enough. He was too overcome with fatigue.

'Is that it for your questions?' Starched Fatigues asked.

'What about Heffernan's death?'

'A tragic coincidence. Conspiracy theorists would have a field day with that one, but it's absolutely true. The guy was a regular at a restaurant and somebody else decided to blow that restaurant up.'

Starched Fatigues reached into a desk drawer, pulled out a bottle and two small paper cups, the same cups Justin had been served water in during his incarceration. The cups were white and flimsy, the kind one got in a dentist's office.

'You know,' the man behind the desk said, 'in my job you have to get used to one thing: how much people hate you. You can see it in their eyes. Their whole face, really.'

'Must be tough.'

'Not really. I never minded very much. It's understandable, their hatred. I talk to people who have secrets. Their job, and sometimes their passion, is to keep those secrets. My job is to find out what they are. Cross-purposes. It's like the Arabs and the Jews. Or cowboys and Indians. It's hard not to hate the person who's trying to take what you've got. I mention all this because I thought you should know, I can see in your face how much you hate me. But there's nothing else you've got that I want to take, so it's wasted effort on your part. And ultimately, it can't do you any good.'

The soldier filled both cups halfway, the equivalent of two shot glasses.

'We are not apologizing to you, Mr Westwood, but that doesn't mean we don't sometimes regret the actions that have to be taken when serving our country.' He handed one cup to Justin, who, as he leaned forward, saw the label on the liquor bottle for the first time.

'Havana Club,' Justin said.

'Fourteen-year-old Havana Club. The best rum in the world. It's like fine cognac.'

'Cuban.'

'We are in Cuba, after all. It's the worst thing about the damn embargo – you can't buy this stuff at home. It's liquid gold.'

'Can't get this in America? Anywhere?'

Starched Fatigues shook his head. 'There's got to be some reward for being stuck in such a godforsaken place.'

Justin took a sip of light brown liquid. It scorched his throat as it went down and filled his belly with heat. But the flame that spread inside his stomach didn't compare to the flame that was raging inside his head. He remembered sitting in Theresa Cooke's kitchen and Theresa showing him the exact same bottle, saying her husband had brought it back from a Midas-related trip to Florida.

This is Cuban, Terry. Not from Florida, he'd said.

341

I know, she'd told him. *Hutch said they sold it in Florida 'cause there are so many Cubans there. Refugees.*

Another one of Hutch Cooke's clues? Another part of the game he thought he was playing to win?

'Ever tasted it before?' Starched Fatigues asked.

'I saw a bottle once, but I never tasted it.'

'And?'

'It's extraordinary,' Justin said.

The soldier stood from behind his desk, downed the rum in one quick swallow, dropped the cup on his desk. Justin watched it teeter before toppling on its side.

'Time to go,' the soldier said.

Justin, too, downed his rum, stood up, and his legs immediately gave way. He stumbled to the desk, grabbed on to it for support. Starched Fatigues grabbed his arm to keep him steady.

'There'll be food on the flight,' the soldier said. 'Sandwiches. It'll give you some strength.'

'Thank you,' Justin said. 'Sorry, the rum must've gotten me.' He gently pulled himself away from the other man's grasp. 'I think I'm okay now.'

Starched Fatigues walked him to a small plane parked on a runway no more than seventy-five yards from where they'd been sitting. Halfway there, they were joined by a pilot. The pilot made no acknowledgment of Justin's existence and Justin returned the favor. Before they boarded, Starched Fatigues pulled a pair of handcuffs from his pocket and indicated that Justin should put his hands behind his back. He did as instructed and was cuffed. No apology was made. Starched Fatigues simply said, 'Precautionary.'

As they stepped up into the plane, Starched Fatigues grabbed the back of Justin's shirt. He didn't grab him too tightly, just enough to hold him back.

342

'Your investigation is over,' he said. 'You do understand that. There's nothing more you can accomplish.'

Justin nodded. 'I understand,' he said.

'Just so you know, if it was up to me, I would have killed you. But I have to follow orders.'

'Orders from who?'

'That doesn't really matter, does it?'

'It does to me.'

'What matters is that the orders are for here and now. You keep screwing around in this thing, those orders won't apply anymore. And I'll be free to do what I think should have been done in the first place.'

Starched Fatigues let his fingers relax. He and the pilot climbed into the front of the plane. Justin was put in the cramped backseat. It was the same kind of plane he'd been flown down there in; the same kind of plane that Hutchinson Cooke crashed. Before takeoff, Justin leaned forward and said to Starched Fatigues, 'Hey, what's today's date?'

'December twenty-first. You'll be home in time for Christmas.'

Justin leaned back, but suddenly moved his head forward again. Into Starched Fatigue's ear he said, 'So, since we're flying companions, do I get to know your name?'

The man's head swiveled around and Justin saw another thin-lipped smile. 'I'm afraid not,' he said. 'Some things do have to remain secret.'

'I guess they do,' Justin said. And as he spoke he could feel the flimsy paper cup that was tucked into the right pocket of his khakis, the cup he'd picked up off the desk when he'd pretended to stumble. He had handled it carefully, barely lifting it with his fingertips, trying to touch only the rim, and gently easing it into his pants as they'd walked.

343

Some things do have to remain secret, Justin thought.

And as the plane began to taxi, as it rocked back and forth and then lifted off the ground, Justin smiled, too.

The first smile he'd managed since he'd been in this hellhole.

It felt even better than the water and the soap and the sunshine because he knew, as long as he was careful, that this was one man whose secrets he was going to learn.

Merry Christmas to me, he thought.

chapter 31

She came running as soon as he called.

He dialed her cell phone because he didn't want to speak to anyone else at the station; the more he thought about it, the more his plan developed in his head, he knew it would be better if as few people as possible knew he was back in town. But he called Reggie because he had to call Reggie.

When she stepped into his living room there was an awkward moment. They had never had a chance to relax as lovers or even savor a moment of the passion they'd shared, so neither was exactly sure how to act. Reggie took the lead when she really saw him – saw the weight he'd lost, and the bruises on his face, and the combination of pain and relief in his eyes. She went to stand in front of him, then put her arms around him. She didn't kiss him, just laid her head down on his shoulder, comforting him and letting him know how much comfort he gave her.

When she backed away a step she smiled at him. It was an anxious smile. She reached back for his face, put her palm on his thick beard and stroked it.

'I'll shave it,' he said.

She shook her head. 'No. It feels like a part of you right now and I want all parts of you to be here.'

'Okay,' he said. 'Okay.'

'There are so many things I want to tell you. And ask you.'

'Me too. But we've got lots of time now.' He touched her chest, the spot where he'd seen her shot. 'How are you?'

'I thought I was dead when he pulled the trigger. But I was just sore for a few days. It wasn't bad at all.'

'That was the worst part of it for me. I couldn't even let myself think about what had happened to you.'

'It's over now,' she said. 'Isn't it?' And when he didn't answer, she continued, 'It's on the Net and we've all been watching the news all day long. They caught all the people responsible for everything, Jay.'

'I know they have.'

'So it's really over. Everything can go back to normal.'

'Yeah,' he said. 'Everything can go back to normal.'

She took his hand and led him upstairs. 'That was the worst thing for me, too, not knowing what happened to you,' she said. 'When I woke up, two of those . . . those men . . . were here. They told me they were FBI and they wouldn't tell me where they'd taken you. They wouldn't tell me anything, just asked me all sorts of questions. What I knew about the plane crash, what I knew about all sorts of things, none of which I knew anything about. They took all the papers you had in the living room, all the files. And your computer. They told me not to say anything to anyone. I said I had to say something, you were the fucking chief of police, and one of them said he'd take care of it, he'd talk to the mayor and take care of it.'

They were in the bedroom now and she sat on the bed.

'I didn't know what to do,' she told him. 'I thought you were dead.'

'So what did you do?'

She looked embarrassed. 'I called your father.'

Justin looked surprised. 'That was smart,' he said. 'That was good.'

'Well, you'd told me a little bit about him, and I'd seen some background when I Googled you. I knew he was rich and I figured rich people would have connections.'

'What did he say?'

'He was very calm, he made me feel better. He said he was going to talk to your friend in the FBI, the one up in Boston.'

'Wanda.'

'Yes. He said she could help.'

'She's all right? Wanda's okay?'

'I guess she is. She must have gotten involved.'

'Did you talk to Leona?'

Reggie nodded. 'Yes. She called me, came to my house, said she'd talked to the FBI, said the one who'd talked to me was named Schrader.'

'What else did she say?'

'She said you were involved in something to do with national security. That you'd be okay, but that you were going to be kept in custody for a while. I was going crazy, Jay. They said I couldn't say anything, if I did I'd be arrested, too. I didn't know what to do. It wasn't until your friend, the big one, came and told me you were okay . . .'

'Bruno.'

She nodded. 'He wouldn't give me any details, said he couldn't. But he came and said you were all right, that I shouldn't worry, and that you'd be back soon. How did he—'

'I don't know,' Justin said. 'But I'll find out.'

'Jay, what happened? Why were you arrested? I just couldn't believe—'

'That's the right thing,' he said. 'Don't believe anything. Just believe me.' He touched her cheek lightly, ran his finger down to her neck. 'How was it handled? What do people think happened?'

347

'No one knows a thing. At least I don't think so. I mean, you're not the most social person in town. So we told the other guys at the station that you were called away for a family emergency.'

'They bought that?'

'They seemed to. No one asked too many questions. Occasionally, they'd ask if I'd heard from you or if everything was okay. But I just said that Leona was the only one in touch with you.'

'Nothing in the paper? No media?'

'No.'

'So no one really knows what happened. Or knows I'm back.'

'No,' she said. 'I don't think anyone knows.' She took his hand in hers and now she kissed the tip of his fingers. 'I was going crazy,' she told him. 'When I woke up and you were gone, I didn't know what to do.'

'There was nothing you *could* do,' he told her.

'But now there is.'

'Yes,' he said. 'Now there is.'

They made love very gently this time. There was none of the passion or the physicality that was there the first time they'd been in this bed together. She gasped when she saw his body – the bruises, how much weight he'd lost – and she kissed him lightly, careful not to hurt him. She made no demands on him, just held and kissed him and touched him until she coaxed him inside her and they came together, shuddering. She held him tightly for a long time after they came. She thought he was asleep in her arms but then he spoke quietly.

'Who was in charge?' he asked. 'Who did Leona put in charge?'

He felt her shift her weight and he heard, rather than saw, her smile, could tell from the quiet way she breathed in and exhaled. 'Me,' Reggie told him. 'I've been the acting police chief. It's a miracle there hasn't been a crime wave.'

They both started to laugh. He kissed her on top of the head.

'I've never been so happy to give up a job,' she said.

But Justin immediately shook his head. 'No,' he told her. 'Not yet.'

'Why not? You're back, Jay. No one has any idea what happened. It'll be fine.'

'I'm just not ready yet. I'd like to stay quiet for a while.'

'Why?' she asked.

He glanced away from her. Instead of answering, he said, 'You and Gary getting along?'

'Sure,' she answered. 'He's a nice guy. I mean, he doesn't like having to report to a woman, but he's been pretty professional about it. Yeah, we get along fine.'

'He's the only one you can tell. In the morning. Ask him to come over here around noon. But make sure he doesn't tell anybody else that I'm back. Okay?'

She raised her head. In her eyes he saw a bit of confusion, an equal amount of suspicion.

'You said it was over,' she whispered.

'I know I did.'

'But it isn't, is it?'

'It's almost over,' he told her.

In the morning, he sent her home. Asked her to go about her business as usual, reminded her to say nothing about his return except to Gary. He knew it wouldn't be a secret for long, someone would drive by his house, someone would spot him through a window, someone would call him up, and it'd be all over town. That was fine. He didn't need to keep hidden for long. He just wanted a brief period of peace and quiet. All he needed was a little bit of time.

The first thing he did was call Bruno Pecozzi. Bruno didn't sound surprised to hear his voice. Didn't seem surprised about anything.

'Bruno,' Justin said, 'you remember that envelope I mailed you? From Washington?'

'It's already in your house.'

'What?'

'Hey, if you're mailin' me somethin' from D.C., I figure it's some-thin' important. Who knows what these sick fucks are gonna decide to do, maybe they're gonna search my house just 'cause I know you. I figured they already searched your place, they wouldn't be lookin' for nothin' new after that. So I did a little B and E and put it some-place safe for when you came back.'

'Where is it?'

'The table to the right of your couch. In that drawer. You should find someplace safer to keep your grass, Jay. I mean, Jesus, you're the chief of fuckin' police.'

Justin said he'd think about it, then asked if Bruno could come over in the afternoon. All Bruno said was, 'Be there,' and hung up.

His next call was to Wanda Chinkle. He tried her at the office, was told she wasn't around. He didn't leave his name, hung up, tried her Boston apartment. He didn't leave a message on her phone machine, decided to next try the number Wanda had given him for emergen-cies – the gym in Boston. This time Leyla answered herself. He gave his name, she said, 'Oh, okay. What's the message?'

He told the woman what he wanted Wanda to do. She said she'd pass it along, and agreed to call back to confirm.

Five minutes later, Leyla called back. All she said was, 'You've got the okay. Wait fifteen minutes, then go ahead. But Wanda said she has a question for you.'

'Go ahead.'

'She said to ask you, "Do you know what the fuck you're doing?"'

He said, 'Does she want an answer?'

'No,' the woman at the gym said. 'She said I didn't have to get the answer. She said she just had to ask the question. She also said to give you a message.

'Okay.'

'She said . . . Hold on, I wrote it down 'cause she wanted me to give it to you right . . . Okay, this is an exact quote: "You're in some serious shit. Try to remember that no matter how it seems, when the time comes I'm on your side." '

'That's it?'

'Except for the number you wanted.'

'Okay. Let's have it.'

'Here's who you're supposed to call . . .'

After she gave him the information, he hung up, waited exactly fifteen minutes, as instructed, called the number of a north shore police station. He hadn't wanted to call Southampton. He was too paranoid to go that close to home. No, not paranoid, he thought. Too smart to risk it. 'I'm calling for Wanda Chinkle of the Federal Bureau of Investigation,' he said when he reached the officer whose name Wanda had given him.

'Right,' the voice said. 'I just got off the phone with her. How would you like us to handle this?'

'I'll get you the two objects that have to be dusted.'

'Two? She said one.'

'You must have misunderstood. Does she need to call you back to verify?'

'Nah. One, two, what difference does it make?'

'Great. Someone from the East End PD'll bring it over,' Justin said. 'We'll need a match for both sets of prints – names and addresses.'

'If they're in the system, we'll get them.'

'One of them should definitely be in the system,' Justin told the cop. 'He's probably military. Might be military intelligence.'

'What about the other one?'

'Strictly a guess, but I think it'll be in Immigration.'

'How deep am I supposed to look?'

'As deep as you can.' Justin gave the officer his home fax number. 'You can fax the info there.'

'Hey, as long as the FBI authorized it, you got it, pal,' the cop said. 'You get me the things, I'll get you the info.'

'They're on their way,' Justin said.

He looked at the small paper cup he'd carried with him from Guantanamo Bay. He'd already wrapped it carefully in bubble wrap and placed it in a manila envelope. He went to the end table to the right of his couch, opened the drawer and, sure enough, found the envelope he was looking for, the envelope he'd mailed from a mall near Theresa Cooke's house, the one he'd addressed to himself, care of Bruno, with the words 'hold for pickup' written across the front. Justin put that envelope inside the manila one, stuffing it under a fold of the bubble wrap. He wrote out a simple list of instructions, added his fax number to be on the safe side, taped the note to the bubble wrap, and sealed the envelope.

A few minutes later, when Gary Jenkins arrived, Justin handed him the package, told him to take it to Riverhead, gave him the cop's name to whom he should hand-deliver it. He could tell that Gary was a little hurt that he was being so curt, so professional after all the time he'd been away and with all the unanswered questions about his disappearance. He softened a bit, said, 'Gary, this is really important to me. You're about the only person I can trust to do this and keep quiet about it. When it's all over I'll take you out to dinner and fill you in and answer all your questions, but right now I need you to shut up and get the fuck over to Riverhead.'

The young cop smiled. 'Already starting to feel like the good old days,' he said.

'Thanks,' Justin said.

Gary gave him a mock salute, flipped the envelope in a 'don't worry' manner, started to leave.

'Gary,' Justin said. And when the young cop turned back to him, he said, 'You know a lot of kids at the high school, right? Through your brother.'

'Yeah, I guess.'

'You know any of the teachers?'

'Sure. A few of them coach Little League and I help out when I can.'

'After you hit the north shore, I want you to go to East End High. I need the best artist in the school.'

'Artist? You mean, like, painter?'

'I need someone who can draw. Ultra realism, that's what I'm looking for. I want the kid who can draw the best portraits in the school. You got that?'

'Yeah, sure. Except school's closed. Christmas vacation, you know?'

'Damn. My sense of time is a little off right now.'

'Don't worry about it. When I went to the school play before graduation, they had an art show, in the admin building. They got people who can draw pretty damn good. Somebody'll know who they are. My brother, one of the teachers. I'll find him.'

'Remember: I need the best. And bring the kid here as soon as possible.'

'I'll bring you the best who's still hangin' around town. That's all I can do.'

'Fair enough.'

'Whoever it is is gonna want to know—'

'Just say it's the same deal that Ben got. Whatever the hell he wants, that's what he'll get. As long as he can draw what I need him to draw.'

'Got it.'

And clutching the envelope, he was out the door.

Leaving Justin to think, *Jesus, I'm taking on the United States government with a bunch of high school kids.*

He went to his fridge, realized that everything there had spoiled except for several bottles of water. He took out one plastic container, drank deeply from it. He was still dehydrated, figured he had plenty of other things wrong with him, too, knew he should go to a doctor soon, but he didn't have time. *When it's really over*, he thought to himself.

What he wanted to do was go back to bed and sleep. Instead, he began to poke around the house, taking inventory of what was missing. The FBI agents had been relatively neat and extremely thorough. The hard drive on his computer was gone. His fax machine had been left behind, but he was certain they'd checked his log of incoming and outgoing faxes. They hadn't bothered to take his phone machine, although he was certain that if he'd actually had any calls, they'd been monitored and traced. There were no messages waiting for him. They'd gone through his mail and, he was sure, found absolutely nothing of interest. Neither did he, for that matter. As he thumbed through the envelopes, there were two solicitations from a chimney repair company. A curt note from Visa telling him he was late paying this month's bill. Nothing but junk mail and bills. At least nothing's changed, he thought.

He went to the phone now, reached down to dial the number for his parents – he knew he should relieve their worry and tell them he'd made it home. But before he could grab the receiver, the phone rang. His caller ID said the call was coming from Washington, D.C. Justin clicked on the talk button and said hello.

'This is Martha Peck,' the voice on the other end said, although Justin hadn't needed to hear her name to recognize that passive-aggressive tone that had driven him so crazy when they'd met in her office. 'From the Federal Aviation Administration. I . . . I know what happened to you . . . I mean, that you've been . . . away . . . but I heard that you've been . . . that you're back home. I hope you're okay.'

'I'm just great,' he said. 'It was just like a vacation.'

'It's important that we talk,' Martha Peck told him. 'Mr Westwood . . . Chief Westwood . . .'

'Try Jay. It's easier, Ms Peck.'

'Then please call me Martha.'

'Deal,' he said. 'Is this just a social call, Martha? Just checking up on my health and well-being?'

He let her silence go on until she decided to end it herself. He had a feeling she wouldn't need much prompting and he was right. 'I . . . I believe I may have been partially responsible for what happened to you, Mr . . . Jay.'

'Responsible for what exactly?'

'For where you've been. For what's been done to you. I think it may be my fault.'

Justin ran his free hand through his beard. He decided to cut it off the moment he was off the phone. It suddenly made him feel filthy and degraded. 'Why do you think that, Martha?'

'Because I called someone. After you left my office. I couldn't believe what you were telling me, and yet some part of me knew that what you were saying was accurate.' She hesitated. Again, Justin waited out her silence. 'I removed Martin Heffernan's file from the computer,' she said.

'But not on your own,' he said.

'No. I did it because someone asked me to.'

'Who?'

'You have to understand the mood in government these days, Jay. After 9/11, particularly after the findings from the 9/11 Commission, and the recent bombings . . . we all felt so put-upon. My agency took a big hit. And there was so much criticism that a lot of it happened because there was no communication between government organizations . . .'

'I understand,' he said.

'So when I got a call, it seemed . . . it seemed important to co-operate. And once I did, I couldn't believe I might have done the wrong thing.'

'Who called you?' he asked softly.

'It doesn't make sense to me,' Martha Peck said. 'It's an old friend. We met at a White House function and we've been friendly for years. When she called, she said it was a very delicate matter, that it had to do with a terrorist alert.'

'She?'

'She said she was involved because the threat involved protected land that fell under her domain. She was working with the FBI and with Justice, she said.'

'Stephanie Ingles. From the EPA. That's who called you.'

'Yes,' Martha Peck said. 'She called me that day and she called me after Heffernan was killed to say that it had nothing to do with me or the file. She said that Heffernan had done nothing wrong but that I was never to tell anyone what I'd done, that it was a matter of national security. Do you know what kind of panic it causes when anyone says the words "national security" these days?'

'Yes, I do,' Justin said.

'Stephanie called me again yesterday. To tell me that the FBI knew

356

you had talked to me and to tell me you were being released. She said that I was not to speak to you under any circumstances. It wasn't just a friendly piece of advice or even a warning. It was a threat. Not an overt one, but I know a threat when I hear it.'

'So why are you calling me, Martha?'

'Because I don't like to be threatened. And because she was lying to me, Jay. She was lying to me from the very beginning. And you were telling me the truth, weren't you?'

'Yes, I was,' Justin said.

'Is this . . . is this helpful to you?'

'Extremely helpful, Martha.'

'Well then, I'm glad I called.'

'Me too,' Justin said. 'I'm very glad you called.'

And I take back everything I've always thought about bureaucrats, he thought. *Every last damn thing.*

He didn't call his parents. Instead he dug out a yellow legal pad and a pen. They'd taken his computer and his files, but he could still write.

It struck him that he should be scribbling in the dirt, this felt almost too clean. But it all came so easily this way. He didn't need a computer for this. Everything was in his head. He wondered if it would be there for forever. He hoped not. But he was glad it was there now.

The names and organizations flitted across his memory as clearly as if they were on a movie screen. He was able to conjure up every list, every variation. He remembered his near breakthrough at Gitmo. And where he'd come up short.

Stephanie Ingles.

She was now in the mix, but what the hell was her role? What was her connection to the others and to what he suspected was going on? He'd overlooked that connection before, but Martha Peck's phone call made it as clear as could be that there was one. But what could it be?

Slow it down, he thought. Go back to the process. Take a deep breath. And another. You're just at another plateau. So think this through. Be logical.

The EPA. Start there. That's where the connection must be. *What was their function?* To protect land, water, and air. Protect wildlife. *Pretty nonthreatening. But what the hell had he been reading about it lately? What had he heard?* Something. He'd read a newspaper story . . .

His mind was racing. Environmental protection. Land preservation. Yes! That's what he'd read. He'd discussed it with Roger and his dad. The EPA and President Anderson had declared a huge mass of land in Alaska off-limits to the oil companies. Stephanie Ingles had pushed for the resolution. Dandridge had supported it. A surprise to everyone. Halliburton was livid. EGenco was furious. But how the hell did that fit? It didn't. It was the *opposite* of everything else that was beginning to add up. It made no sense.

But it had to. It had to . . .

Go slowly, he told himself.

Think clearly. Everything has a reason.

Just get to the next plateau.

It *had* to fit . . .

Millions of acres unavailable for oil drilling.

He began scribbling furiously on the pad.

What was the result of that decision? Environmentalists were thrilled. The permanent preservation of land and wildlife. Possible political gain, a nod to a constituency that wouldn't normally vote for Dandridge.

What else? The oil companies were up in arms. Less drilling. Less potential for domestic oil. More dependence on overseas oil.

So what? So what? What did it mean?!

Less oil, prices go up . . .

Higher prices were bad for the administration. It was harmful to their normal constituents, which meant it was politically damaging . . .

But when oil prices rose, *someone* was making a lot more money.

Bad politically. Very good personally.

He remembered Roger Mallone, lecturing him in the living room of his East End house. 'SPEs,' he'd said. 'A great way to hide a lot of crooked things.'

EGenco. Midas. Special Purpose Entities.

He jumped up and ran out to the front lawn. His newspapers had never stopped being delivered, and he scrounged through the several dozen papers that were scattered around, found that morning's *New York Times*. Justin turned to the business section, found that day's oil prices.

Sixty-four dollars a barrel. A record high.

Justin swore at the guys who'd stolen his computer – he no longer had access to his computerized address book – then called Rhode Island information, asking for the number for Roger Mallone. A minute later, he had Mallone on the phone.

'Jay, Jesus Christ, what the hell's been going on? Are you all right?'

'Roger, I don't have time to explain. I need some information and I need it now.'

'All right, all right. Go ahead.'

'EGenco. Remember we were talking about their Special Purpose Entities?'

'Sure.'

'Well, what kind of entities would they be likely to set up?'

'Depends on who they were being set up for.'

'Government officials. High-up government officials. And Saudis. A combination of the two.'

'That doesn't narrow it down much.'

'Okay,' Justin said. 'Go with me for a second, Roger. Is it possible that oil prices could be manipulated—'

'What, to go down? You mean to help these guys win the next election? Sure. There's been a lot of speculation that, when the time comes, that's what's going to happen—'

'No. To go up. How could the partners in a company benefit if oil prices go way up?'

'Are you kidding? If you're a supplier, you make a fortune.'

'Tell me.'

'Well, several ways. A company like EGenco has the government contacts to get huge contracts to rebuild Iraq and Afghanistan and anyplace else over there we might invade.'

'Keep going.'

'So they have to provide oil and fuel to rebuild the factories and infrastructures there. If oil prices go up, the government has to pay more. The company could make tens of billions of dollars extra.'

'Okay, that's the company as a whole. How about something smaller? An SPE now.'

'Well . . . you mean if I were being really devious about this?'

'Be as devious as you possibly can.'

'Well . . . a company like EGenco doesn't really explore anymore. They're so big, they're in so many other areas, it's not cost-effective for them. So what they do is they buy from small and medium companies. If they wanted to, they could set up an SPE that's a small or midsize oil drilling company. If they had to, they could justify it legally by saying that they're taking a percentage of the findings, which they would – probably fifteen to twenty percent. Then the company – and the partners set up in the SPE – take the other eighty to eighty-five percent of the profit.'

'What kind of profit are we talking about?'

'Well, the partners've got to put up some dough, but it's something relatively minimal. The way it works, when it's really sleazy, is guaranteed money up front. That's the suspicion about Dandridge right now, that's where some of the lawsuits are headed, and it's why people think he's being so secretive. He could have put up a million bucks and gotten a deal where his share of the SPE guarantees him ten million – no matter what the SPE's profits are. In exchange, he arranges the sweetheart deal for EGenco to rebuild the Middle East for billions and billions. That kind of shit goes on all the time.'

'Now let's say the partners also want the SPE to be profitable, over and above that guarantee. What kind of money could we be talking about for a midsize oil exploration company?'

'If oil prices go up? Huge. Let's say EGenco says, "You put up a million bucks each to be a partner." The Saudis generate about eight million barrels of oil per day. Three years ago the price of oil was twenty bucks a barrel. Now it's sixty-two, sixty-three, or some unbelievable thing. So their gross has gone up from about a hundred and sixty million a day to around five hundred a day.'

'Five hundred million dollars a day?'

'Hey, it's why it's nice to be a Saudi royal. You pick up a nice chunk of change from that.'

'Three years ago it was almost a third of what it is now,' Justin said. 'That was around the time of Dandridge's big secret energy conference.'

'You got it.'

Justin shook his head in amazement. 'How about a medium-sized American company?'

'Well, if EGenco puts these guys in a midsize company that's working, that's a success, that kind of company can generate about a hundred thousand barrels per day.'

'Which they're selling for sixty-plus dollars a barrel.'

'Yup. Comes out to six million dollars a day. Of course, that's not profit. EGenco takes their percentage, there's operating costs . . .'

'You know what, Roger? It's still a shitload of money left over.'

'No question about that.'

'And one more thing: give me a simple rule of thumb about how to manipulate oil prices.'

'It's actually pretty easy. Especially if you're someone like Dandridge where everyone would expect him to manipulate downward to benefit the administration and make himself look good politically.'

'Well, explain it to me both ways, up and down.'

'There's just one way, Jay. Once you have production in place, there are only two components: volume and price. The more volume, the lower the price. It's just simple supply and demand. Less volume, the more people have to pay. And vice versa.'

'And the way you alter the volume?'

'You lower the number of producers and producing sources. If you want to be really paranoid, you can say we blew up Iraqi oil wells in the various Gulf wars so the Saudis got a bigger share of production.'

'How about declaring oil-producing land off-limits to drillers?'

'You mean American land? Sure. Anything that limits production is going to raise prices. You know, you're starting to scare me, Jay. This doesn't sound so hypothetical.'

'Do me a favor, Roger. Call my folks and tell them I'm okay. Tell them I'll call them as soon as I can.'

'Want me to wish 'em a Merry Christmas for you?'

'I'll do that myself, thanks.'

'Did I give you what you need?'

'You gave me exactly what I need. I'll make it up to you.'

And when he hung up, he knew he had it. Not every detail. Not every piece of the puzzle. But the overall scheme. It was crystal clear. He had it cold.

And then he began to write. He no longer cared about his missing computer and the lost information. He remembered the last two lists he'd scrawled into the floor of his prison cell and quickly jotted them down on his pad. The first list was Dandridge and the various ways he was connected to the pieces of the puzzle.

DANDRIDGE
Midas
EGenco
Cooke
Anderson
Stuller
Ingles
Mishari

The next list was one where he'd split all the names into two categories – people and companies.

Cooke	Midas
Anderson	EGenco
Stuller	
Ingles	
Mishari	

Cooke was a victim. The others were survivors. The others formed the core group. So he rewrote the list, eliminating Cooke's name. He stared at what he'd written, realized that Dandridge was missing. He was the link to everything and everyone else and he belonged in this grouping. So he quickly scrawled the name at the bottom.

Anderson   Midas
Stuller   EGenco
Ingles
Mishari
Dandridge

He didn't have to stare at it for long before it came to him. Before it hit him like a sledgehammer on the back of the head. He turned to a new page. He wanted this clean and clear. And he rewrote the names in the left-hand column so it read:

Mishari
Ingles
Dandridge
Anderson
Stuller

Shaking his head, he underlined the first letters of each name on the list, first just one line, then two, then three. Each time he drew a line, he slashed down harder and more furiously with his pen.

<u>M</u>ishari
<u>I</u>ngles
<u>D</u>andridge
<u>A</u>nderson
<u>S</u>tuller

There it was. In angrily underlined black and white.

'Son of a bitch,' he whispered.

Who was Midas? That question was answered.

What was Midas? He was pretty sure he knew the answer to that one, too, now.

A hundred thousand barrels of oil per day. Over sixty dollars per barrel.

Over six million dollars a day.

Follow the money, his father had said.

Follow the goddamn money, Justin thought. Everything else is a mirage.

But the money gets you there every time.

chapter 32

He was just missing a couple of pieces of the puzzle. And by the time Bruno Pecozzi showed up in the late afternoon, he was certain he would have one of them.

Gary Jenkins arrived back at Justin's house around 3 P.M. with a sullen-looking blonde girl in tow. She was lugging a large leather case. When she took off her coat, Justin saw she was wearing the usual uniform of fifteen-year-old girls everywhere: jeans that were cut way too low on her hips, a tight shirt that didn't cover her midriff, platform shoes that looked like refugees from the '80s, and a lit cigarette hanging out of the corner of her lips.

'You're my artist?' Justin asked.

'So what is this, some kind of deal where I draw you naked?'

'I'm the chief of police of East End Harbor,' Justin said. 'I'm asking you to help me solve a serious crime.'

She sounded almost disappointed. 'Yeah, that's what Gary said.'

'Officer Jenkins,' Gary said sternly.

'Yeah, whatever,' the girl said.

'Will you help me?' Justin said. 'It's important.'

'I liked it better when I thought you were gonna be naked,' the girl said.

'I don't blame you,' Justin said. 'What's your name?'

366

'Darla,' the girl told him.

'So you gonna help me, Darla?'

She turned to Gary. 'Did you tell him what I want?'

'How could I tell him? I've been with you, haven't I? Don't worry about it.'

Darla turned back to Justin. 'A year's membership at the Museum of Modern Art. In New York.'

'That's what you want?' Justin asked, surprised.

'For a whole year.'

'I'll make it two years,' Justin said. 'If you can draw what I need.'

'Whatever it is, I can draw it,' the girl said. 'So let's get goin'. I don't, like, have all day.'

While Justin stayed with Darla, he sent Gary off on one more errand, handing him a credit card and giving him instructions. Gary was back in an hour with a brand-new laptop computer.

By that time Darla had gotten it right.

No, Justin thought, more than right. Perfect.

'Remember me when you're hanging in MOMA,' he said. 'I'm your first patron.'

'Whatever,' she said. 'Can I go now?'

A few minutes after she'd gone, the doorbell rang. It was Bruno.

It was a strange moment for Justin. He didn't particularly like Bruno Pecozzi. He was not immune to his charm or his easygoing, entertaining manner, but he understood that the man was a killer. Your basic sociopath. Justin had always expected that, one day, he'd have to arrest the man, and he had to admit that up until now, he would have said that would be a day he looked forward to. But there was a good chance this man had saved his life. Certainly, he'd saved his sanity. And there was one other thing: he needed Bruno now. He needed something done and he didn't have the strength to do it himself. Arresting Bruno was the last thing on Justin's mind now. He had something quite different he wanted to discuss with the strong-arm hood turned movie consultant. Something much more in keeping with Bruno's particular talents. Justin was about to cross a line and he didn't really care. He had crossed this line before. So he stuck out his hand, and when Bruno took it, Justin simply said, 'Thank you.'

Bruno didn't say a word, just shrugged. Finally, as they stood in the living room, Bruno said, 'You got a beer?'

Justin brought him one and they sat down.

'How?' Justin said, sipping from his own bottle of Sam Adams. 'How the hell did you do it?'

'You know, Jay, people in my profession, we're like magicians. We don't like to give away our secrets. Makes it look less impressive, you know?'

'Bruno,' Justin said, 'it's gonna be pretty hard for me to not be impressed. You got through maybe the most secretive government installation we have.'

'Without goin' into too much detail, you gotta keep in mind what my business associates specialize in. Remember I told you I was good at judgin' when people were afraid?'

'I remember.'

'Yeah, well, I'm not too bad either when it comes to pickin' people who are . . . how shall I say . . . greedy.'

'Corrupt?'

'That's another way of puttin' it, sure.'

'I'm still not following.'

'All right. I use this lawyer, she's good people, Shirley Greene. She's saved my bacon a coupla times.'

'She represents the guy who contacted me down there.'

368

'She represents a lotta those guys. It's what she does, you know? She's one of those liberal do-gooders. You know, I told her, I don't approve. I mean, all those Arab fucks, who knows what the fuck they're doin' to our country, but hey, she helped me out enough times, who am I to say no when she needs a favor.'

'What kind of favor did she need?'

'She couldn't talk to her clients. It's the way things work now. They got 'em in a place like that, there ain't too much you can do. So she asked if I could help.'

'And you could.'

'Jay, here's the thing. You got a basic honest point of view. You can't help it, it's just who you are, the way you was raised. Me, I see things a different way. And the way I see it, wherever there's any kinda hierarchy . . . good word, right? . . . there's gonna be somebody who's gettin' shafted. Someone's makin' more money than someone else, someone's not gettin' the promotion he thought he should get, someone's not gettin' the girl he thinks he deserves, you know what I mean?'

'Yeah. I know what you mean.'

'So it's usually not too hard to find someone who's pissed off. Who'll do you a little favor in exchange for somethin' he wants. And you'd be surprised how what people want is usually money.'

'But Gitmo?'

'Hey, it's prison guards, right? If there's one thing, I know, it's prison guards. Don't matter who they work for, it's still a shitty job and they all could use a favor. So it's just a matter of findin' out what they want. After Shirley came to me, way before you were there, it took me a couple of months but I found somebody. In fact, I found two somebodies. So she had a pipeline, could get word to her clients, get some information down there, get some back. Shirley's the one suspected that's where they took you. After that, it wasn't so hard. I already had the connection. I called your father, told him what I knew—'

'You and my father?' When Bruno nodded, Justin said, 'I have to say, I'd like to have heard those conversations.'

'He'd already spoken to your girlfriend and he was pretty sharp. He's a businessman, you know what I mean? He knows how to cut to the bottom of things. I enjoyed dealin' with him.'

'I'll be sure to tell him.'

'Well, you should thank him, too, 'cause once he decided I was givin' him the legit story, he called your lady pal up in Boston and they put some serious pressure on.'

'Yeah, Wanda, I know. What kind of pressure?'

'Don't know exactly. A congressman, a senator, between the two of them they got some access. All I know is, your Feebie friend called me and said things were lookin' good.'

'Jesus. Now Wanda's calling *you*?'

'Makes you believe in the Big Guy upstairs, don't it?'

Justin rubbed his fingers across his dry lips. 'Wanda said things were looking good? What did that mean?'

'I was hopin' it meant she had the connections to, you know, monitor the situation. And give you some protection. Which is what happened. She's got some juice, that girl.'

'I guess she does.'

'You owe her, buddy.'

'Yeah. And I guess she'll be making me pay her back for quite a while.'

'So, anyway, once someone with juice knew what the story was, I knew they couldn't do nothin' too bad to you, and I figured that knowledge might come in handy while you were incarcerated.'

'It did.'

'Good. That pleases me.' Bruno was finished with his second beer by then. He seemed to suck the liquid out of the bottle in one big gulp. 'So is this just a pleasant sit-around and thank-you kind of a thing, or you got somethin' else to discuss with me?'

'I have something else to discuss with you.'

'So let's hear it.'

Justin nodded. Held up his hand to say it would just be a moment, went to the phone, and dialed the Riverhead police station. When he was put through to his contact, he said, 'I'm calling for Wanda Chinkle again. How are those prints coming?'

'You fuckin' guys,' the officer on the other end of the phone said. 'You sent me a bunch of jacks to get prints *off* of? You know how fuckin' hard it is to get prints *off jacks?*'

'Do you have anything?'

'We're workin' on it. Maybe some partials. But we don't have a match yet, if that's what you're askin'.'

'How about the other thing?'

'The paper cup? Yeah, we got that. I was just gonna fax the info to you but you called when I was getting up.'

'If you can fax it now, I'd really appreciate it.'

'No problem.'

'And how about the jacks?'

'Hey, I know with you Feds everything's a fuckin' emergency. I said we're workin' on it. If I get somethin' soon, I'll let you know.'

'Thanks a lot.'

'Yeah, yeah, yeah. Go stand by your fax machine. I'll send the stuff in a minute.'

Justin hung up, told Bruno to wait one more minute. It took less than that for his fax machine to start humming. A piece of paper came through. Justin stared at the information on it, then handed it to Bruno.

'I'd like to hire you to use your particular skill sets,' he said to the big man. 'Normally, I'd do this myself, but I don't think I have the strength.'

'Lieutenant Colonel Warren Grimble,' Bruno said, reading from the faxed piece of paper. 'Military Intelligence.'

'I need some information from him,' Justin said.

'Uh-huh. You meet this guy while you were vacationin' down south just now?'

'That's where I met him.'

'What do you need to know?'

'In early November, a day or two before the bombing at Harper's Restaurant, an Air Force captain, Hutchinson Cooke, flew someone out of Guantanamo Bay, and flew him to the East End airport. I'm pretty sure that person was a prisoner there. I want to know who it was.'

'Okay.' Bruno scanned the faxed piece of paper. 'This Grimble's home address?

'And his military base in Louisiana.'

'I don't suppose you got anything to show me what he looks like?'

'As a matter of fact,' Justin said, and went to his desk and got Bruno the sketch that Darla had drawn. 'It's an exact likeness,' he said. 'As good as a photograph.'

'So, Jay, I'm more than happy to be a nice guy sometimes, but I'm still a businessman and usually I'm compensated for this kind of work.'

'Name the price.'

'I like dealin' with you Westwoods,' Bruno said. 'There's no bull-shit.'

He told Justin the price and Justin didn't hesitate. He just nodded and said, 'Done.'

'I got a couple of questions for you,' Bruno said. 'Bein' the thorough professional that I am.'

'Go ahead.'

'You want this guy . . . Grimble . . . to know the . . . how shall I put it . . . the subtext of our conversation? I been hangin' around the screenwriter of the movie. I like that word, "subtext."'

'Do you mean, do I want him to know that the question's coming from me?'

'That's what I mean.'

'Absolutely,' Justin said. 'That's a prerequisite of the job.'

'Then I need to know one more thing.'

'Okay.'

'When I get the answer to your question, do you want this Grimble to be able to discuss this situation with anyone else?'

Justin hesitated for only a moment before saying, 'It's why I'm hiring an expert. I want you to do whatever you think is best.'

The big man rose off the couch now. It took him a couple of attempts to get his full bulk back on his feet. And when he was up, Justin was startled to see as large and as dangerous a man as Bruno Pecozzi wink. 'Like I said, no bullshit when you're dealin' with the Westwoods.' Bruno stuck out his hand. 'I'd love to stay and chat, but I got work to do.'

Justin took the big man's hand. Felt the callused skin of Bruno's palm as they shook.

As soon as Bruno was gone, Justin went upstairs to his bathroom, covered the lower half of his face in thick coils of shaving cream, and pulled out his razor. It took him about five minutes to shave his beard and leave his face completely smooth.

He rubbed his chin and then both cheeks and he looked in the mirror at his reflection.

The beard was gone, Justin thought to himself, but he still didn't feel clean.

On the other hand, he realized, he didn't feel too bad, either.

chapter 33

Justin picked up the phone on the fourth ring. His caller ID told him who it was. He didn't want to talk but he knew he had to. The caller was, he believed, going to tell him whether he could finally put an end to all the madness. He was afraid she was going to say that he couldn't. But there was only one way to find out.

'Wanda,' he said into the receiver.

She was a lot calmer than he expected.

'I'm calling to tell you something, Jay,' Wanda Chinkle said. 'We're not actually as stupid as you might think.'

'Thanks,' Justin said. 'That's very comforting.'

'It's not meant to be. It's meant to be a warning.'

'Is this about something in particular?'

'It's about several things. For one, Warren Grimble has disappeared.'

'Who's that?'

'Lieutenant Colonel Warren Grimble. Military Intelligence. His specialty is prisoner interrogation. He's spent a lot of time in Iraq. But he's intermittently stationed at Gitmo.'

'Huh,' Justin said. 'That's a coincidence.'

'How'd your fingerprint ID turn out?' Wanda asked.

'Not very helpful,' he said. 'Kind of a wild goose chase, I guess.'

374

'Both sets?'

'What?'

'You told me you were running one set of prints.'

'Oh. I just figured I'd sneak in a second set. An old case I've been working on.'

'I'm doing you a favor now,' she said. 'So listen to what I'm telling you.'

'I'm listening.'

'You can trust me.'

'I know. You've told me.'

'Well, it's important that I tell you again. I want you to remember that specifically. If a time comes when you're not sure, just remember what I said. Please.'

Justin massaged the area directly over his eyes with his right hand. 'Is there some kind of secret message in all this, Wanda? What are you trying to tell me?'

'I'm trying to tell you the only thing I *can* tell you. You can trust me and anyone who's with me. *Anyone*. Okay?'

'Sure,' he said. 'Sure. Okay.'

She took a deep breath. 'I've arranged the meeting we discussed.'

He exhaled a huge sigh of relief 'Thank you.'

'Before I give you the details, are you sure you don't want to tell me what this is about?'

'You're much better off not knowing.'

'Final answer?'

'Yes, Regis. I've got no life lines left. Final answer.'

'I'd also like you to remember that you said that.'

'Okay. I'll remember that, too.' He knew he was letting his impatience show through. 'Now what do I have to do?'

'He doesn't want to see you at the Justice Department.'

'So where?'

'New York.'

'The city?'

'The Waldorf Towers. Suite 1603.'

'When?'

'Tonight. Seven o'clock.'

'I'll be there.'

'Jay . . .'

'Uh-oh. Sounds like another warning.'

'Just some advice. And I hope you take it seriously. You won't be allowed in tonight if you're armed. But once you leave the hotel, make sure you have a gun on you at all times.'

'Sounds like pretty sound advice,' Justin said.

'The best you're gonna get,' Wanda Chinkle told him.

'Pretty soon, I won't even be able to count how much I'm gonna owe you.'

'You know me, Jay. I'll hardly ever mention it.' When there was a silence from his end, she said, 'You still there?'

'Still here,' he said. 'Sorry. I'm just thinking how well I know you.'

Justin was sitting in front of his new computer, staring at the screen, at the notes and lists he'd entered since he'd returned to East End Harbor.

All he could think about was how everything was a game. People played at life and they got cute and, as a result, some other people died who didn't have to.

Bruno had returned about an hour earlier, rang the doorbell, and when Justin answered it, Bruno had handed him a piece of paper with a name on it. Justin read the name, said, 'Anything you want to tell me about what happened?'

Bruno shook his head, said, 'Anything you want to ask me about what happened?'

Justin shook his head back. Bruno said, 'Next dinner's on you,' turned and went back to his car.

Now Justin looked at the name he'd typed into the computer, the name that Bruno Pecozzi had brought back to him from Lieutenant Colonel Warren Grimble. It was the name of the person that Hutchinson Cooke had flown from Guantanamo Bay to the East End airport.

Mudhi al Rahman.

He looked down at the piece of paper that had recently been faxed over from the Riverhead Police Department. The note read:

Next time give us something better than a bunch of fucking jacks.
Because we're so damn good, we got you something anyway. The
partials belong to Mudhi al Rahman. Saudi big shot. Good luck.
Merry Christmas. And fuck you again about the jacks.

It was confirmed.

Mudhi al Rahman was the man who had played jacks with Hannah Cooke.

He was the man who'd been flown into East End by Hutch Cooke.

Justin was certain he was the man who'd rigged all three bombs and the man who'd made the cell phone calls to set them off.

As soon as he'd gotten the confirmation, he'd gone on the Net, to Google, and typed in 'Saudi royal family'. He was sent to a page that said there were 312,000 entries. The first one on the list – 'Explore Saudi Family Trees' – looked like it would do just fine, and he was right. It didn't take him long to scour the unfamiliar-sounding names until he came to Mishari al Rahman, Dandridge's friend and business partner. He clicked on that. The names of dozens of brothers and sisters and even more children appeared. The tree listed one of Mishari's sons as Mudhi al Rahman.

377

Part of the game.

Terry Cooke had known all along.

He remembered the notes he'd typed into the computer after he'd come back from D.C. He'd asked Terry why her husband had flown into East End.

I don't know, she'd said. *I guess bad guys have to live somewhere, don't they?*

He'd asked again.

Things are just so muddy, she had said to him. *That's what Hutch would have told you. Things are muddy.*

Hutch Cooke had said, *I fell down the tower,* to let her know he was in Paris.

She had played the same game.

Everything's muddy.

Muddy. Mudhi.

Everything was muddy, all right.

Mudhi al Rahman.

Why East End? he'd asked Terry Cooke.

I guess even bad guys have to live somewhere, don't they? That's what she'd said.

Some fucking game.

Justin picked up the phone, called information, then dialed the number of the top local Realtor. She had an office on Main Street as well as one in Bridgehampton.

As the phone rang, he remembered when he'd first moved to East End Harbor, seven years ago. He'd had a day off and it was a beautiful morning in July. He'd gone to Gibson Beach in Sagaponack. Lay down on a blanket, maybe twenty feet from a group of mothers and their small children. The beach was crowded but he'd carved out a nice little space for himself, quiet. He'd soaked in the sun, eyes closed, left alone with his thoughts, for a good hour, and then he felt a shadow cross his chest. He opened one eye and squinted up. A man was carrying a folding beach chair, setting it down in the sand just a few feet from Justin. The man smiled at him and Justin smiled politely back. Justin closed his eyes again, drifted back to his thoughts, and that's when he realized that the man sitting next to him was Salman Rushdie. There was a million-dollar *fatwa* out against him; the entire Muslim fundamentalist world had sworn to find and kill him. And here he was sunning himself on one of the choicest, most crowded beaches in the world. Rushdie stayed about two hours, nodded and smiled at Justin again when he picked up his beach chair and left. Justin followed him with his eyes until the fugitive writer disappeared into the tarred parking area. He remembered shaking his head in amazement.

Just as he was shaking it now.

If a man on the run from the fundamentalist world could hide in plain sight in the Hamptons, why not the most feared terrorist in the country?

Someone answered the phone on the other end: 'East Ender Realty.'

'Rose?'

'You got her. Who's calling?'

'It's Justin Westwood, Rose.'

'Funny, I was just talking about you. Do you remember my friend Lisa? She was asking about you. I think she's a little bit interested in you, if you know what I mean. I told her I hadn't seen you around. I even asked Leona, I bumped into her on the street, and she said you'd been out of town. Some kind of family emergency . . .'

'I need some information, Rose. This is official business and I'd appreciate it if you'd keep it quiet.'

379

'Uh-huh . . . sure . . . I didn't realize . . . I mean . . .'

'I have a name and I need to find out if he owns or rents a house in the Hamptons. Can you find someone if I give you a name?'

'That's a big can-do. Give me fifteen minutes, I can find anyone you want, tell you how much square footage he's got, and how much less than the asking price you can buy his house for.'

'All I need's an address,' Justin said. 'For someone named Mishari al Rahman.'

'Gazillionaire Arab, right? I'll call Claudia over at Hamptonian Realty. They seem to handle most of the Arabs. Don't know where they got the connection, but it's a mighty profitable one, lemme tell you.'

'It's kind of important, Rose. Can you make the call now?'

'You know it's Christmas Eve, right? People are gonna be takin' off pretty soon.'

'Then you should probably call before they leave. And Claudia has to keep this confidential. If she mentions this to her client, I'll make sure she spends the next few Christmases in jail.'

'Jesus. You in the market? Is this about you wanting to buy? 'Cause if there's a sale in it, the holiday goes right out the window—'

'It's police business, Rose. Important police business. Call me back as soon as you've got something.'

'Right. Call you back in a nanosecond.'

His phone rang in under three minutes. Rose's harsh, nasal voice pierced the receiver. 'Lucky bastard's got a house on Gin Lane in Southampton. You know, it's too bad *my* family wasn't in the oil business. I'd like a house on Gin Lane myself.'

'You have an address?'

She gave it to him. 'You'll see a big house, well, hell, they're all huge over there, aren't they? But the guy you're lookin' for, Mr A-rab, his joint's next to the house with the golf hole on the side. The par three that leads down to the water. To the left of that, that's your guy.'

'Can you call Claudia and tell her to stay put for a little bit? I need one more thing from her.'

'Sure. But how long? She does have a family, you know. Well, not exactly a family. But a boyfriend and he's—'

'Tell her to wait for me for half an hour, okay? No longer than that.'

'Okay. I'm sure she'll do that.'

'Thank you.'

'Don't thank me. Just let me know when you're looking to upgrade, okay?'

'You got it,' Justin said.

He looked at his watch. Almost time to get moving, he thought. But he still had a few minutes. He made the call he'd been wanting to make all day.

'You have Christmas plans?' he asked Reggie when she answered the phone. He was a little stunned to realize how glad he was to hear her voice.

'I was going to drink a six-pack and watch *It's a Wonderful Life*. Got something better in mind?'

'I might.'

'That as specific as you gonna be, Jay?'

'Yeah. I think so.'

'Okay. Sounds good to me.' She laughed. 'So much for playing hard to get, I guess.'

'It's a little late for that, don't you think?'

'What about tonight? We might as well go all the way and do Christmas Eve as long as we're doing it.'

He looked at his watch. 'How unhard to get are you gonna play?'

'About as unhard as it gets.'

'Then I'll try to call you later, okay?'

'Whenever, Jay. I'll be here.'

He was happy when he hung up the phone. He didn't know how long it would last but he was happy. He had to admit it probably wouldn't last very long.

It was time to head into the city.

Justin started out the door, turned back, went to his desk and pulled out his Glock. He thought about Wanda's warning. He'd leave it in the car when he parked in the city, lock it away in the glove compartment. But she'd said to stay armed as soon as the meeting was over. Wanda wasn't an alarmist. No need to be a fool about this.

He went out to his car, stuck the gun in the glove box.

He realized he was hungry, figured that a high-and-mighty government official wouldn't plan on serving him dinner at 7 P.M. in his hotel suite, he'd be lucky to get a glass of water, so after he'd gotten what he needed from Claudia the Realtor, Justin stopped at the Burger King on Montauk Highway. As he drove toward Manhattan, he munched on a cheeseburger that tasted like cardboard and some chicken fingers that weren't bad if heavily dipped in the honey mustard sauce. He poured two full shots of bourbon into his large BK Coke, somewhere around Exit 52 he checked his glove compartment, just to make absolutely sure the gun was still tucked inside, and then he drove straight and fast along the LIE. He only stopped wondering whether anyone would possibly believe what he was about to reveal when he popped in a Bob Dylan CD, *Oh Mercy*, and turned it up full blast to play the song 'Everything Is Broken.'

It seemed like the right sentiment, so he played it five times in a row, as loud as he could, until he drove through the Midtown Tunnel, turned uptown on Park Avenue, and found himself in front of the Waldorf.

Stepping out of the car and taking a ticket from the guy at valet parking, he hoped Dylan was wrong.

Most *things are broken*, he thought, *sure. Absolutely.*

But please, he hoped, *not everything.*

chapter 34

Ted Ackland, the assistant attorney general of the United States, sat on the coarse, tweedish couch in the living room of his hotel suite sipping from a highball-sized glass of scotch and water. He was impeccably dressed, from the crisp starched collar of his white dress shirt to his perfectly tailored black wool Armani suit, to his black dress socks that didn't have a millimeter of sag to them, and his black, highly polished Cesare Paciotti shoes. He crossed his legs, lifted his eyebrows in approval of the scotch, and motioned for Justin Westwood to sit down.

'Merry Christmas,' he said. 'I apologize for the security you had to pass through. You wanted to see me alone, that's what it takes in this day and age.' He raised his glass in Justin's direction. 'To crazy times.'

Justin sat. 'Thank you for seeing me.'

'My wife wasn't too damn happy. She's wrapping our kids' presents by herself. And having a candlelit dinner for one.'

'I'm sorry.'

'Agent Chinkle is someone everyone respects tremendously. For her to call and say that I should see you, and say that it's urgent, well . . . I wouldn't be very good at my job if I didn't respond to something like that. No matter what day it is.'

There was something ingratiating about the man. He drew you in with his warmth and his passion. Justin almost felt sorry for him. Ackland's life must already be somewhat nightmarish. What Justin was about to tell him wasn't going to ease his burden. 'You look tired, sir.'

Ackland's lips formed a distracted smile. 'Well, my department's been a little busy lately. Perhaps you've noticed.'

'Busier than I think even you've noticed,' Justin said.

The smile faded from Ackland's face. 'Are we getting to your business now, Mr Westwood?'

Justin nodded.

'Good. If possible, I'd at least like to have a sip of egg nog with my wife before the night's out.'

So Justin launched into his story. He began slowly and continued in as detailed a manner as he could manage. He left nothing out, beginning with Jimmy Leggett's death at Harper's, Marge's request at Jimmy's funeral, and the plane crash. He told the story step by step, just as it happened, and as he talked about investigating the crash and finding out about Hutchinson Cooke and Martin Heffernan, about Chuck Billings's suspicions and suspicious death, about Ray Lockhardt, about talking to Colonel Zanesworth and Martha Peck, he saw Ackland go from curious to concerned to pained. He saw the fury begin to well up in the second-highest-ranking law officer in the land. And when Justin went into detail about the big boys, as he explained the growing connections to Dandridge and to Ackland's direct boss, Jeffrey Stuller, and even to Thomas Anderson, the president of the United States, he saw the kind of deer-in-the-headlights expression that Justin knew he himself had been wearing for too many weeks now.

Justin described his time in Guantanamo Bay and Ackland began to pepper him with questions, but Justin asked him to please let him finish. It was the first time he'd put the entire puzzle together out loud and he wanted to complete it.

'This is the end of it,' he told the assistant attorney general. 'Over the last two days I've been able to connect all the dots. I can put it all together backwards and forwards now. When Dandridge left as CEO of EGenco to run for vice president, he made a deal with Bradford Collins, the new CEO, and probably other key executives. They set up a Special Purpose Entity, a spin-off of EGenco, as an under-the-table payoff.'

'To what end?' Ackland asked.

'To a couple of ends. They made Dandridge and the other partners rich. Wildy rich. In exchange for which, EGenco received tens of billions of dollars of no-bid contracts for work in the Middle East. Which they needed because they were in danger of going under.'

'My office has been investigating them for nearly two years.'

'I know. It's how Brad Collins was set up at Harper's. He was talking to your people, he was about to blow the whistle.'

'Mr Westwood, you're saying that the attorney general of the United States, Jeff Stuller, not only knew about the bombing at Harper's in advance, he helped to set it up as a way of silencing Brad Collins?'

'That is what I'm saying, sir. It's why you couldn't make any real headway into the EGenco investigation and it's why you never got the kind of information you should have gotten from Chuck Billings. Stuller's been stopping the investigation every step of the way.'

'Jesus Christ.'

'I agree. But please let me finish, I don't have much more to go.'

'Go, go.'

'The SPE that EGenco set up had five partners: Mishari al Rahman, Stephanie Ingles, Phillip Dandridge, Thomas Anderson, and Jeffrey Stuller.'

Ackland groaned.

386

'They called the company Midas,' Justin went on, 'and what I think they were given was a small to medium-size oil production company.'

'You can prove *all* of this?'

'No. But you can. It's all accurate, if not provable yet.'

'Go on.'

'Somebody – my guess is Dandridge because he knew the most about the oil business and is probably the smartest one in the group – realized they could all make an almost unreal amount of money if they could make oil prices go up. And they did. Mishari was their link to OPEC, Dandridge and Anderson could obviously manipulate policy and limit oil sources, and Ingles could help limit oil sources domestically, like she did recently in Alaska. I think all this was worked out at the energy meeting Dandridge called when he first took office. The one the Supreme Court ruled he could keep secret.'

'What about Stuller?'

'Hard to say. He obviously doesn't have much of a role in manipulating oil prices, but he was a crony and it's logical that they'd bring him into this kind of business deal. Plus, once things got out of hand, he was the most valuable person they could have on their team.'

'Got out of hand how?'

'As I said, it started with Brad Collins. He was going to talk. The way I think it went down is someone in that group realized Collins had to go. At the time, Anderson's popularity was way down and it looked like he might drag Dandridge down with him politically.'

'Dandridge's poll numbers were low.'

'He was going to get blown out of the water in the next election. Until the explosion at Harper's. They literally killed two birds with one stone. They got rid of Collins and when they made it look like a suicide bombing it not only threw off any suspicion that Collins was a specific target, it was a brilliant political move. The more afraid people are, the less likely they're going to want a change. Dandridge's poll numbers rose.'

'And the other bombings?'

'More of the same. Heffernan, the FAA guy, was small potatoes, but he could be a problem. He knew too much and he didn't have any kind of big stake in the game, so it made sense to get rid of him. It worked perfectly for Collins, why not do it again?'

'It's so . . . cold-blooded.'

'You know them. How much of a stretch is it to believe they'd be capable of this?'

Ackland didn't answer for quite a while. He took two more long gulps of his scotch, filled the glass up again and took another drink. Then he quietly said, 'It's not very much of a stretch.'

'The last real person who knew anything was Hutch Cooke's wife. They basically knew she was too terrified to speak . . . until I showed up to see her. Then they got nervous. And by then they also realized that every terrorist attack made their poll numbers go sky-high. Unless they looked ineffectual. So now they look even better – they caught the terrorists and suddenly they're the only real guardians of the country. As long as no one finds out they were the cause of the whole thing to begin with.'

'But you don't believe they caught the real terrorists.'

'Hell, no. It's why none of them survived. It's hard for dead men to protest their innocence.'

'So, who did they use to—'

'His name is Mudhi al Rahman. He's Mishari's son. He has a history as a radical. I wouldn't be surprised if he really does have Al Qaeda ties. At some point he was picked up and removed to Gitmo. Mishari must have pulled some serious strings. What I'm pretty sure happened is that Dandridge or Stuller or Anderson put two and two together and realized they could get Mudhi out of prison and have themselves the perfect terrorist. They gave him the targets and then they gave him free rein.'

'If you're right—'

'I *am* right.'

Ackland excused himself, stepped into the bathroom. Justin heard water run and Ackland came out toweling off his face, looking slightly more refreshed. He sat back down on the couch. 'So what's their next step?' he said, tossing the towel onto a countertop.

'This is guesswork on my part now. But it's the only thing that makes sense. They don't need this Mudhi al Rahman anymore. He can only do them damage now. Because he's Mishari's son, I'm guessing they won't kill him. But they sure as hell are going to get him out of town.'

'Do we know what town that is?'

'Down to the street address.'

Ackland stood up. Paced behind the couch, rubbing the back of his neck with his right hand. On his third or fourth round trip, he stopped. 'I think I should be calling you by your first name,' he said.

'Please.'

'Well, Justin . . . I want to thank you for coming to me.'

'I didn't see that I had a lot of choices.'

'No. But at least you made the right choice.' Ackland looked very uncomfortable now, as if he weren't sure what he should or shouldn't say. The struggle was a brief one and he began to speak freely. And the more he spoke, the more relieved he looked. 'I wish I could tell you you're crazy, that what you're saying can't possibly be true. Unfortunately what you've told me is not a complete surprise. But my nuts are between a rock and a hard place. And have been for a hell of a long time.'

Now it was Justin's turn to look shocked. 'You've known this?'

'Not all of it, not by any means. I'm extraordinarily impressed with some of the things you've come up with, because my team and I have been working on this from the very beginning and you got things we didn't. You also took them a hell of a lot farther than we've been able to. And you've filled in some gaps, clarified some motives, certain actions. Just so you know, I'm not convinced that President Anderson knows anything about this. And you haven't given me any new facts to convince me that he does. I think he's been manipulated and lied to. But I am damn sorry to say I've had a very quiet investigation going on to look into the vice president. Jesus, it makes me sick to even say that out loud.'

'I understand that,' Justin said.

'I don't know if you can. I'm close to Phil Dandridge. In many ways, he was my mentor. But the things we've uncovered are not so far off from the story you presented. I believe you.'

'And Stuller?'

'We've been closing in on Jeff, too.' Ackland started to say more. Seemed to be unable to speak, so he just shook his head from side to side. 'My problem now,' he finally said, 'is that I feel a little bit like I'm in the middle of the *Caine* Mutiny. I don't know who to trust. I don't know who I can go to who's above me and I don't know who I can go to who's below me. You're saying even top FBI agents are involved in this.'

'Working under Stuller's orders. I suppose it's hard to turn down an order from the attorney general.'

'I've even fed Stuller information. When I began investigating. Before I began to suspect that he was involved.' Ackland rubbed his eyes. 'Are you sure about Hubbell Schrader?'

'Yes.'

'I've worked with Hubbell. I've worked with Hubbell on this case.

He's been privy to . . . Goddammit.' Again, Ackland didn't seem to know what to say. He began pacing again. When he stopped, he said, 'Do you have any idea what's going to happen when this becomes public?'

Some.

'But you don't care.'

'No, I don't,' Justin said.

'I don't either,' Ted Ackland said. 'Not anymore. Wanda said you'd have something specific in mind. I don't mind saying that I will gladly take any suggestions you'd like to give.'

'Mudhi al Rahman,' Justin said. 'I want to pick him up.'

'Pick him up, hell,' Ackland said. 'I want to kill the son of a bitch.'

'And I'll help you pull the switch. But not yet. For one thing, he might be the only witness we can find out of this thing. If they move him out of the country—'

'—we'll lose our proof. Do you know that he's still here?'

'No, I don't. It's just my hunch.'

'Can you get him?'

'If he's still here, I can get him.'

Ackland poured himself one more stiff scotch, took a healthy swig. 'Wanda Chinkle says you're a hell of a cop.'

'I'm glad she thinks so.'

'Tough guy, huh?'

'Not that tough.'

'Just tough enough?'

Justin nodded. 'As tough as I have to be.'

'You know,' Ackland said, and Justin thought the scotch was beginning to get to him. 'I've spent a lifetime in law enforcement. I was a pretty tough guy, too But I knew how to put a good face on it. I tried to be fair. Tried to see different points of view. It's how I got to the position I'm in.' He started to put the glass to his lips again, thought better of it, and put it down on the glass coffee table in front of the couch. 'You know Phil Dandridge put me in the mix to be on his ticket.'

'I've read that.'

'Not bad for a cop from Wisconsin.'

'No, sir. Not too bad.'

'I guess I can forget it now, can't I?'

'Looks like it, doesn't it?'

Ackland picked up his glass again, took one more drink. 'What the hell,' he said. 'How about we both show how tough we are. How about you do your job and I'll do mine.'

'Sounds like a plan,' Justin said.

He turned and left the assistant attorney general of the United States. Before Justin walked out of the room, he glanced back to see Ted Ackland staring out the hotel window, looking lost and confused and a little bit desperate.

Justin didn't blame him one damn bit.

chapter 35

The mansions on Gin Lane in Southampton reminded Justin of his childhood in Rhode Island. The rich people in Newport, where his parents had a second home, lived like this. On a different, almost unimaginable scale. In a pristine location. Isolated. Unaware that outside their gates and away from their manicured lawns, the real world was lying in wait.

Justin felt very much a part of the real world right now.

And he'd never been quite so anxious to bring this reality behind those electric gates.

It was eleven-thirty at night. He was on foot, walking beside Reggie. They'd driven separately; Justin had her meet him two blocks from the house they were now heading toward. He'd told her to just park on the grass shoulder of the road and wait for him. As he drove the last few miles into Southampton, he'd noticed a car that had been behind him for several turns. He made a point of going past his destination, taking a winding road that led into the local college. That campus was a flat expanse, and as soon as he made the turn he accelerated, heading straight south to the Old Montauk Highway. He crossed over, hit eighty on the speedometer, made a quick left turn, and waited. If anyone had followed him, he'd gotten clear. He forced himself to sit for another three minutes, then wended his way back to his original destination. There were no headlights behind him. It had probably been nothing, but Justin was not in the mood to take chances.

He and Reggie walked past the golf hole that Justin had been told about. It was a respectable par three that led straight to the ocean.

'Isn't there a lot of security for these houses?' Reggie whispered.

'Sure,' Justin said.

'So do we have a plan to get in to this guy's place?'

'We do.'

'What, we just walk in the front door?'

'The back door,' he said.

They were at the house.

'Follow me,' Justin told her. He didn't turn at the front gate that was meant to keep out cars, instead kept around the block toward a side entrance of the house. Running along that side of the property was a low brick wall, just three or four feet high. He pulled himself up to the top of the wall, reached down to give her his hand. She waved him away and easily pulled herself up beside him. A quick hop down and they were both in the vast manicured yard that belonged to Mishari al Rahman.

'Can't be this easy,' she muttered.

'Getting into these places isn't usually all that hard,' he said. 'It's getting out. If you can't get a car up the driveway it's difficult to carry out anything too large. So they mostly care about guarding the driveway. Besides, there's a state-of-the-art alarm system. Anyone goes in the house the police are here in about three minutes.'

'And you're brilliant enough to know how to disable the alarm?'

'Already been disabled. Didn't take brilliance. Just took a call to the Southampton police and the security company that installed it.'

'So we can just waltz right in?'

'Pretty much,' he said. 'But I'd pull your gun now. In case our guy's not in a real dancing mood.'

Although guns were not standard issue for the East End PD, Reggie had a registered firearm. She had told him she was not a bad marksman, which was the main reason he'd called her instead of one of the kiddie cops populating the East End station. She told him she'd never fired the gun in real-life action but she was good on the range. He figured it was the best he was going to do. They both had their pistols in their hands when they reached the back door. He turned the knob, but the door was locked.

'Should we try a window?' Reggie asked.

Justin shook his head, reached into his pocket and took out a key.

'How the hell did you get that?' she demanded.

'The Realtor. She had it from when she showed the house.'

He unlocked the door, stepped inside, his arms up and his gun pointed.

Nothing.

They were in a foyer, the lights off. There were lights on upstairs and in the kitchen, which was off to their right, but the house was quiet. No buzz of a television, no sense of any movement.

'Now what?' Reggie whispered.

'We'll take this floor first,' he answered, also in a hushed tone. He pointed toward the kitchen. 'I got a rough layout from the Realtor. There's a dining room, then the kitchen. Off the dining room is a doorway that leads to a den. The kitchen's actually three rooms.'

She nodded.

'I'll go first,' he said. 'You follow. Don't be trigger-happy, there have to be servants somewhere around. Maybe bodyguards. But don't be afraid to shoot, either.'

She nodded again, nervously. Then he stepped into the dining room.

Moonlight filtered through the windows, casting shadows on the huge room. His arm jerked up, gun pointed toward a corner of the room, then he realized he was looking at a sculpture. Each corner of the room had a marble sculpture in it. They were all of naked women. There was enough light in the room that he could make out the fact that the women's pubic hair had been painted in.

He heard Reggie exhale with relief. Then he saw her roll her eyes in disbelief.

He motioned to her that he was moving into the kitchen. She nodded her okay and followed him.

Justin went through the doorway. The first room of the kitchen had a small stainless steel table and cabinets on all four walls that were stockpiled with liquor. The al Rahman family clearly did not follow the non-drinking dictates of the Muslim religion.

He glided into the next room, where the light was on. The first thing he noticed was the enormous stainless steel eight-burner stove that dominated the room. The second thing he saw made him turn away and made his stomach lurch. He turned toward Reggie, who had seen it, too. She had gone ghostly white. Justin reached out to touch her arm but she pulled away. The skin on her face was drawn tight and her eyes seemed to sink into their sockets, her breath was coming in short, thick gasps, but she nodded at him that she was okay. He turned back to the center of the room.

Four Arab men and two women were lying on the floor in a pile. All of their throats had been cut.

He told her to wait, not to move, and he made a quick search of the rest of the downstairs of the house. There was no one, either living or dead.

He made his way back to the kitchen, took her arm and guided her back to the foyer and the bottom of the stairway.

'The Realtor says there are fourteen rooms on the second floor and twelve on the third,' he told her. 'We'll go up together. At the top, you go left, go to the end of the hallway and work your way back, room by room. I'll take the top floor.'

'Got it.'

'Reggie, be careful. It seems like we've missed him, but we don't know that for sure.'

'Okay.' That seemed to be as articulate as she could manage.

They tiptoed up one flight. At the landing, he nudged her to the left and he kept climbing. Justin followed the same plan he'd just given Reggie. He went left, to the room at the end of the hallway, nudged the door open with his foot, stepped inside. Nothing. The same with the next room he came to. And he did the same at the third door. Stepped inside to a lavish bedroom suite. The front room was empty. The master bedroom wasn't.

Sprawled on the bed, lying on and tangled in blood-drenched sheets and blankets, was a man he was certain was Mudhi al Rahman.

Justin stepped forward to the body. There was no point in checking vital signs. The man had been shot several times in the chest and face. Whoever had killed him had been brutal and thorough.

Justin was overwhelmed by a sense of emptiness and defeat. He'd lost his witness. Lost his proof.

He'd lost.

Justin sagged. Took a step back . . .

And felt a prodding at the back of his neck. He didn't need to be told what it was that was pressed against his spine. A gun barrel. Justin closed his eyes.

'Drop the gun,' Special Agent Hubbell Schrader said quietly. 'Drop it now.'

Justin followed instructions. There was no other play.

The FBI agent poked Justin again. 'Move away from the bed,' he said.

Justin moved until Schrader told him to stop. There was one goal and one goal only now: stay alive as long as possible and hope that something happened to interfere with the inevitable.

The gun in Schrader's right hand didn't waver, it stayed pointed straight at Justin's head, while Schrader used his left hand to toss a second pistol on the floor by Justin's feet.

'Bend down and take it,' Schrader said. 'It's empty, so don't get any wild ideas.'

Justin crouched and picked up the gun. At the very least, he thought, he'd have something he could throw. Not much of a chance but better than nothing.

Schrader indicated the second gun. 'If you don't cooperate I can set it all up after you're dead just as easily. So please don't try anything. I'm already exhausted.'

'You want it to look like I shot him?'

'Very good,' Schrader said.

'Why?'

'Paranoid cop goes psycho,' the agent said. 'Driven over the edge by treatment at Gitmo. I can see the headline now. Maybe "terrorist cop" instead of psycho. It could go either way.'

'It's over,' Justin said. 'It's too late for you. They know what's going on.'

'Do they?' Schrader said with a smirk.

'You know how it works. You got in over your head, you trusted the wrong people. If you cooperate, it'll go a lot easier on you.'

'I am cooperating,' Special Agent Schrader said, the smirk still on his face. 'And you know what drives me crazy?'

'What?' Justin asked.

'Talking. Happens in movies and television all the time. Too much talking. I never had that urge.'

'What urge?'

'The need to explain. I just like to get things over with.'

There was no warning from Schrader, it was Justin's instinct that made him move. He didn't get far, just managed to twist his body because he sensed what was coming. The movement saved his life, at least momentarily, because Schrader fired without another word. Justin felt the fire in his left side. It spun him around and took his breath away. His hand reached for the wound at the same time he stumbled against the corner of the room, as if somehow his fingers could stop the flow of blood. They couldn't.

Justin didn't look up at Schrader. He didn't want the smirk to be the last thing he saw.

So Justin didn't see the smirk on Schrader's face fade when he heard the word 'Freeze!'

Reggie Bokkenheuser stepped into the bedroom, her gun aimed at Special Agent Hubbell Schrader. 'Put it down,' she said.

His gun didn't waver. It stayed pointing directly at Justin. Schrader took two quick, dancer-like steps to the side, swiveled his head to the right to glance back at Reggie.

'Shoot him,' Justin said.

She was frozen.

The smirk came back on Schrader's face. To Justin he said, 'Don't get your hopes up. She's not going to shoot.'

'Kill him,' Justin said. 'Kill him now.'

'You won't shoot,' Schrader said to Reggie. 'Will you?'

There was no movement. The expression on the agent's face turned into a full-fledged smile. He nodded toward Justin, a brief gesture of respect, an acknowledgment of a game well played. Justin tried to gather his legs for a lunge, if he could move maybe Schrader would miss, there was a chance the next bullet wouldn't be fatal, and Reggie would have a chance to take him out. He prepared to fling himself sideways but he knew the burning in his side would slow him down. And the smile on Schrader's face said it didn't matter anyway, he wasn't going to miss.

And then from downstairs there was a crash. A door being busted open. Footsteps running, many sets.

Justin heard someone, a woman's voice, scream, 'FBI! Jay, can you hear me?! Can you hear me, Jay?!'

Schrader looked disbelieving but still the smile didn't fade completely. He had shifted his gaze toward the noise downstairs, it was impossible not to, but his inattention didn't last long. Justin shifted his weight, screamed when the pain came, and threw himself directly at the agent, hurled his body as best he could, but he knew he'd blown it because Schrader had plenty of time to recover and fire. The agent was going to get him in midair, he wasn't even going to get close, then Justin heard a gun go off, waited to feel the agony again, but it didn't come. He looked up, saw Schrader staggering backwards, heard another shot, watched Schrader go down. Justin looked at Reggie, whose arm was still extended, her gun still pointed at the agent, and she fired a third time, and then Wanda Chinkle burst into the room, followed by three FBI agents, guns in hand.

'Drop it!' Wanda screamed. 'Drop it now!'

Justin saw Reggie release her gun and let it fall to the floor, and then watched her being forced to her knees. Two of the agents had their weapons pointed at her, Wanda and the fourth agent had theirs pointed straight at Justin's heart.

'Call 911,' Wanda barked at one agent. Then, to Justin, quieter, but not gentle: 'Put it down, Jay. Put it down and we'll get you help.'

It didn't even register that he was still holding Schrader's pistol.

All he focused on was that another man had come into the room, a man who stood behind Wanda and said, very quietly, 'Put the gun down, Mr Westwood.'

Justin stared disbelievingly at Jeffrey Stuller, the attorney general of the United States.

'Remember what I told you,' Wanda said. 'Please.'

Justin remembered. *Trust me*, she'd said. *And anyone who's with me.*

Trust me.

He remembered something else, too, as he tried to figure out what could have happened, how Schrader could have been lying in wait for him, how Wanda was telling him to trust the man he knew was behind Midas and the entire terrorist scheme.

He remembered a little nine-year-old girl saying, *He was an assistant general.*

You mean like a colonel? Justin had asked.

No, she'd insisted. *An assistant general.*

Ted Ackland.

An assistant general.

Assistant attorney general.

Ted Ackland had been in Hutch and Terry Cooke's house with Mudhi al Rahman. Mudhi had played a game of jacks. Ted Ackland had been the one who frightened little Hannah Cooke.

'Put it down and get on the floor, Jay. Now,' Wanda said.

Ackland. The A in Midas.

Justin said, 'It's empty. Don't shoot. It's empty,' and he let the gun fall out of his hand.

The next thing he knew, he was falling to his knees and Wanda was saying to him, 'You had to get cute. You had to lose me in the fucking college. I had your back, you asshole.'

And then Reggie was holding him and he was thanking her for

saving his life and telling her to be careful, not to get his blood all over her.

'The ambulance'll be here soon,' he heard Wanda say. 'Just hold on.

'What time is it?' Justin thought to ask.

Jeffrey Stuller, confused, looked at his watch. 'Twelve-thirty,' the attorney general said.

Justin looked at Reggie, who had her arms wrapped around him now and was holding him as close to her as she possibly could.

'Merry Christmas,' he said.

chapter 36

At Southampton Hospital they kept telling him how lucky he was. Justin wondered what it would take for someone to be considered unlucky, but none of the nurses or doctors answered him.

The wound was a clean one; the bullet had gone straight through, doing relatively little damage. They told him he wouldn't have to spend more than twenty-four hours there. After eating his first hospital meal – possibly chicken, he thought, and some kind of white tasteless custard – he thought maybe he actually was lucky after all.

Justin could tell how impressed the staff was when the attorney general of the United States showed up, posting two FBI agents at the door of the room to keep any potential visitors out. Justin hoped their newfound respect would translate into giving him a better meal when it came time for his next feeding.

Justin listened as the attorney general stood by the side of his bed and talked. It didn't take long for the tale to unfold. Stuller had been investigating the conspiracy within the administration for months. He'd recently included Ackland in the investigation as he'd become aware of his deputy's involvement. When Justin had called Wanda to set up a meeting with the assistant attorney general, she

403

had checked with Stuller. They'd decided to use Justin to flush Ackland out. They'd decided to use him as bait.

'I'm sorry, Jay,' Wanda said. She was sitting in the straight-backed chair at the foot of the bed. 'You wouldn't tell me what you were up to, although I had a reasonable idea. I couldn't tell you anything unless you'd confided in me.'

'I would have done the same thing,' Justin said. 'No apology needed. But how long have you been part of this?'

She glanced at Jeffrey Stuller, who nodded his okay. 'Not long,' she said. 'But long enough. At some point during the attorney general's investigation, he realized the level of corruption within the Bureau. He decided I could be trusted and he called me into his inner circle.'

'Good call,' Justin said.

'It's one of the reasons I was able to help you out periodically,' she said. 'I was under orders to. We thought you could prove things that even we couldn't.'

'So you're telling me not to get used to your assistance,' Justin said. And Wanda Chinkle nodded emphatically.

Stuller then ran through the rest of the story.

Justin had basically been correct in his assumptions and his conclusions. He'd just miscalculated on a couple of the players.

Stuller *had* been part of Midas. He'd been brought into the SPE because of his long ties to Phil Dandridge. There was nothing illegal about that, Stuller said, and he'd felt no compunction about making money from EGenco or his old friend's connections. It was a legitimate business deal, his holdings had been placed in a blind trust, and he would defend his decision to this day to participate.

But he hadn't known anything about the manipulation of oil prices. That was Dandridge. That was just pure greed.

Justin had been wrong, too, about President Anderson. The outgoing president had been duped and betrayed by his closest advisers, he was guilty of naiveté and stupidity, but not of criminal behavior. His administration would now go down as the most corrupt in American history, but his punishment would probably have to come from future judgment, not from the legal system.

Dandridge's situation was a little trickier. Stuller intended to prosecute him on several levels of financial fraud and misappropriations of government funds. There was no question he'd arranged for no-bid contracts for EGenco and violated the trust of the American people with his fraudulent energy policies. Morally it was repellent, but it was a vague and gray area of the law. Stuller said he'd already begun conversations with the vice president and with Stephanie Ingles and it was clear that, whatever their crimes, they had not instigated the violence or terrorist activity, although the attorney general believed that Dandridge had figured out what was going on somewhere along the line and had decided to do nothing about it. The man was not just weak, he was corrupt, and he belonged in prison, Stuller said, the disgust resonating in his words, but he wasn't sure if he could put him there. Stuller told Justin he might have to settle for Dandridge's and Ingles's resignations and some form of plea bargain, along with his testimony about Midas and Ackland.

Ackland had already been arrested. Stuller had arranged that immediately after Justin left the Waldorf hotel suite. If Stuller had his way, Ackland would not just spend the rest of his life behind bars, he'd receive the death penalty.

Justin asked a few questions and Stuller gave him further background on his investigation.

Ackland had been made a Midas partner at the very beginning when the deal was structured. That was Dandridge's choice. It was a reward for loyal service – and an attempt to ensure future service. But Ackland was more concerned with his future than anyone could have foreseen.

It was Ackland who first realized what would happen if Hutchinson Cooke talked and EGenco came tumbling down. Since it was all coming out of Justice, Ackland was privy to all the levels of the investigation; it was not difficult for him to circumvent it.

Dandridge had arranged for Cooke to fly for EGenco and Midas. But it was Ackland who'd arranged for Mudhi al Rahman's release from Gitmo; it was Ackland who had drawn Cooke into flying Mudhi first to Washington and then to the East End airport. Chuck Billings had been right about the cargo. In addition to the Saudi radical, the small plane had transported Semtex that Cooke had picked up in Colombia before flying to Guantanamo. He hadn't known exactly what he was involved in, but after the Harper's bombing he'd quickly figured it out. He'd contacted Ackland, whom he'd trusted. It was a poor choice of allies. Ackland had immediately arranged for the pilot's murder.

It was Ackland who'd conceived of the scheme to use Mudhi to destroy anyone who could have cut into Midas's profits, and simultaneously to terrorize the country.

Ackland had realized that Dandridge was going to lose the election. And Ackland wanted the vice presidency. Not just the nomination. He wanted to win.

He knew if Dandridge's Midas manipulations came to light, both of their careers were over. So he killed two birds with one stone. No one was around to blow the whistle on Midas. And Dandridge's popularity soared in the midst of the nation's fear.

After Harper's, it was not difficult to repeat the process.

And when he realized his hand could be overplayed, Ackland arranged for the scenario he'd created to come to an end: the decimation of what he claimed was the key terrorist group.

The murder of Mudhi al Rahman was meant to close the circle cleanly and permanently.

Except that Justin had gotten in the way.

Money and power, Justin thought. Nothing new, nothing different. The world will end over a battle for money and power.

When it was over, Stuller asked if Justin had any further questions. Justin said that he had a few.

'What about Hubbell Schrader?' he asked. 'How did he get involved?'

'Ackland,' Stuller said. 'Ackland drew him in slowly, got him appointed head of the New York bureau, which is quite a prestigious position. I'm sure Ackland promised him a shot at being head of the entire Bureau. And Ackland manipulated the man's sense of patriotism. I believe that Agent Schrader was convinced he was doing something for the good of the country.'

'An awful lot of damage is done for the good of the country,' Justin said.

Stuller said nothing. Justin knew the attorney general's political beliefs, knew what a hard-line patriot he was, and knew how torturous it must be for him to accept what had happened. The men he was bringing down weren't just his friends, they were the core of his political and philosophical foundation. But Stuller was able to put his politics aside in this instance. Honesty and a commitment to his public duty had managed to win whatever ideological battle had to have gone on within him.

'It was Schrader who killed Billings, wasn't it?'

'Yes,' Stuller said. 'We can prove that.'

'And Ray Lockhardt, too?'

'I believe so. But I have no conclusive proof yet. We're still working on it, although I don't know what kind of priority it will receive, now that Schrader's dead. Anything else?'

Justin hesitated. And Stuller noticed.

'Is there something else you need to know?' the attorney general asked.

'I'm not sure,' Justin told him. 'But I'd like to reserve one last favor if I need it.'

'What is it?'

'If I need some further information, I'd like to be able to get it from Agent Chinkle. I just need to ask a few questions before bothering her again.'

'Let it rest, Jay,' Wanda said. 'It's over.'

'Probably,' he said. 'But if I need you to run something for me, I'd like to know I can do it.'

When neither of them answered, Justin said, 'Then let me ask you something right now.' He turned to Wanda, waited until she met his gaze head-on, and said, 'You arranged for me to get out of Gitmo.'

She nodded and said, 'I helped.'

'How?' he asked.

'I went to the attorney general. Told him what had happened, that Ackland had ordered you to be picked up. Attorney General Stuller intervened directly, made it clear that there was a lot of political pressure being applied and that if you did not emerge unscathed there would be repercussions.'

'Unscathed. You mean alive? They would have killed me otherwise, once they found out what they needed to know?'

'Yes.'

'So they let me go after that.'

'Yes,' Wanda said quietly.

'But not immediately after that.'

Neither Wanda nor Stuller spoke.

'You let them keep me down there,' Justin said to Wanda. 'You let them keep me until you needed me back.'

Wanda turned away from him, could no longer look him in the eye. 'Yes,' she said. 'You told me once that good cops are the ones that make the right connections. And I know you're a good cop.'

'So you let them keep me there . . .'

'. . . until I knew you'd figure it out. And would have to help us out.'

'Until you could play me and send me in to do your dirty work, to set up Ackland and Schrader.'

She nodded stiffly. Her mouth was too dry to speak.

Justin held his gaze until her head hung even lower, then he turned back to the attorney general. 'About that favor I might be needing,' he said.

'Agent Chinkle will be available for that,' Jeff Stuller said, and his words were meant for both of them.

'Then I'd like to get the hell out of here,' Justin told him.

'One more thing,' Stuller said. 'There is going to be an unprecedented uproar when this becomes public. There are going to be resignations and prison terms. The future course of the country will in all likelihood be altered.'

'Is this a question or a statement?'

'It's a question. I'd like to know what your involvement will be. Will you be talking to the media? You could be lionized as quite the hero. And you can reveal things I'm not positive yet that I wish to reveal. I'm also sure you will be able to capitalize on this financially if you want.'

'Do you have a preference?' Justin asked.

'I'm sure you're aware of my preference,' Stuller responded. 'But I have no right to impose that upon you.'

'I'll tell you what,' Justin said. 'My preference is to keep as quiet as possible. I'd like no one to ever even know I was involved.'

Stuller nodded, relieved.

'Unless,' Justin said, and Stuller immediately stiffened. 'Unless you screw up. Unless I think these scumbags aren't getting what they deserve to get.'

'And then you talk?'

'And once I start it's really hard to shut me up.'

Jeff Stuller stuck his hand out awkwardly. Justin Westwood shook it.

And then he asked if Wanda would call for the nurse. The friendly redhead, not the scary brunette. He said he wanted a little more morphine. That as long as he was going to spend the rest of the day there, he might as well enjoy it.

Justin was released the next day and spent the two days after that sleeping. The pain wasn't bad, he was just exhausted. Drained. He barely ate, and he moved as infrequently as possible. For the first time in a long time, he didn't crave alcohol. His system wanted to be left alone. By everything. And everyone.

He spoke to Reggie on the phone several times but he needed to be apart from her, too, just now. She obviously felt the same way. What they'd shared in the Southampton mansion had been too intense, both intimate and redolent of mortality, and neither of them wanted to relive it just yet. So Reggie went to work and ran the East End station, still in her position of interim chief, and Justin stayed home, sleeping and thinking and listening to music.

On the third day, he called Gary Jenkins and asked him to bring over some reports that Justin had been keeping in his desk at the station. Gary asked if there was a rush, he was heading out to lunch, and Justin said no rush whatsoever. So Gary showed up around two and handed over the folders.

Justin read through the report he wanted to focus on. When he was done, he took a bath, filling the tub with only a few inches of water – his bandages still prevented him from showering – and got dressed. Then he drove toward the East End airport, turning onto a side street about half a mile before the airport entrance. The street had been cut into the surrounding woods. A strange location, Justin thought. It didn't look natural. It seemed as if nature should close back in on the new, pristine houses and swallow them up.

He pulled into the driveway of the third pristine house on the left and knocked on the door. He spent fifteen minutes inside talking to the owner, had a glass of water, and asked a few questions. All very easy and pleasant. Then he left.

At five o'clock he knocked on the door to Leona Krill's office.

'Justin,' she said, 'this is a surprise.'

He gave her the friendliest smile he could muster.

They chatted for a few moments, he gave her some of the details of what had transpired in Guantanamo. Attorney General Stuller had called the mayor to tell her that Justin had been cleared of any and all accusations, that he had, in fact, acted in heroic fashion. She told Justin that she'd been asked not to talk about the matter further with him, so instead they discussed the arrest of Ted Ackland – the entire country was discussing the arrest of Ackland and the emerging scandal – but Justin gave no indication that he knew anything more than he'd read or seen on television. Leona asked when he'd be returning to work and he told her he thought it might be as soon as tomorrow. She said she was glad.

Justin said good-bye, stood up, and then said, 'Oh, by the way, I do have one question for you.'

He asked it, a question he should have asked a long time ago, and she gave him the answer. He told her he'd definitely be returning to work the next day.

He had one last thing to do before nighttime.

Justin called Wanda, said he was cashing in the favor he'd requested. He could hear the shame in her voice, her awareness of the way she'd crossed the line and altered their relationship forever, but all she said was, 'Okay, what do you want to know?'

'I want the ME's report on Hubbell Schrader.'

'What the hell for, Jay? Christ, you saw what happened. Your girlfriend saved your bacon.'

'You want to fax it to me or e-mail it?' he asked.

She sighed. 'Check your e-mail in ten minutes,' Wanda told him. And after a brief hesitation, she said, 'And Jay. I . . . I . . .'

'I know,' he said. 'You were doing your job.'

'Yes,' she whispered.

'I might have done the same thing,' he told her.

Neither of them said anything after that, they both wondered in silence whether what he said was true, and then they hung up.

That night, Reggie came over for dinner. He was staggered when she walked in the door. She wore a short black dress that clung tightly to her body. Instead of her scuffed boots or heavy work shoes, she wore an elegant pair of high heels. Despite the cold, she wasn't wearing stockings. He could see little shivers of goose bumps running down her legs.

She kissed him before she even took her coat off, and he responded. They sat together on the couch and he poured a glass of red wine for each of them. He'd had the bottle for quite some time, a '90 Haut-Brion.

'What's for dinner? she murmured.

He answered, 'It depends.'

She smiled and said, 'On what?'

And Justin said, 'Tell me about Ray Lockhardt.'

Her eyes squinted in confusion. 'You want to talk about that now?' she asked.

He nodded.

'I was thinking this was going to be a little more romantic than that.' When he didn't answer, she shrugged and said, 'Okay. What do you want to know?'

'You interviewed a witness who saw a car parked on the road to the airport.'

'I'd hardly call him a witness. He bicycled past a car on his way home.'

'Your report says he "turned off the road on his way home." '

'Okay. It probably does. So what?'

'It's just odd phrasing. "Turned off the road" is something you'd say if you saw it happen. It's not a usual way of describing something.'

'I'm sure that's just the way he told it to me. What are you trying to say, Jay, that I didn't do my investigation properly?'

'No,' he said. 'You did a really good job.'

The silence lingered between them. He broke it by saying, 'I spoke to the witness, Reggie. It wasn't exactly the way you wrote it up.'

'What did I get wrong?'

'He had a pretty good memory of the car he saw.'

'Did he?'

'The way he described it, it could have been your car.'

'What?'

'I talked to Leona today, too. I realized I'd never asked her who gave you such a good recommendation for the job.'

The expression on Reggie's face didn't change all that much. Just a little. 'Oh?'

'I never would have thought to ask. Except when I met with Ted Ackland he said something that struck me.'

'What was it?'

'He was talking about possibly getting the vice presidential nomination. He said, "Not bad for a cop from Wisconsin." Just made me think. Suddenly I knew two people from Wisconsin.'

Reggie didn't speak or move.

'Leona didn't speak to him directly, she told me. But it was someone from Ackland's office who recommended you. Who called her out of the blue and urged her to hire you. They needed someone on the inside. Someone to keep an eye on me.'

'Jay . . .'

'It was Schrader who gave it away. It happened so fast and I tried to drive it out of my mind, but . . . he was so damn confident that you weren't going to shoot him. At first I thought he was too arrogant, or he was bluffing, or maybe he thought it because you were a woman. Then I realized no, he was way too much of a pro to take things that lightly. It was because he knew you. It was because he's the one who told you to kill Ray Lockhardt.'

'Jay . . . you have to listen to me . . .'

'I went over the timing and it all worked out. You could have done it before you came over here that first time. Maybe it's one of the reasons you were so upset. Killing can do that to some people. Then I got the FBI forensic report back, for the work done on Schrader. You shot him with a .38. The same gun that was used to kill Lockhardt.'

The silence was stifling. Reggie raised a finger to her eye. Justin wasn't sure if it was a nervous response or if she was brushing away a tear. 'I was recruited by the FBI,' she said quietly. 'By Ackland. When I was still in Milwaukee. I didn't know what was going on, I swear to God. They told me it was a question of national security . . . I was working for the FBI and doing my job. That's what I thought.'

'The night we made love the first time,' Justin said, 'the night they picked me up and took me away . . . That's why you went back to your house, wasn't it? To tell them that you could keep me here.'

Reggie took a long time before answering. 'It's not why I made love to you,' she said.

Now it was Justin's turn to stay silent. He took several sips of his red wine. He knew it was delicious, but it tasted bitter to him. He suspected that many things would taste bitter to him for quite a long while.

'Do you have your handcuffs?' he asked.

She smiled. Briefly, the gleam came back in her eye. 'No,' she said. 'But I can get them.'

'Never mind,' he told her. 'I've got mine. Put your hands behind your back, please.'

It took her a moment to realize what was happening. The gleam disappeared as she felt the cuffs snap on her wrists.

'Jay,' she said, 'I was working for the government. I thought I was under orders from the president of the United States. I thought I was doing the right thing!'

'You weren't,' Justin Westwood said. Then he began to recite, 'Regina Bokkenheuser, you're under arrest for the murder of Ray Lockhardt. You have the right to remain silent. Anything you do say can and will be held against you. You have the right to an attorney . . .'

And as he recited, he helped her up and marched her toward the front door. He was taking her to the East End police station.

He decided to return to work a day earlier than he'd planned.

chapter 37

Justin knew he had two more chores before he could say it was completely over.

The next day, at lunchtime, he drove over to Marge Leggett's house, walked up the cement path that cut its way through an over-grown lawn and led to the front door. He knocked and saw the surprised look on Marge's face when she opened the door to let him in.

She made him a cup of tea, which he didn't really want, but she wanted to make it, so he let her dip the Lipton's tea bag into the steaming hot water and then he drank from the caffeine-stained mug. While he sipped he told her what he knew. He didn't give her all the details – she didn't need to know most of it – but he told her what he could. Said it was confidential. But he said he'd made her a promise and he was keeping it. So he explained that while most of what she'd been reading in the paper and hearing on the news was accurate, some of it wasn't, and he filled in a few more blanks.

When he was finished, she said, 'Thank you,' and then she hesitated, looked very uncomfortable.

'Is there something else?' Justin asked.

'He was with that woman,' Marge said. 'At Harper's. He was having lunch with that woman.'

Justin closed his eyes for a second, tried to come up with a name. Something clicked in his brain and he had it. 'Carolyn Helms.'

'That rich woman. The divorced one.'

'Right.'

'Was he cheating on me?' Marge Leggett asked.

Justin cocked his head. 'Marge,' he said, 'is that what you wanted to know? Is that what this was all about?'

'Yeah,' she said. 'It's all I can think about, Jay. All this other stuff, it's horrible, I know, but—'

'But what you really wanted to know was if Jimmy was cheating on you.'

'Yeah.'

Justin took a last sip of the tea, which was now lukewarm. 'No,' he said. 'He wasn't.'

'How do you know?' Marge asked.

'I knew Jimmy,' he said. 'He was an honest guy. And I'm good at my job. You asked me to find out and I did. He was just having lunch.'

'You talked to people? You know that for sure?'

'I know it for sure,' Justin said.

Marge Leggett kissed him on the cheek and said, 'Thank you.'

'It was nothing,' Justin said.

At St Joseph's Hospital, Justin stood in the doorway and looked in at the little girl lying in her bed.

'I'm doing one more skin graft,' Dr Graham said. 'That should be the last surgical procedure.'

'Painful?' Justin asked.

'Extremely,' the surgeon said. 'But she's strong. She's very strong.'

Justin nodded, as if her strength was no surprise to him.

'So is it over?' Dr Graham asked.

'Excuse me?'

'When you were here before, you said you'd talk to her when it was over. Is it over?'

'Yes,' Justin said. 'It's over.'

The surgeon gave him a pat on the back – a half pat, half gentle shove into the room. Justin walked over to the bed, pulled up a chair and sat. He took the girl's hand, the one not covered in bandages, and held it.

Hannah Cooke shifted her head so she could look in his direction.

'I remember you,' she said.

'I'm glad.'

Her eyes closed. And her head relaxed again on the pillow. But she didn't attempt to pull her hand back. He could feel it soften in his grasp.

'Thank you for coming,' she said.

'I can't stay long,' Justin told her. 'But I can come again if you'd like me to. I can come and visit and we can talk.'

Hannah didn't say anything. For a long time, she didn't move. But then Justin thought she smiled.

He wasn't positive, so he just waited, her hand in his.

And then he saw it again. This time he was sure.

Definitely a smile.